The Moonlit Path

a novel

Peter P. Goodman

THE MOONLIT PATH

Soledad Canyon Press
P.O. Box 3288
Mesilla Park, NM 88047
SoledadCanyon@mail.com

All the characters in this book are fictitious,
and any resemblance to actual persons,
living or dead, is entirely coincidental.

Cover design by Richard Ljoenes Design LLC
Interior design by Integrative Ink

ISBN: 978-1-7353412-0-0 (Paperback Edition)
ISBN: 978-1-7353412-1-7 (eBook Edition)

Printed in the United States of America
September 2022

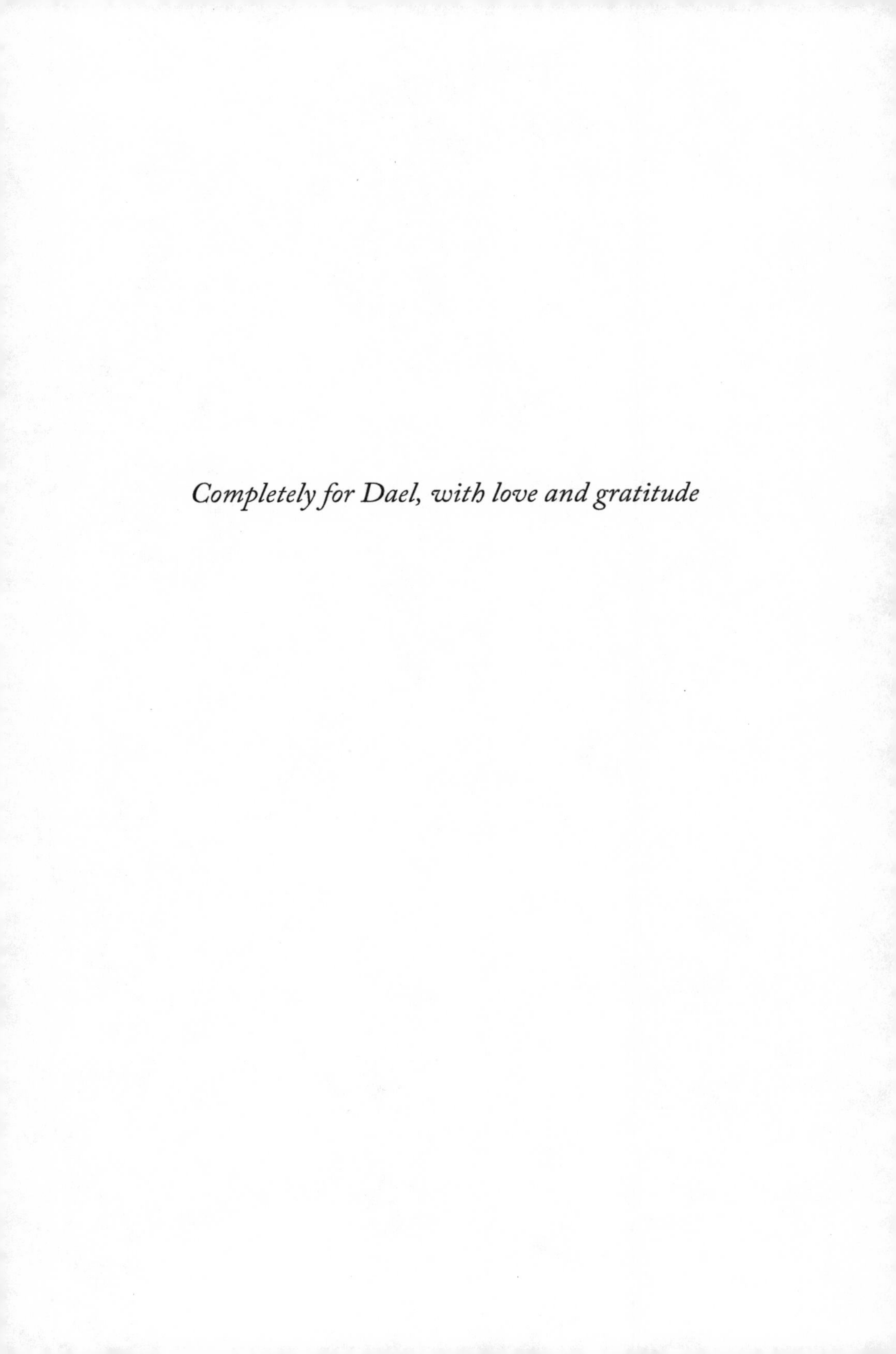

Completely for Dael, with love and gratitude

December 31, 1913

New Year's Eve, about 4:30 in the afternoon. The sky is grey and ominous. Our set has taken tables at the new Oakland Hotel for the first New Year's Eve gala there. Everyone is pleased that we need not go over to San Francisco to celebrate. The town is comically puffed up about having such an impressive new place, which does not quite match some of the old San Francisco hotels. However, it will be fun and quite the event.

Helen gave me this garden journal, to keep a record of all that I plant in the gardens surrounding Father's house. Yet as midwinter offers mostly wind-blown rain against windowpanes, the warmth of the fireplace, and seed catalogs spread out on the table, I cannot see why I should not reflect on other matters. The mind is a kind of garden. I have kept no diary since Richard. Yet I did so as a young girl, and in college. To begin again feels awkward, and a little exciting, although I have nothing exciting to write.

I suppose I ought to write something of what I hope to accomplish during 1914.

I cannot say I am resolved to accomplish anything more than growing the garden and ceasing to let other demands interfere with my painting. I do feel better when I paint everyday. Otherwise, I am aware of no need so urgent that it requires a resolution, although I should like to travel to at least two major exhibitions.

I must be more kind. I must not let my sharp tongue wound people. Every day I shall say at least one kind word that I might not have thought to utter, and shall silently swallow a word that might wound, even a well-deserved word. I will not exhibit my "wit" at the cost of anyone's composure. I will suffer fools gladly—and try not to notice that they are fools.

It is the unanimous view of my friends that I should not so quickly dismiss men's attentions and should be more receptive to what might become a marriage proposal. (No one knows that a man proposed marriage to me last year, or that two others, one married, have hinted at other sorts of proposals!) It may show little resolve, but I suppose I ought to maintain a more open mind on the subject. However, it would hardly show a resolute character to bow to my friends' will and some man's plea (not that so many are beating a path to our door) when my own heart and will hold to the contrary.

I am also determined that my father shall enjoy such time as remains to him. He can be a difficult man, yet I love him. Whatever else he may have done in the world and, thereby, to himself and his dreams, he and Mother gave me much, as I realize more clearly each year. And I must be more patient with Elizabeth.

1914 will be a very fine year. New ideas are carrying the day: playwrights and novelists are doing meaningful work, we have a progressive professor of history in the White House instead of a corpulent Tory (although I should have preferred Colonel Roosevelt), and we women are beginning to shed corsets and tresses and take some share of our responsibilities (and rights) as citizens. The Progressive movement is growing, particularly here. New scientific developments appear faster than we can count them. We have had a decade and a half of peace, and I believe Mr. Wilson will avoid being drawn into the Mexican situation.

January

Thursday, January 1

Spent the Grand Occasion in the ballroom of the Hotel Oakland, having taken two tables. It was a fine evening, yet at times my mood was more restless than joyful. Perhaps what I had seen earlier sapped a bit of the joy from me.

I was to ride to the hotel with Bret. When he called for me, he announced that he was unexpectedly required to stop for thirty minutes or so on the way. Shifting his weight from one foot to the other and nearly stammering, he asked whether I would mind. I wondered why he was embarrassed. As well as we know each other, of course it was all right. Then he added, "At Sixth Street."

With all the festivities I had forgotten that the segregated district was to be closed last night. Naturally the newspaper was interested. The man who was to write the story was ill. It is not, of course, a district I have seen much of and only by day. The long row of one and two-story shacks has always seemed tawdry and depressing; and whatever happens there at night only more so. I had rarely thought about it, except to wish those women free of it, if they wished to be.

By accident I witnessed something sadder and more moving than I can say, something I would not have chosen to see but am glad I did. We could hear singing and laughter and music from automatic pianos. Even as a cordon of policemen slowly but insistently moved the men and boys out of Sixth Street into Broadway, they were still waving bottles in the air and laughing. Then there was silence, except for the intermittent rain; but soon the women began to leave, singly or in pairs, then in greater numbers, like a rag-tag army defeated in battle. Few carried an umbrella.

However they may have looked to men who visited them, with their paint and cheap finery, they were wretched and unhealthy. Whatever joy they may have feigned in their unspeakable work, they looked sad and hopeless now. If ever a young girl imagined there was something glamorous or exciting in such a life, I would have her see such a scene. And their faces! Although many were old, some were so young they seemed mere girls.

"Where will they go?" I asked Bret.

He frowned and shook his head. "That is a fine question that never gets asked when the public is clamoring to close the districts." He added, "Some may take honest jobs; but few such jobs are offered, and even fewer are offered without unspoken conditions that make them little different from the houses. Most will go across the bay, or to other cities, other districts, until those are closed, and then to still others, until they grow too old."

By now there were many women. The police herded them like cattle, showing less concern than cattle might have inspired in them. Few women were dressed warmly against the rain. One studied me for a moment. Her insolent stare told me she wanted to say something insulting if she dared. Instead, she turned to the girl nearest her and, tilting her head toward me, said loudly, "Now it's a stop fer lady tourists. Or else she's from the Decency League." She gave me a last quick look, to make sure I'd heard.

Bret and I said little about what we had seen and were soon with our friends. Everyone turned out. It felt comfortable to be sitting among them celebrating one more good year. Much laughter and guying.

At times I sat silently, letting my eyes roam. Bret showed none of the concern that creases his brow when we talk alone. When my gaze reached Elizabeth and Tub, I smiled, feeling none of the irritation my dear sister often inspires; simply pleased to see her contentedly married. Tub is a good man, and a kind brother-in-law, though I'd run away to teach in Alaska if told I had to marry him. Jack Choate is more witty than wise and sometimes exasperating with his mischief; yet good-hearted beneath it all. Helen and Edward. Helen is so simple and good! And has been since we were in pinafores. (The love of good friends is like a coat one leaves mostly in the closet, but which means everything when the weather turns cold.)

At other moments, I felt wholly out of sorts: annoyed with Bret because the charming and cynical Bret keeping everybody in stitches was not the more sensitive Bret whose newspaper stories sometimes trouble him deeply and who dreams of fashioning a novel from what he sees on Oakland's streets; Elizabeth, superficial and vain, has let her mind atrophy; William Whitmore holds his marriage in such disregard that he has made illicit propositions to me (and to others). Only Julia's insincerity prevents me from telling her of them; Robbie Livingston, sitting beside me—as he always will, if I permit it—can annoy me by his mere existence, though Lord knows he has never worked up the courage to do or say anything at which I could reasonably take offense. He has plenty of money and knows all the facts you could ever need, but on the day God handed out spirit, his nose was buried in some instructional booklet.

I realized that but for the accidents of personal history—neighborhoods we lived in as children, parents who were friendly, schools, and mutual friends—we might have nothing much to say to each other. In San Francisco, Seattle, and Boston, groups just like ours were gathered, laughing with friends they considered unique, but if one exchanged half the members of one group for half of another, it would make no difference at all after a week. We gather according to some instinct we learned as monkeys, and our chattering resembles that of our simian ancestors.

In that mood I arose from the table. When I passed the Jacksons at a nearby table, along with that cousin of theirs, Suzanne Coolidge, I paused.

Suzanne was engaged in a spirited argument with the older Mr. Jackson over the English court decision denying a highly accomplished woman admission to the bar because "a woman is not a person" under English law. He said that it was up to the English courts, not militant suffragists, to construe English law, and that neither he nor Suzanne nor Mrs. Pankhurst was any expert on ancient statutes and precedent. "It requires no expert," Suzanne shot back, "It's no different from the Dred Scott decision that a black man had no rights that white men had to respect, and four years of violent militancy wiped out that decision, rather before my time." She was nearly shouting over the din, and her eyes flashed, but Mr. Jackson seemed to take no offense.

As midnight drew near, with everyone clinking glasses and singing songs and bunny-hugging about the floor, some standing on chairs shrieking like wild Indians, I suddenly felt quite removed, though but a moment before I had been laughing and pouring wine (even into the glass of some tall stranger who shrugged at me and smiled). I perceived everything as from a great distance that diminished the din only slightly but eliminated my ability to feel. Watching the joyous, whirling serpentines fly about the room, I thought only of the poor waiters, one of whom dropped a very full tray as a serpentine coiled about his knees.

I suddenly felt a vague foreboding. How quickly the year 1913, which we had greeted with similar joy in San Francisco, had flickered out! I saw my thirty-two years of life as a row of burnt-out candles. Everyone's joy seemed a wall we had built against the terror of time's passing. Time is so fearfully far beyond our ken, and so implacable, that we mask our fear by celebrating it, as if by making a friend of Time we could soften its ruthlessness. It was a chilling thought but passed in a moment.

At just midnight the lights went out. Everyone roared so that the room shook. When the lights came on again, everyone joined arms and danced among the tables. Someone pulled me up, and I too laughed and swayed like a madwoman.

The storm made us doubly thankful we were not out on the Bay in such high winds. Bret joked that the weather was a judgment on our wickedness.

Friday, January 2

Helen brought two bits of startling news: Suzanne Coolidge has been injured in a motor accident, and that elderly Bishop woman who amused us all so much on Christmas Eve was arrested this morning!

The accident occurred New Year's Eve, very late. Leaving the Hotel, we saw Suzanne with a boisterous group climbing into an automobile. She waved, and gestured for me to join them, but I declined. It seems they went off the road, destroying the machine and injuring several people. Suzanne is in hospital, but Helen thinks she is not seriously injured.

How startling that Mrs. Bishop has been passing fictitious checks all over town. Apparently, Salt, the day clerk at the Hotel Oakland, found her out. Yesterday, as she left the hotel, she stopped to order supper for fourteen on New Year's night at $10 a plate, lecturing the Maître de that he had better have several hundred dollars worth of champagne ready. Mr. Sternberg at Laymance Realty discovered she had been sent to San Quentin for that sort of thing. Taxed with that, she shrugged and admitted that she'd served three or four different terms there.

According to this evening's *Enquirer*, she said her criminal record has broken her daughter's heart. (She no longer knows where her daughter lives!) She had formerly known very fine people in San Francisco society, including the Spreckels, and says she committed her crimes to escape poverty and recover a moment of the old life of refinement and luxury.

This evening, we talked about Mrs. B at length. I laughed and joked too, at first. Later, I felt repulsed by our smugness and fell silent. Who can say which of us might descend to worse crimes than passing bad checks if we lost access to all we take for granted? Finally, Jack, who had been eyeing me queerly, started guying me, saying I was so silent and serious that I must be in league with Mrs. B. I felt a sudden rush of anger, and I replied that indeed I was, that we had used one of her checks to purchase from Jack's groom that colt he keeps telling us will win the California Stakes next year, and that he'd have a difficult time laying hands on it again if he didn't keep a civil tongue in his head. Everyone laughed. I should have told him what I really thought, but I did not wish to end everyone's merriment.

Saturday, January 3

Today I visited Suzanne in the hospital. The Gordons were with her, and a nurse. She looked rather pathetic, all bandaged and bruised. Despite her circumstances, we talked like tornados—once we were alone. I had wondered if she would even remember me, or welcome the visit, but she greeted me by name the moment I appeared and smiled warmly.

Suzanne mocked the newspaper report, which described her as "a pretty girl" before reciting her injuries. "Why do they always write such things? Are my injuries supposed to be more tragic because I am 'pretty?'"

Mrs. Gordon pointed out that they always said such things, and it signified nothing.

Suzanne laughed. "I should like to edit a newspaper for a month. "Judge Smith, a bald man who combs his few remaining strands of hair pathetically across the top of his head, today sentenced Jake Brown to…, or Mr. White of Amalgamated Widget, who has not seen his stomach since Harrison's Presidency, met today with union president Harry Riley, a debonair gentleman with a seductive gleam in his eye around the ladies..., or Mayor Mott..."

I laughed. Mrs. Gordon smiled nervously, and Mr. Gordon shifted position in his chair and glanced out the window.

When the Gordons left, I rose too, but she signaled me to stay. I asked if she was not too tired for further conversation. "Not if the conversation is amusing," she said, smiling. "And so long as you don't mistake my occasional groans for comments on your wit." We soon fell to chattering like schoolgirls, but she did sometimes groan, her eyes glazing over briefly.

When Dr. Williams arrived, she mentioned her pain, but his brow furrowed, and he declined to provide morphine or laudanum or some other medication sufficient to curtail her pain. "He is too strict," she complained, looking at me. "You know him. Can't you talk to him?" He immediately shot me a frown that would have silenced even a fellow physician.

Suzanne is an interesting woman. I had thought she was merely visiting, but she has plans to open a photographic studio here. She talked more of the nuts-and-bolts of photography, and its commercial potential, than of the artistic possibilities that would intrigue me. But she is quite enthusiastic, and it is exciting to think of her starting her own business.

I left when the doctor did but declined his offer to drive me home in his automobile. I have determined to avoid automobiles. Why court such danger merely to arrive somewhere a little more quickly? Suzanne's accident set me thinking how different the automobile is. It is not merely faster. The commands to turn or stop a horse are simple and few and known to all. Everyone, even in a panic, knows what to do, although we may not always persuade the horse.

An automobile is both complex and mindless. The horse at least has some sort of brain, and an instinct for self-preservation. Although he may run too fast and care little whether his rider slips off, he will not leap off a cliff into the sea, nor gallop into the wall of a bank. So far as I have been informed, an automobile has no such instinct. If something goes awry, the motor will initiate no action to preserve itself from complete destruction.

Father said that I ought not to speak in absolutes. He believes we will all be using automobiles one day, and there will be few horses left in use on city streets. Certainly, their use has increased rapidly. Nevertheless…

Sunday, January 4

Father Mayne spoke on Christ and Bergson. Even scientists begin to see that the process of life transcends science and escapes reason. And even Bergson does not claim that mathematics and the sciences can explain everything.

Sunlight occasionally fought through the clouds and brightened the stained-glass. I began to lose the thread of the sermon. I let the feel of things take over: the pew's plush cushions, the music, the rich colors in the windows, the Bible's leather cover, Father Mayne's soft, fleshy hands, the smooth dome of Mayor Mott's bald head between the flowered hats of his wife and daughter. I watched the light play on the backs of those around me, as a cat or a dog might, bereft of understanding and seeking none.

Suddenly I saw and heard this familiar service as if it were a series of plates in *National Geographic*. I wondered how the scene would strike a visitor from some other world. A sun-burnt newsman from Mars or Venus, trained to interpret strange customs, say. What would he make of the songs and silences, or of the collective scraping of shoes as the entire congregation knelt? Of the minister's garb? Would he suppose the creatures surrounding him were celebrating or mourning, or being instructed or entertained? Were they willing participants or prisoners, herded together for some unknown purpose?

Father Mayne warned us that Bergson's message is particularly seductive in our modern era of hustle and confusion. Bergson holds that we ought not to grieve over changes in our lives, or over the role of chance, because these are the very substance of the life process. Many of us see life as an island protected from the sea's waves, but to Bergson, life is the waves, changing and breaking and re-forming at each instant. Father Mayne says Bergson opens exciting doors, but offers no plan for passing through them, and "Makes totems of evolution and chance."

He sounded as if it greatly mattered. Does it truly, to him? Or do pastors learn, as actors and politicians do, to portray unfelt passions? I felt sorry for him. A pastor must write and deliver a staggering number of sermons and talks, for little money, yet must interest and instruct.

I wondered how many of my fellow parishioners truly understood him, and how many would be elsewhere if no one would notice their absence. "All of them," Father would growl if asked. "Except your Aunt Emily. And you, for reasons I never can fathom." Indeed, I would remain for the singing and the cool, reassuring quietude.

God granted us a break in the weather, as afterward, we exchanged pleasantries. I admired Elizabeth's new bracelet and caught up with a few people I hadn't seen since before Christmas.

Cousin Susan looked particularly sweet in her pink dress. Mr. and Mrs. Cooke ambled toward us and remarked with astonishment that she had shot up like a beanstalk. Susan winced, sparking memories of *my* reaction in similar situations. (After Mother's death, such remarks had a wholly different meaning, as they were links to Mother made by people who might help solve some of the mysteries she left behind—but as I could not articulate my questions...)

I perceived in Susan's eyes an alertness I had never noticed. She studied each of us carefully, like an immigrant learning a new set of customs. This change seemed as remarkable to me as her height did to the Cookes. When they remarked on her maturity, she cringed.

(Some further thought about Susan keeps forming and dissipating before I can catch it.)

Walking home, Aunt Agnes and I discussed Father. She said he was never much of a believer. "I think your grandfather's strictness drove him away from the idea of God. When he got out into the world and learned how rich and varied it was, religion seemed part of the narrow life he'd escaped. Then there was the War. And when your mother died..."

I said I'd seen him in church only for funerals and weddings.

"And as few of those as he can decently manage. I asked him once whether he still believed in God. He looked at me so very queerly that I feared for his soul. Finally, he replied, 'If I did, it would only be to curse Him.'"

Monday, January 5

Met Helen for lunch at Cobb's. She is over the moon about her engagement to Edward, though she tries to hide it. She must have harbored real concern that her father might try to forbid the marriage, rather than merely grumbling into his beard. They are to be married on Saturday, March 28. She asked me to be her bridesmaid. Of course, I agreed. Helen is terribly excited but hearing her remind herself of all she needs to do between now and then, I was glad not to be in her place.

Gushing about Edward, Helen checked herself, concerned that she might cause me pain because of Richard, then she rushed on, as if her happiness might inspire me. I do not envy Helen her situation. The gifts of reflection and imagination that render life worth living, render it also more complex and difficult. Good and kind and handsome and earnest as Edward may be, and right for *her*, when Helen goes on about their long walks, I can't imagine what Edward and I would talk about, were I in her place. I should return home numb from his earnest lectures on business and polite but awkward questions about painting, never mind the long silences punctuated by occasional efforts by one of us to point out something of mutual interest!

When Helen gushes, I smile, and mean it; but when she questions me, explicitly or otherwise, I feel like shaking her and shouting, "Don't you understand?" Some of us have shadows over our hearts that others cannot see. Some of us are blessed (cursed?) with questions that cannot be resolved simply by pairing off, raising children, quietly subordinating ourselves to the demands of his business and their education, and every Saturday to Idora Park and every Sunday to church.

I love Helen deeply, but we are quite different. I invited her to go with me to see Suzanne. She looked surprised that I was visiting again. Helen is too good to speak ill of anyone, but I wonder if she disapproves of Suzanne.

Suzanne asked, not unkindly, whether it was true that Edward had asked Mr. Powers for Helen's hand in marriage. I told her they'd have married anyway, and that although Addison doesn't much care for Edward, he gave permission. He said he had not expected to be consulted, adding, "If you don't know her well enough to know she will do as she damned pleases, I'd advise you to reconsider."

Suzanne has strong opinions but asserts them without offending. I remarked that even while arguing passionately with Mr. Jackson, she was obviously not angry with *him*, but with certain of his ideas, and he took it all in good spirit. She laughed. "Are you sure it hasn't more to do with his appreciation of young women with clear skin, rather than with any tact of mine?"

<u>Tuesday, January 6</u>

I invited Suzanne to join us Friday evening.

"I don't get a membership cup?" She teased when I told her how informal our Fridays are. When she cross-examined me about our group, I could only say that we are grown but not yet old and many of us have known each other as long as we've known anything. We vary in our interests and employment, yet we value each other's company all the more as our daily lives bring us together less and less often.

"They are all people with whom you grew up?" she asked. As I thought about Bret and Jack, and others who've joined us over the years, I demurred. I explained that we often gather on Friday evenings for cards and supper and talk. Some find that our conversation keeps us too long from bridge or gossip, and others that our bridge-playing and other frivolities interrupt the conversation too frequently. We annoy men who can't abide women who think; and we offend women who refuse to put up with the sort of nonsense men talk. We are not all couples or all unmarried. We are merely ourselves.

Suzanne remarked that we all talk together, men and women.

"Don't you approve?" I teased.

"Oh, of course I do. I just . . ." Her voice trailed off.

She laughed uproariously when I suggested she had assumed that being all together just wouldn't do out here in the provinces. She said it wasn't so much a geographical distinction as one between her bohemian friends and her conservative relatives. Here, as elsewhere, most separate after supper, the women to chatter about domestic matters and children, and the men to grunt and smoke cigars while discussing clever transactions involving stock or horses or automobiles.

"But not on Fridays."

I nodded, adding that in my father's house, it has never been the custom to separate after supper. As a child, I noticed that gatherings at our home differed from others', but since Mother's death, Father has hosted few gatherings.

Wednesday, January 7

Suzanne asked why I painted. She asked not because she found it odd, but to understand what painting means to me, which forced me to contemplate that question, yet again. I tried to explain that colors and light and the way life composes itself have intrigued me for as long as I can remember. Now, having gained some experience and training over the years, I find that if I sit in the studio, or as I walk, my mind or the scene around me sets little problems I can solve only by painting. I paint daily because I cannot imagine *not* painting.

She was curious about the absence of a man in my life and probed for information but did not offend. Of Richard, I said more than I intended. What I didn't tell, she guessed. She confided that she has been intimate with *two* men. She is decidedly not a "loose" woman. Yet she spoke frankly, does not regret her conduct (although one man treated her shabbily), and does not consider her actions wrong. She turned the conversation back to Richard, in a way that invited further confidences, but I said little.

"Where is he now?"

"We haven't heard from him in some time. I believe he is in Australia."

"He is not in Alameda County then."

I nodded. "I suppose he has made a wonderful life for himself, somewhere; he must have found someone to share it with."

Went to Kahn's later. Bought a dozen rose bushes for $1.50. Three each of Clint Meteor Red and Duchess Albany Red, and a half-dozen White Manean Cochet. It seems a sad symptom of our values that a bottle of wine is dearer than a pair of rose bushes! The roses were half the price of a gallon of brandy but will last far longer and provide a deeper pleasure.

Sarah Bennett invited me to a meeting at the Brooklyn Presbyterian Church this evening to discuss the saloon ordinance. I am not persuaded to become involved. I say little on this issue and find that I oppose whatever view is urged upon me.

When I contemplate the damage drunkenness can do to the wives and children of the drunkards, I cannot quarrel with the temperance movement. Although I enjoy a glass of wine now and then, if abolishing saloons would truly produce a finer world in which drunken men did not beat their wives, and laborers' children did not go hungry because of the money spent in saloons, how could one stand opposed?

I cannot abide the saloon men, who profit from others' weakness and stuff their bank accounts with money that should have bought schoolchildren's shoes, milk, and pencils. Yet the anti-saloon forces have lips too often pursed with a very un-Christian self-righteousness. Nor can I fully share their faith that laws will accomplish their goal. If liquor is such a powerful demon, then surely men who wish to drink will do so, whatever the law may say.

Thursday, January 8

More and more, everyone fears that a battle will break out between the classes. It is difficult to imagine, perhaps because we know quite well so many people from various classes. Would John Gorman suddenly appear at the back door with his rifle to rob us of the piano, merely because we are relatively well off? Never! Yet I suppose a mob of workers to whom we were strangers might do so with clear consciences, if selling the piano would buy a month's food for their wives and children.

Made a plan to see "Blindness of Virtue" next Monday. Julia sniffed that she had already seen it at the Cort in San Francisco.

Reading Mr. Harrison's *Queed*; enjoyable but of uncertain merit. After scores of pages, I have no idea how he intends me to feel about the be-spectacled Mr. Queed—precisely so when first meeting someone, as we cannot always foresee how we will feel about that person when we know him. I'm less impressed by the author's laziness in telling us that Sharlee's face appeals to men or that Mr. West is "good-looking." Such conclusions remind me that there *is* an author. Why can he not simply describe the man's features and let me make up my own mind?

Friday, January 9

Saw something startling this afternoon. Two aeroplanes kept flying into flocks of ducks above Merritt's Lake. Someone in one aeroplane shot them and the other aeroplane swept down to the water's surface and snatched them up! I spied Jack Choate and several prominent people laughing and cheering in automobiles.

Had I possessed a rifle, I might have pointed it at the aeroplanes.

This spectacle diminished my pleasure in anticipating Mr. Beachey's aeroplane race against Mr. Oldfield. Both men are said to be able to travel at marvelous speeds, more than a mile-a-minute. Mr. Beachey claims he will not only win the race but do a "loop-the-loop" in the air. It sounds great fun, but I cannot forget the slaughter of those hapless birds.

The ducks are my friends. In Whitman's words, "They are so placid and self-contained." Walking lakeside recently with Elizabeth as she prattled on, my eyes met a duck's eye, and I imagined he understood how silly she is.

My lakeside walk was interrupted by Mrs. Livingston who offered me a ride home in her five-passenger Packard. I heard a motor pass, then pause before it moved slowly alongside. I told her what she ought to have understood—that I was walking for the pleasure of it and in no hurry. She lectured me on the evils of excessive exercise: it makes us mannish, upsets the natural balance of our bodies, and reduces our natural desires to marry and have children. A doctor has determined that women footballers in New York suffer all sorts of health difficulties from over-exertion. Mindful of my determination not to give offense, I suffered her lecture in silence. As she drove off, I waved to her driver, which annoys her.

Of course, it is nonsense. Even if it *were* true, I should walk, as walks are a solace. How could anything so invigorating to body and mind be unnatural or harmful? Mrs. L. saddens rather than annoys me. She so wants her dear boy to find a woman to love him—and I am not that person.

Saturday, January 10

The post brought a checque from Bell's. Just before Christmas they sold two of my paintings! A wind-shaped cypress on Mount Tamalpais, and "Harbor Dawn," from our stay in Bodega Bay last fall. I am always startled that someone has purchased a painting. Startled, gratified, and a bit sad, as if parted forever from a friend.

Suzanne joined us last night. She fit in quite naturally. She speaks up readily, but not to show off, only to make some point, ask a sensible question, or make people laugh—and she'll argue with anyone about anything if she's in the mood.

When someone mentioned Oakland's change of heart about the Poundmaster giving live dogs to Stanford University for scientific experiments, Suzanne and Charles fought like dogs. Charles listed a host of diseases and conditions such experiments might help ameliorate, but Suzanne said that would mean nothing to the poor dogs' suffering. Bret said that curing all the diseases plaguing human beings would only result in more human beings, of whom he reckons there are far too many, a sentiment I often share. Jack asked Suzanne if she had written the anonymous note threatening Commissioner Turner with "tar and feathers and a lamp post"—and whether she proposed to hang Mr. Turner from the lamp post (or to tie him to it) for passing dogs to use as they might.

Robbie and Tub got into it about the Navy. Robbie recited a host of numbers proving that our Navy, once second only to Britain's, is behind Germany and France, and will soon be less powerful than Japan's. He says Germany has more than double the number of our big-gun dreadnoughts and would make quick work of our conventional ships. Tub said that it would be splendid if all the European powers spent their money on such things and left the United States free to invest in industrial production.

Bret and Jack argued about who would win if Jack Johnson, the negro prize-fighter, fights Gunboat Smith this summer. They call Smith the "White-Heavyweight Champion." Bret said Smith might follow John L. Sullivan's example in refusing to risk fighting a negro. This sparked a spirited discussion among the men over whether such conduct was simply right, and even fair, or reflected a lack of courage. Jack predicted that if a white boxer could beat Johnson, he had better impose such a line if he wished to keep his championship, "or he'll be looking up from the canvas at Joe Jeanette, or that Langford dinge from Boston." William said it is unfair for a white man to have to fight a black because the negro boxers are so recently removed from the jungle that their instincts for survival remain stronger than in more civilized peoples; but Robbie argued that Johnson's depraved life in Paris will likely have eliminated that advantage.

Suzanne remarked that if the jury in Los Angeles convicts Willard for the fight that killed his opponent, California will abolish the boxing game. Bret said that although people call prize-fighting repugnant, whenever two men fall to fisticuffs in a market, every eye is upon them. I do not see why men care to watch other men pummel each other bloody. But if these "gladiators" are men's heroes, then let them be heroes, and fight whoever may come in their way.

Earlier, we watched Lincoln Beachey. Astonishing! He flew upside down, and we could read the name "Beachey" on the top of his machine. He did his "loop-the-loop" and a series of twists and turns and spirals that nearly made me sick to my stomach. At one point the machine dove straight toward the ground, and everyone gasped, certain we were going to see something horrible, but then he pulled upward at the last moment. Evidently this is a standard part of his performance. He calls it the "Beachey bore"—but it wasn't boring.

It must be marvelous to fly.

Tub was disappointed that we have not yet seen Mr. Beachey race Mr. Oldfield's automobile. I said that I should love to have him take me up with him and wished I could learn to fly such a machine. Tub laughed, "Our own Harriet Quimby? I should think her fate might dissuade you." I pointed out that men have also crashed to their deaths. Jack teased me about wishing to fly when I refuse to ride with him on his motorcycle. To my amazement, all the rest, save Suzanne, said that nothing on earth would get them up in such a contraption. Elizabeth said she valued her life too much—perhaps I do not sufficiently value mine. Suzanne predicted that one day we will all be riding in aeroplanes as naturally as in trolleys or hansom cabs.

Sunday, January 11

After church today the Cahill's little boy, Christopher Timothy, was baptized. I was nearly as bored by the proceedings as Christopher Timothy. I found myself watching Adeline Gardiner's face, certain that she must be recalling the baptism of her own infant son, who has been in the grave hardly six months. Her face displayed a sad dignity, and did more than Father Mayne's chiding could have done to remind me of life's fragility. Yet afterward, as we all congratulated the Cahills, Adeline's face was radiant, as if through pure determination she had put away her sorrow at life's unfairness. When our eyes met, she smiled. I could think of nothing more imaginative to say than that it had been a very nice baptism. She replied, "Today had a particular auspiciousness to it, as if he is a special child. Perhaps this being the anniversary of Christ's own baptism made it more momentous."

At dinner, Elizabeth mentioned my excitement in watching Lincoln Beachey. Father, ever the skilled trial attorney, fixed his eyes on me. Softly he asked if he had heard correctly what I had said about avoiding automobiles, then whether Elizabeth's report was accurate. He then repeated both facts, his face feigning amazement at my inconsistency. (Fremont Older said Father questioned adverse witnesses like a coiled rattlesnake without the courtesy to rattle.)

Feeling like an awkward witness, I tried to explain that while to soar like a bird through the heavens would be a thrilling experience—for which I might risk death—I was not prepared to risk life and limb merely to arrive a few minutes earlier at Kahn's. If I died for such a trivial reason, I should stand before St. Peter absolutely mortified. I admitted, however, that I could not avoid automobiles forever. Father seemed to enjoy his victory.

Monday, January 12

I asked Aunt Agnes this morning why our family hadn't followed the custom of having men and women separate after supper. Her initial reaction echoed my own to Suzanne: she asked whether I meant to complain that my parents had failed to teach me appropriate social conduct. We laughed.

"Your father did not much like to be separated from your mother; and your mother relished spirited arguments and was determined to miss nothing, though she did loathe the smell of cigars."

I very much liked this from *Queed*: "For there are men in this world who will run ten city blocks in any weather to avoid talking to a woman who knows more than they do, and knows it, and shows that she knows it."

This afternoon we saw "Blindness of Virtue", the play Mrs. Bennett had railed against. I thought it well-intentioned, though too earnest. I am rarely captivated by plays designed to support a point-of-view, even one with which I generally agree. If the play does not add some magic—some surprising turn, or intriguing character, or moment of true poetry—then I should rather glance at the statement it supports than waste hours dressing and getting myself to and from the theater.

Tuesday, January 13

Helen, with some diffidence, spoke to me today about Richard. She had inferred, from something Suzanne said, that I had spoken of Richard as if he might return to Oakland—and to me. She hoped I did not still harbor such dreams.

I asked how she could be so certain that he would never return to Oakland.

"You have not heard from him that he may—or even that he is alive!"

I continued mixing paints, concentrating more intently than was necessary. Without looking up, I said, "I did not tell Suzanne that I expected him."

"You cannot read his years of silence as a sign that he will return to carry you away. If ever he returns to Oakland, it may well be with a wife and children."

I asked whether she thought the painting I was working on captured anything of the peace of Merritt's Lake at dawn.

"Do not be angry with me," she said, then added, "I wish only to be certain that you do not hold up your memory of Richard as a shield against arrows from Cupid."

If sometimes I wonder if Richard will return to Oakland, or whether he and I might come to care for each other again, well, I wonder about many things.

Helen was not fully satisfied, but she said nothing more.

Wednesday, January 14

Father guyed Elizabeth about the City Council's amendment of the liquor ordinance to permit sales at dances upon the police chief's approval. His voice fairly thundered as of old, reading from the *Enquirer*, which likes the new rule no more than he does. Chief Peterson may permit sales "upon 'his discretion,' so that the 'socially elite' of Oakland may dispense liquors at their dances."

With a nod to Elizabeth, he continued: "A delegation of the prominent society women, planning to inaugurate the 'Dansant' in this city, waited upon Mayor Frank K. Mott recently and requested that it be made possible for them to serve liquors at these affairs, saying that it was always customary, as a supper formed an important part of the dansant... The commissioners agreed with him that the society people should not be deprived of serving a regulation supper with wine at their affairs. Then it was discovered that the first of these fashionable affairs was scheduled to be given Thursday, whereas it would take 10 days for the ordinance to become law. Here was a dilemma. But the commissioners decided to solve the problem by countenancing a violation of their own laws. Commissioner Baccus moved that liquor be allowed to be sold at the dansant in the Hotel Oakland... It passed unanimously."

Looking up from the page, Father growled at us like a bear with a fish in its paws and repeated, "delegation of prominent society women" in a falsetto voice, wriggling his shoulders. He knew Elizabeth's views, even if he was uncertain that she had been in the party visiting Mayor Mott.

"Pure hypocrisy," he added, looking at me.

I protested my neutrality but couldn't help smiling.

When Father turned back to Elizabeth, Tub gallantly attempted a diversion, asking: "Isn't it exquisite irony that the very commissioner most associated with this whole controversy over liquor at dances should be named after the God of Wine?"

Father uses silence to better advantage than any speaker I've ever heard. He studied Tub as if his attention had been called to some rare species of insect with an oddly shaped mandible. Then, very distinctly, he dropped the word "Yes" into the silence, like a rock into a lake.

Not to be deterred, Father turned to Elizabeth and said, "Dansants? Dansants?" turning up his nose and mimicking a lady's British accent. I take it we've grown so sophisticated in Oakland that mere 'dances' won't suffice." Even Elizabeth laughed.

Father said he could understand the view that we should make whiskey illegal. "That's damn foolishness, but consistent. But protecting the working classes from themselves while setting a contrary example… Do you really suppose that you are somehow better suited than a housemaid or a laborer's wife to enjoy liquor without doing yourself harm?"

"Why yes, Father, because of my excellent upbringing," Elizabeth replied.

Father snorted merrily. "But your excellent parents didn't raise the entire herd that will attend these "dansants."

Tidying up after supper, I was struck by the following:

> William B. Tucker, a negro, who has been in jail 122 days on a charge of forgery, was yesterday sentenced to one year in the penitentiary. Tucker, who has been demonstrating his skill as a water color artist since his incarceration, today made an excellent plea for probation, but was refused, partly on account of the probation officers considered him a bad risk because he has no friends.

I had never thought of a negro learning to paint water colors. I wonder what sort of paintings they are, and where he learned. Does he paint from nature, or make portraits of the persons with whom he associates? And how terrible it must be to be in jail and without friends! Now that he has been convicted, will they still allow him to paint?

Thursday, January 15

Sat up late finishing *Queed*. Though I foresaw how it would end, I could not go to sleep until the problems had worked themselves out. Queed's character interested me. Though he was a bit too fine at times, I appreciated his unconventional integrity and social awkwardness; and of course Sharlee seemed like a sister; but also, now that I reflect, other characters, while guilty of misconduct, were not pure villains from a ten-twenty-thirty melodrama, but real people who managed to see things in a light that justified their conduct. "Minor" characters were portrayed with wisdom, humor, insight.

Mrs. Bennett and Reverend Finch turned their luncheon visit into a protracted effort to convince Father the magazine should take a strong position on the anti-saloon measure, and on November's prohibition referendum. As a mere bystander I enjoyed the match between their earnestness and Father's sense of humor.

"What did you buy the magazine for if not to use the power it gives you for good?" Reverend Finch asked.

"I bought it in a fit of pique, and have lived to regret it," Father replied.

Mr. Finch looked puzzled. I had thought everyone knew the story. Father explained that he was furious when the newspapers spent column after column on Blaine's death and merely half a paragraph on General Doubleday's. "Blaine entered Congress a pauper and left a massive estate after decades in public office, while the General was a gallant officer, cool under fire, often wounded, and later patented the cable-car. My wife dared me to stop fulminating and *do* something about it. So, I bought the magazine—and never have figured out what to do with it."

His visitors protested that he had done quite a bit with it and argued that he should do a bit more. Father referred them to Arthur Sullivan. They pointed out that Father remains chief shareholder. He conceded the point, but added that so long as he owned it, "the magazine will take the side of freedom—against political machines, dishonest government, trusts, and the railroads. For the negroes, the poor, and immigrant workers. Asking some flatfoot to take charge of morality invites him to arrest a Slav worker for his bottle of beer and look the other way while Patrick Calhoun sips a glass of wine—and powerfully tempts him to line his pockets in the process."

Mrs. Bennett asked, "What about the freedom of wives whose husbands give their pay envelopes to the saloon men? What of the freedom of children who tremble when they hear their fathers stumbling home at night? Why fight the trust that overcharges us for necessities but not the saloon man who makes men slaves to drink, robbing them of both money and mind?"

Father suggested that perhaps they could persuade Art, "or Katherine, who I keep hoping will take the thing over." When they turned to me, eyes bright, I said that I limited my role to occasional reviews of books and art exhibitions. As if watching a lawn-tennis shot, they turned their heads back toward Father, paying me no further attention.

When Mrs. Bennett invoked Frances Willard and expressed disbelief that anyone who shared "that great name" could decline to stand up for temperance, Father nodded, as if in agreement, and said, "Yes, I've been reading a lot about *Jess* Willard of late, but I shan't take up prize-fighting." He reminded Reverend Finch that Jesus's first miracle was the turning of water into wine, rather than the reverse. Still, he was courteous and did not say all that I know him capable of.

After they left, Father said I might do well to consider taking a more active role on the magazine. He is right, of course, yet I can never bring myself to do so.

Tonight, was Art Appreciation Club. We are gaining some enthusiasm, I think. Professor Clark gave a fine lecture on the value of artistic efforts to interpret nature in black and white.

Friday, January 16

I am not yet sleepy. Nor do I wish to read. My mind is busy musing over this evening's gathering.

I am pleased with Edward for Helen. He is manly, strong, and handsome; capable in his work; and progressive in his political views. Above all, he seems truly to love her, and does not see her as a mere housekeeper, outlet for his sexual energies, and mother to his children. In matters that concern him, he weighs her opinions seriously. He listens courteously concerning other matters and allows her spheres of interest that need not involve him.

Do I damn him with faint praise? I do not mean to. He is not the man I might have chosen for Helen—although Helen is more practical than I, and moved less by artistic impulses, what she does have of imagination he will not encourage her to develop. He will not disparage or discourage her; but, lacking such qualities himself, he is as unaware of its value as a horse is of whatever it crushes under its hoofs. Edward is driven to innovate in business, accumulate wealth, and live a comfortable family life, and what is not essential to those he may fail to appreciate.

Still, Edward is the finest specimen of the type of man he is. Few businessmen condemn so sternly the violent crushing of miners' strikes or the conditions that cause tragic factory fires. Where Mr. Powers regards the national government's policies on trusts as a declaration of war, Edward sees a healthy and natural regulation that, as one weeds a garden to encourage flowers and vegetables, will help smaller businesses to prosper and new ideas to find the light. Where Mr. Powers complains that requiring better working conditions will jeopardize profits, Edward sees a prudent route to industrial peace—and eventually to higher productivity and profits. He speaks like a preacher of the need for capitalists and workers to make common cause.

Bret called *Queed* "a reconstructed *Deliverance*." I was startled, but I see what he means. Each brings together a man and a woman from opposite sides of a southern feud, the noble child of a fine but impoverished family, and the child of the dastardly man who wronged and ruined that family during the Civil War or Reconstruction. In each, the child of the villain insists on making things right. However, *Queed* passes but lightly over Reconstruction itself, as something the local white gentry fought, without beating into us that all carpetbaggers were vicious, negroes all stupid, and white gentry noble hearted. No cloying sentimental portraits of former slaves loyal to their former owner's widow and children, even longing for ante-bellum days. The few negro characters serve dinner or go about their business, without making stump speeches for Jefferson Davis. Except for a few passages, *Queed* might take place in any small city.

Jack told a remarkable story about his cousin Fobster, a balloonist, who took his fiancée to Siberia, where they made an ascent from Vladivostok but met with dangerous weather. His fiancée grew distressed. He made an emergency landing near a river; but when he jumped out, holding the balloon by a rope, he noticed a Siberian tiger. He threw himself to the ground. The tiger, much more interested in the balloon than in the man, leapt at the car, and clung to it with his claws as the balloon began to ascend with the poor girl still inside! Fobster, pulling the balloon along like a kite, jumped into the river. With the balloon above the river, he urged his girl to jump into the water. After she did so, he released the rope and let the balloon ascend, much to the amazement of the tiger!

Bret says it's nonsense, pointing to the frigid temperatures of a siberian river in August. Still, it makes a wonderful story, which Jack swears is true.

Saturday, January 17

I dreamt of Siberia: beautiful countryside, with much snow and ice. I had fallen out of a balloon and been left behind; shivering, hungry, and without clothing, my body was covered with sores. I had to find the village. This grisly scene felt oddly familiar.

I recalled a dream I often had as a child. I had seen a magazine picture of a Siberian leper dragging food through the snow. Mother explained that hungry lepers would cry at the edge of the village, and when one woman leper persisted in sneaking into the village to steal food, the authorities took all her clothes—but still she attempted it, until she was found lying frozen under a tree. There were also bears, and a clever dog that danced and barked and led the bears away from the lepers' camp, deep into the forest.

Sunday, January 18

Grey clouds and rain. The greyness suits me, or do I suit it, as a lake's color varies with shifting skies? The day seems unable to commit itself either to a downpour or to letting up—as do I. Thoughts of Richard distracted me in church this morning... For whom am I writing all this?

In girlhood, I began a diary as a record of what I saw and heard and wanted to tell Mother and Father about when they came home. When I learned that Mother never would come home, I kept it up—my silent, stubborn resistance to her death. By the time Father came home, the diary had become a habit I then maintained even at Mills.

I suppose I fell out of habit while keeping company with Richard. When he left, I resisted the urge to begin again. I don't know why. Pain? Even then I had doubts about his return and wanted neither to indulge my maudlin self-pity nor to deny it by writing hopeful nonsense.

Now I have no one to address. Mother is a vague memory. Richard is nearly as distant. Yet I feel I am speaking to someone… I have no child. My painting will never earn me such renown that some future student will search these pages for inspiration. Perhaps there is in each of us a second mind, or voice, formed by the collective words of parents, teachers, and companions, our dreams and imaginings, and what we suppose we ought to be. Perhaps I write to *that* Katherine: explaining, justifying, questioning. Painting requires no reason. I do not ask myself why I paint—why ask why I write? I enjoy it!

When Elizabeth stopped by this afternoon, she was wearing a hat with a brilliant aigrette. Not ostrich, but egret! I was shocked. As she intended. She concentrated so fixedly on the task of removing and setting it on the hall table that there was no chance her gaze would meet mine.

I bit my tongue at first but could not resist remarking on it. She feigned surprise, then made excuses as weak as the millinery industry's old claim that no egrets were slaughtered for their plumes, that the plumes were picked up from the grounds of "egret farms" in Tripoli or somewhere. She blinked her eyes several times and murmured that even if laws now forbade importing or selling such things, no law prohibited purchasing them.

"These feathers are from birds killed before the laws were passed," she said, tossing her hair and flashing a smile that seemed to contain at least 72 teeth. I urged her to confine her ornamental purchases to ostrich feathers from ostrich farms. She replied that as everyone would be wearing ostrich, she could not.

Father remarked, "As Elizabeth has the centuries-old instinct of women that life can no more exist without bright adornment than without bread, a few distant warblers hardly signify."

Elizabeth's account of the dancing last night elicited an impatient lecture from Aunt Agnes on how tiresome the tango craze has become. "We have tango hats, tango waists, tango stockings, and tango shoes, and I have read that 'tango' is a color now. Soon we will be consulting Doctors of Tango and depositing money in the Tango National Bank."

"The tango mania will run its course, just as roller-skating did thirty years ago, or the six-day walking matches that preceded that," Father predicted.

Wednesday, January 21

I did not manage even three weeks before neglecting to write anything at all for a day, then two. I had no thoughts worthy of expression. (Are any of my thoughts worth expressing?)

Supper with the Powers family. Addison asked my opinion of Edward. I had not supposed he much cared for the opinion of an unmarried woman whose only children are tulips and landscapes. I carefully expressed neither my private misgivings nor the qualities I appreciate in Edward's views, which would surely not recommend him to Mr. P! I said Edward was high-minded and determined, that anyone could see that he loved Helen, and she him, and that since he was set on making his way in the world, the marriage seemed promising. When I asked what he thought, Mr. Powers smiled and said, "Had I been appointed chairman of the selection committee, we might have reached a different result; but I was not. Perhaps it will be all right." I sensed a softening in him toward the idea.

Mrs. Powers was still shaken by her experience in San Francisco yesterday evening, calling it, "nearly a revolution." The streets were seething with crowds shouting, smashing windows, and singing revolutionary songs, and even battling with the police. The Wobblies, Charles says.

She says they gave her a fright on the way to the theater and delayed her carriage returning. "They all kept shouting about 'free speech' and 'free assemblage,' but they didn't mind interfering with *my* rights of free assemblage." She was angry that Mrs. Parsons, widow of one of the Chicago Haymarket rioters, was involved, and insisted that California should not have permitted her to enter the state. Charles eventually got her to admit she knew of no law by which the state could have kept the woman out. He also said that if police had permitted the original meeting, there would have been no rioting.

"Of course, they are just your sort," she replied. After glancing upward for heavenly assistance, she stated, not for the first time, that Charles's law practice required closer contact with criminals and policemen than was healthy or wise. She went on that she knows he will not take the Southern Pacific job but asked why he must represent "sweaty immigrants whose noxious odors keep decent people from riding the trolley cars," when their employers pay better and speak English. Charles said nothing and kissed her cheek. When I asked him later why he prefers his sort of practice, he said, "It can be heartbreaking, but it is always interesting. I like that they don't speak English or know which fork is for which course. What would I learn from being closeted with Borax Smith or Charles Weyerhauser, let alone Herrin?"

The post-supper rainstorm washed away my avoidance of automobiles. I had intended to walk home, but it was pouring, and Charles offered to drive me. He is a careful driver, although how he could see anything is a mystery. I asked how he liked Edward. "Edward who?" he joked. He says his father "will end by liking Edward better than any of us."

It rained until the streets ran like streams!

Thursday, January 22

The ground was soft, and the sky clear this morning as I sketched in the garden while Helen told of distressing floods in outlying areas; and Bret spoke bitterly of the "battle parties" in Texas, in which society folk are taken to hilltops to view the fighting in Juarez. I could not take my eyes from two snails on the path behind him engaged in procreation. Suddenly it seemed that neither floods nor carnage could possibly be more worthy of attention than the calm that follows a storm, and the scent of fertility everywhere. Then the rains started again, sending us indoors and leaving the snails their privacy.

Friday, January 23

Bizarre day. I awakened early and took advantage of a lull in the storm to go walking earlier than usual. Near Lakeshore I became aware of tremendous excitement: several firemen and others ran past me toward where some men were shouting. I followed and beheld a bear hunt in the middle of Oakland! Apparently, the poor thing had escaped from someone's home in Alameda. It was still not light, and the men were stumbling around with torches, and making lassos out of clothesline. Finally, they shot it. How sad.

In the afternoon I accompanied Bret to interview Lincoln Beachey. He and Barney Oldfield are back to perform more stunts and will race tomorrow and Sunday at Emeryville, if the weather allows.

Aviators are different from the rest of us, and must be, to do what they do—living so close to death. I could see it in Mr. Beachey's narrowed eyes and his determinedly offhand manner. He refers to death as "it", as if it were some creature lurking in the clouds, and says, "It will get me when it wants me, but so far I haven't struck it as tasty enough." Did his fatalism draw him to flying, or have the deaths of so many fellow fliers, and his own close brushes with death, made him a fatalist? Strong wind rattled the canvas tent; an angry spirit warning us what it could do to a man who dared brave it in a flimsy aeroplane?)

A mechanic told Mr. Beachey that a French aviator had died, and Mr. Beachey's cobalt blue eyes seemed to dull, and he fell silent, looking down fixedly as he lit a cigarette. (Earlier, while telling us about nearly falling asleep from the drowsiness the cold induces at high altitudes, he had lit a cigarette as easily as taking a breath.) A friend urged him not to go up. He shook his head. "It won't want two of us in the same day." Bret raised an eyebrow, and Mr. Beachey added that if "it" wanted him, it could find him as easily in a railroad car or an automobile.

"Do you think about it while you're flying?" Bret asked.

"Just before going into a dive, I've looked down at the crowd and thought that half of them expect me to die, even crave the thrill of seeing a man die, and the pleasure of telling their friends. But, no, you can't think about it. You'd lose your nerve. A flier who thinks about it invites it."

Asked what he feared most, Mr. Beachey laughed and replied, "Sneezing." Bret asked if he were serious. He said he wasn't, "But if you've once had a sneeze make you momentarily lose control, you know how easily sneezing could make a man suddenly jerk the controls and be unable to recover."

When I offered Mr. Beachey a four-leaf clover for luck, he raised his hands and shaking his head said weakly, "No, thank you." We were told later that fliers do not care for four-leaf clovers. A few years ago, someone painted a four-leaf clover on a French monoplane and the two fliers in it were killed soon after becoming aloft.

This evening, I told everyone about the bear. Jack laughed at my sympathy for the owner. He knows the man, and says he was planning to use the bear in a hunt and was selling tickets at three dollars to men who wanted to hunt down the poor animal!

Bret is always so full of lively accounts of human foolishness. Tonight, he told us of a man coming into the police station and shyly reporting that while he was walking on Franklin Street near 12th at about midnight, a girl dressed in man's clothing held a gun in front of his face. He stuck up his hands, and after she searched him and found no money, she kissed him and told him to run along home and tell his wife about his adventure. The policemen started laughing, and the man ran off without giving his name. Not ten minutes later Sean O'Hara came in and told the policemen that on the same block he'd been held up by a girl who took $2.40 and a watch—then returned the watch. She then returned forty cents, saying he probably needed a drink before going home to the wife.

"I'm in love!" Bret shouted over our laughter.

Saturday, January 24

Returned to Emeryville to watch the race. How strange to see Mr. Beachey and his aeroplane trailing Mr. Oldfield's Simplex racer, like some huge eagle swooping down after a rabbit. Mr. Oldfield's "rabbit" won, but it was a close contest. Suzanne photographed them together, Mr. Oldfield in a plaid coat and waving a cigar, and Mr. Beachey neatly turned out in a dark suit.

In today's mail there was a cutting from *Munsey's Magazine* of an anonymous article entitled "The Plaint of a Spinster" in which "by one of them" was crossed out and replaced with "by Katherine W?" Unlike the author, I don't feel "stunned wonder" about my unmarried state; but I certainly wonder who sent this. At first, I was annoyed, then amused. Then annoyed again because I spent much of the day answering in my mind the implicit charges of my anonymous correspondent.

"There is no tragedy like that of the woman who wants a home and has none, who dreamt of motherhood and never knew the reality," writes the "spinster." I wished to reply that while it may also be "tragic" to fail in one's dream to play baseball with the New York Highlanders, or invent an automatic starter for automobiles, I do not aspire to any of it.

I was particularly annoyed by the interlineations. Just below a passage on childless women someone had written, "painting landscapes or planting the entire state in tulip bulbs and pansies;" and underlined, "Because I disdained asserting myself to catch the eyes of men, I am sitting alone, with the useless riches of my nature mildewing and festering in the damp of my own tears and the fever of my rebellion."

Foolishness! So why am I so irritated? The spinster's self-portrait (if the thing was not written by some man) resembles me not at all. If it hit closer to the mark, I should be unable to laugh at it. Whoever sent it has not only invaded my privacy but badly misread my character. How forward! And yet I cannot reply.

Sunday, January 25

Sometimes the power and solemnity of the music in church makes me more reverent (rather as granite and marble enhance a building's grandeur), and sometimes a hymn will remind me of mischief committed in childhood while I pretended to sing it.

This morning, as I sang, I let my eyes wander. All around me, familiar voices were singing familiar words. A few pews over were Mr. and Mrs. Anderson and their three children. She held the hymnal, glancing up now and again with a look of pure adoration and delight that he was by her side, which she tries to mute to avoid inspiring in him remorse for his frequent absences. He glanced down at her, their eyes meeting briefly, his face a study in embarrassment at being in church and being touched by her pleasure. (I could not see his face, but I know that look well.) Beside her, Mary, the eldest, held a hymnal for herself and Patricia. Billy, the youngest, his high-pitched voice unable to confine itself to any one key, doggedly held his own hymnal, though it dwarfed his little hands. God probably delights more in his voice than in many a polished baritone.

In the pew in front of us were William and Lucy Cooke. I could not see her sightless eyes, but I know her face was the picture of sincere devotion. She sings fervently, head up and shoulders back, still the good little girl reciting her verses in the one-room schoolhouse in Williamstown that burned down more than half a century ago. Mr. Cooke's face I could see, and for a moment I could not look away, though I felt like an intruder. Of course, he paid me no mind, for his eyes are always wholly on *her*. He even seems to sing to *her*, not to God—or to God in thanks for her? When we sang, "New every morning is the love," I almost think he believed we were celebrating *Mrs. Cookes'* loveliness and goodness and strength.

I looked over at Aunt Agnes beside me, her voice as sure as ever. As a child, I had looked around stealthily, but now she has no duty to correct me, and if she sees that my attention wanders, it is because her own attention wanders too. I let my gaze rest again on Mrs. Cooke. What if I were to be afflicted thus? I closed my eyes and heard the many individual voices, a cough, a nearby child kicking at the legs of the pew in front of him. Everything sounded louder and closer, as if we were in the belly of a big fish.

Tub and Elizabeth came for lunch despite the horrid weather.

Father mentioned a newspaper story about a man found in his lodging house with a bullet in his head, and a note saying that doctors had told him that he would not recover from a paralytic stroke he'd suffered two years ago. He then read aloud two lines from the note: "I have long held to the belief that one in such condition should be afforded every facility for an easy exit. I know this is heretical to accepted doctrine and to that on which I was brought up, but I am right." Elizabeth shuddered. Tub looked uneasily around the table.

"Sensible fellow," Father concluded with a smile and that slight jutting of chin that suggested he anticipated a debate. If anyone disagreed, no one rose to the bait.

"Do not let us speak of such things," Elizabeth said quietly. Father gave her a queer look but said no more.

Monday, January 26

Confused dreams this morning. I was with Mr. Beachey in his aeroplane. He wore his neat, dark suit, and the same charming smile, but his head was that of a bear—and men kept throwing things at the aeroplane, trying to make us crash! Then I was standing on the ground, near Merritt's Lake, watching. Men with long sticks and guns forced Mr. Beachey's aeroplane into sharper and sharper turns in the air, until finally he crashed into the lake. Later, the men goaded me, prodding me with sticks, one shouting, "Simpering spinster!"

Tuesday, January 27

The storm seems to be over. Eight people are dead—the most deadly storm in California since '89! Railway traffic still has not fully resumed. Near Merritt's Lake, where branches lay on the ground, I tried to capture the unsettled mood of the world lightening up again after a violent storm. I do not think I succeeded but will see what I can make of it tomorrow in the studio. Afterward I tidied up in the garden, which the storm had also disturbed.

Supped with Helen and her parents. Her father and Edward argued over Mr. Ford's startling announcement that he will distribute among his employees ten million dollars from this year's profits. Mr. Powers called Ford "a damned fool" for advertising that his prices are so high he can "squander millions to prove his saintliness." Edward said that was not saintliness, but enlightened management designed to hire better men than the competition—and it would motivate the men to produce as efficiently as possible if higher profits for the company meant an increase in a man's own income.

Charles agreed but was appalled by Mr. Ford's announcement that men who smoked cigarettes or drank alcohol might be unable to share in the distribution. He added that the men's morals away from the factory are their own concern. Edward replied that drink is responsible for a great percentage of industrial accidents. Mr. Powers interrupted to say it was "a lot of damned nonsense," calling Mr. Ford a frustrated preacher.

Despite being at odds, Mr. Powers may be coming to respect Edward. As I was leaving, Edward said that Mr. Powers had requested that he call at his office on Thursday. He was brusque and gave no clue as to the subject. "He is convinced that I am some sort of fortune hunter," Edward said. "Perhaps he will offer me a substantial sum of money to leave Oakland."

"Are you hoping so?" Helen asked, smiling.

"I only hope it's a generous offer," Edward said. "I'm a reasonable man."

Helen's grandparents were there as well. Mr. Cooke walks as erect as ever, but seems smaller, and moves slowly. Mrs. Cooke has always seemed old—and young. I try to imagine her face at sixteen, crossing the plains by wagon. She could hold us spellbound with stories of when she was captured by Indians, then rescued after a battle. "Suddenly a handsome young man with blue eyes was holding me in his arms, and that was William," she would say, giggling like a schoolgirl.

It is distressing to read everywhere of censorship, the outcry against "The Lure" and "Fight" on the New York stage, and Mr. Comstock's railing against *Hagar Revelly*. The novel is sad and unappealing, indeed; but if it be even remotely accurate, then that very ugliness is its virtue, rather than cause for burning it. What young girl, contemplating Hagar's sad figure, could wish to emulate her?

It seems that the two plays' serious study of the relationship between White Slavery and politics has caused the outcry. Suzanne says there's not a word in "The Lure" that could provoke a leer or snicker. Rather, it makes the case that some of our most powerful political figures benefit from the exploitation of young girls captured on city streets like wild beasts in the jungle, although that news almost seems old-hat after recent events in Los Angeles and Seattle. (Have the newspapers attacking "The Lure" forgotten the huge profits they made by printing every sordid detail of the Thaw case?)

I do not presume to select what others ought to see or read, and I am an unmarried woman who has taken no interest in such matters for several years now. While I understand Aunt Agnes's views—the dramatic changes between men and women confuse many—I do not see how serious drama or literature could avoid the topic. The women's movement, which is radically changing the relationship between the sexes, may be the most important aspect of our time. How could theater worthy of the name let the Pecksniffs and Chadbands limit it to pretty, little comedies and dusty tragedies from earlier times?

Wednesday, January 28

The petition for a ballot vote abolishing prizefighting has more than 32,000 names! Mine is among them. Father's is not.

I see no good in two men beating each other senseless. The loser, if beaten badly enough, may become a public charge; the winner becomes the idol of schoolboys—who dream of beating someone senseless, and begin practicing on their weaker schoolmates.

Father waggled his finger at me. "If I abolished painting, would you not manage to paint? What would I improve by enriching the criminals who smuggled in the paints or rented you a studio at inflated rates? Or the 'cop' who turned a blind eye for a few dollars when he surprised you in a meadow with your easel? I should make you, the smugglers, and the policeman great friends and push the whole activity underground."

Dr. Williams supped with us. I must have looked put out with him because as soon as the opportunity arose for private conversation he asked, "Did you think me harsh with your friend?"

I nodded. "Were you not?"

"Superficially, yes. Sometimes the strictest doctor, in refusing to give habit-forming drugs to relieve pain, is in fact the most tender-hearted, whereas the kinder fellow is so cowardly he constitutes a danger to the community."

"Do you suppose Suzanne would have become a drug fiend?" I asked.

"I had a patient whose family condemned me roundly for trying to take the edge from his pain with ice bags, fly plasters, liniments, oils, and other external applications; but he's a healthy man today. A woman suffering the same sort of infection at the same time, attended by a 'kindlier' physician, remains a confirmed habitué of laudanum, despite twice being weaned at an institution. And to everyone she advertises her physician as a great healer."

Thursday, January 29

Worked in the studio on "After the Storm" to no great effect. If ever I improve it sufficiently to name it, I shall find a less banal title; but I have never been very good at titles. Nor was I very good at painting this morning. It reflects the flatness and disorder of the storm's aftermath, but not the promise of sunlight starting to burn off the clouds—and how that feels, which *can* be painted somehow, though not as yet by me.

Helen and I lunched at the Hotel Oakland, chatting of family and wedding plans. She and Mrs. Powers have already amassed quite a storehouse of clothes and useful objects for her trousseau. As we finished dessert, Edward arrived to report on his interview with her father. Helen had thought her father would offer Edward some sort of partnership. Edward thought that Mr. Powers wanted to make one last effort to discourage the marriage. I had guessed that Mr. Powers simply wanted an opportunity to talk with Edward man-to-man.

Mr. Powers asked Edward many pointed questions about handling workers, financial prudence, and developing business relationships, with much coughing and harrumphing at Edward's answers. Finally, Mr. Powers offered Edward a position, though hardly a partnership. Edward conceded that it was a generous offer.

Helen was delighted, but Edward quickly advised her that he had respectfully declined. "I told him I was honored and grateful, and that if ever the time should come when he felt inclined to make such an offer based on his appraisal of my value as a businessman, I should be likely to consider it favorably. Your father protested that he would not make the offer unless he believed I merited it, but I suggested that the offer was based solely on his love for you and his concern that you be well provided for—and his concern that I could ensure that. I strongly doubt that such a business relationship would work out very well for any of us, and said I hoped he understood."

"Was he angry?" Helen asked.

Edward stroked his chin with his thumb and forefinger, then looked away, as if trying to recapture the moment. "I don't think so. He showed little feeling. He simply stared at me, puzzling something out. Then he rose and extended his hand and said rather formally, 'Well, thank you for coming in.' I repeated my thanks to *him*. And here I am."

"Do you suppose he regrets your decision?" I asked.

"Frankly, I think he made the offer with regret, and hadn't dared dream I might decline," Edward replied.

I wondered aloud whether Edward thought Mr. Powers respected him more now, and therefore might feel some remorse that they would not be working together.

Edward laughed. "That's a kind thought."

Friday, January 30

Informed Helen yesterday of the anonymous letter. I felt oddly uncomfortable speaking of it. She was appalled and sympathetic.

Helen wishes for me the kind of happiness she is rushing toward with Edward. But whom would she have me marry? Jack Choate is handsome and devilishly funny, but I deeply distrust him. I sense that if I submitted to him there would be a kind of triumph in his eyes that would verge on meanness. (I am a prize to be won and then?) William offers something quite different from marriage. Robbie is kind and trustworthy, but as imaginative as a hat-rack and as lively as a wet mop, and I could hardly brook having Mrs. Livingston as "family." Bret is the least offensive candidate. I respect him and enjoy his company, and I hope we will be friends all our lives; but it has never occurred to me to regard him in that way, nor has he ever hinted that it has occurred to him. (I recall reading of some old British clergyman who said that many people marry to lose themselves, a game that neither wins.)

Saturday, January 31

A new man brought the manure today. He was very dark, Greek, or Italian, and spoke little English. As I took him a glass of water with lemon juice, I thought to remember how his skin positively glistened from the effort of unloading the cart. Just then, Jack Choate arrived on his motorcycle.

"Who's your friend of the Black Hand?" he asked me, as if the man could no more understand Jack than the horse could. I said I did not know his name. Shaking his head, Jack asked, "Why is it that all throughout California the Greeks and Italians are taking the lion's share of the laboring work from honest working men?"

"It's not as if *you* need the work," I said a little sharply.

"Hardly," he agreed. "Still, it's disquieting."

He then rattled on and on about how the 1914 Indian was the perfect motorcycle: cradle springs, a two-speed gear, folding footboards, an electric starter, and numerous other wonders. He might as well have been speaking to the horse.

February

Monday, February 2

The first bulbs have begun thrusting little pointed leaves up through the soil. Each year they surprise me, like small creatures, just born, poking a curious green face into the world. Fortunately, the bulbs seem to like what they see well enough to investigate further.

Helen is furiously sewing, crocheting, and embroidering in anticipation of the Great Day. She showed me a selection of handmade nightgowns and tablecloths and towels. If their prayers are answered for a "fruitful union," her frenzied activity will have served as preparation for a Blessed Event. (God help me for being grateful I am not in her position!)

Went to the Cookes' open house to celebrate their sixty-second wedding anniversary. The Cookes astonish me—not only for the strength and length of their bond, but they look and behave as if they were much younger. Had I not seen Mr. Cooke hammering away, I would never believe he built their home, and in his eighties! Mrs. Cooke is a treasure of old-fashioned "wisdom," such as, "Always wear your prettiest clothes, and never allow yourself to get careless in your appearance" and, "Neatness and pretty clothes are the secrets of youth"—yet she has done more interesting work than many men. She was a newspaperwoman in Oregon for years, published a book of poems well before I was born, and says she has another volume ready in manuscript!

Conversation turned to their first meeting while crossing the wilderness in covered wagons, well before the Civil War. That chance meeting, like a tiny seed drifting on the wind, has grown into six decades of married life, with four children and many grandchildren and great-grandchildren. I cannot imagine what it would be like to have shared intimately with a man twice the number of years I've been alive. Mrs. Cooke was seventeen when they married, nearly half my age!

Went out this evening with Suzanne and Ann Swinburn to a little restaurant called "The Gipsy Wagon" hidden away in the back of the Miller Building. It is said to be like restaurants in Greenwich Village, where writers and artists congregate. The women who operate the place all wore bobbed hair and smocks and berets. I had not realized that there was such a place in Oakland. Light at the tables was limited to candlelight from red candles fixed in wicker-frocked wine bottles covered with drippings. Back numbers of *The Masses* and *Metropolitan Magazine* lay on a table in the rear, although the light was too dim for reading.

Miss Swinburn cross-questioned me about what I paint and was quite disappointed to hear that I paint landscapes.

"Why?" she demanded, looking down her nose at me.

"Must there be a reason?" I asked.

She snorted. "There must. Not because I would have one, but because there always is. Whether we choose to *know* our reasons, well that is another matter."

I replied that the beauty of the land calls to me, much more so than people and our objects.

Miss Swinburn says that "Art for Art's Sake" is "a vicious formula of the reactionary dilettantes," and means "art for the sake of pleasing the privileged classes," whereas *true* art must struggle to expose the ways the privileged exploit the people. "Your distaste for the nature of man's world, that is precisely what you should paint."

I pointed out that I paint pictures, and do not write tracts. Still, her manner amused me. She cares as little for courtesies as a brown bear, but she means well and does much good work. It was an invigorating evening.

Tuesday, February 3

Elizabeth and Tub and I supped with Uncle Thomas and Aunt Emily. Uncle Thomas was blown up like a blowfish about Mexico.

"Just as I predicted, the Mexicans have given in to us and released Harwood," he said. We all agreed that this was fine news. "I knew Huerta could be made to understand that Harwood had powerful friends in this country—and it would be very poor judgment to offend." He leaned back in his chair and snapped his braces with his thumbs, as proud as if he himself had gone to Mexico and rapped Huerta's knuckles with a ruler. "Now if only the damned Congress were as tractable," he added.

"What have they done now? Aunt Emily asked.

"Defeated the Hayes Amendment. Soundly. 'Oh, goodness, we wouldn't want to offend the Japa-KNEES,'" he added in a simpering tone. "Refused to do anything regarding Asiatic exclusion, even after the amendment had been very much weakened. One eastern Congressman accused Californians of waging a Japanese war. I'd like to hear what tune he'd sing if *his* state were being inundated with the Yellow Tide."

"Independence Day speakers and political candidates praise this country for welcoming adventurous immigrants with the courage to leave their own hidebound countries," Tub said, mischievously. "The Constitution doesn't mention the Asiatics."

"Yes, but Japan was only opened during the past half-century. Madison and Jefferson knew nothing of it. They knew good solid farming folk from Western Europe," Uncle countered.

It's not an argument that interests me greatly, but I have been told it would if I were in business. I *have* read that there are marvelous gardens, and marvelous paintings of gardens, in Japan.

As I often do when Uncle is talking, I wandered off into some other part of my mind. "Woolgathering," he used to say with a snort. I learned early to wear an attentive expression, as one might leave a pleasant note for the milkman.

I tried to picture Oakland with so many Japanese that we had Japanese gardens everywhere. It was a lovely vision: peaceful, meditative. Then I pictured Uncle in the robes of a Shinto priest, looming in front of me, that expression on his face, like a greedy boy grasping for candy. I had a sudden fit of nerves, the sort I sometimes feel around Uncle Thomas.

Wednesday, February 4

Spent the entire day in gloves and gardening hat, carefully turning over earth and sifting out stones and old roots, then working the manure into the soil. Our clay soil is so stubborn. How satisfying, when with my own two hands I manage to turn a hard, unmalleable patch of dirt, soft and nourishing. As free of cares as a child in a sandbox, I dug up each clod, shook it out, picked through it, raked the surface, dug it up again with the hand-trowel—all the while full of thoughts that now elude me.

We ought to treat everything as a good gardener treats the soil, yet most of us lack the patience. How wonderful it is that a flower depends upon the most unglamourous commodity on God's Earth—dirt. I am so grateful for the garden. It has increasingly become my refuge. In the garden, there is only earth below, and

the birds overhead, and if we're lucky, a light breeze catching the wind-chimes.

Elizabeth was watching me from the porch for some time before I rose and noticed her there. "You must be mad," she said and shook her head. I replied with the importance of good soil, and she replied with, "You take it beyond all reason. Not only in doing the work yourself, but in sifting and re-sifting as if you were making an apple pie for President Wilson."

Elizabeth has not the capacity to imagine how good I feel in the garden, where there are no subtle social rituals, hidden schemes, or hurt feelings. The stones I remove do not spit jealously at the clods of dirt I retain; and while the weeds try to get the better of me, there is no malice in their struggle.

What I can hardly admit to myself, never mind sharing with Elizabeth, is that more recently, the garden has become a welcome distraction from worrying about Father, who seems less and less vigorous, like a snapdragon after flowering.

Consequently, I have been thinking more about the magazine. Others have occasionally forced me to consider it: Mrs. Bennett exclaiming of the good I could do; Ann Swinburn chastising me for squandering my energy and talent on painting landscapes instead of painting word pictures of child-laborers and squalid sweatshops; Art Sullivan asking whether I might contribute to the examination of the Woman Question—which Father put him up to, I suspect. (Is it horribly selfish to focus on capturing beauty and playing with soil when more meaningful work needs doing? Fiddling while Rome burns?)

<u>Thursday, February 5</u>

Worked all morning on improving a mediocre landscape of ducks at Merritt's Lake, and all afternoon in the garden, making unsatisfactory progress on both. Is this a life? Most days both provide some measure of contentment, even moments of joy, but it hardly feels so, today.

Bret stopped by after a day spent covering the Pearsson trial. Ida Pearsson testified, and Bret, ever the cynic, said she was "got up to look so mournfully innocent that she'd have to shield her eyes from a flower's stamen." She was dressed all in black, and her mother and father helped her to the witness stand as if she were an invalid.

Friday, February 6

Dreamt I was testifying in a vast courtroom in only my bathing costume. I had been violated by a young man while intoxicated and was mortified to recite the sordid details. The lawyer asked extremely precise questions, and when I could not recall some detail, the bailiff presented a top hat from which I picked a scrap of paper instructing me to pay some embarrassing forfeit—as in the game we played as children. I was also made to stand on a desk and name the members of President Wilson's cabinet. The judge was Uncle Thomas who listened intently, all the while greedily gobbling Hub Wafers from a paper sack. My lawyer was William Wilson, the Secretary of Labor. I apologized for never having read his poetry. "That's all right," he replied, in a kindly manner. "Your heart will be in the right place once you plant it."

Every time the opposing lawyer wished to approach me, he had to place his feet in a particular sequence of squares, as in hopscotch. Once when the lawyer failed to do so, I looked up at Uncle Thomas, expecting him to order the lawyer to begin again, but he merely ordered me to answer the question. Suddenly only Uncle Thomas and I remained in the courtroom, and I woke up. (Perhaps Bret's sad account of the Pearsson girl affected me more than I realized!)

What a startling turn in Adeline Gardiner's life! Last night as she and her husband sat in their living room, she heard a baby's cries. She supposed her grief was playing tricks, as she has not recovered from the death of her son last year. Victor and Edith heard the cries as well, and upon investigation, found a baby boy wrapped in silks and a blue baby blanket on the porch. From the handle of the basket hung a note on very fine paper, saying the child was "little Mr. Nobody, born January 28, 1914, at 9 p.m.," and entrusting the Gardiners with his care. Adeline is delighted and hopes the police fail to determine the infant's parents.

Met Roger Leslie, the gentleman from New York who is traveling to China to rescue his younger brother Bob who married a Chinese girl in Shanghai. The family is prominent, they don't care for the marriage, and they believe Bob may have been drugged with opium. Mr. Leslie swore that breaking the marriage and extricating Bob would not take him three weeks. I believe he enjoys the drama. He was charming, but he clearly considers New York society, particularly his own society, innately superior, not only to Chinamen, but to Oaklanders.

Tub says Amundsen has ordered two ships to be built in San Francisco for use at the North Pole! The Fram II will take supplies enough for seven years. How strange to contemplate years of ice and snow, without a single flower.

<u>**Saturday, February 7**</u>

Harwood has written his story for the *Enquirer*. Now I understand why the Mexican authorities arrested and nearly killed him. He says a man in Los Angeles, backed by American capital, hired men to go into Mexico, supposedly for a motion picture. They camped twenty-five miles from Tia Juana. The organizers intended to create an armed force to capture part of Lower California and form an independent state. It is no marvel that Mexican authorities arrested Harwood when he walked into Tia Juana to buy food. He appears to have been but a pawn, thoroly ignorant of the plot.

Mr. Leslie joined us for supper. He must have wondered whether he would survive to sail on Thursday after Suzanne asked whether New York will vote for equal suffrage next year, and he dismissed the topic with a wave of his well-manicured hand. He then tried to put her off with, "Western States have always allowed women almost anything in order to persuade them to settle in rough country, whereas New York, with its wealth of cultural assets, need not resort to exceptional means." Only after it became clear that Suzanne was not to be humored did he show his true colors by asserting that letting women vote breaks up homes, and that most women do not vote, or vote based solely on emotions. He then delicately suggested that "bad-women" dominate the women's vote in some western states! Suzanne cleared her throat and rolled her eyes before turning her attention to her plate. Father closed the subject by commenting that at least "bad women" vote with a deeper knowledge of human nature than most of us.

Sunday, February 8

Quite a gathering for Sunday dinner in honor of Aunt Agnes's birthday. Afterward, I stood at the window and watched the children play in the garden. I saw such a look of alarm cross Susan's face that I looked to see if one of the younger children had fallen, but she appeared to be reacting to Uncle Thomas pointing to his watch. When I turned my gaze back to Susan, she was nodding obediently, and the panic had all but faded from her face—but her expression nagged at me all evening. Was it my imagination—what Helen calls my "sensitive nature"—or was Susan's look much more than a child's displeasure at being called away from her playmates?

Monday, February 9

Another odd dream. I was standing at a window looking out on the street when I heard the bells from old Watson's junk-cart, and saw his two big, sleepy horses pulling the cart down 22nd Street. Then I was outside, looking into the cart as Watson watched me carefully. He wore a clerical collar and smiled unctuously, then nodded toward the used goods. Though I never buy from him, I looked politely at the items. Some were under a dirty tarpaulin, and when I reached to pull it back, he shifted uncomfortably and attempted to draw my attention elsewhere. His apparent disquiet made me curious, and I lifted a corner of the tarpaulin.

A clock-face lay among the tools. On its face, I saw Susan with her eyes cast down, singing softly to a yellow flower in her hand. "I should like a clock," I said to Watson. "I have none," he replied sharply. "Are you certain?" I asked. Watson struck the tarpaulin with his whip, and I lost my hold on it. "That one's no good," he said with a sneer, and the cart abruptly pulled away, nearly knocking me to the ground.

I awoke with a start and knew that I could not fall back asleep. After putting up water for tea, I sat in the early-morning shadows. My head was as foggy as the bay, and it took many minutes to realize that the persistent whistle of a vaguely familiar bird was in fact the shrill call of the teakettle.

I took my tea out to the garden, mesmerized by the steam rising from the cup—and from the dew. Overnight, a spider had spun an especially fine web on the banister, which took on all the colors of the rainbow in the morning light. I later tried to paint what I remembered from the dream, despite a lingering uneasiness—but to little effect. Even working in the garden could not relieve me of my disquietude.

Tuesday, February 10

Helen and I took tea at the museum, then retired to the porch where we could speak more freely. Suzanne, who was out walking, stopped by.

Spotting *The Century* open to the article on the Mona Lisa, Helen asked if I'd read the short story about a Japanese god who bestows upon only the most devoted the ability to take on the illness of another one wishes to save. When I nodded, Helen asked, "Can you imagine?"

I told her I could not imagine doing so—but was there a time when I might have, for Richard? I was foolish enough then. I reminded Helen that even after three hundred years, the lacquer on the floor in front of the statue is hardly worn.

"I suspect the lacquer would be wholly untouched, in this country," Suzanne remarked.

Helen agreed, "People always say they would die for someone else, but you never hear anyone saying they'd take the white plague in someone else's place."

Suzanne pointed to the Wells story in the same number, about a future war decided by great air battles, in which aeroplanes drop horrible atomic bombs from the sky, destroying whole cities. "That's much truer to life than assuming another's illness."

Suzanne then asked how the story ended, and Helen explained that the girl who takes on the illness of a handsome young man is in turn saved when a young monk gives up his own good health so that the girl may marry the man she saved. "Sometimes the good we do *is* repaid by unseen forces," Helen suggested. (I should like to think so!)

Wednesday, February 11

Kneeling in the garden this morning as I scratched over a bed in preparation for peas and tomatoes, I was disturbed by vague memories that were at once strange and oddly familiar, having felt their presence most urgently when I was with Richard. Even now, I cannot bear to write of them in any detail. It is impossible to believe such things could have happened—could have been done *to* me and could have been done *by* me.

Thursday, February 12

Must wear gloves. After working in the garden today, I stared at my rough hands, as if I had never seen them before. Would Richard still kiss them? I suddenly felt that everything—my hands, Father's health, the broken wheel on the old wagon—was deteriorating. I had myself quite worked up. Then a gust of wind blew the small mirror off the window-sill, and it fell and shattered, as if adding an exclamation point to my thoughts. I could not help laughing, it seemed so darkly poetic. (Does this mean seven years of bad luck?)

Suzanne came for tea and conversed with Aunt Agnes for the first time. I could see Aunt assessing Suzanne: the absence of corset, the bobbed hair, the frankness of her conversation and her manner. I noticed a slight tightening of Aunt's lips when Suzanne used phrases that did not meet her grammatical standards.

They had quite a discussion of the frankness in books and plays regarding sex. When Aunt complained that it seemed to be "Sex o'clock all over America," Suzanne said it was high time. When Suzanne poked fun at the older generation, Aunt asked, "Why do you assume that because we do not chatter incessantly about a thing that we have never heard of it? Have you never considered that there may be a certain charm to reticence?" When Aunt pointed out that even children could now read things that would once have been under lock and key, Suzanne said there should be *more* discussion rather than less, and that schools should forewarn children about sexual matters.

"Why in the world should they?"

"Because children are deeply curious about such things. Thwarting their curiosity stifles the mind and can pervert a natural feeling into a covert and prurient one,"

"How do you *know* that children are deeply curious about such things?"

"Search your own memories," Suzanne replied with a smile.

"I have done so, and I was quite well occupied with how soon our next school holiday might be, or with trying to dive to the bottom of the swimming hole or coast down a snow-covered hill without breaking my neck, and other matters far more beguiling than the laws of propagation," Aunt retorted.

"They will have to understand these matters in a few short years when temptations arise. Forewarned is forearmed."

"There's something to be said for the reverse."

Suzanne looked puzzled.

"My parents' generation might have said, 'forearmed is forewarned,'" Aunt went on. "They sought to nurture in us a clear sense of right and wrong, and some measure of self-restraint, in matters seasonable to our childish minds. They trusted that if we learned to behave appropriately with regard to cats, dogs, our younger siblings, and to our appetites for chocolates, mud-puddles, and others' toys, then as we matured, we would apply that same learning to such new temptations as might arise. They trusted that if we were brought up in honor and goodness, we would act honorably and goodly, and absent solid moral resources, any warnings of the sort you suggest would fall on rocky soil."

Wisely, we let Aunt Agnes have the last word on the matter. While I disagree with much that Aunt says, her eloquence impresses me. Yet when she speaks of the innocence and goodness of her upbringing, I am left with a mystery. I can picture clearly the world she describes, and my memories of Mother support her account. Then how is it that their sister could marry such a man as Uncle Thomas?

Suzanne seemed determined to provoke Aunt and remarked that she was furious with the Suffragette leaders for shaking hands with President Wilson when they marched on the White House. "It's the most pompous foolishness, to march on the White House and be told that it's all very nice, but there's nothing to be done because of the Democratic Platform, and please, may I shake your little hands. They might better have refused, telling him that loyalty to their sister Suffragettes forbade it."

"I recall a bicycle tea they planned for the Claremont, in New York, just before I moved here. The bicycle craze was at fever pitch among men, but the idea of women riding was still a novelty; in the countryside, people would stop and stare. The men and women were to meet at the Michaux Club to wheel to the Casino in the Park for luncheon, then on to the Claremont for tea—still in biking togs. But in the event, only two of us did so. The other dozen or so women all wheeled home after luncheon, changed out of their short skirts and shirt-waists, and appeared at the Claremont in the full glory of their latest spring frocks." Aunt punctuated her account with a disdainful snort that made us laugh and added, "Women will always ask whether the revolution might be delayed for an hour to permit a change in costume."

Suzanne asked if she admired men more than women.

Aunt stared at Suzanne as she used to stare at me when I had come home soaked from walking too far in the rain. "Speaking of bicycles, Katherine," she began, as if ignoring Suzanne's question, "A year or two before you were born, the high-wheel velocipede was quite the fad. Its front wheels were five feet in diameter and the rear wheels sixteen inches high. Men would wheel about proudly until that enormous front wheel hit a stone sending the rear up in the air, and the cyclist forward on his head, much to the amusement of passersby.

"Well, men grew tired of always taking headers. When new bicycles came out with a small wheel in front and a large wheel in back, they sped about on those—frequently falling backwards and cracking the *backs* of their skulls. Then, around 1884, we saw the first of the safety bicycles, with wheels of equal size—the original Rovers. Low, and ungraceful, but safe. The men insisted that those bicycles would be fine for *women* and continued crashing on bicycles with wheels of unequal sizes. Yet somehow men have developed the idea that it is *women* who lack the intelligence to cast ballots!"

Saturday, February 14

Mr. Edmonds's man was here again. Antonio.

He is so dark that Elizabeth took him for a Mexican. He has long, black hair, and coal-black eyes. I admit that I felt a slight fear of him at first. I think he knew it. Once, when he came into the kitchen for a glass of water, I noticed he was still holding his knife. Keeping his eyes on mine, he said, "This is good knife. My father gave it to me. It is a working knife, not for criminals." He smiled broadly, to reassure me, I presume.

Monday, February 16

Just days after two experts announced that thoughts of ever flying across the Atlantic were wholly unrealistic, Glenn Curtis says it will be done next summer. To think it is just nine years since man first flew—we have seen such a dizzying rush of inventions. During my childhood, no home had a telephone. Even ten years ago, when Uncle Thomas had one installed, there was a flurry of envious curiosity. Now they are common. At twenty, I rarely saw an automobile. Now many people I know have machines, and some of the men even act as their own chauffeurs. Might the rush of scientific changes alter our basic nature?

The *Enquirer* says hundreds have applied to join Sir Ernest Shackleton's new Antarctic expedition. Tub says anyone who would leave a warm fire and a good cigar to flail around in the snow and ice should be given an asylum to explore instead. I disagree. If my gender allowed, and I had any experience, I'd apply. When I asked Tub whether the moving pictures of the earlier expedition had not amazed him, he said that only a lunatic would risk his life merely to see something he could see in perfect safety at the Oakland Photo some months later.

At supper I confessed my complete bafflement at the evening paper's report of a claim made by a British professor of Astronomy. He insists that if one could go to a near star with a sufficiently powerful telescope and look back at Earth, one would be able to see oneself as a child departing the house for the first time. From a more distant star, one might even see one's grandmother as a baby! Something about the time light takes to travel from Earth to a star. Tub shrugged and said that scientists had known this for decades, but when I asked him to explain, it was clear that he understood nothing of the matter.

Excitement is high over the voting tomorrow on the Hart Initiative Ordinance. Opponents rely solely on claims that it is loosely drawn.

Tuesday, February 17

It appears today's voting will exceed the vote at any such election in the town's history. Does it say something of our nature that a special election, in which saloons are the major issue, should bring us to the polls in greater numbers in than any previous such election? I am not persuaded we must outlaw saloons, but I voted to limit their number.

Thursday, February 19

Art Appreciation Club with Professor Kenyon lecturing on art history was a bit dry. As I understand it, high art was created for a small public that wanted and discerned it, whereas modern art was created for a public that neither wants nor understands it—by artists who despise the public. Aestheticism (Whistler as dreamer), scientific naturalism (Monet abandoned subject, preoccupied with light), or self-expression (Cezanne's whimsical improvisation), and regarding Matisse: "We have no need to deplore the deliquescence of a great talent, for we have no reason to suppose he ever had any."

Professor Kenyon belongs early in the last century. I hope our efforts to interest people in art will survive his lectures. Suzanne looked as if I were mad to have brought her. While everyone was chatting, I challenged her to make a presentation on photography. I think she would have declined, had Mrs. Livingston not sniffed disdainfully and said that photography is "a sort of science, not an art."

Luckily Professor Clark turned to us just then and said of the return of the Mona Lisa to the Louvre, "Why does everyone refer to it as 'the' Mona Lisa?" It's more likely that the one hanging in the Prado is the original portrait, and the one in the Louvre a copy. Apparently, Vasari, who wrote in detail about the portrait, was just five years old when Leonardo followed Francis I to France. As Vasari never visited France, he must have been writing about the Prado painting.

Professor Clark went on to say that her mourning attire suggests sittings in 1499-1500, when the Prado portrait was done. Lisa Gherardini had given birth to a daughter who was still-born or died soon after birth. As Lisa herself nearly died of grief, some believe that the portrait was commissioned partly as an effort to amuse and distract her. Professor Clark's comments were so satisfying, I could almost forgive Professor Kenyon for being dull.

Friday, February 20

The light this morning had that special quality of sun shining between clouds after a heavy rainfall. Even so, calla lilies have a simple grace I can never quite capture. Suzanne gamely placed one

of my efforts behind a single cut calla in a vase and photographed them together—nature's put mine wholly in the shade. Too often I must overcome the terrible certainty that my work is so superficial as to be insulting to Art. From one to whom more talent is given, more is demanded. A man, if he faces that challenge honestly, may well be excused minor weaknesses which in some other man should seem unbearable.

I think I could forgive a man almost anything if he were truly an artist. To paint or write poetry requires more imagination and courage than the explorations of Christopher Columbus or the battles of Lord Nelson. Our enemies—time, internal emptiness, lack of faith in one's capabilities, death—are more implacable foes than Napoleon. Yet the artist must fight alone—no navigator can guide the poet along the shoals of his own soul, and when the impulse comes to turn the ship around and speed away, no one will see his absence.

Saturday, February 21

As I was setting in the nasturtiums this morning, a little negro boy paused outside the gate. He stood so still, that at first, I failed to notice him. He gave me quite a start, and I dropped my trowel. Irritated at myself, I nearly shouted. He seemed not to notice, his eyes huge as saucers and fixed solely on the flowers. I was charmed and covertly watched him watching me. I thought of saying hello and asking his name, but when I looked up, he was gone. I rather hope he returns.

Tuesday, February 24

Twice in as many days, masked robbers have robbed trains and killed passengers. Robberies seem uncommonly frequent of late;

we've been inundated with news of murders based on passion and jealousy; and the Drown trial starts this week.

Are we all going mad? Are automobile exhausts and factory smokestacks affecting our minds? Or does moving so rapidly, with faster ships and trains, and now automobiles (and even aeroplanes), cause in us some deep uneasiness? Perhaps we were never meant to move quite so fast. I said as much the other day, and Jack flippantly replied, "Meant by God?" He so irritated me that I wanted to shout back, "YES!" But I had been thinking of Nature, not God.

Wednesday, February 25

Tub got after Uncle Thomas about Oakland securing a convention of colored people next year—some national conference of Baptists. Apparently, the Chamber of Commerce invited them last year, but the Commercial Club didn't join in. Tub and the Chamber are in high spirits over 10,000 visitors to Oakland. Uncle, naturally, wonders whether it is wise.

Thursday, February 26

Laura Reynaud has died in London. I recall when her knowledge of a former life created, as the *Enquirer* put it, "a great sensation" in Paris, where she was a nurse. She recollected dying of consumption at the age of nineteen, in 1840, in another country. She even described the town and house—although she had never left France. Her account piqued my curiosity, and we had robust discussions of whether such a thing was possible. Father surprised me by shrugging and saying he had seen enough strange occurrences in his youth to keep him from dismissing such a thing out of hand. This evening he said that as he draws nearer to crossing over, he wishes he could believe there is something after this life—but cannot.

I have long been curious about "thought transference" and "telepathy." When I was eleven years old, Aunt Emily took me to see a French lady and gentleman. They gave various audience members a list of hundreds of names of famous people; then, as the man stood blindfolded before an easel, the lady walked among us. When someone whispered to her a name from the list, she pointed at the blindfolded man, saying nothing, and he instantly sketched a portrait of the person. Then the man walked among us while the lady was blindfolded, and she instantly named any article shown to him, even the dates of coins and the numbers of railway tickets. Aunt Emily allowed me to show him the locket with a miniature picture of Mother. The lady called Mother "beautiful." Uncle Thomas, upon hearing of my elation, declared it was all done by ventriloquistic whispers.

<u>Friday, February 27</u>

Our discussion of Madame Reynaud this evening was likely a repeat of what we said at the time of the "great sensation." Edward expressed polite skepticism, prefacing everything with, "I certainly wouldn't close my mind to the possibility," and proceeding to do precisely that. Helen scoffed, playing the sensible farm girl she oftentimes imagines herself to be. Julia, Madame Reynaud's most passionate proponent, pointed out to Edward that when doctors took Madame to Siena, without informing her of their destination, she was able to walk directly to the house she had described, and to the church, where she went straight to the tombstone of a girl who died of consumption in 1840 at the age of nineteen, and then fell in a faint.

Bret said Madame could have read something of the girl years earlier, retained the facts, and later taken them to be her own memories. Jack thought the whole affair concocted with the doctor and surmised that the doctor hypnotized her and gave her the information while she was in a trance, so that she sincerely believed everything she said. Suzanne noted that Madame Reynaud refused to profit from all the fuss, and that although she was able to effect cures of certain nervous maladies, she refused payment.

Bret related a strange event at the jail. They had arrested a man for armed robbery, and his brother for assisting him. After the two were placed in a cell, the "brother" confessed to a guard that in fact he was a she—and had been masquerading as a man for months as they traveled about the country! It might be interesting to pass as a man, but I doubt I could manage it for long. I enjoy men well enough but would not care to be one.

Saturday, February 28

Painted morning light catching sails on the bay—San Francisco almost wholly hidden in a cloak of white fog. With each painting, I confront problems, feel frustration, satisfaction, and even joy. Yet, whatever painting calls forth has no need to be further conveyed in writing.

Set in more annuals: coreopsis, for the butterflies; celosia. The negro boy came by again. I wonder who his people are. He watches me as if trying to memorize how to do it just so.

Set in delphinia starts this afternoon. As I was finishing, I looked up to see the little negro boy. I still do not know where he comes from. He simply appears. "Hello," I said, smiling. He did not respond and stared at the flowers. Holding a delphinium, I took a few delicate steps toward him, as I might approach a fawn, and paused several feet away, the fence between us.

His huge eyes looked at me as I said, "This is a delphinium." I held it up, repeating the word slowly. He echoed me, in little more than a whisper. (His effort sounded like "Divinity.") "Del-fin-ee-yum," I repeated. "Devinamum," he said. I smiled. He smiled and watched closely as I set in the plant.

When I asked his name, he had to repeat it twice before I understood: "Lucius." I asked where he lived, but he just looked at me. The third time I asked, he rattled off a torrent of words, presumably English. I asked him to speak more slowly. (How can these people have lived for generations in this country, and yet cannot be understood? We have done them a great disservice—the education of negroes is abysmal. Yet their persistent foreignness seems almost willful.)

March

Sunday, March 1

"The Inside of the White Slave Traffic" has sparked much talk, and the film is filling the theaters. Repeated news headlines ("YOUNG GIRLS MAY BE IN HANDS OF WHITE SLAVERS"), probably help. They advertise the film as a lesson for parents on the dangers of an "Out of the House!" policy on "daughters who have temporarily strayed."

I don't understand the fuss. Plays and songs make light of infidelity and mock clean thinking, and even portray prostitution as stylish and *fun*. Why shouldn't a truer portrait be shown that might discourage young girls?

Suzanne asked Bret about Hazel Lux, the woman who says she's glad she killed her paramour. (He was a bartender, and they ran some sort of brothel.) She killed him in Emeryville, where they had lived since the red-light district was broken up New Year's Eve. She claims that he brought her into "the life" and lived off her earnings, and she killed him when he told her he "couldn't marry a woman of that kind."

Bret replied with, "They close the resorts and tell the girls to reform; but few want to reform. Most know that they *can't* reform. Shall they become domestic servants? As soon as they're found out,

Mrs. Jones won't have them in the house—or Mr. Jones will take liberties, and she's forced back into the same game. The so-called 'social evil' can't be abolished until men's and women's hearts are changed."

Suzanne retorted, "Women's hearts have nothing to do with selling their bodies to stave off starvation. Nor do men's hearts have much to do with satisfying their lust with some poor creature who has no real choice in the matter."

"Of course not," Bret said. "I mean the hearts of parents who can't forgive some poor girl who gives herself for love, leaving her no choice afterward but to rent out her body to lonely men."

Wednesday, March 4

Supper with the Jacksons. Suzanne enjoys baiting the elder Mr. Jackson. He is still angry that women haven't disavowed Mrs. Pankhurst. "I'm sympathetic with someone who suffers for the sake of his opinions, but people of her ilk are punished not for opinion but for deliberate transgressions against elementary principles of civilized government. They have no regard whatsoever for property or for those whom they may inspire to use violence to redress real or imagined grievances—the workers, immigrants, negroes. What use is discouraging lynching in the south, or murder in New York, or the lawless violence of miners, when just the sort who should be displaying a finer path are applauding these lawless women? When Mrs. Pankhurst speaks to mad applause in a packed house, why shouldn't some negro, affronted by the insults of a southern railway company, feel justified in dynamiting the track?

"And yet," Suzanne asked in her sweetest voice, "Wasn't it your Lord Acton who said, 'It seems to be a law of political evolution that no great advance of human freedom can be gained except *after* the display of violence.'"

"Are you referring to Mrs. Pankhurst or to the miners and negroes?"

"I suppose you would have to ask Lord Acton," Suzanne replied. "I am a mere woman."

Thursday, March 5

Suzanne was our presenter at Art Appreciation Club. She began by describing how early experimenters created images of leaves by placing them on paper soaked in silver nitrate and dried in darkness. Sunlight reached the paper only where the leaves didn't block it—recreating on paper the pattern of the leaves. But when they removed the leaves, the page quickly became black because of the additional light. In 1802, Daguerre accidentally made a sharp black-and-white photographic image by leaving a partially exposed photographic plate in chemicals. Those who posed for photographs had to endure having their heads covered with flour and clamped between iron rods, then sit that way on a roof for nearly half an hour!

She suggested that photography presents with special clarity the basic problem of "art." Because photography can imitate reality, its slightest departures from reality must be intentional expressions of the artist's views. Why do some argue heatedly that photography cannot be an art? I should have thought the whole controversy settled a decade ago.

I was especially taken with two prints of photographs by Alvin Langdon Coburn. One, "Spider-webs," was of a small sailboat, *sans* sails. The water reflected its rigging, and rigging from larger, unseen ships. The patterns on the water were both a faithful representation of reality and something new. "House of a Thousand Windows," was of a tall city building viewed from a taller building or aeroplane—also a visual pattern freed from context.

She showed prints of Coburn's portraits of Meredith and Henry James and noted that Coburn must admire his subjects, or at least find them interesting, to make satisfactory portraits. If he dislikes someone he photographs, his emotion shows up in the photograph. I have noticed the same to be true when painting—but painting is not a scientific process.

Suzanne stressed that she values personal vision over the standards of any particular school, revealing that she has studied with Clarence H. White in Maine and with Stieglitz in New York. I appreciated her talk and made sure to tell her so.

Saturday, March 7

Beatrice McCall writes that "The Inside of the White Slave Traffic" is a lesson to all of us who will vote on the Redlight Abatement Bill, and she insists that the picture reflects conditions as she has seen them in her work. The crib system seems too horrible to believe, but she personally knows a negro woman who paid $140 per month to a San Francisco boss to rent a ten-by twelve-foot crib. It is shocking that anyone goes back to that sort of life because honest work doesn't pay enough, but Miss McCall says she cannot find young girls department-store jobs that pay adequate wages.

"Care has been taken to eliminate all suggestiveness," Bret read aloud, eyes twinkling.

Aunt Agnes snorted, "When everything is told, there is no need for suggestion."

Aunt Emily pursed her lips then exclaimed, "I cannot see how mischief can fail to result from exciting in young men curiosity about brothels and their inmates, while demonstrating graphically to young girls the value they might command in such places. They say the greater part of the audience is groups of boys and young men, sniggering and whispering. Theater managers cannot pretend their purpose is to teach moral lessons. They are out to make money—and are making a great deal of it."

Aunt Agnes said she neither wished to see the "movie" nor objected to its being shown. "Unfortunately, at present, the public cares only for novelty. They are a stampeding herd, their hooves sure to crush good taste."

Aunt Agnes then guyed Bret unmercifully about purporting to be a writer, yet using interchangeably "continual" and "continuous," or "complete" and "finished." She ended her lecture saying, "Slang is like the measles or chicken-pox: contagious, though short-lived, and most severe where the sanitary conditions are most favorable to its development."

Father responded, "Twenty years ago you probably reacted the same way when people fell into the habit of pointing out some minor mishap by saying 'Your tire is punctured' rather than 'You have slipped your trolley.' Before the bicycle craze, if you'd said two young people were 'riding tandem,' or called their chaperone a 'pacemaker,' or referred to a man living at a fast pace as 'geared a little too high,' no one would have understood you. Language must change and grow, just as life must."

As Bret was leaving, he quietly remarked that Aunt Agnes is "the only person in America who speaks always in complete sentences, each element of which is always both correct and tasteful, and she never hesitates a moment in search of a word."

Sunday, March 8

Elizabeth says the next "thing" (Fad, Elizabeth!) will be brightly colored wigs aping the Lady Washington style: hair high on the head, full of feathers and combs, and carrot-colored, French blue, Zona Bond red, or Leila Young green. She says we'll see such wigs at any smart function after Lent, though only at night. Apparently, daylight heightens the artificiality, making the arrangement too comical. New rule for conduct: only what will stand the light of day!

Monday, March 9

Set in delphinia and schizanthus near the circular bed where the red and white tulips will soon flower. I had placed lily bulbs in the same area last fall and dug carefully. Upon finding the tip of one lily working its way toward the light, it was like meeting an old friend. The garden's peace was a contrast to the afternoon's news. Sacramento is calling for the militia to deal with the unemployed armies, whose leaders are under arrest. San Francisco warns Sacramento not to send them back to San Francisco.

Someone suggested that each city collect the unemployed daily and send them to another city. The men would spend so much time on trains that they would have no energy left for agitation. But would cities not go bankrupt paying railway fares? Sounds like the medieval practice of putting mad people onto boats and sending them to some other town!

No one cares for my suggestion that for less than a city spends on police and militia, pay the men to beautify it by weeding and planting. Jack laughed of course, and Tub said the men would refuse. Bret quite sensibly replied that by the time the money made its way through city government, the men would barely earn enough to buy a tin of tobacco.

Tuesday, March 10

Uncle Thomas fairly preened as he informed us about the gathering of San Francisco and east bay officials and businessmen at the grounds of the 1915 Exposition. He said that the direct ferry to the site took just 22 minutes from the Key Route Pier in

Oakland; and that visitors from Oakland will be able to reach the grounds more quickly than many residents of San Francisco itself. Furthermore, if the direct ferry is instituted, half the visitors to the Exposition will find rooms on this side of the bay.

Tub is on the road with the Lincoln Highway Boosters. Elizabeth said that they are drawing enthusiastic crowds, but she is concerned by the trouble with the unemployed. Sacramento drove the men into Yolo County and posted hundreds of armed guards at bridges leading back into the city. In Loomis, the men smashed windows, blew open the post office safes with nitro-glycerin, and stole $3,000 in money and stamps after a gun-battle with the postmaster and citizens! Elizabeth fears that the posse might chase them right into Tub's group.

Uncle snorted and said the men are "professional idlers" who sneered at work in orchards and are determined to propagate class hatred. (Locally, they tore down some fences and stole wood for campfires.) He maintained that only Chief Peterson's decisiveness saved Oakland worse disruption—hardly reassuring for Elizabeth.

Susan was quiet throughout the meal, and I could see nothing that strengthened or eased my concerns. After she asked to be excused, I asked Aunt Emily how she was doing.

"She's so like you in certain ways." She went on to explain that about six months ago Susan had developed a sudden fetish for cleanliness. "Nothing would do but she must wash repeatedly, more than a dozen times in a day, on some days. Do you recall going through a similar stage?" I recalled, too, Aunt Emily's remarking on it at the time—and that she never appeared curious as to the cause.

Wednesday, March 11

Elizabeth dragged me to Kahn's for the spring showing of gowns. With Tub away, she seems so "blue" that I could not refuse. Eight New York models strutted about on a raised platform while

Madame Cattle described the gowns to a crowd of onlookers. Everything looked charming on the girls but would surely look far less so on me. Morning frocks, afternoon frocks, evening gowns—Elizabeth's smart friends must spend half their days changing costumes. Elizabeth fell in love with a Paul Poiret dress of white imported crepe and green golfine.

Afterward, we witnessed a terrible runaway. The frightened horse dashed down Grove Street, while the driver (a woman), tried desperately to check the animal with one hand, the other holding onto a young girl. The girl was so frightened that she tried to leap from the rig. The poor woman's furs and hat flew into the street as two motorcycle patrolmen closed in. We heard later that no one was injured, though the flight continued all the way to Adeline and Harmon.

Thursday, March 12

Tub is back and quite worn out, though he denies it. Elizabeth is much relieved. In Lodi they were warned that the unemployed army was headed toward them and might attack them from ambush. Feeling like warriors, they prepared themselves to run down anyone who tried to block their way, but they never saw anyone. They got separated in the hills and straggled into Placerville one automobile at a time, hours late—and were met by a brass band and a crowd of 2,500! When they reached Sacramento, they were distressed to learn that they could not get a shave. The city was under martial law because of the unemployed armies, and the barbers were all out trying to watch the riot.

When I asked Tub if he would do it all again, he said the trip was worth many thousands of dollars to Oakland and cemented Oakland's place in the chain of national highways. He sounded almost fierce as he ended with, "Southern California can never replace us as the Pacific Coast terminus of the Lincoln Highway."

"The Plaint of a Spinster" has generated a storm of further comment in *Munsey's*. I rather like one "sister spinster's" response: "If one would listen to the birds and the children (even though they belong to others), to brooks and music, to the stars, the clouds, the trees, and the poor, one would not have time to hear 'the slow drip from her broken heart as she waits for the years to pass.' I haven't."

Friday, March 13

Went with Helen to Garrett's. She and Mrs. Powers are absorbed in preparing for the wedding reception and deciding on decorations for the church, as well as arranging visits from family. Such a tidal wave of petty details is washing over them that I fear they may drown.

As I stood with Helen, who was deciding between two hats, I put my forefinger to my chin. The moment I touched my chin I felt a chill. I had done exactly this already today—and yet I had not. In the dream Richard was waiting for me to decide whether I would move with him to Chile. He was still flush with success as the first man to drive an automobile across some high mountain pass from Argentina along a mule trail.

We walked to the Hotel Oakland to meet Helen and Edward and Suzanne and Bret. I remember thinking that Helen would be amazed that Richard had returned. The head clerk brought out Mrs. Bishop to greet us, but when she removed her hat, she became a younger and much prettier girl, and smiled at Richard. His hand suddenly felt icy, and when I looked down, his fingers were webbed and wrinkled, like a reptile's. He gestured at the girl, introducing her as his wife. I woke up troubled but fell back asleep quickly. Thank goodness such dreams no longer leave me wholly unable to sleep.

In the afternoon, Mr. Edmonds's man, Antonio, delivered manure to enrich the soil on the 22nd Street side of the house—where I hope the sundial will soon stand.

Jack arrived during the delivery. Watching Antonio, he remarked that Antonio was a true Sicilian: "A swarthy fellow whose ancestry no one can trace." When I asked Jack what he meant, he laughed and said, you have the evening newspaper at your feet. Look at 'The Wayfarer.'" The columnist described Sicily as "the world's melting pot," a heterogeneous population, including Africans and Asiatics, that "mixed, melted, married, fused, and produced race-mixtures such as the world had never before seen."

I looked over at Antonio and agreed that he is rather dark-skinned, but his complexion suits a man who works outdoors. If chance encounters over centuries produce such a manly race, perhaps our leaders have been on quite the wrong track. I expressed no such thoughts to Jack, as I should never hear the end of it.

When I brought Antonio a glass of lemonade, he was on his knees showing Lucius how to set in the delicate plants without breaking their roots. He was surprisingly gentle for someone so strong. Mr. Edmonds had mentioned that he has a way with plants and animals. Children too, perhaps. I'm certain that he did not mean to be impolite by keeping me waiting—he was simply caught up in what he was doing, and even as he thanked me, he was watching Lucius trying to do exactly as he had been taught.

Antonio finally looked over at me and smiled, which I have seen him do only once before. "He is good boy," he said.

"You have wife and family in your country?" I asked.

"No." He looked at me and spoke slowly. "No wife. No sons. Only trouble."

"Were you a farmer?" I asked. When he did not answer immediately, I added, "Work with the land, animals?" I made a hoeing motion, then mimed the milking of cows. He shook his head vigorously, almost angrily. I asked what work he had done there.

Eventually he drew his index finger briefly to his lips to suggest secrecy, and said, "In my country, I study to be a teacher."

I was startled. I had not imagined this dark, muscular man who speaks broken English to be a teacher. "But why . . .?" I realized that he might not like to be reminded why he was no longer a teacher and took the empty glass inside.

Saturday, March 14

Took groceries to Lucius's mother. They were clearly needed, and I was clearly unwelcome. She was polite, but her eyes avoided mine, and the stiffness with which she moved and spoke let me know that she was uncomfortable. I said that Lucius had been keeping me company while I worked in the garden. She thanked me for the foodstuff, and then we stood in the sunlight, sharing an uneasy silence. She clearly wondered why I had come. I had been silently asking myself just that, until I started talking. I heard myself explain that I should be glad of a little assistance with the gardening, and that if Lucius could help me on the weekend, or after school, I would gladly pay him for his time.

She looked me over trying to discern what secret motive I might have. I could not have enlightened her. Lucius is unlikely to be much help, and he might be something of a distraction. Still, I want to help Lucius, and he and the garden clearly belong together. I met her gaze and waited, despite wishing I had left well enough alone.

"I s'pose that be alright, if he want," she said. She spoke casually, as if there had been no interval of silent suspicion between my offer and her response. "How much you gwine pay?"

I had not foreseen this rather obvious question. I did not wish to pay too little, or too much, yet I thought I must answer unequivocally, or her suspicions would deepen. "I can't say yet. A man gets about 25 cents per hour for that sort of work these days. Lucius is inexperienced. Shall we see how it goes? I will pay him fairly." I heard in my tone my mother's gentle firmness and felt better. I feared she might take offense, but she nodded, then smiled and said softly, "My Lucius a good boy."

Walking home I was nearly knocked over by a motor-truck that turned the corner so sharply its wheels were briefly on the curb. Not two blocks later, a child rushed past me toward the street, intent on joining playmates. Had I not reached out and seized the child's arm, he would have been run down by a Mercer driven by a well-dressed man who was either terribly late or thought it "smart" to display his daring to us mere pedestrians.

I was glad to see that the English gave that woman six months' hard labor for mutilating "Venus" in the National Gallery. I sympathize thoroly with Mrs. Pankhurst, but I can't countenance destroying a famous work of art. Velasquez's "Venus" did not cause the subjugation of women; and whatever this madwoman left of her will be around to edify us long after we have gained all the rights that men have. Meanwhile, I must brook old men, such as Mr. Jackson, hectoring me about it whenever the discussion turns to women.

Sunday, March 15

Lake Shore Park this afternoon. First band concert of the season. After Intermission, two fine solos by Anita Heymans: "Sunshine and Roses" and "A Good Old-Time Sleigh Ride."

I spoke with Mr. Edmonds yesterday about Antonio, remarking that conditions in Sicily must be quite harsh for a teacher to seek work as a farmhand. Mr. Edmonds nodded, pulling thoughtfully on his pipe.

"What did Antonio tell you?" He asked.

"That he had been educated as a teacher. I started to ask more, then bit my tongue, lest I hurt his feelings."

Under his steady gaze, I felt like a fidgety young girl. "That was kind of you," he said.

"But to your mind not necessary, I take it."

"I wouldn't worry about hurting Antonio's feelings. He's a thoughtful young man, and he knows just how things stand for him,

and why." The horse shook its head, as if impatient with our chatter and eager to begin the journey home. Mr. Edmonds looked at the horse, then at me, then shrugged his shoulders at his helplessness in the face of the animal's will. I laughed. With a wink, he tipped his cap and departed.

Tuesday, March 17

Moving things about, I came upon a box of old diaries. It was nearly a half hour before I resumed my chores. Many entries might have been written by a stranger. Some I clearly wrote in the throes of strong emotions, yet the precise circumstances are irretrievably lost in the folds of memory. Some (involving Richard) are cryptic because there was much I did not dare write. Many are purely of the moment ("The quality of light early this morning seemed almost holy"), while others are too brief to make sense of ("Deep and moving conversation with C" and "Such a strange night at Maud's").

The entries from the diary I kept in 1909—when Richard and I were keeping company (Riding tandem," as Mrs. Condon used to say, a '90's phrase that amused me at first, then embarrassed me once Richard and I were intimate)—brought back the joy and pain, and why I had not opened the diary since we parted ways. Reading through also made me wonder if I secretly hope that Richard will return, and that we might marry and our children one day read this. (How I wish for a similar account from Mother's youth!)

Supper with Elizabeth and Tub and friends. When I mentioned my visit to Lucius's mother, Elizabeth asked whether she performed any rag-time songs for me. I saw precious little of youthful joy in the eyes of Lucius's mother, but I simply turned the conversation to Tub's latest exploits. I believe Elizabeth was sincere, but her thoughtlessness recalled the froth that abounded when "Honeymoon Express" played, a bunch of nonsense about southern darkies having the fountain of youth in their rag-time music.

Tub is still glowing over his adventures with the Lincoln Highway Boosters and singing his usual hymns to the automobile. He bragged that horses are fast disappearing from city streets. "In fact, the number of licensed horse-drawn vehicles decreased by 4.8 per cent in San Francisco last year," Robbie stated, averting his eyes with *faux* modesty.

I tried to bring in the human costs. "Well, of course bad drivers should be punished," Tub conceded. He shares the modern view that streets belong to the automobile drivers, and pedestrians must dodge and scurry like squirrels or pigeons. I said that fining the drivers is like trying to stop a bull with a fly-swatter. Dangerous drivers should be imprisoned and forbidden to drive, and their cars confiscated if they have been particularly careless.

"Doesn't your sister realize there are runaway horses as well?" Elizabeth's young friend Jane stage-whispered to Elizabeth, then added in a louder tone, "I'm sure your parents shook their fists and said the same things about drivers of trolleys and stages."

I replied that anyone who couldn't or wouldn't control his horse in a crowded street ought also to be stopped. Jane's fiancé, Dean Allen, smiled indulgently at Jane and remarked that she is so enthusiastic that she has taken to driving her own car. Later I overheard Jane say to Elizabeth, "Your sister is quite the old maid."

Am I quite the old maid? Today's events have left me wondering if she might be right.

Wednesday, March 18

Thinking about a garden sundial. They are old-fashioned; but consulting a shadow rather than some incomprehensibly intricate mechanism is natural and strips time of the great importance we moderns have given it. A simple sundial atop a white pillar, with a small hedge of holly around it, as well as red tulips and scarlet phlox.

None of the mottos I have seen appeal:

"Through alle the yeare
I tarry here,
To mark ye minutes
Of good cheere"

Bland and far too "fulle of cheere" for mee!

Rather liked the reference to "secrets of forgotten days" on the dial at Harwood's:

"Hours go!
But all the secrets of forgotten days
And all the joy of still untrodden ways
I know"

Care not at all for the backward-gazing sentiments:

"For dayes gonne bye
That cannot die,
And golden houres
Amid ye floweres
Forget me notte"

Olde English feels too pretentious. I am not creating this garden for some distant ancestor, but for *itself*.

Found myself pondering why the writer in *American Homes and Gardens* deemed this gloomy:

"I tell ye houres
Till lyte doe cease,
And praye they bringe
Bothe joye and peace"

Both "lytes" must fail, eventually. A peaceful end is the best we can hope for.

As it is to be my sundial, perhaps I must write its motto:

Time's finger writes but letters in the sand.
The earth's a ball a child holds in his hand.

(Wild/child/beguiled?)

Time's finger writes but letters in the sand.
The earth's a ball a child holds in his hand.
Yes, pause and glance and say you know the time,
The way a child repeats a silly rhyme.

I quite like that, but where did it come from? And how do I fit in wild/beguiled, and the sense that a garden might beguile us away from our fears of what the wild child might do with the ball on some sudden whim?

"And let the garden's dancing hues beguile / you back to childhood for a little while."

(Follows without stating the ominous sentiment that we may exist at the whim of a petulant child.)

Time's finger writes but letters in the sand.
The earth's a ball a child holds in his hand.
Yes, pause and glance and say you know the time,
The way a child repeats a silly rhyme.
And let the garden's dancing hues beguile
you back to childhood for a little while.

(Would not Time's finger write numbers? "And" in the penultimate line, with a comma after "rhyme"? Professor Eastman would mock my muddled metaphors and repetition of "child" thrice in six lines, but that's easily solved: I shall invite no professors of poetry to my garden.)

<u>Thursday, March 19</u>

Lucius is a sweet-natured child, and quite bright. It is a mild surprise to find such sweetness in a child of his race, and a greater one to find it in a child of his gender. He seems to love the flowers, and even talks to them! I am wholly unable to understand him when he speaks softly, as he does to the flowers—it is as if I am witnessing some secret foreign rite. Whether the foreign nation is the Congo, Childhood, or Nature is more than I can say.

Supper at Addison and Clara Powers'. Mrs. Powers complained of the displacement of theater by the motion picture and exclaimed that even London's oldest theater, Sadler's Wells Theatre, has been turned into a picture palace. Mr. Powers complained that saloons may disappear. His droopy smile and befuddled air reminded me of Helen's St. Bernard when it knew it had done something wrong, but not exactly what.

"No disrespect to women, I fear that the male animal, as we know him, is in danger of extinction. No saloons. None of those unmentionable places on Fifth Street. No prizefights. Soon, no cigars." Mr. Powers went on to say that he fears the "feminization" of America will make men an addled and nervous lot, not confident of their roles, and incapable of making war, and even of maintaining businesses and public offices.

Charles pointed out that no state that has adopted women's suffrage has ever rescinded it. Mr. Powers said he believed in the vote for women but had concerns. "What if our whole foreign policy and military defense become 'maternal?' Will impractical idealism and illogical emotionalism replace reasoned dialogue? That may be all well and good with respect to child-labor laws, but it would be an unfortunate way to manage the battle of Gettysburg."

Charles replied, "Isn't men's real fear that women are sufficiently superior that if they are allowed equal status in the political arena, the average man will have to bring himself up a notch or two in order to compete with them?"

Mr. Powers (wisely I thought) changed course and said he fears that electing senators by direct vote of the people will ruin the Senate. "The original scheme was carefully thought-out: one body elected directly by the people, and responsive to their changing passions, and another composed of wiser, more reflective men. Now, senators will be younger and more active, but less experienced and therefore less wise. Getting things done appeals to the man in the street. The capacity for careful study of what it might be *wise* to do, that is a quality too ephemeral for the stump. Senators will have less judgment, less distinction of manner, and far less true quality, than we are accustomed to."

Charles quipped, "Herrin and Southern Pacific may choose intelligent and reflective senators, but if they dedicate their intelligence and contemplation to promoting the interests of the railroads and the timber industry, what use are they to me, or to my clients?"

Mr. Powers means no disrespect to women, but his respect is for the Idea of Woman, as he learned it from his father, in a day when women were moving from hoops to bustles. When I said as much to Aunt Agnes later, she shook her head and replied that it always amused her to hear women of the past dismissed as chained to the spinning-wheel. "You would be surprised to learn how many eloped in those days," she said. "I think it was Alexander Black who said that 'How much we regard as distinctive in the modern woman may depend upon how little we know of the woman of our grandmothers' and great-grandmothers' time.'"

Friday, March 20

Went to the Liberty this afternoon to hear Helen Keller, the famous deaf, dumb, and blind girl, lecture with her teacher, Mrs.

John Macy. What she said—and that she "said" anything at all—was inspiring. "The only truly lightless dark is the blackness of ignorance and insensibility. It is not the number or power of our senses that distinguish us, but the uses we make of them, and the imagination and courage with which we do so."

Miss Keller said that learning to spell so delighted her that she spelled to her dogs. For years she did not realize that the dogs did not comprehend when she apologized for stepping on them or tried to ask them whether they too liked ice cream. She also said that she wept in sympathy with the flowers as they grieved for their lost blossoms. (She has not sight, but she has wonder!)

Professor Clark met Miss Keller a few times in Boston, nearly twenty-five years ago, after he finished at Harvard and was working as a newspaper artist. She was five years old. When they were again introduced, her fingers found the elk's tooth on his watch charm, and she said immediately, "Yes, Mr. Clark of Boston. The newspaperman with the elk's tooth." She said, with tears in her eyes, that Professor Clark had produced a lump of clay and guided her hands to form it into something doglike.

Many large parties attended. There was even a musical program. (Helen Mesow, the blind soprano.) Miss Keller said that even a deaf-blind child has inherited the mind of seeing and hearing ancestors, a mind accustomed to five senses, and thus is influenced by light, color, and song even if he cannot know them.

Saturday, March 21

Spent the morning in the studio. How I wish I could have sketched Miss Keller's face as she was talking yesterday. I consoled myself with a sketch of a bemused young newspaperman watching the wonder on a young girl's face as her fingers explored the mounted head of a tiger. I liked it well enough to begin painting, but then it began to resemble a commercial illustration, so I turned to perfecting a view of the trees and sea from atop Mt. Tamalpais.

After I emerged, Aunt found me in the kitchen making a cup of tea. She told me that she worries about my solitariness. "Understand, I do not mean your solitude. A woman's solitude is one of her most important possessions. To be able to be alone, without rushing always to the side of one's friends, is essential, as is being allowed to be alone, either by financial circumstance or a husband's whims. While still impressionable, you saw your father always alone, and you saw me alone, a mature woman. Just as you learned to clean your teeth and choose the right silver, and to say 'haven't' rather than 'haint', you might—had your mother lived—also have learned the role companionship in marriage can play."

As Aunt paused and looked searchingly into my eyes, I wondered fleetingly if she had sent me the "spinster" article. "Not every woman should marry. Not every woman finds her deepest fulfillment in marriage. I worry that you may not be hearing what your instinct is telling you about your deepest nature." Her words were grim, but her voice was full of love.

As I listened, I saw a rapid succession of images: Aunt Agnes waiting for her tea to boil, a wistful expression on her face; a fireside with Richard; the cross look, rolled eyes, and barbed silence between a husband and wife in an unguarded moment; myself, painting, alone and pleased to be so, over on Alameda, with herons and other birds and the changing light on the bay; the Tremont's three-legged dog, getting on marvelously, unable to recall that he'd once had four legs.

Was Aunt correct to fear for me—did my unfortunate experience living with Uncle Thomas and Aunt Emily teach me that men cannot be trusted? Did I not retain with Richard a certain reserve that interfered with our passion?

<u>**Sunday, March 22**</u>

Mentioned to Mr. Edmonds my sense that plants come to know the one who cares for them. He didn't think it silly at all. "Some folks draw others, while some create a sense of uneasiness, no matter how earnest and kind they seem. Dogs instinctively love some people and loathe others. Why shouldn't plants also react to us? Mr. Burbank, who knows more about plants than any other human being on earth, believes they do."

Mrs. Bennett came by while Suzanne and I were visiting. When she complained of the sorts of moving pictures out these days, Suzanne summoned up an impressively solemn face and asked, "Why do you find vice so alluring?" Mrs. Bennett looked as if she'd been accused of running a bordello. Sputtering like one of those two-cycle motorboat engines that never get anywhere, she replied, "I fail to take your meaning, Miss Coolidge."

Suzanne, looking as innocent as a child in a Mary Cassatt painting, went on, "You devote great energy to keeping people from knowing about vice, whereas I should have supposed that the way to keep people from vice is to teach them all about it, so that they understand it thoroly enough to have no illusions that it is more than it is."

Fortunately, Mrs. Bennett did not see my copy of *Hagar Revelly*, which I had left on the bench. After she left, in a huff of course, Suzanne guyed me about letting fashion guide my reading. Fashionable or not, I'm enjoying it.

I recalled Aunt saying that the three greatest literary women in England—Jane Austin, Miss Edgeworth, and Miss Mitford—were all old maids. After Suzanne left, I reminded Aunt of that. "I don't recall saying so, but I've no reason to think otherwise. They were what I call 'natural old maids:' unmarried not merely through circumstance—ill health, early disappointment, or self-sacrificing devotion to duty—but women whose lives were complete without the emotion we are taught is our prime motor. Women who, as someone once said, 'walk from the cradle to the grave, handling their lives with delicate satisfaction and content.' Austin, notably, was lively and gay, and attractive to men, and attracted by them in turn." Aunt paused, then smiled. "As are you. Whatever I may have said, I did not mean to suggest that eschewing men would advance your painting."

From Father Mayne's sermon today: The famous deaf-mute Laura Dewey Bridgman was very fond of birds, and once, while residing at the Perkins Institute, she reached out a window and by chance touched a sparrow which had alighted on the sill. The sparrow allowed her to caress it, and even returned frequently. Delighted, Laura feared letting anyone else take part, lest they scare the bird away. Eventually she did permit another blind girl to pet it, confident that her friend's fingers would have a similarly reassuring touch. We may pity the blind for their affliction, but they pity us for our clumsy, awkward ways.

Monday, March 23

Gipsy Wagon with Suzanne and Ann Swinburn. Interesting discussion of suffrage, and the vote in Washington, rejecting the Anthony Amendment. (I know so little!)

"The vote itself proves the importance of suffrage," Ann asserted. "Of the 96 Senators, 47, one less than half, favored the Amendment. Senators from states where women have the vote were nearly unanimous in favoring it, because women matter in those states. Just as the opposition to restricting immigration is strongest among congressmen from the Northeast, where large numbers of immigrants are already present and voting."

The Shafroth-Palmer Amendment would require a referendum on suffrage whenever at least eight per cent of the men registered to vote in a state petition for it. A majority voting in favor shall establish women's voting there. Since no state could be forced to extend suffrage to women against the will of a majority of its male voters, this should not offend states' rights. Rather, this would leave it in the hands of the states but would facilitate states voting on it.

In November, equal suffrage will be on the ballot in several states!

Tuesday, March 24

The morning's walk filled me with love for Oakland and its people, with all their silly foibles. Children and old people smiled as I passed; even the morning sun seemed to smile. I found myself charmed by the care with which a dog sniffed a lamppost; and the intense gaze of an infant studying his new world, alert as a Hawkshaw for clues as to how to live in it. If asked why I felt so buoyant, I have no answer. Father is ailing, Richard has abandoned me, and my life has become some stunted object of curiosity.

After Mother's death, when I would not even speak of her, lest it make me cry, Aunt Agnes asked me, "When she and your father were away from home, did you put them out of your heart and drop their names from your vocabulary?" I agreed I had not. "Then why should you do so now? Do you suppose you show your mother love by extinguishing the smile she so loved to see?" (I now understand that Aunt was exaggerating her loneliness so that I would see the joy I brought her, and thus begin to feel joy in my own heart again.)

Wednesday, March 25

Walking today, I stopped and watched an old Japanese man attending to odd-looking plants in a small shed beside his house. On his work-table was a small plant that looked like a cypress tree, the sort one sees "trained by the wind" on Mt. Tamalpais, high above the shore, but this one was hardly ten inches tall.

Lifting the pot, which seemed too small for the tree, he lightly tapped on the sides and then carefully removed the plant and examined it through his thick eye-glasses. Deep lines in his face expressed a kindness that made me wish I had my sketch-book. With a small sharp implement, he scraped the ball of roots, hardly bigger than the palm of his hand. I took a few steps closer, and he acknowledged my presence with a nod. If I offended, he gave no sign. Then he smiled. His teeth were yellowed, and some were missing, but his smile was so engaging that I smiled too. He held up the plant for my inspection. A cypress, indeed. A miniature cypress.

"It is very beautiful," I said. He pointed at his ears, shook his head and shrugged, then said, "Sollee. No speak." I bowed slightly. I felt silly, but he smiled and bowed back. I continued my walk, oddly cheered by the encounter.

Thursday, March 26

Finally went to see "Traffic in Souls" this evening. I cannot see why anyone should think it a danger to morality. I had avoided it not from prudery, but because it seems a fad. There was nothing joyful about the establishments pictured. Instead of coquettish young beauties consorting with dashing men, we saw women thrown into rooms like prison cells and intimidated by threats. We saw nothing that could cause a young woman to feel anything but horror, muting her curiosity and strengthening her wariness in the company of strangers. Nor did we see these women in a pose or mood that could appeal to men's lust, unless one enjoys seeing a woman in misery.

The picture's most shocking element is the suggestion that such establishments are often owned by the very citizens who shout loudest that they be closed. Some even say that the furor has been created by those who fear exposure. It has also been suggested that the same sort of men who accused women voters of "puritanism" and "emotional voting" in the Gill recall are now behind the campaign against these motion pictures. (I had best keep these thoughts to myself, or Father will surely urge me to pen something for the magazine!)

I do not know whether the problem is as widespread as they say, but how can anyone call it far-fetched that the head of the decency league secretly owns the brothels, when just five years ago Los Angeles abolished its "crib district" because of the city administration's scandalous connection with it? Have people forgotten that the first use of women's suffrage in Seattle recalled Mayor Gill and jailed his chief of police for two municipal brothels operating openly? (Father was beside himself that a friendly judge quashed the indictments against the "higher-ups" because commas were omitted.) Fremont Older always claimed that in San Francisco the Ruef Administration was interested in such an establishment on Jackson Street.

I begin to understand the fuss over *Hagar Revelly*. It deals honestly with common conduct between men and women—and does so with simplicity and clarity. As with the other plays and novels the Comstockians have lit into this year, I suspect *Hagar Revelly* offends for reasons different from the ones most often stated. I anticipate an unhappy ending for Hagar, and perhaps for her sister. Precisely because Hagar's vulnerability and fall are accurately portrayed, and the consequences foreseeable, the novel could have a cautionary, rather than degrading, effect on girls. Rather than forbidding them to read it, perhaps we ought to require them to do so. (I sound like Suzanne!)

Unfortunately, I do not care for the characters. Hagar is pretty and naive, and self-absorbed like her mother. Her sister's character is more interesting, but murky. If I sympathize with anyone, it is Greenfield, the old roué pursuing Hagar. He is at least passionate, and unlike the others, torn by conflicting impulses. In his way, Greenfield is a searcher for self-knowledge.

Friday, March 27

Went to see the old Japanese man and his miniature plants. Having recognized the trees as fully mature in miniature, I felt a sudden thrill followed by repulsion. How must it be to have one's growth stunted? So powerfully did I feel for the trees that I nearly fainted. The old man paused in his work and regarded me expressionlessly. When our eyes finally met, he held up the plant and stroked it, as if it were a cat or a dog. Then he tilted it and pointed at the roots, which looked quite healthy. He seemed to understand my discomfort and was reassuring me that the tree was in no distress. I smiled, although only by a bit of an effort, and he went back to his work, and I to my walk.

Attended Helen's wedding rehearsal, and, having endured the tedium, was subjected to numerous introductions to visiting family. I shall be glad when tomorrow has passed! Helen looks lovely in her white dress, but I shall feel very foolish in my matching bridesmaid costume. "But you must," Aunt Agnes said, with a wry face. "Why must I?" I grumbled. "You do know why bridesmaids wear costumes mirroring the bride. Long ago, people believed that evil spirits were jealous of happy couples. Wearing similar dresses, and confusing the spirits, was one of the ways to protect the bride. Disguising the bride behind a veil was another precaution. They even rang the church bells to frighten evil ones; celebrating the couple's happiness was secondary."

I asked if tying shoes to the back of the car was also aimed at intimidating spirits. "Folks in Tudor England believed that by throwing shoes and hitting the carriage, guests could guarantee good luck to the new couple. But sometimes the couple got hit by the shoes, so the custom was modified." I then asked about the custom of not letting the groom see the bride before the ceremony. Aunt laughed before she answered. "That has a very practical explanation, from the time of arranged marriages. Often the betrothed couple had never even met. Hiding the bride from the groom gave him no time to run away." The irony of our conversation was not lost on me.

Saturday, March 28

Returned from Helen's wedding feeling tired yet determined to paint. The event set loose strong feelings: love for Helen, joy at her happiness, a curious sense of loss. (Time passing? Something we shared? Feelings, strong but nameless. Restlessness!)

Retreated to the studio. At first, I tried to draw something that had startled me during the ceremony. As we stood in the front of the church, Father Mayne leading Edward through his vows, which Edward repeated with such deep emotion that he was briefly unable to speak, I glanced at his friend, Alfred, and read the expression on his face as one of pure rage. I told myself I must be wrong. When I tried to draw the two of them, I could not capture their expressions as I wished, so I turned to a painting of a white horse in a green pasture, pine trees in the background. I still feel unsettled, but a touch less so having painted.

Sunday, March 29

Finished *Hagar Revelly*. I better understand the outcry now. Hagar's fate, while hardly every young girl's dream, is far from the "just deserts" Mrs. Bennett might wish on her. Hagar makes a cynical bargain, trading the value of her body for a better life. Though she experiences fear and loneliness, and nearly becomes a lady of the night, Mr. Greenfield is a wealthy, kind man who loves her, and even marries her. Their marriage is hardly presented as a punishment; rather, the writer suggests that they may manage a sort of love.

I suppose I agree that the overall portrait is not much suited to young people; but the novel's defects do not justify banning it. Besides, such outcries accomplish little beyond increasing the publisher's profits. I remember the furor over *The Woman Who Did*, banned in many cities, and that year's most profitable novel. There was such endless debate over Herminia Barton and her disdain for marriage that I stole Aunt Agnes's copy after she had finished it and read the whole thing in one night.

Yesterday affected me more than I had anticipated. I'm happy for Helen and Edward, though a bit worried. I have known Helen nearly as long as I have known anything. Standing at her side, it struck me that to marry takes a kind of courage. Life is uncertain, our lives fragile, and pledging one's troth is a startling act of faith.

"A dreamer is one who can only find his way by moonlight, and his punishment is that he sees the dawn before the rest of the world." (*Hagar Revelly*, pp. 410-411)

Monday, March 30

Looking at the horrible photographs of operating boards in the April number of *Cosmopolitan* made me wish we had these pictures when Charles and Suzanne were arguing about giving dogs to hospitals. How could anyone look on such torture instruments without shivering with fear? It boots little to say they give the dogs anesthetics, when the mere sight of the instruments would be terrifying.

I've been mulling over the sundial motto.

Time's finger writes but letters in the sand.
The earth's a ball a child holds in his hand.
Yes, pause and glance and say you know the time,
The way a child repeats a silly rhyme.
And let the garden's dancing hues beguile
you back to childhood for a little while.

I like the first four lines, but the final couplet lacks the slightly ominous "world as a ball in the hand of a whimsical child"—was I too beguiled by the rhyme?

Tuesday, March 31

Mr. Edmonds mentioned today that he will be making a trip to Santa Rosa to see Luther Burbank about some seeds. How I should like to meet Mr. Burbank!

April

Wednesday, April 1

Elizabeth asked if anyone planned to go to Aubert Cook's one-act farce at the Broadway. I said she could tell me about it afterward. Elizabeth has no choice but to go. Not only do they know Aubert, but Tub's a friend of the Wollitz girl's father.

"It seems odd to think of the undertaker's daughter having her Vaudeville debut," Elizabeth said.

"When she's on stage, one doesn't think about her father," William said. "I had to attend 'The Maneuvers of Jane' at the High, because my niece had a few lines, and Miss Wollitz starred. Thoughtful-looking blonde, quite attractive."

"I ought to go so that I can say so when I run into Cook in the city room," Bret said. "But the idea of the would-be suitor disguising himself as a Newfoundland and being hired as a watchdog seems a bit thick."

Bret's editor has asked him to attend the execution of "Thomas Green," the young man who won't give his true name lest the news break his mother's heart. It will be the first execution Bret has watched. I should not care to join him.

Thursday, April 2

Pleased to see Father exhibiting more of his old feistiness as he derided *Life Magazine* for describing Westerners as crude and scatterbrained. Holding the magazine as if it smelled of old fish, he read us excerpts calling the Pacific coast "a sociological laboratory for political experiment, hospitable to all novelties and lacking moderation and sophistication," and "a geological afterthought, thrown up long after the rest of the continent was dry," and thus subject to earthquakes, adding that being an afterthought "gets into the people."

Father dropped the magazine on the floor and shuddered. "Someone might tell the writer that if indeed God created the West after making New England, then He created it having learned from that earlier failure. 'Welcoming novelty and distrusting stability' *is* what the English said of New England, back when New England still had some life to it."

Lucius worked in the garden with me after his school day. At one point, I found him staring at the green-flies on the leaves of the rosebush. He was quite caught up in watching the ants milk them, but misunderstood what he saw. "Who wins?" he asked. When I realized what he meant, I said that the ants weren't fighting the flies, but use them as we use cows. I explained about the honeydew, and the ants coaxing, or milking, the aphids with their antennae. He thought for a moment, then asked, "The green-fly don't mind?"

I explained that the aphids must eat far too much sugar from the plants—as if we had to eat a barrel of treacle to get an ounce of meat. "They're delighted to have the ants take it, because it's so sticky that it interferes with their movement." His interest spurred me to explain how the ants herded the aphids, whose placidity is like that of miniature cows. His wide eyes reminded me how wonderful it all is. I felt almost guilty about destroying so many thousands of the aphids with tobacco-water.

Friday, April 3

A strangely muted evening. Everyone was full of gaiety, joking about people in some Nebraska whistling-station taking up the tango. The Women's Club owed $12,000 for a new clubhouse and decided to pay it off by holding tango dances, but no one in town had the least idea how it was danced. One enterprising woman journeyed to Omaha for a week's lessons, then taught the rest. Half the town was salivating over the prospect of seeing how it was done, while the other half had learned from their pastors that it was the most depraved evil of the 20th Century, so the whole town turned out. The town is named Valentine. We concocted various visions of how badly the "teacher" had taught the rest. Jack and Elizabeth performed an imitation of the tango as we guessed it might be danced in Valentine, the "Tango Mecca of the sand country."

Bret was unusually pensive, then left the room. I found him in the garden, sitting on the tree swing, staring into his whiskey-glass. He did not look up as he said, "If only you could paint the patterns of light dancing in the bottom of a glass."

"Are they so beautiful?"

"Even the smallest of life's pleasures should delight us. Although I could not manage to be delighted by this evening's fashionable prattle."

I recalled that he had spent the morning witnessing the execution of "Thomas Green."

"He seemed more boy than man. He was steady, open, ... manly. Said he was not afraid to die. He'd prefer to live, but as he couldn't, he was sorry to see the mountains no more."

I reminded him that the boy had killed a man in a bank robbery.

"Oh, yes, he did something very wrong. He made no excuses, although it started as a lark, and the shooting happened so fast he hardly knew what he did. Still, the act seems so different from the man that it seemed a terrible waste to extinguish a second life."

Bret's voice was so soft I could barely hear it over the oak branches rustling in the breeze. I recalled that "Green" and another young cowboy had traveled somewhere for a rodeo that didn't come off, and as they rode through El Centro (or Blythe), they decided to rob the bank. I wondered what "Green" thought about last night, lying awake in his cell, and whether he regretted not letting them tell his parents where he was. I could just hear everyone chattering happily inside. Someone came clattering out the back door, laughing, then apparently changed their mind.

When Bret spoke again, his voice was flat and cold. "As they adjusted the noose he smiled wistfully. His eyes were so clear I couldn't meet them. I hated myself, hated all of us gathered there like zoo visitors. Even the guards shifted about like schoolboys hoping not to be called on. He looked straight at us until the hood covered his eyes. He never swayed or trembled. He just stood there with a frightening stillness. Even Warden Johnson was as pale as a consumptive and walked unsteadily. He had spent an hour alone with the boy, and they say the boy may have told him his real name. For ten minutes after Dr. Stanley pronounced him dead, none of us spoke. Even Fred Williams, who'd probably never been silent that long since he learned to talk. Jed Lane, who might have invented gallows humor, stood around like a church deacon."

I asked if he now opposed capital punishment. After a moment, Bret answered, "I *feel* as if I should. But I can't say that I do. Had it been any of the other four, I should not have minded nearly so much. Bundy, though he's only 18, seems to have nothing to recommend him. Ralph Fariss is a charmingly candid rogue who deserves to die. I dare say neither Lee Man Chin nor that Allen fellow will affect any of us near so much when their turns come."

"Bundy's the one who killed the 15-year-old boy?"

Bret fairly snorted. "Yes. He shared Green's cell. They didn't get on. Green, as do most of the prisoners, thought little of Bundy for killing someone so young, but as soon as Bundy heard of Green's death, he burst into tears. Not for Green, you can be sure."

"Eighteen seems awfully young."

"Younger every year; but think of it: Bundy telephoned the pharmacy to have some drugs delivered out in the middle of nowhere; he watched the younger boy leave to make the delivery, then bicycled to the spot and beat him to death for the money he was carrying."

After a moment's silence, we went inside.

Saturday, April 4

Edward Sturm stopped for tea and invited us to join him later this month on a visit to his friend Luther Burbank. I revere Mr. Burbank! He's created so many new and better varieties of fruits, even fruit-bearing cactus. His russet potato helped save Ireland. Friends say he is a very simple man, dedicated to furthering man's cooperation with nature. He has done things with plants that even the great scientists cannot explain. How should I *not* wish to meet him? Agreed with Edmonds to combine our journeys.

Sunday, April 5

Father Mayne preached on "The Soul's Triumph Over Science"—or the triumph of soul and science over the materialists' claim that scientific discoveries show that all we imagine to be "soul" is merely the telephone-exchange called "brain." Although souls have been for some years "out of fashion," as James put it, Father Mayne says learned opinion has grown less unanimous in holding that we have no souls. A growing minority see the latest modern scientific discoveries as strong evidence that we are more than the sum of our parts.

He mentioned Broca and others who have found that the brain is mapped in precise areas, with tasks such as speech and reading, and different types of vision, assigned to specific centers, like offices in a factory. (With a special center for perceiving music!) When an injury harms just one "office," the others go on as before, but that one function disappears—like the elderly woman who woke up one morning unable to read, but otherwise unchanged.

He explained that these discoveries, which had seemed to negate the concept of a soul, are now said to reveal that the brain is merely the soul's instrument—else how to explain cases such as Reverend Hanna, who was suddenly unable to recall anything of his past life, nor recognize even his fiancée, but could form new knowledge, and was quickly educated again. The Reverend could sometimes recall events since his accident, but not before, and at other times the reverse—yet in dreams, he would see, and later describe to his physician, images and people as to which he was wholly amnesiac when awake!

If the brain is the true and only seat of memory, such things could not occur; but if the brain is a mere instrument through which the soul expresses memory, then such cases are simply temporary problems on the "telephone lines." Scientists say that the stuff of our brains is constantly passing away and being replaced. After seven years, all the cells in our brain are new. If memory is attached solely to cells, how could an amnesiac's "new" brain recover "lost" memories after as long as fourteen years?

Tuesday, April 7

Supper with Uncle Thomas and Aunt Emily.

Poor Susan. She was developing into such a pretty girl and now seems so awkward, walking with shoulders hunched, dressing unbecomingly, and staring at her plate all through supper. Almost as if she *sought* to look unappealing.

Wednesday, April 8

Got up a group to see the Bishop Players' production of "The Common Law." I was surprised by how vehemently we differed when discussing it afterward. I saw nothing in it to which even Aunt Emily could have taken exception, but Julia spoke angrily against it.

"Painters' affairs with their models are normally tawdry and meretricious arrangements, not lasting love. Few of the women who remove their clothes for painters would have the intellectual or moral resources to hold the interest of such a man as Louis Neville beyond the first glow of lust. The playwright stacks the cards wholly in Jane's favor. She is such a perfect saint that only a terrible snob could oppose the marriage. And Louis Neville . . . How many men in the real world would behave with his restraint? How many poor girls forced to earn their bread in distasteful ways have Jane's moral strength, intelligence, education, and self-control?" Realizing she hadn't convinced us, she added, "Think of the impression Neville and Jane leave with young men and women."

Had I been much impressed, Julia's arguments should have lost all force when she used William as an example. "You don't see William getting entangled with students," she asserted. (How little she knows of William's true nature!)

Suzanne liked the play but found little romance in it. "If you boil it down to essentials, it teaches us that a woman alone, without family or wealth or standing to insulate her, is at the mercy of such men as Querida, and has little choice but marriage."

"But she loves Neville," Helen protested.

"Yes," Suzanne agreed. "But given his family's prejudices, she refused marriage until Querida's misconduct brought her face-to-face with the depth of her vulnerability."

I saw the merit in Suzanne's view but reminded her that *she* didn't believe that a woman alone had no alternative to marriage. Suzanne replied that while *she* did not—and conducted herself accordingly—I would understand her point more readily if my father were a malter or longshoreman. "What *I* think boots little. If a woman in that position believes that she has no other avenues open to her, then it is so."

Helen asked Suzanne if she believed in "free love." I noticed that William grew quite attentive. "Good for you," Elizabeth interjected. Suzanne said she wasn't running for office and needed no labels, but since she wasn't a man-hater and planned not to marry, her life might grow unconventional. "Never marry?" Helen asked, as if she could hardly believe such a thing possible. Suzanne laughed. She said that she wasn't fool enough to make any guarantees, but that marriage is part of the legal system that makes women second-class citizens.

Elizabeth asked if we were going to the Macdonough Sunday to see Evelyn Nesbit Thaw. "It's to be our only chance. She's committed to appear in Europe for years."

Suzanne laughed. "Why should I go to stare at a woman because she was involved in a celebrated murder case?"

"It does seem wrong to help make her wealthy solely because of that," Helen agreed.

"They say she's highly talented," Elizabeth protested. "And she waited six years before appearing again on the American stage precisely *so* the talk would die down and no one could accuse her of exploiting the murder."

"So, they say," Suzanne agreed. "As should I, if I owned the Macdonough."

"I'm afraid her only talent is her beauty," Helen sighed.

"And her willingness to reveal it further for the right price," Suzanne added.

Thursday, April 9

Susan is staying with us for two nights. She is a sweet-natured child—but so shy! She rushed into the house after school, breathless.

When I offered her iced tea, she insisted I not go to any trouble, but she held the glass in both hands and consumed half of it in one gulp, then giggled and looked apologetically at me. "Wholly unladylike," I agreed, reassuringly. She smiled and sipped the rest of her tea. Sitting at a high stool at the counter, legs dangling, and tracing circles on the counter with her fingers, she could have been some magazine artist's creation. "Joe, draw us a real old-fashioned American girl? You know, freckles, gangly, colorful frock, winning smile."

When I mentioned that Lucius would be arriving shortly to help me in the garden, Susan was eager to join us, but her energy far exceeds her knowledge. Overhearing Lucius explain to her how the ants milk the aphids, I felt an odd excitement, the sort a teacher must feel. His obvious pride in explaining something of importance to Susan, who is older and white, was comically sweet; but his enthusiasm for the natural world is nothing to laugh about.

In the evening, Susan and I painted. She loves to paint, but whenever I praise her effort, she demurs. She painted a cottage by a lake, with a forest behind. Animals stood at the edge of the forest, or peered down from the limbs of trees, and their oversized eyes seemed to watch the cottage intently. On a lawn in front of the cottage, a woman, and man with a neatly trimmed beard, sat reading. Beyond them, a girl stood beside a small tree surrounded by a small iron fence. At first, I supposed that the girl's legs were hidden, but she simply had no legs, as if Susan had been interrupted and then forgot to add them when she took up her brush again.

I cannot for the world imagine asking her what I feel I must. To speak of such a subject, to such a *child*, is unthinkable. When I let myself consider the likelihood, I feel a kind of outrage I never felt about Uncle's conduct toward me, perhaps because I never felt as young and innocent as Susan looked. I always believed I was quite grown up, even when I clearly was not. I find myself examining her every word and gesture for a hint of what she might wish to tell me—yet cannot. I hope she does not feel as if I am a scientist, studying her.

Friday, April 10

Luncheon at Elizabeth's. Hannah asked about Lucius, whom she had seen about the house last Saturday. When I described how we had met and why Lucius came to be my helper, my pride and affection must have seemed odd.

"Katherine spent too much time listening to Father's stories," Elizabeth said. She explained to Hanna that Father grew up on the Wisconsin frontier, carrying a Sharp's rifle before he could spell, and often camping out at night with escaped slaves who stopped with Grandfather on their way to Canada. "Grandfather believed in God and abolition. He read only the Bible and the New York 'Try-bune' and considered it his duty to help runaways. Sometimes he and Father used their weapons to delay the authorities while some poor fugitive got away. Grandfather was even jailed briefly after a pitched battle over some runaway."

I wish I had known Grandfather better. I can call up but two or three memories. The house's deep silence when he napped after dinner, and I barely daring to move for fear I would awaken him, although Lord knows I was in no danger of being punished. His teaching me to sign my name. He made the "K" in Katherine outsized and graceful and told me I must always be proud of my name and myself.

My strongest memory is of walking through town with him and everyone greeting him with great respect. (He was the mayor, or sheriff, or magistrate?) On one terribly hot day a prisoner was working in the town square. Standing in the dust, he looked like a scarecrow except for the leg-irons. His frayed clothes were soaked, his hair stood straight up as if something had shocked him, and he stared at the ground as we approached.

"A mite warm, ain't it?" The prisoner, likely stifling some less polite response to such a question, on such a day, said, "Yes, sir." Grandfather then asked, "How many days did I give you for that drunken stunt?" After the man answered, Grandfather said, "Come with me." The man followed us into Grandfather's office. He smelled like a public outhouse. I was a little afraid of him, not understanding that he had been jailed merely for public intoxication and was no danger. I watched carefully as Grandfather unlocked his shackles, then told him to go back out in the square with his broom and, when no one was in sight, kick off the shackles and get clear of town as quickly as he could.

Within no time, Great Uncle Joseph appeared in the office doorway, shouting, "Escape!" Grandfather looked up like a lizard dozing on a log. "DO something!" his brother shouted. Grandfather stared at the back of his hand as if seeking instruction, then back at Joseph. Normally decisive, Grandfather asked a few questions that seemed silly even to me, then said, "Well, he's likely gone." Joseph shouted, "Then he must be caught!" Grandfather looked up at the ceiling and said, "I haven't anyone to send after him just now. Unless you'd like to undertake it?" Joseph declined, made a brief speech about Grandfather's indecisiveness, and exited, grumbling. Years later, when I asked Father if my memory could be accurate, Father said it sure sounded like Grandfather.

There was a pregnant silence when I returned from my reverie.

"Hello, Central. Can you not get through to Katherine?" Jack said with a laugh.

"Anyway," Elizabeth said, "Father is short with anyone who slights negroes, and insists on using Mint's instead of some nicer barbershop. Now Katherine seems to have adopted a colored son."

I felt oddly put out with Elizabeth, but I forbore to point out that I have no maternal aspirations, and that what impelled me to take on Lucius was the way he takes to the garden, not the color of his skin.

Saturday, April 11

Mrs. C. has cancer. Helen said that Doctor Williams shook his head sadly and mumbled that no one knows its true cause.

Robbie asserted that the latest scientific view is lack of light. Apparently, aborigines in Africa and elsewhere are almost wholly free of cancer because dark skin absorbs all phases of the light spectrum, reflecting no color at all, while the light skin of the more advanced races absorbs only ultra-violet rays, and perhaps violet.

Bret called that line of thought nonsense. Robbie insisted that the X-ray and radium help stop the progress of a cancer because they penetrate white skin and supply the light-food for which our internal tissues and cells are starving.

"American negroes die of cancer," Bret scoffed.

"That just proves my point. Our negroes wear clothes, insulating their bodies from light. Man is the only creature who does so, and the only creature in whom cancer is common. If lack of fresh air produces tuberculosis, might not lack of light be equally damaging?"

"Shall we all run about naked?" Bret asked. "I can see few advantages to that."

"The Greeks often did so, and even Galen doesn't mention extensive suffering from cancer among them," Robbie replied, adding that some professor believes future races will be even more purely white—and more vulnerable to cancer. Bret replied that evolution seemed to be a way that species, through trial-and-error, developed their best mode of survival, while the prof's theory would have the reverse effect. I confessed I had no idea but did not expect to see Oakland's most prominent citizens parading about naked.

Sunday, April 12

Easter Dinner with the whole clan *chez* Uncle Thomas and Aunt Emily. The festive nature of the occasion made difficult because of my concerns for Susan—who looked lovely and busied herself overseeing the smaller children rolling their eggs. A timeless picture of childhood, as if to reassure me. At table, Susan sat beside Uncle. When he patted the top of her head, she looked highly uncomfortable—simply embarrassment at being treated so?

My fears for Susan have awakened memories I had "tucked away" behind baby shoes and pinafores, and the old ice-skates Mother had brought here, to a world without ice. Now that I've opened the "cluttered closet" of my mind, the dusty memories are tumbling out, like hatboxes from an overloaded shelf. I must face them if I am to help Susan. I must also be sure not to misread her situation because of my own. I foolishly assumed that I had somehow tempted him, but now I fear that, as a drinker is drawn to alcohol, or a glutton to food, he will do as he does as he can.

Monday, April 13

Took painting tools with me on my walk. I have thought often of painting the Japanese man, his deeply lined face concentrating on those tiny trees. At first, as before, he showed no awareness of me. Then, without moving his head, he glanced at me out of the corner of his eye, then back at the plant in his hands. We share no words, but he sees I am fascinated by his world of miniatures, and by the graceful care with which his old hands tend to them. He turned the plant slowly, holding it up for my inspection. A tiny juniper. (A mature tree in such a tiny pot is both beautiful and eerie; it is the natural tree and not the natural tree.). He showed me how he scraped the roots. His strokes were gentle, yet firm.

In painting, I do not judge. If I can portray the old man's concentration so that others perceive its purity, I have made something from which others can learn, or take pleasure. Let some philosopher or botanist opine on his strange activity. He must believe that he is helping the plant become something new and beautiful, though I do wonder why the trees do not die.

I set up quickly. I did not ask whether I might paint him. I trusted that he would know that I would stop immediately if he objected or appeared uncomfortable. I *thought* none of this while working. Once, early on, he raised his head and studied me for a moment, perhaps satisfying himself as to something. Thereafter he ignored me, as I had hoped he might. Later, I wondered what some unseen watcher might have made of my intense concentration on the Japanese man's intense concentration on a tiny plant.

Painting can be deeply emotional. I am often beset by churning emotions: one moment, exhilarated to have captured the subtlety of a shadow, or the grace in a cat's posture, nearly convinced that I have some idea what I am doing. The next, chagrined at failing to translate into brush-strokes the quality of the light or the expressiveness of a face, I reproach myself for pretending to be an artist. Moments later, all thoughts are swept away by breathless concentration. Only the painting exists.

When I showed him the sketch, he studied it, then shook his head and rubbed his cheeks to suggest that his old face was not worth so much attention. Still, he seemed to appreciate my effort and nodded, then bowed slightly, and looked into my eyes, as if they too were a painting. I sense a strange wisdom in him—or is it merely his age and our lack of a common language? Proverbs teaches that "Even a fool, when he holdeth his peace, is counted wise; while he who shutteth his lips appears a man of understanding."

This evening, we went to hear Reverend Crawford speak at the First Methodist.

Tuesday, April 14

Father's birthday. We celebrated quietly. Tub, Elizabeth, and old Mr. Dinwiddie joined us at supper. Father has never been much for celebrating his birthday, although he always manages to make a special occasion of ours. As it was his 70th ("An age which, during my youth I had neither expected nor aspired to reach"), others looked in briefly for cake. Elizabeth showed off her new "hoop" earrings, rhinestone set in platinum. Father growled, "Not long ago one didn't *see* a woman's ears. Now they're decorated like Christmas trees."

About the Easter festivities, Father remarked, "It's not clear to me how frills, flounces, and feathers commemorate the Christ's agony, or how ruffles, scallops, and balloon skirts illustrate the spiritual humility He taught."

"But you'll agree that it's quite a pleasant show?" Tub asked.

"A bit out of my line for some time now."

Bret toasted with, "To April 14, a distinguished day in history, not only the day on which Wendell Willard entered the world in 1844, but the date Maximilian and Carlotta set sail for Mexico fifty years ago, John Wilkes Booth shot Mr. Lincoln forty-nine years ago, and the Titanic sank two years ago. Whether these four disasters are of equal rank, I cannot say."

Sometimes I fear that newspaper work is ravaging Bret's heart. While being a newspaperman may add spice to what he sees as life's stifling hypocrisy, might it also kill the sensitivity that enabled him to perceive life so? Like a policeman, he sees the human race at its worst, when our faults and passions explode. The naked greed of a man with a gun, not the businessman's more subtle thievery; the fatal knife fight between two Italians over a woman outside a saloon, rather than the averted eyes and social "cutting" with which higher classes handle such conflicts; not to mention insane people and abject poverty. (Yet Bret chose the work, and it *is* a wonderful trove of characters that may someday add richness and depth to his novels.)

Father and Uncle Thomas disagreed about whether President Wilson's ordering the fleet to Mexico means war with Mexico—or should. Father said he hoped it was a bluff and that Huerta wouldn't call it. "But I don't believe in bluffing so baldly, nor do I see how a minor indignity to a few soldiers warrants risking the lives of many more, particularly when Huerta has apologized."

Uncle Thomas replied, "The Mexicans have been asking for it. Benson, the crucifixion of the Bishop, all the atrocities. You don't parade captured American soldiers through your streets with impunity. Yes, he's apologized; but if a man slapped your face and instantly apologized, would you feel satisfied? And we can't continue with matters so wholly unsettled down there. I hope Huerta persists in refusing to salute Old Glory and gives us justification to go in and clean things up—a job that very much needs doing."

Mr. Dinwiddie, who was a soldier for many years, said, "You'd talk quite differently if you were a young man, sir. No disrespect, but we'll see tens of thousands of our boys slaughtered if we try to fight inside Mexico. All those Mexican factions will suddenly turn brothers to fight the Gringo." He punctuated this prophecy by dumping out the ashes from his pipe and staring at Uncle Thomas, as if daring him to offer a contradiction. (I thought of Bret's jest about Maximilian and Carlotta. Will people look back and say that today we initiated an equally foolish adventure in the same country?)

The occasion of Father's birthday forced me to wonder how many he has left.

Wednesday, April 15

What must it be like for a white woman in the heart of the African jungle to live like a monkey, eating with her hands and wholly unclothed? I might have doubted the story entirely, but for Mr. Crawford's sincere manner and precise description of her in his talk Monday. (Fingernails like an eagle's claws!) He said that her wild ravings contained recognizable fragments of an old English rhyme. (How came she to be there? In her child-like state, is she happier or unhappier than she would be in civilization?)

Mr. Crawford construed her ravings and cursing at him as proof that she had chosen a life among the animals because some man had wronged her; but perhaps she lost her way or was carried off by animals when young. There are stories and myths of wolves raising human children. Can African apes do so?

I cannot imagine her life. Yet her very existence testifies eloquently to the inessential nature of so much that we believe necessary! Is there a kind of freedom in contentedly gobbling down a snake, wholly unconcerned about whether it is cooked for the proper time, or enhanced with the best spices, let alone whether one is dressed correctly and uses the proper fork? So long as it nourishes, what matters the rest? We have been taught that it should—but if we had not?

Thursday, April 16

Art Appreciation Club. My turn to speak, on color. I got through it, and Professor Clark was quite complimentary. So were others, but he is the only one who really knows anything.

Judge Ogden attended with his wife. I did not expect him to pay much attention, but as we drank tea, he asked, "Have you thought about the similarities between your art and my profession?" I certainly had not. He continued, "I was interested in your explanation that we unconsciously fail to see precisely the color of a face or a curtain—that the face by firelight or moonlight has not the same color as the same face at noon, and that the curtain borrows colors from a nearby rug or painting. You said that one needs rigorous training to see only what is actually before us. That is precisely what the jurist must do, suppressing all memories, prejudices, and perceptions not arising directly from the evidence, so as to decide guilt or innocence solely based on that evidence. A different field, but the same rigor."

Judge Ogden even said he might use my example in his charge to a jury! "Quite frankly, I had not contemplated the discipline required of an artist. I had accepted at face value all that romantic nonsense about inspiration, but I begin now to glimpse something more in it."

I asked Professor Clark more about his plans. They leave hardly a week after the term ends! All is readied. "The clothes you see on me I shall wear for the next 43 days." The farmhouse is in a little village called Penchard, somewhere between Paris and the German border, fairly near the Marne. "You won't find the village in Hare," he laughed; "and no railroads deigned to lay track to it." He said that a neighboring village, Crecy, is walled and still surrounded by a moat, so that all the little houses with their gardens have their backs at the water, and each has its own little footbridge that can be pulled up.

Someone asked why he should retire to France, when California is the nearest thing to Paradise that God ever made. Professor Clark smiled and said that as he will not be very well off, and his pension is small, in France, he can live cheaply and with dignity. "France is the easiest country in the world in which to live as a pauper." I have heard him describe the farmhouse as little more than a peasant's hut, but it is nearly two hundred years old, with stables and an old grange and other outbuildings, and commands a marvelous view of the surrounding countryside.

When Elizabeth asked whether he wouldn't be sorry to leave our modern conveniences, Professor Clark laughed so hard that he nearly spilled his tea. He said that our conveniences seem less and less convenient every day. "Yes, it's wonderful to have so much going on, and to be able to know so much so quickly, but I feel so burdened by the duty of keeping up that I can never stop long enough to contemplate all that I am constantly learning. We may soon see an evolutionary change in the American brain: the part of it capable of concentrating on any task for more than six minutes will atrophy, and we will flit from sensation to sensation like hummingbirds."

Professor Coates teased him about his absent-mindedness, and how he concentrates on his work to the exclusion of everything around him, telling us, "The world of drawing is more real to Lester than the one we walk about in. I recall once in San Francisco, after signaling to a cabman, he was about to enter the cab when he realized it was attached to a truly miserable specimen of horseflesh. I could see he doubted we could complete our journey safely. The cabman beckoned impatiently. Pointing at the horse, Lester looked up and asked, 'What's this, driver?' to which the man replied, 'A horse, of course, sir.'

"Lester shook his head and said, 'A horse, eh? Well, rub it out and do it over again.'"

Professor Clark smiled sheepishly.

Judge Ogden claimed that when he told old Watson that Watson's horse looked old enough to vote, Watson quickly replied, "Waal, Your Honor, he has voted two or three times."

Sunday, April 19

I am weary but also exhilarated and grateful that Suzanne and I were able to travel to Santa Rosa with Professor Sturm and Mr. Edmonds. By six-thirty, Mr. Edmonds and his man Antonio had arrived in Mr. Edmonds' new motor truck, and Professor Sturm in his automobile. Traveling so far by automobile was tiring, yet I was absorbed in watching the farms and forests and towns fly past.

I had read of the miracles Mr. Burbank works with flowers. He knows them so well that he can manipulate their sizes, colors, and even seasons! They say his potato adds millions of dollars a year to our farm production, and he improved the prune so much that we export prunes rather than importing them. (Men who disapprove call him "plant gambler" or "wizard.")

We found Mr. Burbank in the village, pedaling his bicycle on some errand. Though pleased to see Professor Sturm, he appeared as if he might have preferred to continue his errand rather than lead us to his home, though he graciously did so. He is full of delight and wonder, like a child, yet speaks of the natural world as beautifully as a poet. He combines the best of the scientist and the priest. A scientist not only in his accomplishments but in his commitment to keen and careful observation; and a priest in his deep, almost solemn, reverence for Nature.

Mr. Burbank is also modest. As we sat on the terrace drinking tea and chatting, I noticed that his extensive vocabulary did not seem to include the word "I." He asked questions rather than dwelling on his own accomplishments, and when asked about those, he implied they had simply happened, or had been managed largely by the gardeners he employs.

At one point our conversation was interrupted—nay, much enhanced—by a lovely incident that illustrated his modesty. Professor Sturm had asked about growing up one of eighteen children, and Mr. Burbank opened his mouth to answer, then closed it again, as if some new idea had struck him. He cocked his head to one side (like the dog listening to a gramophone in the advertisement), and he seemed to be listening to something; but the only sound was the singing of the birds. Someone started to speak, but Mr. Burbank held up his hand and shook his head ever so slightly, then smiled and arose from his chair. Silent as a cat, he slunk to the railing while we watched, puzzled. After a few moments, he gestured for us to join him.

At first, we saw nothing out of the ordinary. Antonio was leaning casually against a wall; the birds were singing—and then I realized that we were hearing Antonio along with the birds! He was imitating the birds so perfectly that his calls fit in with theirs. But for Mr. Burbank's keen ear, none of us would have known. After a while Antonio looked up at us, then away, embarrassed.

Mr. Burbank beckoned him to join us. Miss Burbank, having put on a blue gingham apron cross-stitched with white squirrels, brought him some lemonade. One might have supposed that Antonio was their honored guest. He and Mr. Burbank chatted like old friends, hardly hindered by Antonio's limited English.

"Can you sing the songs of other birds?" Mr. Burbank asked him.

Antonio glanced down at his feet. After a moment we heard the soft hoot of an owl, followed by a loon's lonely call, then the trill of a nightingale. Antonio remained expressionless. Mr. Burbank's face filled with sheer wonder. His sister stood behind him; from her face, she might have been in church. After a few minutes, Mr. Burbank called to the gardeners nearby, inviting them to approach the terrace and listen, and then bade Antonio continue.

When Antonio paused, smiling shyly, Mr. Burbank said, with great enthusiasm, "Nature has taught you to sing like a bird. Come into the garden and see what she has taught me." With that, he gave us (or rather Antonio, but allowed us to follow), a tour of the wonderful novelties with which he has astounded the world: the thornless blackberry; a bed of amaryllis he had coaxed to new colors, blossoms thrice the size of any we had seen; several new varieties of strawberries, each delicious; the spineless cactus of which we had read. (The cactus pear, as its fruit is called, is bright red, and grows in thick clusters, and is as juicy as a watermelon, with a strange taste that is unlike any other fruit.)

The visit was thoroly delightful and inspiring.

Monday, April 20

When I think of the visit with Mr. Burbank, I am filled with wonder. He is a sage, yet unpretentious. He talks simply yet eloquently on many subjects and holds strong views on all.

Bret fears his editors may be coming to share the widespread view that muckraking is over despite his view that there remains much to be done in that line. He says that regardless of Mayor Mott's ability, Oakland's government is as corrupt as ever. "How could saloons operate illegal gambling establishments a block from the police department without paying the police? I've seen police officers in some of those saloons after work."

"Hell, I play poker against one of them in Ollie's place," Jack interjected. He pointed his cigar at Bret and grinned. "But don't think you've got a beat! You print that, I'll deny it."

Bret said that was small potatoes. He's convinced he can get the goods on the city council and some of the franchises. But will his editor back him up?

I suggested Bret stay for supper. Father asked about his work, and he seemed pleased by Father's interest. When Bret criticized the newspaper's waning interest in muckraking, Mr. Jones, of course, said that although he'd enjoyed the early pieces by Steffens and the others, it seemed now that most everything of importance had been uncovered. Father snorted.

Mr. Jones continued, "Oh, I don't say there aren't still things being done that aren't right. There could be some rotten things in Denmark, still," he conceded. "But businessmen are working hard to bring things into line with the new business conscience, and readers are wearied of reading only mud and dirt."

Father argued that although the faces had changed in the last few years, the game itself hadn't changed much. "Your editors may be right that readers are weary of it. Novelty was part of what made muckraking go at the start. People were surprised that things were so corrupt, and it was fun to shoot at the 'Big Men' everyone envied. But people always lose interest, and your editors see that. That's not to say that corruption has vanished."

Tuesday, April 21

Today is John Muir's 76th birthday.

I can never hear his name without smiling (though I have met him but thrice), for I have hardly been happier than during those two weeks in the Sierras. (He must have been 70!). Hardly a day passes in which I don't recall something he said or smile at a memory of him teasing us. (I hadn't expected him to be such a fun-loving sort.) His adventures sounded like that wild ride on the avalanche. After he narrated some hair-breadth escape and remarked, "I'm not a reckless man," Mr. Burroughs laughed and asked whether we could imagine what a *reckless* man might have done.

The final night, we sat around a huge campfire at Camp Ahwahnee, contemplating the spruces and firs and listening to the Merced River chortling on our right, while the Falls roared somewhere to our left. I took a long walk with the full moon for company. It was like walking through a painting. I tried to impress it all deeply on my heart, as on a photographic plate, sure that if I could but carry this moment within me through whatever awaited me back in Oakland, I should be all right.

Mr. Muir asked at length about Father, although they had not known each other particularly well in Wisconsin. (Mr. Muir was years older.) Mr. Muir's father sounded even more difficult than Father makes Grandfather sound. A cross between a military officer and a preacher: strict and stern and humorless. Mr. Muir's mother was quite well-educated for her time and loved painting and poetry and nature.

Tonight, while Uncle Thomas went on about the Japanese, I thought back to something Mr. Burbank said that was quite different from the usual views. He said that he did not see why the same principles of crossing species of plants, combining and modifying, merging a totally wild strain with one weak from over-civilization, and developing the strongest strains might not apply to the development of the human species. "We have such a grand opportunity in our country!" he exclaimed, beaming. "Unparalleled, throughout history, such a vast mingling of races from every corner of the world. Why do the newspapers quiver with fear about immigration? We have an opportunity to create the finest, strongest race in history, a magnificent race." He turned to me. "I will not live to see it. You wait, though. A couple of generations. You will see."

"But would you do away with the physically weak?" Mr. Edmonds asked.

Mr. Burbank replied, "I would shore them up, make them self-reliant, train them to be the best they could be. Some of our greatest leaders have been physically weak, particularly in childhood."

"What about the mentally defective? Would you do away with them?" asked Professor Sturm.

Mr. Burbank shook his head. "I grant you, in theory, the human race would be improved by removing the burden of those who can never learn to reason, but have you ever looked into the face of a woman with an imbecile child? You see the same bright light of love as in any mother's face. What man could willingly extinguish that for a mere ideal? And who is to say that with all the progress being made in medicine and surgery, that someday we may not be able to train even those unfortunate souls?"

Thursday, April 23

Frances Ballard is here.

Friday, April 24

Frances is not a happy person. While I awaken each morning pleased to be alive and curious about what the day may bring, she awakens as if someone had rudely snatched her from the world of dreams and set her down roughly in a foul-smelling place rife with hidden dangers.

This afternoon we had a long talk. At least, she talked at great length about her life in Fresno. It saddened me. She is the sort of girl who wanted nothing more than to marry, build a home, and nurture children; and she'd have done it eagerly and well; but her mother taught her about homemaking, and nothing about men's

natures, then turned up her nose at every boy who came to call. Jenny managed to find friends with a surplus of beaux, and learned how to attract men, although she's no prettier than Frances.

Once Frances felt she had a sympathetic listener, she expressed very bitter feelings toward Jenny. She portrayed her as a somewhat casual mother, far more preoccupied with her position as a leader of what passes for the smart set in Fresno than with caring for Phyllis. When Jenny went East for a month, she left Phyllis with Frances, who was delighted and even sewed several new outfits to fill gaps in Phyllis's wardrobe. When Jenny returned, instead of thanking Frances, she smiled superciliously, muttered something about Frances having "nothing else to do but fuss with patterns," and seemed annoyed at the bond that had developed between her daughter and her sister.

"It was a cruel lesson," Frances said. "I didn't realize how lonely I was, how much I wanted to be a mother, until Phyllis came to stay." She thinks it terribly unfair that men marry not the women who might best suit them and nurture their children, but the women who appeal to the worst in them. Such women, she said, have men in abundance to choose from, while those with the character for marriage and motherhood have none.

"Did you never have a beau?" I asked. Frances laughed, but without joy. "Oh, yes. Howard Aldrich visited me four times, but Jenny laughed at him for a "slow-poke," and Mother was appalled at keeping company with a mere clerk. He was intelligent and ambitious—owns two factories today—but I was never good at going against Mother. Then Jenny started flirting with him, guying him about this and that, blinking her eyes, laughing so foolishly that I feared he'd think less of me for having such a frivolous sister, he was so earnest and serious himself. Well, I was worrying about the wrong gun: the next thing I knew he was head-over-heels in love with Jenny. Of course, she didn't care a fig for him.

Saturday, April 25

With much chaffing, we tried to decide what to do to entertain Frances. Helen plumped for DeRemee's horses headlining at the Broadway. "They're beautiful, big white horses with flowing manes. One of them is supposed to be intelligent, and answers mathematical questions."

Tub thought we should see Al Jolson's "The Honeymoon Express." Edward scoffed that it was "some silly froth about a divorced husband and wife taking up again together by mistake." "Who cares about the plot if you're laughing all the while," Tub replied. Elizabeth had heard it was a bit spicy and feared it might offend Frances, but Tub said it was so good-natured that no one could take offense. "She'll be laughing too hard to be offended." (Does Elizabeth assume an "old maid" from Fresno must be a prude? Did Frances say something prudish to Elizabeth?)

We took Frances to the Pantages. They claim Mlle. Adgie is the only woman lion-tamer in America. At first, I wondered why there are not more women lion-tamers, the lions seemed so overfed and lazy; but once Mlle. Adgie got them whipped up, and put them to various tricks to irritate them, there certainly seemed a good deal of danger, and when she drew them back into the cage, she barely escaped through a little door. (Or was that all pretense?)

Frances appeared to enjoy the show. Relieved by the hope that war with Mexico may be averted after all, we laughed all the more at a show I normally shouldn't have cared for—although I did like de Toska, the garrulous juggler.

Sunday, April 26

Missed church today. After seeing Frances off, I felt fatigued, and sat all morning in the garden. Father was in his office, and no one else was around. It seemed as if all the world, but he and I, were in church. (I *was* in church. *My* church.)

Some of the irises seemed regal in their purple splendour. The slender spires of the white fox-gloves rose tall and pure, their heads bent slightly as if in prayer. Humming-birds and other small birds flitted about to cool themselves in the water.

How enchanting it would all appear if we were but eight inches high, and the colorful flowers were as tall as trees! Then no one could miss the miraculous beauty of God's world.

Gardeners require a special ruthlessness, to put to death their own children without even Medea's jealous passion to justify the carnage. Who am I to decide that the nicotiana (which rise up like vaudeville clowns, their white blossoms hanging in disorderly fashion like disheveled hair, and delight me by staying long after most flowers have given up and left the party), must yield to the irises and lilies? Sometimes the awesome responsibility almost paralyzes me. (Is this how a judge feels at sentencing?) At other times, I root up plants as indifferently as the sheriff of Nottingham rounds up the King's enemies.

Monday, April 27

Aunt Agnes has no patience with Frances. "Being unmarried is no excuse for idleness or loneliness. It never has been, and surely isn't now."

I told her Frances longed for children. "There are more than enough ragged specimens on the streets of Oakland and San Francisco whom she could adopt. I suspect that's so in Fresno. If not, you might advise her that there are stagecoaches and trains."

"Or the parcel post," I quipped. (How we laughed last year over the Alabama farmer who didn't understand that the parcel post wouldn't accept live shipments and wrote to an adoption service that it could send the baby by the new parcel post service, if it were under eleven pounds!)

Aunt asked if I understood the difference between Frances and myself. I said that I was fortunate to love painting and gardening. "You find joy in life. Frances does not. The air in Oakland is no better than in Fresno, and I doubt that your father and I, and your friends, are so much more fascinating than the people she knows. Your nature is to take delight in people and things, and to share that delight, while hers is to find faults and slights, and to twist her mouth with pain and distaste. Naturally people smile back at you—and avert their eyes from Frances."

I told Aunt that she is too hard on Frances and a good deal too rosy in her view of me.

Tuesday, April 28

Elizabeth demonstrated for us her new "Three-in-One." Father teased, "It should prove quite useful should you take up shoplifting. When floorwalkers and policemen trail you from the store, dressed in your chic black taffeta and robin's-egg blue, you can turn the corner, pull that string, and voilà—you are in bright red from ruffle to toe, and can walk right past your pursuers in perfect safety." Then, eyeing her new purse, one of those small, square leather boxes that looks like a little medicine bag, Father pretended to confuse her with Dr. Williams, and persisted in asking poor Elizabeth about his medical condition. I was glad to see him so light-hearted on that subject.

Mostly the men rattled on and on about the marvels of the six-cylinder motor they say is replacing all others. Tub tried to explain it to me: apparently each cylinder wastes most of its time getting ready to do whatever it does, creating lulls in its production of power. The use of six cylinders allows for continuous power, which makes for a much more comfortable ride.

Tub claimed the motor-car is already an astonishing boon to the nation's economy. "A motor-car traveling at the speed limit can cover four times the ground as a horse. Suppose a thousand men who formerly used horses changed to automobiles and saved four hours every day. How much is an hour of a man's time worth, conservatively?" After I ventured a guess, he calculated the increased productivity for a thousand men, working six-day weeks for fifty weeks, and proudly announced a savings of nearly a million dollars per year.

"Maintaining an automobile is much dearer than feeding a horse," Father said.

"Yes, but those expenses are no more than a flea bite on the savings," Tub replied.

When Aunt Agnes asked what all this additional time was to be used for, Tub gulped, then said, "Why, anything at all. Building more buildings or dams or maintaining accounts. Playing whist, even. I don't care if you read books or learn the tango. The point is there's a rich vein of time and energy to be mined. And I don't think we yet see the half of it."

After Tub had "run out of steam," Father said quietly, "It doesn't matter how fast you go if you don't know where you are going." Father always praises scientific advances, but something in his tone sounded pensive and weary. Is his faith in science and reason waning as his own future shrinks?

Wednesday, April 29

This morning I began a painting of the garden in all its disordered beauty.

The lilies are a foot or two high, healthy, and strong. A lily seems to have a seriousness of purpose. Rigidly erect, she seems determined to move straight toward the sky, without distraction.

Most of the calla are lying down, weary from keeping their cheerful mien while guarding the garden and waiting for all those other slug-a-beds to join them.

The columbine, bright yellow against the green iris leaves, resembled tiny lamps showing leprechauns the way home from their saloons.

Clamoring for attention are the gladiolas, only the red so far, as if the other colors have agreed to wait for May.

The tomatoes are a foot tall; but the carrots and cucumbers are moving slowly, like the always-stalled motor-trucks one saw ten years ago.

Thursday, April 30

In September I shall go to Chicago for the great art exhibition!

May

Friday, May 1

Odd article and photographs in the current *American Homes & Gardens*. The author built a special glass box, set tulip bulbs at various depths inside, then photographed the bulbs through the glass as they grew toward the surface of the soil. One bulb was set eleven or twelve inches deep, more than twice the right depth: and its leaves just barely managed to breach the surface. Its poor flower lay like a stillborn foetus an inch or two below the light, and the leaves shriveled up after an "unhappy existence of about ten days." Another, thirteen inches deep, was "beaten completely," never reaching the surface.

I stared at the photographs as if in a mesmeric trance. Although I understand the usefulness of such an experiment, I felt as if I were watching a foetus struggling desperately to be born, only to expire, clawing desperately at the obstruction.

This evening Bret reminded me of that poor woman who shot the man with whom she lived for going back on his promise to marry her after keeping her in a brothel for years—then asked why her situation hadn't provoked in me nearly the concern the tulips had. I had no ready answer, but my sympathy with the natural world sometimes exceeds my sympathy for my own race.

Saturday, May 2

Annual family picnic this afternoon. Croquet, horseshoes, whist—and lots of sandwiches and conversations. I was troubled by what I saw of Susan. Whenever Uncle Thomas drew near, she flew off elsewhere, rather like a hummingbird. When chance placed them in proximity, her body grew stiff, like that of someone much older, and she moved sluggishly, without her usual grace. This seemed so remarkable that I could not imagine others failed to notice. But then, no one saw anything amiss with me. How blind we can be!

Yesterday evening we discussed the series of essays on spinsters in *Munsey's Magazine*. I do not think anyone in our group sent me her original piece, nor did anyone appear to think of me in connection with it. Most of us do not sympathize with the "spinster" who wrote it; the women more impatient with her than the men.

I pointed out that all through my childhood people sneered and joked about "old maids" and "spinsters" because they couldn't get men, but nowadays everyone's angry at "bachelor women" because they *decline* to marry.

Julia agreed, "Men writing in magazines make fun of all women: married women are too respectable, bachelor girls too advanced, old maids too prudish, and suffragists too aggressive. If you stay at home, you lack imagination; but if you work, you're mannish."

Charles observed, "The problem isn't spinsters, but parents who push a girl to say, 'Yes' whether she would or not, reminding her she's nearly 'on the shelf.' Result? A high divorce rate and a great many more homes where there should be divorces."

Julia replied, "I resent the view that maternity is a woman's chief calling, and invariably ennobling. I don't see much lacking in the characters of Jane Addams and Clara Barton, and some mothers hardly bring 'nobility of character' to mind."

Suzanne was unwontedly silent. When Bret inquired, she tossed her hair and said with a sweetly defiant smile, "Marriage is one of the chains with which men keep women 'in their place.' It's a pathetic vestige of the days when you hit us over the head and dragged us off to your cave. It hardly comports with Twentieth Century reality, or what *should* be Twentieth Century reality. I don't want to be anyone's property, or to own anyone, and refuse to make promises I can't keep."

"Like the heroine in *The Woman Who Did*?" asked Julia.

"Rather, although with no illusion that I'm Striking a Blow for Woman."

"And with a happier result, one would hope." Julia said.

"Clearly," agreed Suzanne.

<u>Sunday, May 3</u>

Frederick Mills visited. He has just graduated from the University, studying economics, and was quite full of the new adventure on which he embarks Monday next. The Immigration Commission has engaged him to investigate how hoboes and migrant workers live on account of that horrible incident in Wheatland last August. He is to take the train down to Fresno, disguise himself as a worker and get in with such people.

Tub said the I.W.W. is set on class warfare. "From pure envy they would light a fire that would destroy our entire way of life. They will use the poorer Americans to destroy the better sort; but if they destroy American business, there will be no work for the lower classes."

Mills disagreed. "Try working in heat of a hundred degrees, a mile from the wells, with ten toilets for thousands of people. That farmer in Wheatland had called for twice as many men as he needed—and wouldn't allow anyone to truck in water or supplies because his brother had a concession to sell lemonade at a nickel a glass to men making just $1.50 for a 12-hour day. He forced them to buy all their food at inflated prices from his store on the farm."

Mills asked Tub if he'd care to be one of those people. Tub said that he would not and was working hard to avoid such a fate, and that while he sympathized, he didn't want the agitators using the workers to destroy life here. "Working hard," Mills repeated, eyes blazing, though he spoke calmly. "Those men work hard too. Do you not realize how critical the accident of your birth has been in helping your work have some happy result?"

Tub opened his mouth to argue, then thought better of it.

Tuesday, May 5

Tomorrow I am to go to Judge Ogden's court with Bret to watch the trial of Hazel Lux. After Bret kept chaffing me, saying that I cared more for some stunted tulips than for a stunted human being, how could I not go?

I had read that when the "red-light district" was closed New Year's Eve, the Lux woman moved to Emeryville with the man who kept her. He continued refusing to marry her as he had promised, and so she shot him dead. Bret says she was married at sixteen and sold into white slavery by her husband two days later, then lived in degradation and hardship for sixteen years. She lived with this Garland as man and wife for four years, giving him all the revenue from her "trade" on his promise that soon they would be married, and she could leave that life behind.

I felt sympathy. (I shuddered in horror; truth be told.) Until Bret urged me to go with him, I had not thought of attending a trial, although since childhood I have heard men recounting stories of trials. I often think they prefer the law courts to the theaters.

I asked whether women attended. Bret acknowledged that it is not customary, but said several women attended Millie Drown's trial. Bret is of opinion that women *should* be interested in "the fate of one of your sex who has been so harshly treated by the worst of mine. It would be a sad tale indeed, if after a life of slavery, she were executed for trying to free herself from it."

I was curious, now. "They will not convict her of murder?" (Uncle Thomas complains that the men on juries always let women off who've killed their husbands.)

"Most likely not," Bret said. "But one can never be certain."

I felt rather as I had when Frederick Mills told us about the workers at Wheatland. I do so little about such things.

Wednesday, May 6

Spent much of the day at the Lux trial. It is all a little unnerving. The gravity and formality of the setting made me feel *I* might be placed behind prison bars for some unknown offense. Among the reporters, lawyers, and men who find trials entertaining, I was the only woman, except for a prison matron. I sat in back, and when Judge Ogden looked around, I wanted to duck, lest he recognize me. Then I was nearly attacked by a fit of hysterical laughter—at my own foolishness, and the stern surroundings, which made everything seem funnier.

"Oyez, Oyez."

I soon understood why men find trials so fascinating. I was as attentive as in the theater. Perhaps more so. Although the dialogue was often slow, and laden with impressive words, this was *real.* A woman's life hung in the balance!

Before Hazel Lux testified (as her only witness), I had doubted her, though I had not said so to Bret. I had wondered if she killed Garland for some other reason (perhaps emboldened by knowing that women are rarely convicted for such killings), then worked out with her attorney a more sympathetic explanation. Her appearance did not reassure me: she looked rough, almost mannish, and as if she had a mocking knowledge of the world. Then I watched, and listened, and I was moved. I believed her.

I believed her tears, too. Her story moved some jurors to share them. I marveled at her determination "to quit the life and be decent."

Garland was truly vile. She had given him $200 a month for five years toward the home they would buy when they married and had believed his story that he was investing it in lots. When she asked for proofs, he replied that he could not receive the deeds until he had finished paying down the mortgages. Told suddenly that she had nothing, and hearing his cavalier threat that if she bothered him about it he would go back to his folks (which she, of course, could no longer do), "and you will have to sleep in the gutter," I too should have felt beside myself, and might well have acted as she did—particularly when he sneered, and chided her for being idle when there were so many fellows hanging around on a Saturday night.

Miss Lux is just 32, my own age, although she seems both much younger and much older. Younger because of her wretched thinness and vulnerability (despite having killed someone), and a sort of naivete, despite her rough speech. Older in the weary expression her face takes on, and because of what she has experienced.

I have been searching her trial (as I might a play) for moral lessons. Without supposing I would enjoy her company, and without condoning all she has done, I feel anger rise in me when a man makes a casual joke about her. Instead of taking pride in my supposed respectability, I feel humbled: I have not been put to the horrible tests she has; I doubt I could have survived them. My own misconduct, with a little bad luck, and without the protection of relative wealth, could easily have left me as defenseless as she. If Richard and I had eloped, and he had abandoned me, or if there had been a child…

The case will go to the jury tomorrow. Judge Ogden instructed the jury today on manslaughter. Suzanne and Helen are to accompany me.

<u>Thursday, May 7</u>

The jurors deliberated for but a half hour before bringing in a verdict: guilty of murder in the second degree. We had thought they

might settle on manslaughter. Miss Lux showed little emotion. The jury recommended mercy in sentencing. Bret said the crime carries a sentence of ten years' imprisonment to life, and that if Judge Ogden sentences her to the former, she may be free in seven years. It seems a terribly long time, yet she did take a man's life. A *sort* of a man.

I stood beside Bret as he interviewed the attorneys for Miss Lux about the conviction. One of the attorneys shook his head and said, "She is a poor woman." Bret contrasted this case with Millie Drown's case. Her trial lasted six weeks and was attended by many prominent women. Where Millie could pay for alienists to appear as expert witnesses, Hazel Lux had none. Bret said that this is only the second time in recent years that a woman has been convicted of murder in Alameda County. She will be sentenced Saturday.

Once out on the street, we witnessed an odd demonstration: city engineers and police were giving a final test to some devices two policemen came up with: using railroad semaphores to control street traffic. They had installed a set at 12th and Broadway. Using some electric push-button apparatus, the crossing policeman operated the semaphores so that arms were raised to signal east and west traffic to stop. After an interval, the arms were lowered, and the north and south semaphores signaled for that traffic to stop, and the east and west traffic proceeded. The signals have colored lights to flash at night. The experiment today proved successful, and they intend to have such systems operating along all the mercantile streets within a week. It seems such an obvious idea—yet no one had thought to do it before.

Friday, May 8

Sitting in the garden and relieved not to be hearing lawyers' voices or being jostled in a hallway—or breathing the close air of a courtroom amidst tragedy and conflict. Warmed by the morning sun, drinking fresh coffee, and surrounded by the scents and colors and bird-melodies of the garden, such sordidness is difficult to imagine.

Where I began planting two years ago is now the wild, vibrant home of irises (a few still blooming); foxgloves (mostly white, but some lavender, more plentiful than last year); lilies (two flowering, the rest rising rapidly to join them); columbine; lobelia; and just there, blue and white delphinia, and a few red glads (where once were bright red tulips); and of course, schizanthus, recent arrivals, happily settling in.

Butterflies flutter coquettishly. Yellow-and-black bumble bees enjoy the dark purple columbine, the color-contrast so startling that I move closer. Tiny green insects explore the lavender-and-white delphinia, a few snails lurk in the depths of the foxgloves' lower leaves (the lattice-work they have made of some leaves is evidence of their nocturnal crimes), and spiders perform acrobatic feats among the lilies. When I return to my chair, a humming-bird darts down. I had not seen them show interest in the columbine before. The humming-bird makes her rounds, from columbine to lily, and on to the Peruvian lilies.

Conflicts in the garden seem more benign, although probably not to the participants. Spiders do not spin webs merely to win prizes at an exhibition; and the humming-bird that so amuses me is a death-dealing dragon to insects. Yet the difference is not mere scale. Their conflicts concern essentials. The roots of foxglove and lily may jostle for space because a foolish woman has planted them too close together; but a fading foxglove does not shoot a lily from jealousy, a lobelia does not sneak behind a delphinium and knife it to death so as to steal extra air and water, and the humming-bird does not beat the columbine to a pulp because it has let another kiss it.

<u>Saturday, May 9</u>

A strange and shocking day. I have sat for several minutes in silence, staring at this blank page. I am troubled by the fate of a woman of whom I had hardly thought before this week!

Suzanne and Helen accompanied me to court today. Judge Ogden commenced by reviewing the sordid facts. He reminded Miss Lux that had Garland been on trial for killing her, the same twelve men would have voted to hang him, rather than convicting him of a lighter crime. I began to fear that he would not be lenient.

His next words will ring clearly in my mind for months: "Should I obey the recommendation of the jury and give you the minimum sentence of ten years, and you were freed in seven, what would confront you? A cold and heartless world. You would again sink into the utmost degradation. You would become the victim and the consort of the lowest and vilest of men." He went on to explain that by giving her the maximum sentence of life imprisonment, he could protect her from that fate, and assure her "a good home for the remainder of her life."

Judge Ogden's tone was almost gentle, and the import of his words struck slowly. Miss Lux put her hand to her mouth in shock, then began screaming hysterically. Judge Ogden asserted that he took the action for her own good, and that if she wished to become a good woman, with the assistance of those in charge, he might someday lend his aid in gaining her freedom. Miss Lux trembled and sobbed as he intoned, "I hereby sentence you to imprisonment in the state prison of San Quentin for the remainder of your natural life."

We rushed to her side and tried to encourage her. She continued sobbing, and screaming, her voice cracking, something about how she could have redeemed herself. We could do nothing for her. She only grew more hysterical, until finally the court bailiffs half-carried her from the courtroom, still screaming and sobbing.

Numb, five of us women trailed behind her to the doors of the jail. When Suzanne remarked that the sentence was as shameful as

Mr. Garland's conduct, a young man smoking a cigar coolly replied, "The sentence was just." Suzanne replied that it was an outrage.

"Not at all," he said. "She killed him because he wouldn't marry her. Just as that fellow Nyalyte killed a woman of that sort because she wouldn't leave the life and marry him. If he pled guilty and was sentenced to life imprisonment, why should this woman go free? Judge Ogden did say that if she does right, he will not oppose parole when she is eligible."

I am resolved to write to Miss Lux in jail, and visit her, and take an interest in her case.

Elizabeth spent the day at the May Festival pageant.

Sunday, May 10

Today is "Mother's Day." Miss Jarvis's invention merely serves to reopen a wound the years have barely scarred over. Now there is yet another day that commands me to think of her! Surely, I am not the *only* motherless child who prefers no such celebration. No one had heard of Mother's Day five years ago, but today there is hardly a village in the country that fails to celebrate. I imagine that they will institute a "Father's Day" sometime after Father has passed on.

Perhaps I was disposed toward sadness today by the memory of Hazel Lux's shrieks as Judge Ogden declared her sentence, and by reading yesterday of the terrible earthquake and volcano eruption in Italy. (How many mothers are digging their babies from the ruins of their homes this morning, wailing and shrieking, as abandoned by God as Hazel Lux?)

As I thought more about Miss Lux's fate, the lack of any corroborating witness, I suddenly understood why Uncle Thomas ceased when Elizabeth returned. He was only too aware (as I was not), that his conduct was criminal in nature. Though he must have felt confident that he could deflect as childish nonsense anything I might say, he must have feared that if even one so young as Elizabeth should corroborate my account, all might be lost. Lizzie was prone to run to Aunt Emily at the drop of a hat, and he must have known that. I even recalled that he suggested to Aunt Emily that we were old enough to sleep in separate rooms. Fortunately, Elizabeth was afraid of the dark, and pled to be allowed to continue sharing a room with me.

I shudder to think how it might have been if we had stayed longer in that house. How perhaps it is for Susan. I cannot testify to what has occurred between them, but I can surely make clear to a court that he is capable. How obvious this all seems now.

Monday, May 11

This morning Father fell.

Tuesday, May 12

Father did not break any bones, but he seems shaken. Weaker. Oddly uncertain. Smaller, somehow. After his fall, he went back to bed, where he remained all day. When I took him supper, he looked at the food, then at me, as if unsure what it was for. Then he set to eating rather intently, but soon stopped, leaving most of his supper untouched.

Today Father left his bed, but he had no idea what to do with himself. He sat in one chair or another, staring at a painting or out the window. If he picked up a book or magazine, he put it down immediately, as if he had discovered it was in Chinese. If I asked a question, he answered sensibly, but as if from a long way off.

May 12th is the date Father took me to my first Circus. There were acrobats, lions, and two funny men—a bald clown with a guitar, and a banjo-playing man dressed in street clothes but with a clown face and wild hair. The clowns sat on high stools and made jokes about events and political figures. I understood little, but I laughed right along with everyone else. Father knew someone, and we were allowed to talk to the performers. The midgets fascinated me. Their wary eyes, rough skin, and lined faces did not belong on a child, but they were no taller than Elizabeth.

Wednesday, May 13

Father is still not himself. Several times he asked, "Why should I have fallen?" Although he has not said so, I fear he believes that he is weakening and will die soon. I sense he is thinking often about death, though he does not seem frightened or unhappy. I have been staying home to keep him company, and have more leisure than usual to paint, or to write. I do neither. I cannot even muster the will to garden.

Thursday, May 14

Went out walking for the first time since Father's fall. Aunt Agnes was at home. I set out and kept walking. My legs were as eager as Mr. Edmond's horse on its way home. Above all, I longed not to think. At first my thoughts raced, but soon the steady sound of my feet hitting the ground trampled my brain into submission, and I just walked, paying little attention to direction. After what must have been nearly two hours, I found myself walking along the Alameda estuary. I paused, startled that my feet had brought me to this familiar spot. Immediately I felt as if the sun had come out. Then tears came to my eyes. A single heron stood in the shallows, searching for fish. He turned toward me, then resumed seeking his lunch.

Mother had wheeled here, with me following on my new Vanguard. I was proud to keep up with her, though quite probably she kept to a pace tedious for her. That the road was unfamiliar, and that I had no idea where we were going, enhanced my sense of adventure. She glided to a stop (while I lurched to a stop), in a small clearing near the water, in which sat a very unusual craft.

A huge man with dark skin and beard stood on the deck, wearing only a pair of short trunks and a belt to hold his knife. I stared silently at him. He stared silently back at me. I wanted to ask him if he was a pirate; but before I could form the words, his gaze shifted to Mother.

"You've brought the pirate queen," he observed. Then to me, "At your service, your Highness." The twinkle in his eye dissolved all fear of him.

The Admiral and his wife were not people one saw socially, but his proficiency in sailing gave him entrée to some of Oakland's "best people" who were fond of the sport. He rarely wore shoes, and I doubt his wife owned a presentable frock. I never heard of their visiting anyone else we knew. I wondered now how Mother happened on them. It had not occurred to me to ask. Uncle Thomas did not approve of Mother's visits, and said so to Father, who muttered that Moses should have announced an 11th Commandment: "Mind your own business."

The Admiral was truly an astonishing figure: six feet three inches and strongly built, with sun-bronzed skin and a thick black beard. Working on his boat, knife on his belt, he did indeed resemble a pirate. Yet how he loved to tease and laugh! He thought clothing a waste of time and money, and unhealthy. He had seen natives in Tierra del Fuego walking naked on the snow, and their buoyant health strengthened his taste for minimal clothing. His wife agreed, and their children wore hardly anything. During our visits, I was permitted to shed most of my clothing, and I felt wonderfully free.

Mother later told me that the Admiral had started wandering because of a woman he loved who could not (or would not) marry him. (I also heard the Admiral had been married to a half-caste woman in the South Seas who died.) He commanded schooners and steamers in the South Seas and around the Hawaiian Islands. He was also a surveyor and engineer and had crossed the Sierras on foot many times.

His wife was warm and gentle and unaffected. She was from Australia, and I loved hearing her speak even though I barely understood a word. Her eyes met mine with such frank intimacy that everything she said seemed both exotic and important.

The Admiral had charge of a steam dredge that was deepening the estuary, and he swam in the estuary often, as part of his work. He joked about being paid to swim when others had to stay caged up in offices and stores to earn their bread. He was building a sloop from his own design, to be called "Whirlwind." Sometimes he let us help—which no doubt impeded the work considerably.

Being in their company was like visiting another country. The children and I made up our own language. We swam mostly unclothed in the estuary, hiding when boats came near. The bottoms of my feet toughened from going barefoot. We were trappers, trapping beaver; we were Hawaiian Islanders, dancing strange ceremonial dances; we were a band of renegade Indians pillaging southern Arizona with the Apache Kid. How painful it was when Uncle Thomas and Aunt Emily forbade me their company. How I longed for Mother and Father to return!

The Admiral won all the sailing races in 1893, and most in 1894, in the Whirlwind, even though a half-dozen sloops were built specially to beat her, using his ideas. When I heard other men complaining that they could not best him, I felt proud, as if I had contributed to his success. I looked for him whenever we passed near the California Yacht Club, or the estuary, but I never saw any of them again.

Friday, May 15

Father stays mostly in bed. The confusion he experienced on Monday and Tuesday has lifted like the morning fog, but he still says little. I sit with him and read from *Pudd'nhead Wilson*. When he dozes off, I read *The Common Law*. Sometimes I look up and find he has awakened and is gazing at me with an expression I cannot interpret. I smile, then he smiles, and we simply look at each other.

This morning I asked him when he was happiest. He laughed and said he had been a very fortunate man. When I persevered, he furrowed his brow, then replied that I might choose among three moments he would nominate. (A lawyer's answer.) His three nominees were: the day Mother and he married; a period when he was sixteen, during the War; and a trial he won many years ago with Thaddeus Stevens.

I then asked what had been the most terrible moment of his life. Immediately, I wished I had not. He frowned and his eyes seemed to widen with fear. I sensed that he was seeing something just beyond me. Suddenly he smiled and said that the most terrible moment in his life had been Mother's death. I nodded, then asked what it was he had thought of initially.

"Are you sure that you wish to know?" he asked. When I nodded, he said that the most terrible moment in his life had also occurred during that short period in his youth when he served with the Union Army. "Do you know how they punished deserters during the War?" he asked.

Father could not have deserted! "Were they shot to death?"

"Officially, 'Desertion is a crime punishable by death.' And that happened. They made a big fuss, to deter others. But desertions were growing nearly as common as casualties. Near the end, more than five thousand soldiers a month were wandering off; to shoot them all would have destroyed many able-bodied men who might yet be made to fight." Father coughed.

"Truly, they didn't shoot many men, particularly among those who deserted only once. They gave punishments that either humiliated them or caused unbearable pain, without disabling them permanently. One of the more common punishments was to brand them. As one might brand a cow. The letter "D" was burned onto the man's backside or hip, or even on his cheek. I heard that in some places they cut the letter in with a razor and filled the wound with gunpowder. In our regiment, a deserter was branded on his cheek."

"And you witnessed this?" I asked.

Father glanced out the window, then looked straight into my eyes. "The task of branding fell to the surgeon. If no surgeon, it was done by the drummer boy, or the youngest soldier. I think they supposed that because of our youth we wouldn't be targets for revenge." He fell silent, then added softly, "Even now, as I drift off to sleep, I sometimes smell seared flesh and see their eyes, which swelled so violently I feared they would explode."

For several seconds we said nothing. Father smiled—in apology, I thought, for telling me such a terrible thing. I squeezed his hand to reassure him.

Finally, he said, "It seems ironic that the same time in my life should be the answer to both your questions. Great danger heightens every small pleasure. After wandering across an acre of dead and putrefying bodies, to hear a sparrow sing seems an extraordinary miracle. When a man who laughs and sweats and curses by your side is suddenly thrown to the ground, lifeless, by a sniper's bullet, it becomes precious simply to breathe the air on a summer evening. A man who is your comrade in war can be forgiven almost anything for the remainder of your lives.

"In that madness, far outside the rules, we made our own. Mine were simple: I would try never again to cause pain to anyone; and for guidance I would look not to statutes, or the Ten Commandments, or to preachers and teachers, but to my instincts, which seemed all I could trust.

"I survived. But I have never forgotten how easily I might not have. I lived for nearly a year knowing that I might die at any moment—and that I must not let that knowledge interfere with the business at hand. And I have felt so ever since." He smiled. "If love or friendship or duty should run contrary to the rules of religion and Society—we have not time to do what we cannot feel to be right."

I felt I was coming to know him only now—when it might be too late. I placed my hand on his. He looked as if he himself had no such feelings, but he was prepared to accommodate mine. We sat so until his eyes closed.

Saturday, May 16

Soon after dawn, I carried my coffee cup outside and sat on a rock, watching the sun enrich the colors. Father's illness preoccupies me, and I dare not paint or garden, lest he need me. This afternoon I had hoped to do several simple tasks, but I never even changed into gardening clothes.

Father came down to breakfast for the first time since the fall. He puttered about in the library, then I helped him return to his room. He had been so pleased with himself at breakfast that I feared he would be disappointed by the quick retreat; but he seemed not to think of it that way.

When Lucius arrived, he was surprised to find me indoors. Contemplating the mid-morning sun on his dark skin, and the shy smile that emerges from his tough little street-face once he is in the garden, I decided to paint him. This suggestion did not meet with his approval, and he stuck his thumbs in his trousers-pockets and studied his shoes for a moment, then made various arguments (he was "not nuttin' to see;" the weather was too warm; we needed to finish weeding the asparagus bed), only acquiescing once we agreed that he could sit in the garden.

Susan appeared soon after I began, and she helped mute Lucius's impatience. Intent on capturing his expression, I barely heard their chatter; but I realized how much I enjoy them. Children are in touch with their hearts, and their imaginations. The wonder of discovery has not yet been riven by disappointment, soiled with greed, nor lost beneath the clutter and dust of making one's way in the world.

A while later, I recognized the sound of Mr. Edmonds's motor-truck and smiled, recalling our visit to Mr. Burbank. I heard Antonio whistling from behind me, until he caught sight of us and stopped. When I asked, without turning, what he thought, he was silent for so long that I nearly did turn around. "You are remind me," Antonio said, as if that were the sum total of his communication. "I remind you…" I prompted.

He haltingly told of driving a British tourist lady to Selinunte. Apparently, she hired him in Bixio to drive her to the ruins to paint. The vastness and decayed grandeur of the place appealed to her, and she stayed a full week, going every day to the ruins to paint.

"I see her first time, she is wearing long, beautiful white dress, walk and walk and walk. So many flowers in April, many colors. No people, only her. She walks, she picks the… how you say? wild parsley? She dances like little girl, she picks flowers, make a circle to put around her neck. Like child, happy, think of nothing. She ask can I take her next day, next day, one week. Always she is wearing the trousers like a man, and she brings many things for painting. She watches everything close, like hawk in the sky above ruin."

Then Antonio pointed to the sunlight on Lucius's face—exactly what had caught my eye.

I tried to explain that when Lucius is in the garden, his face has a special brightness. Something more than sunlight. When I looked over to see if he understood, he was smiling.

"Who puts this in boy face?" he asked.

I was not sure how to reply. "It is his nature," I said. "It is there."

"It is there before the boy know you?" he asked, then walked off to unload the plants and manure without waiting for a response. When he returned, I was concentrating on capturing what I could recall of the light on Lucius and wished he would go, but at least he watched silently.

When I was nearly finished, I turned my head, winked at Antonio, and said meaningfully, "I thought I heard an owl." Antonio

responded by providing a hoot. Susan and Lucius looked around, startled. It was great fun to watch the wonder on their faces.

Susan's friend, Helen Holmes, came looking for Susan. She had a terrifying morning: a boy with a knife tried to rob her of some rings she wears. She struggled, even though he had the blade of the knife pressed against her, and managed to knock the knife from his hand and free herself. She is unhurt, but still, how frightening! The footpad himself is but fifteen. When he jumped from behind a tree and shouted, "Hands up!" she thought it a joke.

At sunset I walked to the top of the hill and sat alone, reflecting. I wondered what I would say if asked the questions I put to Father. I was happiest with Richard, and unhappiest after he left, when his letters ceased. Then I thought about our visits with the Admiral and his family, suddenly being deprived of them, and Mother, all at once. Then living with Uncle Thomas—was that the worst my life has been? I think so.

The setting sun turned the bay into a golden bowl of light surrounded by hills, the clouds became soft, colorful quilts, and the breeze blew just cool enough to freshen the warm air. I thought of the lilies in the late light, and Father's whimsical smile, of Lucius's curiosity, Susan's sweetness, and their awe at hearing Antonio's bird-calls. As if one of the trees had asked me to identify my happiest moment, I murmured, "Now."

Tomorrow is "Go to Church Sunday." I had thought the whole thing rather silly at first, but I agreed to spend the afternoon assisting at a service in the jailhouse.

Sunday, May 17

How frightening to hear the jail's metal gate clang shut! How wearying to speak with men trapped like zoo animals, though they may deserve it. I learned that the warden has discretion to place a life prisoner into solitary confinement for the rest of his life. Some of the men were sullen, but others' desperation to please us seemed even sadder.

When I told Aunt Agnes and Elizabeth about Helen Holmes, Aunt said that two eleven-year-olds recently robbed an eight-year-old of 35 cents. Then they grow up to be Bundy. Elizabeth reminded us of that terrible incident the other day, in which two brothers were playing "Mexican War." Of course, that was an accident, but I cannot imagine how the boy felt who was playing at executing his "Mexican prisoner", only to learn when he saw his brother fall to the ground dead, that their father's gun was loaded! Aunt says it is a result of today's parents' disinclination to instill religion and moral precepts.

Saw Mary Pickford at the Oakland Photo, playing a ragged squatter girl, willful but good. After the sombre day, I laughed all the harder, but now when I recall those poor men, I feel guilty about my frivolity.

Monday, May 18

When Dr. Williams looked in on Father today, Father urged him to speak frankly. "I believe that I am dying. I don't wish it, but my wishes are immaterial. I hope to die as I have lived, looking straight at the road ahead, whether it's muddy or dry or impassable."

Dr. Williams seemed relieved. He said he has seen dying men whose doctors and relatives and friends all conspired, with fine intentions, to deny death's imminence. "It's damned silly. The dying man, if still attentive to his surroundings, recalls playing a role in similar conspiracies and recognizes the game."

When Father pressed him, Dr. Williams said that, unfortunately, Father was not a bad diagnostician. His heart is weak; his lungs are full of fluid; and he will continue to weaken. How long? He could not say with certainty. "I do not expect you to die this month.

However, I would not suggest you spend much time writing New Year's Eve toasts."

I gave a small, involuntary cry upon hearing Father's situation stated so baldly.

"So, I had supposed," Father said, as if Dr. Williams had predicted rain.

Tuesday, May 19

Had Professor Clark for tea. Retirement has him beaming: after decades of dreams and plans, and much chaffing that he would never do it, he is moving to France! I quite envy his fulfillment. As we sat on the green bench by the fuchsia, I asked him how it felt.

"Ah, you cannot imagine it, my dear. All my life the culture and history of Europe has called to me, as has the peace and calm of the French countryside. Now that countryside will be home. Paris, Berlin, Amsterdam, London, even St. Petersburg will be a mere train ride away. And the farmhouse we have purchased in Penchard is just a short train ride west to Paris, yet not so far from Germany."

Elizabeth was chattering about him later, emphasizing that the "we" included his friend Charles Hare, the bank teller, with whom he has often taken vacations. I suppose that what she meant to imply, and what Richard used to say about them, is quite likely true. If so, perhaps they will be all the happier in Europe, where such things may be more accepted. They have stayed together longer and more harmoniously than many married couples.

Wednesday, May 20

Visiting the estuary has revived childhood memories.

Some of Mother's friends were appalled that she rode a bicycle—and even let me do so. It was not "ladylike." Others bicycled with her—and imagined that the riding of bicycles would free women. "I've taken my stand," I heard her say one day to Father, to which he replied, "and your seat." No one thinks twice about a woman riding a bicycle today, but few would say Miss Anthony was right that the bicycle would do more for the emancipation of women than anything else.

I understand something now that I could not have articulated during those carefree days playing with the Admiral's children. Most of the faces we see are masques. Uncle Thomas's masque of righteous civic leader hides another face few could imagine; but he is an extreme case. Is it the rushing about and crowds of modern life? Is it the inner pressure to live up to the morality we are taught in church, when we are simple beings who, not long-ago, lived-in trees? Our inner uncertainties? Aunt Agnes blames parents "too kind" to impose the standards of eighty years ago, leaving us without clear road-signs to navigate life's twisting paths. *Something* creates such a deep uneasiness that we present to the world a different person from who we are. The difference may be vast (as with Uncle Thomas or William), or slight.

The Admiral was exactly what he seemed, always. How do I know this? Children seem to know. Over time, we forget that we are divided, distracted by the task of perfecting our masques. Or becoming them. So intent on performing, we forget that it is a performance. The Admiral was himself. I cannot think of anyone else... Perhaps Mother?

Thursday, May 21

Suzanne's reverence for the moving pictures irritates me at times. This morning she exclaimed that watching a new art develop makes our time as invigorating as the fifteenth century, when the art of printing books developed. She then asserted that the most beautiful painting, or the finest statue, is "a ridiculous caricature of real life" compared with "the most tattered film in a side-street nickelodeon." As she knew it would, that caught my attention. She then quoted some writer's claim that our descendants, accustomed to moving pictures, will care nothing for Mona Lisa's smile, frozen on her lips for four centuries. Adding, "A smile is a fleeting thing. The fixed smile in a painting is not a smile at all but a grimace. Only by a determined effort can we ignore the inherent artificiality and limitations of paintings."

Suzanne is right as to the direction the world will take. To oppose it is as hopeless as Wordsworth's discomfort with the intrusion of steam engines and railroad tracks crossing the verdant British countryside. Yet a good painting matters precisely because of the fleeting nature of that smile—which disappears instantly in life. That is precisely what renders the painting invaluable. Our lives are fleeting. The painting freezes forever one artist's vision of one moment. Moving pictures cannot accomplish this—diverting and even thrilling as they may be.

Art Appreciation Club. No speaker, but a brief flare-up (again) over whether photography is an art. It is remarkable how slowly ideas permeate the social brain. If we reprinted the debates from Steichen's "Camera Work", we should generate exactly the letters people wrote then on why photography did or did not deserve to be called "Art." The "New Woman" was also new in 1905, and 1895, and perhaps before I was born. *The Woman Who Did* was a sensation in 1895, as was *Trilby*, and the same shocked outcry that made the publishers wealthy then is filling the seats at "The Lure" and helping bookstores sell copy after copy of *Hagar Revelly*!

Does contemplating the fleeting nature of Father's life have me on edge?

<u>Monday, May 25</u>

Father has spoken more about his youth during the past few weeks than in the decade preceding. Nearing the end of his life, he recalls the beginning, as if life were a circle that has brought him back around to childhood. He is now sometimes so weak that I must assist him with bodily functions he had performed unassisted since boyhood. He is not as embarrassed as I might have feared. Once I thought he was about to ask whether it embarrassed *me*. (A man's body is not so unfamiliar to me as he supposes.) I am glad to do it. It makes me feel very close to him. Sometimes I feel almost what I imagine a mother feels for her child. Sadness too because I will soon lose him.

This morning Father spoke of an incident near the end of the War. The two sides were camped so near each other that the pickets from each side could yell across the river. They ceased bothering to snipe at each other, and eventually began trading. Yankee coffee for southern tobacco, and such.

One day Father swam across the river to visit and trade. Before he could return, General Gordon rode up. (As Father learned much later, General Gordon had instructions from General Lee to put an end to this unseemly friendliness.) Father dove into a bush, but the General noticed his men were nervous, and decided to investigate. One man told him that they had been preparing to present arms if he should happen by. The General said that was commendable, then asked why the bush just beyond them was shaking when there was no wind.

Father had no choice but to show himself—quite literally, for he had removed his uniform for the swim. As he stood there shivering, "not sure whether I felt more foolish than scared, or more scared than foolish, but aware that I was a good deal of both," General Gordon asked sternly, "Have you not noticed that there's a war in progress in this neighborhood?" Father agreed there was, but said that as it wasn't active just then, he'd not thought it would do any harm to have a friendly chat.

General Gordon announced that he was going to have Father thrown in the guardhouse as a spy. His men protested that they had invited Father across as their guest, and that it would dishonor them

and the General to treat him otherwise. General Gordon started to ask Father whether, if allowed to swim back to his own side, he would promise to stay there. Before he could finish the question, Father shouted in the affirmative and dove into the water.

June

Monday, June 1

Another grey day. This morning I did not feel inspired to paint or to walk.

My interest in *The Custom of the Country* is waning after less than 150 pages. Ralph loves the peace and simplicity of Italy, while Undine longs for the excitement of a sophisticated city in which to show off her beauty. Ralph has finally begun to realize that in "the small half-lit place in which his wife's spirit fluttered, her mind was as destitute of beauty and mystery as the prairie schoolhouse in which she had been educated." I sigh at the prospect of spending a further 450 pages with these people!

The May 29th number of the *Mirror* came. I was quite taken by some poems by a Webster Ford. The poems ring clear and vivid and true. He knows human nature.

Tuesday, June 2

We seem to have reached our summer pattern of cool, grey mornings that give way to bright, warm afternoons.

Why does it surprise me so when the light tarries late into the evening? Every year it seems a novelty. How we used to love the long summer evenings of childhood! Bursting with energy, we played till unheard-of hours. Even Mother and Father could not bear to put us down to bed while it was still light.

Now I am 32. My mind knows that June 21 is our longest day. Nevertheless, each year the longer days are an invigorating surprise.

Wednesday, June 3

In no time at all, the motion picture has grown from a curiosity to a major industry. They say it ranks fifth among the world's industries. Watching the elaborate 'movies' of today, it is hard to recall how recently we lined up to watch a few minutes of a train moving on the screen! The picture-publicists boast that we can digest an entire novel in two hours and fifteen minutes; but, as Aunt Agnes says, if the goal were to eat in quantity, we could all consume loads more than we do, but we would not be better off. The picture may give us the plot and a glimpse of the characters, but much of the writer's art we never see, let alone "digest." It hardly seems right that something a writer labored over for a year should flicker past so rapidly and be gone.

Thursday, June 4

I wonder that Elizabeth can keep up the endless rush of gossip, bridge, tango, and social and charitable activities. Aunt Agnes says we are so intent on knowing the most up-to-the-minute news, with newspapers and magazines and books proliferating like spring weeds, that thoughtful conversation is a lost art. She insists that things were much better when she was young; but even in my own time we have forgotten how to maintain solitude and thoughtfulness—or has reaching my thirties taught me to cherish contemplative moments?

I had nearly forgotten that *Munsey's* nonsense about spinsters, but the new issue has another piece by the original spinster, who has now provided her name. I am fascinated by her views of the responses the magazine has published—and by the letters to her. With all the talk about her misery and loneliness, I had never thought of men sending her proposals of marriage! It was unsettling to find that her name is Katharine too, though with an "a." No doubt my anonymous correspondent is much amused.

She's sounding more capable. Less of a whiner. Is it merely that, as she says, her first piece was written in a deep valley of depression and loneliness—or has all this changed her? Is she stronger for having spoken up—or more confident with a parlor-full of marriage proposals? We shall never know, unless some years from now *Munsey's* publishes her account of journeying to East Whistlestop, Montana, or looking into her first child's eyes.

The letters sound so genuine:

"Your story in *The Munsey* sounds mighty good to me. I've been ranching alone out here for about four years; was sent out to die. But I'm not dead—not by a good deal. I'm more alive than I ever was when I was harnessed to a broker's office in New York. The climate's great; but climate is not all a man wants… I'm forty-seven, have three thousand dollars in the bank, and seven hundred acres of good land. I would build a new house."

"Your Plaint revealed such depths of womanly sweetness that I am fired with courage to try to know the lady who possesses such attractive qualities… Perhaps I should tell you that I am fifty-one years old, with no vices except the devotion to my work and the bashfulness I have mentioned."

"I am lonely too, and would fairly worship a good, loving wife. Age, sixty, height five feet nine inches… don't smoke and detest whisky, drink a glass of beer in the summer sometimes, one the limit, can walk ten miles a day and keep it up all week if I had to.... I enclose the names of the Governor of one of our papers, and a banker. To them you can refer as to my respectability."

Also, a sweet letter by a widower who praises her sweet character, adding he expects her to receive many proposals and would add his to the lot but has promised to consult his two children before undertaking marriage again. One she seems to be considering!

I am less than halfway through *The Custom of the Country*. The remaining pages loom like a long hill from which the view may not warrant the effort. Mrs. Wharton's prose is clear and strong, but I cannot care about the tedious lives of her people. Even Ralph's poetic longings are drawn so vaguely that Mrs. Wharton must mean us to understand them as ineffectual.

I find myself longing for Trollope's characters. Although many were silly, greedy, or narrow, one *cared* about them, perhaps because they were a mixture, as we are in life, or because he let us into their minds, to witness the process by which they reached decisions.

Friday, June 5

The men quack like ducks about their fighters. Tonight, much about Gunboat Smith and a Frenchman named Carpenter, and of course the negro, Johnson. He is to fight Moran. Robbie insisted that the "big Zulu" is so strong because his ancestors were still wild and uncivilized just a few generations ago. William argued that Johnson's depraved life in Paris may have dissipated his strength. Jack said Johnson "loves his championship the way a southern darky loves his lodge regalia" and knows how America would laugh and jeer if he should lose. They descended to such inelegant locutions as, "The Gunner packs a kick in each mitt."

"Does anyone here speak English?" I asked. (Do they memorize sports pages as we used to memorize lessons in our McGuffey Readers?)

This afternoon I was tempted to toss *The Custom of the Country* across the room. I am unable to believe that Undine forgets her son's birthday party. While she might be chagrined at the prospect of spending an evening at such an event, I cannot credit her forgetting it altogether. She is too sensible to forget that she was to take her son to her husband's family for his party. I can't help but think Mrs. Wharton wished to stress Undine's selfishness and settled for a very lazy way of doing so. I *was* interested by Mr. Bowen's soliloquy that the average American looks down on his wife and won't let her participate in "the real business of life." However, it seemed to have little to do with the case at hand.

Saturday, June 6

Susan came to help in the garden today. She delights in Lucius. When I praised her ability to communicate with him, her face lit up. I asked whether she has a good life with Uncle Thomas and Aunt Emily. For a moment her eyes rushed madly about. Then she cooed, "Oh, yes. They are wonderful," adding, "We're just like any other family." (Does she protest too much?)

I cannot fathom how to ask her directly about Uncle. I understand too well the fear and shame, and the pain it might cause her to have anyone else know; and if my fears are unwarranted, I might cause great harm, poisoning her mind and raising concerns that should not yet trouble her.

Sunday, June 7

Remain annoyed with *The Custom of the Country*. Ralph's suicide comes from nowhere. It simply suited Mrs. Wharton's convenience.

Trollope would have shown us the gun long ago, and portrayed vividly Ralph's secret melancholia.

Monday, June 8

Spent hours with Helen and her grandparents today. I fear Mrs. Cooke will not live more than a few days. Mr. Cooke says little. He is of that generation when men *did*, rather than said. He is pale, his skin sags, his cheeks almost sunken, and his eyes dart about, then fix desperately on someone, as if grasping for help. There is no help in this.

Mrs. Cooke seems to dream, mostly. She spoke to Helen by name today, and said she was in little pain but felt a terrible itching. At one point, she awakened and raised her head and turned it from side to side, looking around with great wariness. When I touched her hand to calm her, she asked, "Are we almost there? It seems such a long, long way." Later in her sleep, she sighed and murmured, "Perhaps we should have remained in Massachusetts."

Finally finished *The Custom of the Country*. I raced through scores of pages just to have it over with. No surprises. I felt chagrined to have wasted good money and better time.

Tuesday, June 9

With Helen at the Cookes most of the day.

As afternoon was turning into evening, we left them alone and sat in the parlor. The ticking of the Aaron Willard clock sounded as loud as a locomotive. Periodically we called through the door, but Mr. Cooke said she was resting and that they needed nothing. We sat, in that numbed state beyond fatigue, listening to the clock and thinking our private thoughts. The chimes drew me from some reverie and turned my attention to the clock. A wedding present to

Mrs. Cooke's grandparents. Missing its middle finial since its trip West across the prairies. It might have lain smashed by the side of the trail after an Indian attack, as she became the unwilling bride of some feathered brave. Instead, it has stood here, like a sentry guarding the childhoods of children and grandchildren.

I had a sudden idea that the clock would stop when she died. A foolish thought quickly dismissed—yet it chilled me and brought me to my feet. I asked if anyone wished a glass of water, but neither did.

"It has been a long time," Helen said. At first, I thought she too had been thinking about the clock, but she was looking at the door. Quietly we opened it and looked in. Mr. Cooke sat by the bedside, holding her hand, just as we had left them. He leaned down stiffly to rest his cheek against hers. As we approached, I could see from her stillness that she was gone. Her mouth was open in a toothless little "O", perhaps having tried for a final breath. Her bluish pallor suggested she had been gone for a while. Nellie caught her breath so sharply that the air whistled. I looked at Mr. Cooke.

"She…" I began, not sure quite how to say it.

He nodded. "Yes. Soon after you went out. We just wanted a mite longer together."

Wednesday, June 10

Jenny Ballard arrived today. (Mrs. Russell, that is, or "Jenny Ballard that were.") She flounced in, dropped baggage and children with Aunt Agnes, and disappeared to shop with Elizabeth. (How like her sister's description!) Jenny's husband is going motoring in the country with Tub and friends.

Reading *Dr. Ellen* again. Refreshing after that slog. I love Juliet's precise language: "A delicate skin and amusing little brown eyes would have made her pretty if she had not used her face much as a more coy generation did its fan, peering through it for effects, presenting it always at a meaningful angle," and "Christine would have defined feelings as facial expressions designed to add piquancy to conversation—if she had been given to definitions."

I savored the passages and thought of Jenny.

Thursday, June 11

Watching the Cookes has reminded me of my solitude. (Are we such "egotists" that we see another's life merely as lights to illuminate our own?) I shall never know another person so deeply, love anyone so much, nor share such companionship. Yet I cannot convince myself that such a partnership could develop with any man I know.

I said as much to Aunt Agnes when she came into the studio while I was sketching the Cookes as we saw them at the last. Aunt appeared quite moved even though I have thoroly failed to capture the emotion in the scene. Aunt asked whether I thought that William and Lucy, as a pair of naive young people beguiled by illusions of California, meeting by chance on the arduous wagon trail, envisioned the depth of companionship we saw decades later. "Do you suppose love is created by royal fiat, or congressional legislation? Or might it grow gradually, like the formations inside a cavern, from an accretion of shared moments that in themselves seem merely mundane or trying?"

I take her point. They say that even when marriages are arranged, love can happen. Still, my heart balks at the thought of decades with the likes of Robbie Livingston. Do people today *love* as the Cookes loved? In our times of hustle and uncertainty, is it still possible to form bonds of such depth?

Friday, June 12

Too often at funerals the organ's majesty seems out of proportion to the unremarkable life that has ended. Not today. Mrs. Cooke's long life, with its interplay of will and chance, was worthy of such magnificent celebration. Father Armour would say that the music celebrates God's magnificent garden, not the individual blossom. Contemplating the Cookes, I wonder if He has let his garden go. We do not measure up: Tub sitting in his automobile, demanding better roads, is not Mr. Cooke crossing a dangerous and unknown country swarming with Indians; Edward and Helen traversing the golf-field are not Mr. and Mrs. Cooke sharing the perils and rough life of the wagons; Even Suzanne's spirited independence may not measure up to Mrs. Cooke, who wrote for newspapers and published her poetry when our own parents were children—all while keeping a house and raising children.

Father Armour's eulogy said all that it should have, but I thought he dwelt too long on their chance meeting. (Marveling eloquently at God's mysterious ways, he seemed too pleased with his own eloquence.) Yet he is right. If that Indian had murdered Lucy, if William's wagon had fallen behind, or absent some other chance occurrence, many in the pews would never have existed.

"If William had not been a manly youth, courageous and resourceful; and if Lucy had not been of strong and determined character; then this 'chance' meeting would have been meaningless. William would not have rescued her; or he would have found a sniveling, broken creature, not the spirited young woman who captured his heart. Neither would have seen in the other that strength of character which drew them together; or they might have quarreled and parted before reaching Salt Lake City. Yes, God's plans for us do sometimes seem to depend on 'chance'; but we must hold ourselves always ready to meet His challenges and grasp hold of those chances He offers us. William could not know he would be called upon to assist in rescuing a young woman from Indians; Lucy could not know that she would face such a crisis; but each became the best William and the best Lucy they could be, to face whatever might come in their way."

Walking home, I thought of Elsa Barker's *Letters from a Living Dead Man*. Her visitor from beyond this world explains that although one's Will cannot evade death, it can powerfully affect after-life. I wonder if William and Lucy formed such a powerful bond in this world that they will manage to travel together through the next?

I am surrounded by death. Mrs. Cooke's death and Father's illness make the thought of it inescapable. Father gets frustrated when his mind fails, but speaks of death frankly, sometimes even humorously. This afternoon I remarked that he seemed remarkably calm. He shrugged and asked what there was to get excited about. Later he said, "Life has been a fine dance. I love you and Elizabeth, and Agnes. I'm proud of the women my daughters have become. It has all been quite diverting, but perhaps I am ready to leave."

Something in Father's matter-of-fact tone stifled any impulse to cry.

Saturday, June 13

Antonio came by today. Sometimes when he delivers plants or vegetables, we share a smile and a simple joke, or I inquire after Mr. Edmonds, or he asks about Lucius. Today, I learned more of his unfortunate past, after asking whether he had considered becoming a teacher in this country. Before answering, he took up his glass of lemonade and looked out at the garden. "Is *difficile*. Yes, I want teach, to teach. *Però* first, I work, I study. I make my English more better. Is *fondamentale*. To write English more better. Then I teach *americano* children. *Però* I am *contrastanti*. I love teach. Help *alleivo*, pupil, find curious nature and grow. Give pupil word and *idee* and *scienza*, like give farmer horse and plough. Is *bellissimo*. You same, paint tree, paint flower. Is *bellissimo*. *Però* no more teacher I think. Is *rotto*, broken? Work farm is *silenzioso*, *facile*. Horse, wagon, land, sky, vegetable, manure, smile, good people, drink cold lemon water. No anger, no *assassinio*, no *tradimento*, no jail.

"This country different? Maybe yes, maybe no. Here is problem. I read is trouble, men speak good for worker. Teach some, *però* no truth *totale* is bad. *Però* teach truth *totale*, make pupil angry, want to change bad, maybe die, maybe go to jail, because I teach truth *totale*, *cose buone*, good things and bad things. More better to live *vita silenzioso*, work farm, work bank, marry, make child, take picnic to lake, *consumare* good drink, good food. No too much think, more better."

Antonio took another long drink of lemonade, then he smiled. His smile seemed to wriggle out from his usually serious mien, like a cat from under a porch, to stretch in the sunlight. "Talk sometimes no good thing. C*omprendere*? Better not know *precedentemente*."

I felt moved by his words. I understood this much: The betrayals and misfortunes he suffered because of his political beliefs caused him to withdraw to the peaceful farm, like a turtle into its shell. I once would have suggested that things are different here. But with such news as Wheatland and the tales Frederick Mills told us, and all the talk of class war and the I.W.W., perhaps our countries were not so different. Still, it is disconcerting to think that if Antonio had remained in Sicily, this gentle, caring man would quite probably have been executed.

Sunday, June 14

Nothing is quite so sweet as a strawberry fresh from one's own garden. Why does that always surprise me so? What we know with the mind is less vivid than what we learn by feeling. No product of intellect matches the taste of that first strawberry. (Would even Father agree? I'm referring to him as if he were already gone.)

Bret lent me May's number of *The Little Review*, after quoting Synge's suggestion that before verse can be human again it must be brutal. Aunt Agnes immediately accused Bret of shortsightedly dismissing everything written before last week. Bret replied, "I only mean that modern poetry, with what Untermyer calls 'the new beauty,' means far more to me, because it reflects the life I see around me, not some abstract concept that only an elect few comprehend."

"And what *is* 'the new beauty?'" Aunt asked.

Bret replied that it speaks to people in language we all understand, whereas the old is decorative, indirect, and overly estheticized.

Aunt demurred. "Beauty is beauty. There is no 'old beauty' and 'new beauty'. What makes Masefield a fine poet is not his brutality, or his vulgarity, but his beauty. Do you imagine that Longfellow failed to 'speak to the people?'"

Bret expressed something other than unreserved admiration for Longfellow. Aunt, shaking her head, remarked quietly, "The wonderful arrogance of youth."

"I want poetry that is an encounter with life, in all its magic, pain, joy, and chaos, not an escape from life," Bret replied.

"You can't credit anyone who rose above his own time because so many of his imitators surround you. Have you forgotten Queen Victoria's testimony of Longfellow's visit? She was so enthralled with his company that she let him stay a much longer than usual. The servants and officials kept making excuses to come into the room, and they stood along his route as he left the palace. Victoria could not imagine that they too were readers of Longfellow. She caused inquiries to be made and found that, indeed, they had all wished desperately to meet him, or at least to see him with their own eyes. Among all her illustrious guests, none had received such a tribute from the common people who served her."

Monday, June 15

After painting all morning from sketches of the estuary, I passed the afternoon in the garden. Jenny dropped in while I was weeding and sat on the new bench after inspecting it for cleanliness.

"You look so…" she began.

I looked up from my weeding. It took me a moment to realize that those three words were all the verbal communication she intended. The silent ellipsis has become a universal adjective that serves the smart set in place of a vocabulary. (How like Aunt Agnes I have become!)

When she realized that I was too dull to "get" it, she said, "Like a painting. 'Garden Woman,' by *Je-ne-sais pas qui*. You look too natural to be real."

I thanked her, because I could think of no other suitable response, and returned to weeding.

She then took out a cigarette and lit it—or I would write of someone else. More accurately: Her long, slender fingers, with their carefully manicured nails, extricated a long, slender cigarette from an engraved silver cigarette case and placed it stylishly off-center between her prettily painted pink lips. She lit the cigarette, then inhaled deeply, tossed her hair, and exhaled so slowly and abundantly that not even the foxgloves could fail to perceive her pleasure.

The smell of tobacco mixed with that of jasmine and damp earth, and I wondered for the thousandth time why women smoke. I thought of asking her but wisely turned my attention to the snapdragons.

"You don't like me as you used to," Jenny said.

Startled, I looked at her. She was studying the cigarette, as if the directness of her words had exhausted her capacity for conversation. Her fingers were trembling slightly, and I could find none of the self-assurance in her face I had seen there a moment earlier. She looked as if a harsh word would shatter her like an antique china plate. I said quietly, "Battle, murder, and sudden death are not as great a shock to some as their own failure to please."

She inhaled hungrily, as if the cigarette contained some essential nutrient. "You've been listening to Frances," she said, without looking at me. "She thinks my life is too easy."

I stood up, cut off a lily blossom, and presented it to her with a bow.

She burst into tears.

"What, Jenny?" I asked gently, our words colliding.

"I don't know that I like me much either." We were silent then, each waiting for the other to say something more. I asked again what the matter was and listened to her unburden herself for the next twenty minutes.

She explained how energetically she supports Preston in his business, how earnestly she is making a place for her children in what passes for society in Fresno, and how actively she has supported improvements in the schools and hospitals.

What I *heard* was that once Preston had won her, his attention turned to his business, leaving her without a challenge that excited her (as securing a suitable husband had done); that being "smart" had cost her much humiliation at the hands of women whose "smartness" was unassailable; and that beneath her feverish energy was a disappointment too deep to dare express to anyone, including herself. Her references to Preston's "needs" suggested that the carnal side of marriage has proven a distasteful inconvenience. I could not discern whether she understood that it could be otherwise. Nor did I think it prudent to inquire.

Most remarkable was her transformation when Elizabeth joined us. Like an actress changing costume, Jenny assumed that attitude of charm and self-assurance Frances so envies. (I briefly wondered which of her aspects was the "real" Jenny. Perhaps she *is* as haughty as Frances would have her, and the "confidences" simply for show, to bring me into her camp—or maybe her girlish wiles won her a prize that proved illusory. I quickly abandoned any idea of knowing the "real" Jenny, silently applauded the performance, and laughed at myself for being a pliant dumping ground.

I was relieved when shortly they motored off, all of us gaily waving. Having abandoned any notion of returning to my weeding, I walked up the hill to watch the sun set over the bay. In the late afternoon light, watching the shadows stretch across the valley, everything was at once more clear and more inscrutable.

Tuesday, June 16

Pondering life's dualities lately. Though I know little of Dr. Freud, I do not make fun of his ideas (as Tub and Elizabeth do), rather shiver with recognition. Others seem content (desperately so) to accept what they see on the surface. Although I may not know what is beneath, I know that there *is* a beneath.

I do not see any surface—Mr. and Mrs. Budlows' placid faces as they walk arm-in-arm; Jenny's smartness; Antonio's distant expression—without seeking to know what is beneath. The Budlows' violent quarrels; Jenny's resentment; Antonio's surprising past; like bulbs pushing determinedly toward the surface.

This morning, after sketching a portrait of an iris, I wondered whether this sense of mine is related to that period after Mother's death when we lived with Uncle Thomas and Aunt Emily. I quickly learned that it is possible to wear two different faces: the stern yet charming face the world sees, and the private one that softens with pleasure when one surrenders control. How could I not develop an awareness of life's inherent duality? (Thank God that Elizabeth's nightmares put an end to my own horror.)

Wednesday, June 17

Attended a lecture by a most remarkable man yesterday evening, Charles Delvin. He was one of three men who attempted to circle the globe by bicycle, without money, covering 20,000 miles on land, all within one year. Last year, on May 1, they started bicycling east from Waco. The other two men gave up before they reached the Atlantic Coast, but Mr. Delvin persisted, even though he has only one leg! (The other was amputated below the knee several years ago.)

He stowed away on a boat to England, crossed Europe, took a boat to Egypt, then bicycled across India. He reached New Zealand well ahead of schedule, and stowed away on another boat, but when he was discovered, they threw him off in the South Sea Islands, some place called Papeeta, where without money or friends, he had little hope of going onward.

He considered suicide. Then he found a box of shoe polish (in a country where shoes were hardly known) and set up the island's first shoe-shining parlor. When some drunken fellow from Seattle bought a shine, the natives were so delighted by the sight that they took turns borrowing shoes and having them shined. Eventually he was able to sneak aboard a boat bound for the U.S., but he arrived a month after the year was up.

His courage is noteworthy, as is his attitude toward losing his chance to win the $10,000 prize offered by a Texas newspaper. He seems genuinely more interested in his experiences and said that they are worth far more than the reward itself.

Thursday, June 18

When French workmen in a little town in German Alsace repaired the main road, they planted blue, white, and crimson flowers so that the summer sun brought forth a vast tricolor flag bordering each side of the road. Outraged German officials immediately tore it all up. What an image: uniformed soldiers making war on forget-me-nots and phlox!

Tuesday, June 23

I must remove Susan from that house, but I cannot see how it is to be done. I cannot tell Father what I fear, for I would have to explain, and that would break his heart. (Perhaps literally, he is so frail.) It would be too painful for Aunt Agnes to hear such a thing about her sister's husband—and whom would she believe if he denied it? I should feel tremendous shame telling *anyone* what I experienced; and yet I would surely do so—if I were confident that I would be believed! Father Armour? He holds many secrets; and he might be able to influence Uncle Thomas and Aunt Emily to let Susan live elsewhere.

Friday, June 26

Listening to Bret's friend, George, I understand why I disliked *The Custom of the Country*.

"It isn't in Mrs. Wharton's nature to be kind to people. Thackeray kept finding excuses for Becky, George Eliot did so with Tito Melema, Trollope seems always to see the real difficulties his characters face in finding the right course, but Mrs. Wharton just skewers poor Undine, like some native spearing a fish then holding it up to show everyone."

He added, "Wells would hold society to account, not silly Undine. For him, a character's weakness is a symptom of a disease afflicting society. Mrs. Wharton seems too fond of the aristocrats to look for the fundamental social causes of Undine's conduct."

Later, I reflected on the choices we (novelists, painters, muckraking reporters) make. Do we look deeply and express what we see? Or do we laugh behind our fans at the silliest of our companions? Father likes to say that Lincoln Steffens always goes to the roots of a thing, or at least struggles to go as deeply as he can, no matter whom it may offend. Too many of his imitators merely pillory one player or another, without fully portraying the context. Novelists like Brand Whitlock and Ellen Tompkins understand and sympathize with their characters.

Monday, June 29

Called on Father Armour, hoping to share my concerns about Susan. In greeting, he said that Uncle Thomas and Aunt Emily had given him supper the previous evening, and he was full of praise for Uncle over some charity drive. (They sometimes go shooting together, I suddenly recalled.) Still, I mustered some hope that he might be of help. I asked if Susan had been at supper, and he responded, "Your aunt and uncle have been simply marvelous with that dear girl." When he then asked how I was, I told him I had been reading *The Devil's Garden*, hoping that might lead us toward the topic; but he said that he did not read novels. I alluded to Judge Weller and the men he had allowed to escape punishment for statutory crimes against young girls. Tapping his fingers together, he agreed that such things were terrible, but added that the root of the problem was ten years of unrestricted immigration.

In the end, I could not do it. I could not even begin! It is not as if I had *seen* something untoward. To explain why I construe what I *do* see as I construe it, I must explain facts of which I have never spoken to anyone. Father Armour must think me an idiot. I circled around the subject for an hour like some hungry wolf around a baited trap. Finally, I invented some foolish question about the auxiliary and made my escape, leaving him wondering, no doubt, at my red face.

Now, what? I could speak to Tub and Elizabeth, but Tub is so ineffectual. I cannot bear to speak of it to Aunt Emily. There is no one to whom I can turn and yet I must do something! If only Father was the inventor in "Traffic in Souls." I could purchase a dictagraph and use his invention for recording the sounds from it onto phonograph records. Then I could invite Uncle Thomas to meet me, start a candid discussion of his conduct when I was Susan's age, and then threaten to play the record unless he releases her to me.

Tuesday, June 30

The Archduke's death reminds one how sadness has stalked that family. His mother died at 28. Someone else was assassinated earlier. Franz Ferdinand was in line for the throne only because his father died and the Emperor's son committed suicide. Emperor Franz Josef was perfectly horrid about Ferdinand's marriage to Sophie, a mere Countess. If they had been in Austria-Hungary when it happened, she could not have been at his side, and would still be alive. It seems something out of a novel, the way fate has stalked them.

Suzanne has no pity for the royal family, naturally, saying they "live by legalized theft on the backs of the simple folk they rule." Aunt Agnes doubts Austria will grieve much over an unpopular crown prince whose wife could never be queen and whose children could not succeed to the throne.

July

Wednesday, July 1

This morning I walked through the garden and with each step felt compelled to make a painting. The wonder of the *Linaria triornithophora* catching the light, looking for all the world like a flying fire-elf from another world; the red velvet lily against the bright green swords of the gladiolas; the rare blue of the cerinthe silhouetted against the alyssum's soft white bouquets. A fuchsia blossom had recently fallen onto an elephant ear, where it lay brightly pink, soon to fade to brown, and then to rot. Our lives seemingly pass as quickly as a fuchsia blossom... Yet on we march, as intent on our various affairs as so many ants, unaware of our insignificance. (How quickly my thoughts turn to Father these days.)

Thursday, July 2

Several of the Webster Ford poems in the new *Mirror* struck me particularly hard.

LOUISE SMITH

Herbert broke our engagement of eight years
When Annabelle returned to the village
From the Seminary, ah me!
If I had let my love for him alone
It might have grown into a beautiful sorrow—
Who knows? —filling my life with healing fragrance.
But I tortured it, I poisoned it,
I blinded its eyes, and it became hatred—
Deadly ivy instead of clematis.
And my soul fell from its support,
Its tendrils tangled in decay.
Do not let the will play gardener to your soul
Unless you are sure
It is wiser than your soul's nature.

HERBERT MARSHALL

All your sorrow, Louise, and hatred of me
Sprang from your delusion that it was wantonness
Of spirit and contempt of your soul's rights
Which made me turn to Annabelle and forsake you.
You really grew to hate me for love of me,
Because I was your soul's happiness,
Formed and tempered
To solve your life for you, and would not.
But you were my misery. If you had been
My happiness would I not have clung to you?
This is life's sorrow:
That one can be happy only where two are;
And that our hearts are drawn to stars
Which want us not.

GEORGE GRAY

I have studied many times
The marble which was chiseled for me—
A boat with a furled sail at rest in a harbor.
In truth it pictures not my destination
But my life.
For love was offered me and I shrank from its disillusionment;
Sorrow knocked at my door, but I was afraid;
Ambition called to me, but I dreaded the chances.
Yet all the while I hungered for meaning in my life.
And now I know that we must lift the sail
And catch the winds of destiny
Wherever they drive the boat.
To put meaning in one's life may end in madness,
but life without meaning is the torture
Of restlessness and vague desire—
It is a boat longing for the sea and yet afraid.

I read the poems silently, then out loud—then sat motionless. Even as dusk fell, I could not rise from the chair. It was not so much the tale of the jilted Louise that paralyzed me, for I am not Louise, and have never come to hate Richard. Even so, the final four lines of Herbert's reply sounded shrilly inside my heart.

I thought about the line, "Do not let the will play gardener to your soul." I have known too many who believe some lover was "formed and tempered to solve their life," then fall into a deep well of self-pity when refused.

It was George Gray, however, I contemplated as if he were a mirror reflecting my soul. I have not dared all that I might have, in art or in life; I too am, "a boat longing for the sea and yet afraid;" I too feel "restlessness and vague desire" well up in me, although my desires are so vague that I cannot say what I am restless *for*. Clearly, I have carried memories of Richard too far down the years for my own good, and they have become an anchor holding me from "catching the winds of destiny. (Yet if I have turned down other men, it is not Richard's knowing kiss that holds me back, but the dull eyes and timid pecks offered me since.)

Much later, same day: Father asked me to help him hasten his end. He had mentioned the idea before, half-jesting, but now he is serious. He is not sure how, and certainly does not wish to do anything that would leave him even more helpless.

I felt both fear and relief. Relief that he may avoid what he most fears: a long period of mental incapacity and physical weakness. Relief that he trusts me. (He forbade me to confide in Elizabeth. Does he doubt her strength, fear her sense of the proprieties, or love her too much to lay such a burden on her?)

Later, as I sat in the garden, I felt a sudden welling of resentment. What if something goes wrong? How could Father put such a responsibility on me? After abandoning us after Mother's death, how could he ask this of me? I thought about life and death, growth and deterioration. Watching the plants and birds and insects in their natural stages—a lily freshly blooming, a blossom brown and sagging and ready to fall; the vibrant late sunlight outlining the pulsing veins of a leaf, while another lay on the ground decaying into food for next year's flowers—I wondered if we have the right to interfere with the natural course of things. Father stands on the frontier between Life and Death. That is God's province, not mine! I trembled, as I did in childhood, pretending that Mother's gowns and petticoats were mine. There too I was trespassing against a power larger than I, wandering among mysteries beyond my ken.

I will do this thing, because Father has asked me—but will I wonder always whether I ought to have resisted? And what of God? Will He understand and forgive me for helping Father with a decision only He should make? (I fail to see how to honor both my earthly father and my Father who may be in Heaven!)

<u>Saturday, July 4</u>

Dr. Williams spoke with me today about Father. Father had also asked him to hasten his journey to the next world. Dr. Williams said that doctors, by their oath, could not do such things, but that the same oath obligates him to alleviate Father's suffering. "Knowing that he is in great pain," he began, then stared sternly at me when I interjected that Father was not in pain so much as frustrated by his helplessness, and repeated, "Knowing that your father is in great pain, I am prescribing a rather heavy dose of morphine. You must keep careful track of how much is given him. If he were accidentally to take just half this bottle in a few hours, such an error would almost certainly prove fatal. You must be very careful." He added that an overdose might cause a violent disturbance of the stomach if certain other steps had not been taken. (Perhaps even this is too much to acknowledge here.)

Dr. Williams sensed the storm of emotions Father's plight let loose in me. He reassured me that it was not unusual for patients in such circumstances to wish to expedite the end; and that although he could not assist, or condone, he did not judge. Looking into my eyes, he added, "I judge a child, who desires to assist in such a circumstance, to be most loving and courageous; and all the more because the heart wants so urgently to speak, when it cannot."

<u>Monday, July 6</u>

This morning I asked Father about proposing to Mother. He smiled the old smile. "It wasn't at all as you'd imagine—and surely not as she'd promised herself it would be, her suitor togged out in evening clothes and kneeling on a rug before a roaring fire. We had gone sleigh-riding and got to talking about the sorts of things lovers talk about, without realizing we'd run onto a long dry stretch of road the wind had swept clean of snow, until the exhausted horse stopped in his tracks. We had to get down and lead him back. Trudging along a country road, with one hand on the bridle, well, that was the scene, wholly unromantic. Your mother used to jest that the cold addled her brains."

Wednesday, July 8

Father joined us for breakfast then stared silently at the same page of the newspaper so long that I felt sure he was unable to make sense of it; and when he put the newspaper down, he knocked over his water glass. After I cleaned up, we sat and every so often looked at each other and smiled. As I was staring out the window thinking that he might never see the garden again, he said my name.

"Katherine. I'm sorry." Thinking he meant for the spilt water, I waved my hand; but he shook his head and added, "For leaving you."

"Oh Father," I cried. "How can you apologize for what cannot be helped?

He seemed to struggle to follow my words, then he laughed. "I mean, before. When you were a child. Perhaps I couldn't help it then either. But I am sorry."

I felt buffeted by a storm of feelings, hearing him say what I should have liked to hear twenty years ago, and saddened by the possibility that he has felt guilty all this time. How I wished that they had never left me with Uncle Thomas and Aunt Emily, that Father had come home when Mother died so that we could console each other, and that when he did finally come home, we could have spoken more frankly. Still, twenty years of love and kindness and shared life so outweighed that unthinkable time apart that I could not concede significance to his apology by saying out loud how unnecessary it was.

"It was all right?" he asked, reaching out to touch my hand.

"It's all right now Father," I replied quickly, covering his hand with mine.

Thursday, July 9

Wonder how Professor Clark is faring. The newspapers report great damage in the heart of Paris from recent storms. I mean to write to him soon to thank him for his willingness to treat me as a fellow artist, even when I was a naive and clumsy beginner; and sharing the secrets of the craft without presuming to dominate my sense of the art. If he sometimes wonders what use his teaching life was, I want him to know how grateful one student is.

Father showed little interest in what I read to him from the newspaper, even the article about the Parks girl answering an ad for a filing clerk position and falling into the hands of three white slavers who took their pleasure with her. He seemed to show a little more interest in the item about the Chicago vice crusaders publishing the names of owners of hundreds of houses used for immoral purposes. I am glad *someone* is striking back at the men who get rich by exploiting the women's misery!

Often now I consider events through Father's dimming eyes. A devastating storm in Paris—Father will never see Paris again. A monoplane sets a record by ascending to 21,000 feet; a predicted record fruit crop—Father will never fly in an aeroplane, nor enjoy any of that fruit.

Friday, July 10

I did not wish to go out last night, having no stomach for laughter and levity, but Helen dragged me away, impelled to rescue me from wholly devoting myself to Father. I mustered little energy for clever conversation, nor could I speak of my thoughts.

Tub traveled with Barry Cool to Lake Tahoe over Independence Day Weekend, covering more than 600 miles in five days, to test gas consumption and performance. (Presumably to aid Mr. Cool in selling more machines.) Tub was radiant describing the marvels of the Lozier Light Four and Light Six, and even remarked on the beauty of the mountains and Emerald Bay. The road across the summit passes through high snow, even in July, so naturally, they had a snow fight! Between the Tavern and Tallac, the road occasionally runs along the water's edge, then is suddenly hundreds of feet above the lake.

I should have preferred to hear more about the natural beauty of their travel than about the cars averaging 13 ½ and 11 miles per gallon—though I admit it is impressive that neither presented any mechanical difficulties beyond two blow-outs.

Tub complained of rough roads around Colfax and beyond Folsom, and of dust, but his major complaint concerned "road hogs" who occupied the center of the road, moving more slowly than his party wished to move.

Bret laughed and explained how he had solved that problem. Having noisemakers and fireworks with which he planned to amuse his nephews and nieces, and annoyed by a slow driver, he tossed a giant torpedo from his Studebaker at the other motorist. "It hit the road under the other car and let go with a bang. They immediately pulled out at the side of the road. As I swept past, the other car's crew was frantically inspecting all four tires."

Not to be outdone, Jack claimed that his uncle finds himself blocked by a load of hay so often that he has equipped his automobile with a horn that neighs like a horse. When the driver hears the neighing, he supposes some neighbor's horse is pilfering a free meal and pulls out. Jack must have invented the story to top Bret!

Sunday, July 12

Father is no more.

I can say nothing of his last hours to anyone. (But for the possibility of consequences to others, I shouldn't care who knew.). I feel grateful for his trust, and for the privilege of sharing his final moments. Nor do I believe the facts shame him. Rather, they do him honor: he died as he had lived, walking as unwaveringly toward death as he did toward life's difficulties. He died calmly, with the true courage that arises from acceptance. Not the courage that proclaims itself as such, but the courage to say, "I wish it were otherwise, but Death has come for me, as it will come for each of us."

I will never again feel such intensity as when I sat with Father as he ingested what he needed to. We spoke little but expressed much. What little we did say rings as clearly in my ears now as the bells in the church tower. I was astonished and delighted that Father could still joke! In a child's voice, he asked whether he would get apple pie and ice cream if he finished everything. He also told me quietly and without drama that he loved me. "I love you too," I replied, and added with mock severity, "I believe you said that only to delay finishing your potion."

Later, Father opened and closed his hand in a silent invitation. His skin felt like the dried-out hide of an animal. I contemplated the weakness of a hand which had once been capable of holding me up toward the sky, and I held his hand more tightly. His eyes, which had fallen shut, opened, and he smiled. Soon after, he slept, and I sat beside the bed, still holding onto his hand, wondering whether he could feel my touch—then with more urgency and some fear, wondered what would happen next. What if he awakened in terror? What if he wished to cling to life, or awakened ill and confused, his mind as withered as his body?

While I fretted, his spirit left his body. A slight shudder, rather like a halted sneeze, then nothing. It was so wonderfully gentle, for which I do thank God. When my time comes, I shall leave much easier than I might have, having watched Father welcome death with his usual equanimity. It was only then, as I realized that I never could thank him, only then did I weep.

Monday, July 13

Aunt Agnes obviously harbors unspoken suspicions. I wonder if at some time when they were younger, she was half in love with him.

Tuesday, July 14

We visited briefly with Father Armour. He and Aunt Agnes carried on most of the discussion as I could not concentrate on the details of the service. (Since we will meet Father again, the funeral is not to mourn Father but to lift him up to God.) It hardly matters, as Father will not hear it—though I dared not say so.

Father Armour will read John 14:1-6 (In my Father's house are many rooms); the hymns are to be "A Mighty Fortress is our God," "Rock of Ages," and "Let Saints on Earth in Concert Sing"; and Aunt will read Rossetti's "Rest." I imagined Father plumping for Marvell's "To his Coy Mistress," which he once shocked a small group of friends by reciting from memory in a comically exaggerated manner. This vision made me laugh, 'til they shot worried glances at me, and I caught myself. Father Armour will also say a brief tribute, which he usually does not. (Because of respect for Father or Agnes's strong will?)

I dread tomorrow! Father must be laughing at us.

Wednesday, July 15

Listening to Father Armour's tribute, I was partly in the church and partly somewhere else. Although he accurately recited the facts, he laid them out as if they formed some sensible, even inevitable, pattern. What had seemed uniquely significant sounded commonplace as Father's life was fashioned into a lesson everyone could digest.

He described Father's rise from humble beginnings to a position of respect and fortune, when Father perceived his childhood on a harsh and violent prairie as unspeakable wealth. He spoke of war as if it were a stage of life Father had left behind long ago; when war colored Father's thoughts and actions every day of his life.

"The early and tragic loss of his wife" was an accurate but pale allusion to Father's loving pursuit of Mother, and to the searing pain and disbelief that caused him to delay so long returning home to his daughters. Nothing in Father Armour's words or tone communicated the peculiar force of Father's love and grief—let alone its consequences to others.

The references to the magazine were stilted, of course. Father Armour does not always approve of its content. He made Father's purchase of it sound like some logical extension of what had gone before, while Father always made light of the purchase as a foolish impulse sparked by his anger over the newspapers' treatment of General Doubleday. One would not have learned from Father that he saved a dying publication, provided a deserving editor with a more comfortable old age than bankruptcy would have, and created a forum for the free expression of ideas, some of which appalled him.

I had thought I might cry. Instead, my brain circled feverishly around the words, gathering memories as a squirrel collects acorns in autumn. At one point, I remembered to look around (Look, Father, just look at the crowd), and was surprised to see that the church was full. As well as family, friends, and close associates, there were people I had not seen for years, such as Roger Taylor. Mr. Taylor had come over from San Francisco and came afterward to the house.

"Surprised to see me?" he asked, smiling. His eyes still had the wicked gleam that, according to Father, made the girls fall madly in love with him thirty years ago. I smiled and mumbled something ambiguous. I *was* surprised. Mr. Taylor was a railroad man through and through. He and Father had been on opposing sides of many bitter battles.

"Your father was a man I truly respected. Of course, that's the sentiment *du jour*, what everyone says after a death, but today more of 'em *feel* it, I'll warrant. And *deeply*."

I remarked that I thought he had known Father in the War. He said that they did not meet until afterward, but that the War created a bond that was sealed by their recognition that each man welcomed candor, despite their differences.

"We saw such things in war—felt such things, *became* such things—that afterward we never wanted to believe so passionately in anything again. Wanting so strongly to abolish slavery and save the Union had driven men to the madness of war, and we didn't ever want that again, not for us and not for our sons. What marked your father was that even though he could no longer believe in 'God,' he still did good."

I thought of Father's last days. He had not expressed the least hope that we would meet again in Heaven. When Aunt Agnes said some such thing, he waited until she left the room to wonder aloud whether she really believed it.

Mr. Taylor added, "Many returned with a distaste for believing strongly in anything, even God, and we used that as an excuse for all kinds of misconduct. Our passionate beliefs had led us into Hell on earth, and we guessed we might be better off without them. But when you throw the rules out the window, and have nothing much to replace them with, that can easily become license to do whatever suits you, and devil take the hindmost."

I ventured that Father had maintained his passion for freedom, with no mention of God.

Mr. Taylor nodded, "A great many of us were agnostic in the '70's. It was the fashion. How could the God we'd been taught about countenance the things we had seen? What little we knew of Darwin confirmed our instincts. But most men couldn't stand the cold for long. They either let their consciences atrophy or crept back into God's warm embrace. Or both."

Our conversation left me feeling I knew Father the better for it.

Thursday, July 16

Now I'll never know why Mother and Father did not leave me with the Admiral and his family. (Yet if they had, I would not recognize what I believe to be Susan's situation.)

I begin to see in human lives the same imponderable pattern as in nature. Things work as they must. Whether by God's design, or Nature's. Does it matter? I hear Father's skepticism and Aunt Agnes's professions of faith and love them both. I do not care who or what brought us together on this planet.

Friday, July 17

I am staying in this evening because we are in mourning; but I also have no taste for frivolity. What I am feeling is private and not for casual conversation. I do not feel mournful, although I miss Father. The constant weight of his passing rests heavy on my heart. Yet I feel joy, too. Joy because we loved each other, and because Father and Mother gave me a spirit that belonged only to them and lives on in me.

Saturday, July 18

"Valley of the Moon" is again at Oakland Photo Theater. Apparently, Sonoma means "Valley of the Moon" in some Indian tongue. Everyone goes to see it because many scenes are laid in and around Oakland and Alameda. There are also many views of the countryside. When the boy, Billy, is released from jail, he and his girl celebrate by seeing a moving picture set on a farm. Drawn to the peace of farm life, they set out on foot and meet the artists in Carmel who call themselves “Abalone Eaters.” I am not sorry to miss it.

Sunday, July 19

Did not wish to go to church this morning, but to stay home would have seemed ungrateful. (Silly me! I do not owe Father Armour anything for doing his duty by Father.) Quite a discussion afterwards with both aunts and Elizabeth. Aunt Emily said (in a tone that made clear she assumed nothing), that she *assumed* that Elizabeth and I would be following the prescribed mourning rules. For a parent, a full year. I had not thought about the rules, as I've been too busy grieving!

She was quite annoyed with our responses. Elizabeth flatly refused, saying modern life is too busy for such things, and I simply thanked her for her thoughts and sympathy. I did not say that the business of mourning has become just that: appallingly commercial and primarily for the profit of milliners, jewelers, and manufacturers of crepe.

While I would readily wear a veil for the next twelve months if it would ease Father's journey to the next world, I am not about to do so to mollify the town's busybodies. I loved Father and will mourn him for far longer than a year. Excessive outward exhibitions of grief seem false and pretentious, as he would be the first to say. I shall wear the veil when going out, but probably not for the full year; and I surely will not forego traveling to Chicago in September for the art show!

Aunt Agnes said that she will do as she would if he were her brother. Six months: crepe for three, plain black for two, and half-mourning for one month. To do more would be unseemly, as she was not his widow, but to do less would be wholly inadequate. She added that in her stage of life, mourning is no great burden. Later, privately, she said she knew better than anyone how much I loved Father, and how much I had done to make his last years a joy. She had no intention either to suggest a course of conduct or to judge me.

Monday, July 20

Sitting at my desk now for twenty minutes, writing nothing. Habit directed my hand to reach for the pen, but habit can only do so much. I feel that I am—that I must be—a new person. Without Father, I do not know who I am or will be.

Tuesday, July 21

As we sang "though now divided by the stream, the narrow stream of death" at Father's funeral, I thought how narrow that stream truly is—and how vast. Watching Father take his last breaths, the line between life and death was so slender I was not certain when he crossed it.

Saturday, July 25

For three days I have had nothing to write that didn't strike me as trite or self-pitying, but I have been painting with an energy almost urgent.

Yesterday evening Helen and the others went to Idora Park for the gala opening of the "Jardin de Danse." I felt free to go, having reflected on Aunt Emily's assumption that we would follow the forms of mourning and concluded that, in light of Father's views, to submit to considerations of "propriety" would be false to his memory. Nevertheless, I could not muster interest in going out. It is too soon, and for reasons no one but Father and I could know.

Richard and I spent many memorable moments at the Idora Park rink. He was a fine skater, and envious eyes often watched us. Warmed by our skating exertions, we had many intimate conversations at the rink as we came to know each other better. After they remodeled the pavilion and replaced the rink with a brightly-lit new dance floor, what we shared there was lost, yet another reminder of time's passing.

I am not who I was then. At 32, life is no longer a roller-coaster ride. I am content with a quieter life. Even without Father's death, it would have felt odd to dance when millions of Europeans might be plunging into history's most violent war. Do I feel this so strongly because of Father's soldiering, and my concern for Professor Clark?

Sunday, July 26

They are saying that a general war may be avoided. Apparently, Servia will make an unconditional surrender, although it all seems to depend on some sort of note from Russia. Diplomats say that Austria may have cleverly stolen the march, using the assassination as a pretext. There was no strong Austrian reaction to it immediately, though it appeared the work of Servians; but once Russia was immobilized by internal rebelliousness, and England distracted by violence in Ireland, Austria seized the moment to do as it wished with Servia, gambling that Russia would not come into it. (What would Father make of this?)

Monday, July 27

I have written little of Father's death, but I do feel less devastated than I might because we got to say good-bye. Every time I feel his loss, I am reminded that I was able to share his last moments.

It now appears that there will be war in Europe after all. Troops are moving into place and may even have begun shooting. The

British are attempting mediation. I hope they can manage it. The European nations seem like so many bullies in a schoolyard.

Tuesday, July 28

Austria has declared war on Servia. I do not understand what this is about, but if it had not been the Archduke's death, it would have been something else. There are deep and ancient feuds between the peoples there. We are fortunate to live far removed from such things, although I should feel far less smug if our government were to do something foolish with regard to Mexico. At least there have been strong statements from Washington that the United States will not be involved in this European war.

I realized today that I have no idea what a Servian looks like. (Dark hair and Tyrolean caps?) The news is confusing: the Austrians are said to have crossed the Danube River; but some say the German Kaiser has accepted Sir Edward Grey's mediation suggestion, while others say Germany has officially rejected it.

Bret is pessimistic. He says that while Britain would like to assist Russia and France, its problems in Ireland may prevent that, and the Germans know it. He pointed to the newspaper headlines—that the King's Own Scottish Borderers fear they'll be killed if they venture from their barracks and that British soldiers face murder charges for firing into an Irish home rule crowd. "If we know that, surely the Austrians and the Germans do. It's like a poker game in which the British are trying to maintain a bluff when the Kaiser has seen their hole card."

Thursday, July 30

I've decided my friends are a necessary distraction. Robbie and Jack sound like schoolboys betting on jumping frogs when they argue about how aeroplanes and dirigibles may change the nature of this war as sky battles will be important. Apparently, the French and the Germans have very different ideas. The French have hundreds of little heavier-than-air machines, each with a pilot and a fighting man or two; but the Germans have only a few machines of that sort and rely on huge dirigibles. Jack envies the French aviators more than he can bear and says they will quickly destroy the Germans. Robbie said Germany's huge Zeppelins and Parsifals, which carry more and bigger guns and a crew of twenty, are superior.

"The French dart gloriously about, but the Germans will own the skies," he insisted. "Being able to lift so much more, they have far stronger weaponry; and their superior stability will permit them to aim and shoot with far greater accuracy."

Jack retorted that they'll be like "a hunter shooting a shotgun at a mosquito buzzing around his head," and claimed that a single aeroplane can destroy a dirigible as easily as a dirigible can destroy an aeroplane. Since France has so many aeroplanes, and Germany only a smaller number of dirigibles, Jack is convinced the French will prevail.

Jack seems to hope the United States will become involved. I shudder at the thought. The riots among Austrians and Servians in Los Angeles last night confirm my fears that if a country as mixed in races as ours should be drawn in, it would have to slaughter great numbers of its own citizens at home before it could do battle across the Atlantic.

Meanwhile, Oakland is rioting, over the Fruitvale street-car. The car has taken to stopping a few blocks before the end of the line for the convenience of the company's drivers. The passengers find it so maddening that last night they rioted! With such tragic events afoot, how can we care so passionately about trifles?

Friday, July 31

Marion Couthouy Smith's poem, "Youth Speaks to Age," caught my eye in *The Century* this morning. I marked it to read over again later. Aunt Agnes pointed at my pencil-marks and laughed. "Are you Youth or Age?" I did not reply immediately. I realized that in my heart I had indeed responded as Age, as one "Whose eyes no longer glisten with quick tears, / Whose lips no longer laugh for love of laughter / … to whom sorrow is a crown of pride."

She read my hesitation more easily than I might have wished. "Hear me, Kate: age is long, and is far from the curse that you modern young folks suppose, and indeed has its quiet pleasures that more than make up for whatever has been lost. But don't be in such a hurry to throw yourself into it. Autumn is a fine season and brings great delights; but you cannot will the leaves to fall in July merely because summer has been a touch too warm."

August

Saturday, August 1

Declined to play in the whist tournament to benefit the Improvement Club. I had given money and promised to play, but whist and dancing seemed neither appropriate nor appealing.

I think often about boarding the train for Chicago next month to spend a week at the big Modern Art Show. How I wish I could leave today! There will be work by Monet and others who have changed our understanding of good art, and I am curious to see *actual* paintings by Cezanne, Gauguin, and van Gogh.

I still regret not going with Professor Clark to the Armory Show last year. It was a chance to see important European art from recent decades, including some very new works, without crossing the Atlantic.

Since Father's death, I paint almost desperately; perhaps seeing how other artists' struggles are expressed on the canvas will bring some peace of mind.

Monday, August 3

Germans are marching toward France through Belgium and from Metz, commencing an attack on Paris. So far as I can determine, Professor Clark is directly in their path. I can only hope he has managed to escape to London!

Jack may have been correct about the French aviators. When a German dirigible crossed the frontier into France on Sunday, a courageous Frenchman swooped down upon it from above, ramming it and setting it ablaze. Both craft fell from the sky, all the bodies burnt up. Another French aviator ascended above a German Zeppelin, fired shot after shot and sent it crashing to the ground, then lost control of his aeroplane and crashed.

This war has become real in a different way for each of us. Jack reads accounts of daring sky-battles. I fear that my dear friend may be trampled like a mouse beneath a rampaging elephant. Tub is concerned about California's trade. They say that German cruisers may engage the British sloop Algerine somewhere south of San Diego, and if the Germans prevail, they will control all commerce bound to and from Pacific Coast ports. The sloop is said to be no match for the cruisers, and the officers of the Algerine do not yet know of the war, as the sloop carries no wireless equipment and sailed from Mazatlan for San Diego days ago. How odd, that we know, and have known for days, and they do not.

Tuesday, August 4

Canceled plan to see premier of Adam Shirk's new musical comedy, "The Oyster Pirate," with Suzanne and Bret. Adam had given Bret a fistful of tickets, and I had promised to go, but that was before Father's death.

Suzanne mocked the *Enquirer* headline, "Dialogue Sparkling and Music Original–Idora Stages a Winner," asking, "Does nobody find it odd that Adam is both the *Enquirer's* main theatrical writer and the playwright whose work it praises?"

Even if I were not in mourning, such a production seems especially frivolous when today's headlines included, "Austrians Lose 300 Soldiers in Battle" / "Paris Looks Upward for Night Attack from Aeroplanes" / and "Cry Havoc and Let Slip the Dogs of War."

The French have given their aviators orders that if they cannot shoot a German dirigible from the air, they should ram it with their flying machines, sacrificing their own lives.

Suzanne remarked, "I suppose that in war it makes perfect sense, as your life is but one, against dozens in the dirigible, which can drop horrible explosives in the midst of a city." She then asked Bret whether he could do such a thing. He replied that, fortunately, he couldn't fly an aeroplane. Then he shook his head and confessed that he had no earthly idea whether, at the last moment, he could do such a thing or not. "Selfishly, I'm glad I'm spared the need."

"I suspect you would sacrifice your life readily, but not the lives of the deeply fascinating fictional characters with which you plan to amuse and instruct the world," she replied.

Jules Dauviler, Chief Chef at the Palace, says he will put down his pots and pans and take up a musket in France. This news affects me more than reading of hundreds of dead Austrians. His is a face I know, a voice I have heard, and a name whose cooking I've praised. Father knew him well before he moved to the Palace and introduced me to him when I was still at Mills.

Wednesday, August 5

Who imagined the Belgians could hold back the Germans! England has declared war. Is there any chance that Germany will agree to mediation? No one seems to think so, although President Wilson was right to offer it.

Supped at Elizabeth's. The men's conversation was predictable. (How I miss Father!) Tub said the war could not have begun at a worse time for California, just as the heavy shipping season begins. If all the California goods on the high seas, headed to one or another of the combatants, were to be destroyed, the state could lose millions of dollars.

Uncle Thomas expressed outrage at Judge Ogden's comments in court about the confessed forger. "I grant that the man committed the offense to save wife and family from starving, or convinced Judge Ogden so. But how can a superior court judge sit on the bench and say outright that he was justified? 'A man is justified in committing almost any crime short of violence when so situated. Society is to blame.' I expect such nonsense from Emma Goldman or Jane Addams, or that fellow Whitlock you admire so much, but not a judge! Is he not inviting any man distressed by his economic circumstances to do as he pleases? He can keep the goods if successful and plead poverty if not."

Judge Ogden's words had startled me as well, but pleasantly so, and yet his sympathy for this man contrasted sharply with his harsh treatment of Hazel Lux. "Any man similarly situated would have done the same thing," he said of the forger. "Any woman would have done the same," I say of Hazel.

Thursday, August 6

Awakened from a dream in which Uncle Thomas's chauffeur had locked me inside a carriage. I could hear the horses' hooves clattering on the stone street, and through the small window, I could see ancient stone buildings. Europe? The time of the Inquisition. The chauffeur said not a word, but I knew he was taking me to be tortured.

At nearly every corner there was a large clock on a tower, through which the King watched what everyone did. There were many bridges, and men poling small boats. People moved as easily by water as by road. Then we were no longer in the carriage. From a bridge, I saw a family on a small Chinese junk, with strange sails and brightly colored clothes hung out to dry. The children were playing happily and waved as if we knew each other. The chauffeur caught me looking at them and laughed. "He said to stay on land. "He's no dub."

I could see the man who could save me pacing on a bridge, but I could not call out to him because of the rag tied over my mouth. Then I was in a dungeon with barred windows and straw on the floor. Uncle entered the cell with a very old Chinese man in a green silk robe embroidered with flowers. The Chinese man carried a tray with strange-looking implements. I was taken to a rack that looked like the operating boards on which they hold dogs during experiments. Suddenly, the room began to move, as if shaken by an earthquake. We were on the water, being towed. I knew that there was safety on the water. Uncle and the Chinese man looked at each other, frightened. Slowly the walls crumbled, and I could see the man at the helm. He was big and strong, with a thick black beard and a sailor's cap. The Admiral had saved me after all! Then the dream became mixed with my thoughts about what should happen next. Uncle's punishment was being debated, though whether in the dream or by my own half-awakened mind, I cannot say.

Once I was fully awake, I understood why Uncle Thomas could not abide my childhood friendship with the von Schmidts. He recognized in the Admiral a man who could see through him. (How I wish I knew where the von Schmidts went!)

<u>Friday, August 7</u>

This morning I tried to paint all of us children playing in the estuary, while the von Schmidts looked on from their boat. Some might find it an appealing portrait of childhood and nature, but it did not satisfy me at all, and perhaps could not.

I've been plodding through Henry Sydnor Harrison's *V. V.'s Eyes*. It seems terribly dense with social nonsense and labored asides that might be clever if they were not so carefully assembled. (I wonder that I so enjoyed his first novel, *Queed*.)

Saturday, August 8

For a moment today I thought old Mr. Dinwiddie had taken leave of his senses. Reading accounts of the terrible fighting in Europe, he suddenly laughed loudly. When I asked what he found funny, he said that for all the modern armaments, the French are finding their best success with a trick borrowed from the American Indians: apparently in many fights, lines of French skirmishers rush forward, concealing from the Germans a very sturdy defensive force; then at a given signal, they retreat, and the Germans who follow are cut down by machine-gun fire. "That's the Sioux all over again under Crazy Horse. That was a favorite sport, a few bucks on horseback attacking a force of blue-coats and getting the greener officers to pursue them into a trap. You'd ride over a hill and see four thousand braves."

Jack is an idiot. He called the Belgians' heroic resistance to the Kaiser, "Almost as surprising as Boston." I looked blankly at him. "The Braves were anchored in the cellar a month ago, and now Stallings has them chasing the Giants so hard that McGraw would ask for a 24-hour armistice if baseball's rules allowed." When I told him he was a fool, he feigned seriousness and said, "The Belgians are holding off the Kaiser with outdated arms. So is Stallings: his best pitcher is Dick Rudolph, who was let go by McGraw."

I see where *V. V.'s Eyes* is going, but doubt I care to accompany it through scores more pages of Callie Heth's determined superficiality. As in *Queed*, the very beautiful but not unintelligent woman who has won the golden prize, a man who is wealthy, charming, handsome, and highly intelligent, will belatedly recognize that a socially awkward but deeply honest fellow (bespectacled Mr. Queed or the lame Dr. Vivian), is her heart's true desire. Yet it all seemed more interesting and pointed in *Queed*: Queed was odder and more interesting than Dr. Vivian, and not so obviously good; Sharlee was at least thoughtful, whereas Callie exhibits no desire to think until at one point she tells her friend, "I'm thinking. It's interesting, I may try it again." In *Queed* we came to know that West was not a "villain" by nature, but in *V.V. Eyes* Mr. Canning remains remote.

It rather seems like a chemical formula: mix pretty, bored young maiden with dashing gentleman, add altruistic young intellectual distinguished by his honesty and compassion, and—poof—a happy explosion.

Sunday, August 9

Father Armour led us in prayers that peace be restored. He also spoke of the petty motives drawing European leaders into so destructive a conflict that it may be the last of wars, persuading future civilized beings to exhaust every possible alternative before resorting to armed force. He then prayed that the European powers would accept the U.S. offer to mediate. No one thinks they will. Everyone calls the offer "fine" and "the right thing to do," before adding that there is absolutely no chance the warring powers will accept.

Tuesday, August 11

A letter from Professor Clark! I'm delighted yet concerned, as his letter was written before the declarations of war. At least he seems up on the news, and likely has escaped to England.

Penchard
July 28, 1914
Dear Katherine,

My sole regret is that you are not here to paint with me. You would enjoy these rolling hills covered in grain fields and orchards. There are only small vestiges of forest, for almost all the land is cultivated. Wonderful vegetables! The French call this sort of country *un paysage riant*; and whether it smiles or not, I surely do when I take my coffee out to the garden and contemplate the peaceful countryside that stretches as far as I can see.

The place itself is a hodge-podge of gables and stables and whatnot. What with putting up the window shutters—solid-wood and quite heavy—and locking the various doors, and the stable and the garage, and bolting the door of the salon, and closing and bolting all the shutters, it takes forever simply to get to bed.

During the daylight hours, we are still sharing the place with a few workmen, but you will be pleased to hear that my studio, in an eccentrically attached one-story addition with a gable, is finished, and has excellent light. It is close enough to the house for convenience, even in bad weather, and yet sufficiently separate that my clutter need not infect the remainder of our home. All the rooms on the ground floor boast red-tile floors, the ceilings are raftered, and the huge beam in the salon is at least eighteen inches thick. A garden surrounds the house, and there is an extensive orchard. It is a comfortable place in which to enjoy a few more years before cashing in our chips and leaving the party.

There are all sorts of rumors flying about that there will be a general European War as a result of the problem in the Balkans. Others say the Government is exaggerating the dangers to draw attention from the acquittal of Mme.

Caillaux. Still, if war does come, I fear it will be the bloodiest in history.

Yours with love,
Lester

Wednesday, August 12

There may be a huge naval battle just beyond the Golden Gate! A steamship captain spoke the Algerine Tuesday evening. According to the *Enquirer*, they had a long chat by megaphone—the British sloop's first news of the war. The British asked that if the Beaver met a German cruiser, it say nothing of the Algerine's presence. (Cannot Germans read the newspaper?)

I continue to struggle through the Harrison novel. At least he portrays effectively the gap between what we strive for and what we really want. Carlisle is a silly example; but we can be wholly unconscious of what we really want and struggle for that which glitters superficially, like a tin can caught in the light from a street lamp.

Friday, August 14

Friday evening at William and Julia's. Aunt Emily would have my head, but I failed to see how sitting home would help Father. I did wear mourning and came home early. The men spent much of the evening discussing the war's disruption of the prize-fighting world. The Frenchman who beat Gunboat Smith is said to have enlisted in the French Army; the big negro, Johnson, said he would also volunteer, but no one believes him. Jack remarked, "He likes his fried chicken and the girls of Paris too much."

Julia said the big fight scene in *The Spoilers* was a real fight: that there was some bitter hatred between Farnum and Santschi, such that each trained seriously and studied secretly under a real-life prize-fighter to learn the right tricks and use the fight "scene" as a vehicle for beating up the other man. The camera operators had no idea they were about to record a true fight, but once it started it was so violent that one of the men broke bones in his hand.

Bret looked as if he were about to be sick and slipped out into the garden. I followed and found him doubled over with laughter. He laughed 'til tears came then said, "I never supposed that anyone actually *believed* all that malarkey the publicists write. How could anyone credit these two men risking their health and the success of the moving picture? The picture would be ruined, and neither man would see the inside of a studio again. Some shill invented the tale to increase the crowd at the Macdonough."

Perhaps I owe Mr. Harrison an apology. I was furious yesterday, sure that Vivian would remain silent when Callie assumed that her rich suitor had done the good deed Vivian had secretly done, just as Queed let Sharlee hold to her mistaken beliefs about him—in a slavish imitation of the earlier work. Fortunately, Vivian is not Queed, and quickly explained that he was the anonymous donor, though he asks Callie to keep his secret. I might well have put the book down for good if he had not explained.

Mr. Harrison articulates a pattern that has marked us all. Callie's mother has taught her to charm the right man and marry above her. It is a fine scene when she goes to the settlement director offering to work, and by asking whether she will live in the settlement, whether she has nursing skills, and what she can do, he allows her to see that she has been raised to be useless.

Thank goodness I was never Callie. Father was far more thoughtful than Mr. Heth, and neither Mother nor Aunt Agnes resembled Mrs. Heth. Yet her concentration on superficial attractions are not unfamiliar to me. We live in a world where girls are expected to be frivolous, emotional creatures. I may have rebelled, but I did not grow up unmarked. (Does Elizabeth irritate me, not because her behavior is foreign to me, but because it is not so foreign as I might wish?)

Sunday, August 16

Mr. Steindorff received a fine welcome back to his conducting: after we applauded him at length, the band manager gave him a huge harp of flowers with a banner that read, "Welcome Home, from the Boys." He seemed pleased to the point of tears. I don't know how near he went to the actual fighting, but after the sounds of cannon, the bustle of refugees, and the tears of families sending boys and men to the front, Lakeside Park on Sunday afternoon must have seemed like Heaven. Perhaps he even doubted that he would see all this again!

Monday, August 17

Aunt Emily came over for tea. She is deeply shocked by the woman professor from Michigan who says that children and adults of both sexes should bathe and dress together with no apology for their nakedness, and that open study of the nude would help cure immorality. Suzanne, naturally, thought there was something in that, and could not understand the opposition to teaching sex hygiene in public schools.

"Just because some wealthy clubwoman hasn't the time to teach her child about life, why should the responsibility be thrown onto the teachers?" Aunt Agnes replied.

Suzanne said that it was not a matter of "wealthy clubwomen" but of "parents who may not fully understand these matters themselves."

Aunt Agnes replied in a mock whisper, "Well, they must have understood something."

Suzanne then pointed out that a horse's ability to reproduce didn't qualify it to explain the emotional, medical, and moral issues that might be involved.

Aunt Agnes indignantly closed the conversation with, "These matters are sacred. If something is to be said, it ought to be mother-to-daughter, intimate and private, not something a teacher lectures on, like spelling and arithmetic."

Tuesday, August 18

Today is my 33rd birthday. Conveniently, mourning standards precluded a large gathering. Over the years I have grown indifferent to birthdays, reminders of all that I have not accomplished and what is lacking in my life, but there being only two of us made it quite sad. Aunt and I both felt it so and said little.

Many women my age have a loving husband and several children. I do not mind that my life has turned out differently, but each birthday revives questions I had thought settled. When I picture life with a husband and a brood of children, I am certain that it all would be a great bother. When would I paint? Painting seems more necessary than ever since Father's death.

Finished *V.V.'s Eyes*. Pleased that Mr. Harrison did not graft a happy ending onto it but agree with a reviewer that he let his style run away with itself after his success with *Queed.*

Wednesday, August 19

The Germans are in Brussels.

Pope Pius X has died. His physicians say he died of a broken heart because of the war. Jack joked that the Pope was a fan of McGraw's Giants.

The police think Helen Smith was murdered by the Japanese photographer, though they have not found her body. I hope she went off to paint some new scene and that we will hear from her soon.

<u>**Sunday, August 23**</u>

Heated Sunday dinner with the Powers family. Discussed primary election, then Addison and Charles argued about prison reform. Charles spoke of a model prison in Ohio that consists of a brick factory with seventy prisoners. Ten skilled brick-makers direct their work, but no guards. They have a big dormitory, and a baseball diamond, but their favorite activity is holding mock trials! Charles thought it a particularly fine sign that the prisoners found legal arguments of such interest.

Addison said he had read about the prison, then added, "I became disgusted when I read about a band furnishing concerts every night. What's the use of a prison that sounds so pleasant most working men would commit a crime just to be allowed to reside there?" Charles explained that the prisoners play in the band. It is not some hired extravagance. Addison muttered that if Helen could induce her children to become shoplifters, she could save on piano lessons.

The newspaper printed a comparison of relative fighting strength. Russia has nearly twice as many available men as Germany, but the Germans are better trained. The total manpower favors Germany and Austria-Hungary, but all combatants are strapped with debt. Charles pointed out the "Available for Duty / Unorg'z'd" column and said, "That is the number that will tell." There are 14,900,000 men available in the U.S., more than the German and French combined. I reminded Charles that we are strictly neutral. "As well we'd best be, for now," he grinned, indicating where the table showed very few men in uniform in this country.

Helen and Edward had seen "Cabiria." Mrs. Powers was appalled by the very idea that a poet who had written "Love's Triumph" and "The Dead City" would condescend to write a "movie." She complained that "legitimate stage actors are selling themselves to Vaudeville." Then wondered aloud "if he is as shame-faced as so many of them."

"Why shouldn't he write a moving picture, if the Italian company is willing to pay him for it?" asked Mr. Powers.

"Yes, and why shouldn't the next Pope get up on the trapeze with Delmore and Lee?" Mrs. Powers quipped.

Tuesday, August 25

Primary election day! I voted at 10 a.m. I have little doubt that Mr. Heney and Governor Johnson will be our nominees, but I never fail to vote. No true woman should. If every woman voted, that would answer the claim of men in Eastern states that we lack interest.

Stopped in briefly at the Englands'. Mary England, barely 21, was having a party to celebrate her first chance to vote. She and her friends were studying the issues with a charming mixture of diligence and levity. I thought of my own first ballot, two years ago now. Quite different to cast it as a woman of thirty, after helping fight for the right. I cannot claim to have "struggled for years," but I did spend time urging suffrage. Mary and her friends cannot know the quiet satisfaction we felt casting our first ballot, whether 21 or 30 or 56, like Aunt Agnes.

Wednesday, August 26

Helen Smith is dead. Murdered by George Kodani, they say.

I think of her sitting above the sea near Carmel, lips pursed in concentration, peering out through her owlish glasses at the waves as if she sought to understand the incomprehensible. Trying to get the light, and the patterns of the waves just right, then turning to say something silly to us, just when I thought she had forgotten our presence. She was always the child, though a dozen years older than I. Always enchanted by what she saw. A strange mixture of shy and bold, which her work illustrated magically. (I wonder if Jennie Cannon will hear of Helen's death.)

The newspapers say Helen was romantically involved with Kodani. I suppose that love comes to everyone in time; yet I had never seen her interested in any man. I find it impossible to credit Kodani's story that they quarreled over another woman. She struck him, and then he picked up an abalone shell and beat her to death in a mad rage. Helen, strike any living thing in anger?

The editorial sounds like Uncle Thomas spouting about "the wily Japs" no one can know or trust. "They are not to be credited with honorable purpose, nor to be considered faithful to any vow." I thought of Mr. Yamashita and his bonzai trees, his gentle touch, and the rapt expression on his face as he trained, re-potted, and carefully pruned each one. They say Kodani was involved with women in the restricted district of Monterrey.

The headlines scream of new carnage, worse than anything in history; yet Lord Kitchener hints that the war could last three years. Unimaginable! Indeed, most of England seems to find it so. The military men say that modern ammunition would run out within months, the financial men say they could never find money to continue the war so long, and the politicians say the people in every European nation would erupt in revolution first. But Lord Kitchener is War Minister and must know something. I told Aunt Agnes I could not imagine how they could go on for years killing tens of thousands of men every few days. She replied that she could not have imagined such carnage for even the first few days.

Thursday, August 27

The House will not consider national woman's suffrage. The Rules Committee chairman from Texas announced that he will not allow suffrage even to come to the floor. No man should have such power! Suzanne said the members should be locked up to vote on suffrage and not let out until we see "smoke from the chimney."

Jack said that if the House were allowed to vote secretly, as the people do, it would defeat prohibition soundly, but that if there is ever a publicly recorded vote, the measure will pass easily. He said it may be the same with suffrage: many Eastern representatives do not want it, but they believe it will come eventually, and prefer not to make too strong a record of their opposition, lest they be turned out of office the first-time women vote in their states.

Friday, August 28

Tuesday, I leave for Chicago! Although I do not look forward to packing or to such a long train ride, and I will miss the garden, I am excited now that the trip is near. To see such art, all at once, here in the United States!

September

Tuesday, September 1

My things are all packed.

It is a drab season in the garden, and the heat discourages me from much that I ought to do. Still, I spent much of yesterday ensuring that the garden will not suffer during my absence.

Last evening at the "movies" they showed the Russian Czar reviewing hundreds of thousands of troops. Normally, no one cares about the Russian Czar, except to shake one's heads about his autocratic rule of a backward country. Last night, people began clapping, first a few and then many, while others hissed. When appeared scenes from the Belgians defending Liege, again clapping and hissing. I felt a tremor of fear that the audience at the Oakland Photo Theater might erupt in violence, but despite the apparent differences of opinion, everyone remained good-natured. Even so, this illustrates why the United States cannot enter the war on either side.

Much jesting about the new pope. His small stature and nearsightedness have inspired a treasure trove of silliness that erupts anew whenever someone thinks of a new twist: that they have made a higher throne so that people can see his face over the shoulders of those kneeling before him; that at first they used an infant's dining chair; that all the motion picture cameras are being fitted with special lenses so that he will be visible in the Pathe reels of his coronation; that he rides round the Vatican on the back of an Irish wolfhound; that he is so near-sighted he once poisoned a whole parish with cleaning fluid he had mistaken for wine.

He is said to be very devout, and so simple in his living that in Rome he was often mistaken for a poor country priest seeking charity. (I can hear Father saying, "They also say each new pope is saintly, yet they all manage to get elected.)

Evening—aboard the Overland Limited.

I am on my way, but I feel more relief than pleasure. Aunt Emily thought it terribly unseemly to go on such a journey so soon after Father's death. Her arguments might have meant more if I had not known that Father wanted me to go, and he was the *last* person to chart a course based on appearances. (She has no idea that he and I discussed the matter on his death bed. Smiling, he called the trip my "great adventure.")

Aunt Emily insisted that others would see the trip as disrespectful. I resisted asking her to identify these "others" who keep such close track of my movements. Her lectures on the prescribed mourning rules make me wish I could ignore them completely. She cross-questioned me about the exhibit, as if I were a criminal who might give herself away if asked repeatedly the same question. She simply cannot imagine why *anyone* would travel two thousand miles merely to see works of art.

Aunt Emily went on to say that for a woman to travel so far alone was not only improper but dangerous. Aunt Agnes agreed with me that such concerns were fatuous. According to Agnes, when they were young, no one ever thought of such a problem. "This nonsense of seeking a *duenna* or a chaperone was never heard of in this country until we grew wealthy, and people had leisure to think about aping the Europeans. Girls have always been able to travel across this country alone. We took pride in it. So far as I can tell, it is still so." She paused, then narrowed her eyes at me.

"However, I doubt that traveling across Manhattan Island alone would be prudent."

I recalled the battle over garbing me in mourning after Mother died. Aunt Emily dressed me in black, although friends told her mourning was going out of fashion. I had no idea what "affectation" meant, but I silently agreed. I should likely have had to wear black the whole year had Father not returned.

Dreamt last night about that old woman near Paris who kept her house shuttered and the lights dim, ever since her fiancé dined with her before going to the front in 1870. Now the windows are open and French flags flutter in each window, and she's asked the commandant to send a man to dine as her guest each evening, because his men are finally going to avenge her fiancé's death.

In the dream I *was* the old woman, but I was also watching her, as in a motion picture. Just before waking, I saw my deeply wrinkled face in the mirror, and when I held up my hands, they were bony claws, and shook uncontrollably.

When Helen saw me off at the station, I told her I had dreamt of the Frenchwoman who had lost her fiancé. "Did the portrait draped in crepe resemble Richard?" She asked, laughing. As we embraced, she gave me an old envelope, saying her mother had come across a letter from Mother, years ago.

A brief incident at the station reminded me that I had yet to come to a decision about Susan. At Sixteenth Street Station a family was awaiting the same train. The girl, slightly younger than Susan, had a doll. She held it casually, as if to suggest she had outgrown it, yet she was not prepared to undertake such a long journey without its companionship. I smiled, and might have forgotten them, except that I noticed a man watching the girl closely. The girl, just out of pinafores but not yet ready for evening gowns, displayed the same mixture of child and budding womanhood as did Susan. Suddenly I saw her lithe, uncorseted body through the man's eyes and had the oddest sensation of seeing Susan as Uncle Thomas might: a girl impatient to be a woman, but with the beguiling sweetness of childhood clinging to her like the last leaves in November. Just then they called my train.

Now, sitting in the dining car, I still see the girl's unconfined grace and naturalness, which will be trained out of her all too soon. Not only our bodies but our spirits and dreams become compressed. Thank goodness my family was somewhat impatient with convention. I remember when Ah Fong told me that in China women bind their feet to keep them tiny, causing such a deformity that they can barely walk. I was horrified, but he laughed. When I pressed him, he said, "'Melican girl, think bind feet vely bad thing; but 'Melican girl… she bind heart, belly, how-say-it, leevir. Cut off feet, still can live. Cut out…" He moved the side of his hand along his belly. "So, who do vely foolish thing? Chinese? 'Melican?" He shrugged.

If I see that family on the train, I will speak to the mother, woman to woman, and beg her to forego the corset with her daughter, no matter how strange she may find me.

Wednesday, September 2

Glad I'm alone in this compartment; having chosen the upper berth for sleep, I can use the lower during the day. Twice during the night, I climbed down to sit awhile and read, and watch the countryside rush past under the nearly full moon.

Just after dawn, the light was magnificent. The sun rose ahead of us, turning the land into a series of elongated shadows pointing back toward California. Were I inclined toward mysticism, I might have seen them as omens to disembark at the next opportunity and take the first train back to Oakland. I simply watched and tried to guess what was casting a shadow before it too passed. I felt grateful for the morning light, and for my solitude.

Yesterday evening, I read the letter Mother wrote to Mrs. Powers on August 24, 1893, and was enthralled by this passage:

Of course, they insisted that riding with the engineers would suffice for our purposes, but we stood firm: we would see so much better, and we understood that several ladies had done it already. They finally capitulated, after requiring us to sign documents stating that we took full responsibility and the railroad none.

It was the most wonderful two hours of my life! The air whizzed past, and the engine panted and grunted at our backs making such a roar that we could not hear each other speak. We were excited by mingled sensations of danger and delight. High up the pass there came a tunnel. You cannot imagine the thrill of entering a tunnel riding on a cowcatcher. The track before us vanished into a little black hole in the mountain. Quickly that black hole yawned like a huge mouth before us, and we plunged into its darkness.

The train rushed on through the Cimmerian blackness with a deafening noise, wholly indifferent to our fears. I held fast for my life. My wind burned eyes stared ahead for the point of light that seemed never to come. The cold, damp air made me tingle, and the train's roar filled my ears. FINALLY there was light, and it drew us onward, and out, as the mouth of the tunnel had swallowed us minutes before.

Was the sky ever so blue, and did the sun ever shine so brightly on green pine trees? Will air ever seem so fresh and warm and pure? Unable to hear each other speak, we waved our hands and laughed with joy at being once more out in the open, and young, and alive. The smiles hardly left our faces during the rest of the ride.

After I finished reading the letter, I looked out the window for a long time. Then I cried tears of joy and fresh grief. Her words were so full of life! I felt as if she were right here with me, riding this train, not as "Mother" but as a dear friend. Her childlike delight in riding on the cowcatcher, and her insistence on being allowed to do so, sounded just as Suzanne and I might. This new view of her pleased me thoroly. Your adventuresome blood runs through my veins, Mother!

I wanted terribly to discuss the letter with Father. What did he recall of the trip, and who was the friend who rode with Mother? I wanted to ask about Mother's spirit and courage. He must have known of the ride. I can see his face relaxing into an indulgent smile, as it did when he discussed memories of Mother. (Did he object? Did he himself ever ride on a cowcatcher?) I felt my loss of him even more strongly.

Later, passing through southern Wyoming?

[Clipped from the September 4 number of the *Mirror*:]

ELSA WERTMAN

I was a peasant girl from Germany,
Blue-eyed, rosy, happy and strong.
And the first place I worked was at Thomas Greene's.
On a summer's day when she was away
He stole into the kitchen and took me
Right in his arms and kissed me on my throat,
I turning my head. Then neither of us
Seemed to know what happened.
And I cried for what would become of me.
And cried and cried as my secret began to show.
One day Mrs. Greene said she understood,
And would make no trouble for me,
And, being childless, would adopt it.
(He had given her a farm to be still.)
So she hid in the house and sent out rumors,
As if it were going to happen to her.
And all went well and then the child was born—They were so kind to me.
Later I married Gus Wertman, and years passed.
But—at political rallies when sitters-by thought I was crying
At the eloquence of Hamilton Greene—
That was not it.

No! I wanted to say:
That's my son! That's my son!

HAMILTON GREENE

I was the only child of Frances Harris of Virginia
And Thomas Greene of Kentucky,
Of valiant and honorable blood both.
To them I owe all that I became,
Judge, member of Congress, leader in the State.
From my mother I inherited
Vivacity, fancy, language;
From my father will, judgment, logic.
All honor to them
For what service I was to the people!

Reading these Webster Ford poems is like reading a novel. I do not cry easily, but I teared up reading aloud Elsa's sad tale; the words "That's my son!" welling up inside of me. Then, as I read Hamilton's words—noble, if a trifle too taken with his own power—I shuddered at the loving bond he and his mother had missed.

My world has shrunk to a metal snake. The walk to the dining car is a great adventure, though a far shorter walk than I take most mornings at home. At lunch I read the newspapers. There *are* happy endings, after all. Mr. Braley, the multi-millionaire who gave so much to the suffrage movement, and spoke out in favor of it along with his late wife, has married Mary Gridley, the Los Angeles suffrage leader. I am glad these two people in their seventies have found happiness in their final years. (Is there hope even for me?)

Roller-skating season begins at Idora today. At least Oakland need not fear a dirigible appearing in the night skies. The Germans bombarded Antwerp again at 3:30 in the morning, putting the whole city into a panic. Another dirigible attacked Paris at the same time. Some say a raid over England is possible.

Thursday, September 3

I had supposed the train might provide time to reflect and write, but I have not felt it so.

Elizabeth asked why I would take a garden journal to an exhibition of paintings, to which I quickly replied that I might see a plant *genus* I should wish to note. I do not know why I dissembled. Perhaps because she might tease me about my "diary," or because it might pique her curiosity to learn that I write more here than planting notes and garden diagrams.

I am missing Governor Johnson's speech at the Piedmont pavilion. Although he's a wonderful speaker, I shall learn far more from the exhibit.

We arrive in Chicago at 9:30 tomorrow morning. Such a long ride, and too much idle time in which to contemplate my sins. Yet it's a wonder that the trip takes only 63 ½ hours! We take modern speed so much for granted. William and Lucy Cooke traveled for months. I think they wintered over in Salt Lake City, so one could say it took them a year.

Friday, September 4

Arrived at 9:45, a mere 15 minutes late. I went first by cab to the hotel, which is small but very comfortable. I recalled the little hotel in Willow with Richard. Checking in as man-and-wife felt a bit frightening and exciting, as if we were outlaws.

Eager as I was to see the show, I above all wanted a bath. After bathing, I lay down to rest for just a moment, half-dressed, and awakened more than an hour later. Not until 1:00 did I arrive at the show, where I wandered among a larger crowd than I might have wished. Most seemed to know little or nothing of art, but were drawn to the spectacle, sensing that they should be seen to be there. Fewer seemed drawn by the opportunity to see paintings they might never otherwise see, but even their comments suggested that few knew much about the painters.

Saturday, September 5

The Cubist room was a revelation, although I find it difficult to state in words what it revealed.

I must admit to a certain ambivalence. I well understand the mockery heaped on some of these works. I even share the uneasiness over whether it might not be all a fraud, or mockery. Yet I do not think the art is fraudulent, or lazy. These artists are after *something*. I recalled Harriet Monroe's observation that although it is not always clear what the Cubists are doing, they are certainly having a lot of fun doing it. I cannot see what they are after. Nor perhaps can they, but they have convinced me that they are after something significant.

Although I would not hang even one of these pieces at home, their inventiveness has inspired me. I am on fire with ideas for painting; ideas not a tenth so wild as what surrounded me this afternoon, but ideas I hope to nurture; ideas from within, my imagination freed by the variety, even madness, of these works.

Can it really be six weeks since the Austrian ultimatum to Servia? It seems a decade. To the Europeans, it must feel like a century.

Sunday, September 6

Sitting this evening in the hotel's comfortable dining room, I recalled my first trip to New York. How shocked I was to find that the hotels wouldn't take a girl traveling alone, and the best restaurants would not admit me after a certain hour. This trip has been extraordinarily pleasant, perhaps because I am so much calmer at 33 than 22.

Look forward to lingering over the Monets. I remember the first time I saw a reproduction of "Impression, soleil levant." It portrays the feeling of a harbor sunrise in a deeper way than a more "realistic" painting might do. "Impressionist" used to be a term people used to make fun of a painter whose work they didn't care for. Now Renoir, Whistler, and Rodin are considered masters. Someday we may view Cubists as such.

Found a kindred spirit where I should never have imagined one. At some point yesterday morning, I became vaguely aware of a negro. While scores, perhaps hundreds, of visitors had come and gone, this negro had remained in the same room as I the entire morning.

For much of the morning, I sat before a painting of two small sailboats suffused in a golden, shadowless light. Although they were said to be moored off Málaga, that would not have been apparent from the painting, for there was nothing visible but sky and water. The painting was not the work of an Impressionist, but it might as well have been.

My mind strayed to a day Richard took me and a few friends out sailing. Fog hid the sky. The sun, when visible, looked more like the moon. Fair-weather sailors had not dared to ventured out, though the temperature was mild. To the delight of gliding over the bay by sail was added an intense isolation. We could see no land and no other boats, and we spoke little. Our small craft might have been the only life on the planet. I could hear nothing but the occasional rustling of lines and clanging of halyards, and the sound of water as the sailboat cut through it. When we came about, the sails clumped and thumped in the swirling wind.

Richard made quite the handsome captain. I am sure he was well aware of the noble posture he presented and intentionally maintained, although he had long since captured all he might wish of my heart. I watched him handling the boat and occasionally giving a crisp command to the friend assisting him. I wished we could continue, past the military prison on Alcatraz, through the yawning mouth of the Golden Gate, to somewhere very far away. Then it came to me that, with no sight or sound to identify our surroundings, we might be in the Mediterranean. I gave a short laugh, and Richard looked at me and smiled and said, "Yes, we are there."

I stared at him. "Where?" someone asked. Still smiling at me, Richard replied, "The Mediterranean, or a painting Kate will make of this day, and long after we are dust, someone looking at the painting in the Metropolitan Museum will imagine he can hear the cries of the gulls, and the water smacking the hull, and he will ask the museum curator about the happy people in the painting."

Though I have often recalled the day, I had forgotten that last remark of his, and lost in reverie, I gasped. Looking around to determine whether I had been heard, it was then that I noticed the negro. It is unusual to see a negro at such an exhibition, and I must have noticed him earlier. I now realized that he too had not moved on with the current of sheep drifting from room to room, bleating to each other whatever the newspapers have taught them to suppose they think. When he still did not move, I thought perhaps something was wrong with him, and that whoever was to assist him had been delayed elsewhere. It did not occur to me that he might be taking time with each painting, as I do. Then he stood up, took out a watch, glanced at it, then around the room. Our eyes met, and he immediately looked away in embarrassment and walked slowly from the room with an odd sort of dignity. I realized then that it was well past noon and that I felt a little peckish.

I should likely have forgotten the negro, had I not seen him again during the afternoon. I had eaten in a small café, luxuriating in the certainty that, so far from home, I am nearly invisible. (I do so enjoy sitting alone and observing others.)

Perhaps because of how I had spent the morning, the restaurant and the street seemed like paintings, available for viewing but with no claim on my attention beyond their merits. Within an hour I was back inside the exhibition. I nearly gave in to the temptation to spend the afternoon with the Monets, which I have been saving for a less crowded day. Instead, I found a quiet corner among lesser-known works.

Spent a long time in front of Matisse's "The Red Studio." At one point, a fashionably dressed man was speaking rapidly about one of the French paintings to a pretty, young woman, and I realized that the negro was sitting on a bench facing the same painting—and that they were standing in front of him, blocking his view and heedless of his interest in the work. When he saw that I recognized his situation, there passed between us the sort of meeting of eyes in which people who know each other well wordlessly share an understanding. He smiled briefly, revealing lovely teeth, and with a slight motion of his shoulders expressed that he was accustomed to such treatment, and that although it was boorish, he had come to accept it. Such things happen to me when I am studying a painting, but it is usually acknowledged with an apology. I doubted the negro would receive such courtesy. Indeed, he did not.

Monday, September 7

Other than the cursory communications required to gain admission to the exhibit, or order food, I have spoken to no one except the negro. This morning we nodded to each other but did not speak. I spent the morning with the Monets and then with five Edith Dimock water colors lent by Mr. Marcus.

It was such a glorious day that I decided to walk to the park with my lunch. At the first park bench I passed I saw the negro from the exhibition. As soon as I saw him, I glanced away, without thinking. He had evidently done the same, each of us aware that if we acknowledged each other there might ensue some awkwardness about whether I might join him on the bench. A few steps later I turned back and asked just that.

"Certainly, ma'am." He rose courteously to his feet, just like any gentleman, and gestured toward the bench. His voice was deep and his accent Bostonian, which surprised me.

I do not know why I chose to join him. I was curious about the anomaly of a negro at such an exhibition. Yet it might have proved terribly awkward if he were not intelligent or well-mannered. I realized how startled (and disapproving) my friends and family would be to see me sitting on a park bench chatting with a negro; but I decided that I had every right to sit with anyone I chose and braced myself for a possibly awkward time of it.

We had rather a delightful conversation. He too was looking forward to the Monet and holding off until a weekday, and he made some sensible observations about the way they have organized the exhibit. Having attended the Armory Show last year, both in New York in Chicago, gave him an interesting perspective.

After a few minutes we fell silent. I heard then saw an indigo bunting on the top of a post and wondered how soon he would fly south. I had begun to question whether we would renew our conversation when I heard him chuckle.

"I have rarely seen a white person invest the time to savor a painting as you do," he said. "White folks seem always in a terrible hurry."

I laughed as I too always wonder how anyone could dash through an exhibition in a morning and suppose they have experienced anything of it, but it had not occurred to me to associate it with race, and I said as much.

"I have been to many museums and galleries, and almost all of the people in attendance are white, and everyone is in a great hurry," he said, smiling, then added, "Of course, many of the people who see my own work are black, and they hardly study it with the care I thought it deserved. However, I have always attributed that to some inadequacy in my work."

"Your 'work?' Do you paint?" I must have let my surprise show, for he laughed again.

"Indeed, they make brown-handled brushes just for the likes of brown-handed painters. A company in Charleston, South Carolina," he quipped.

I burst out laughing. His response was frank, but his eyes said he meant no harm.

"In most southern states, it's illegal for a negro to paint with a white-handled brush," he went on, his tone light but edged with pain, even anger.

"Californians are more concerned with the colors at the other end of the brush," I replied. He smiled, and I asked him to tell me more about his painting.

Wholly to my surprise, we had a thoroly invigorating talk. Despite our differences, we have wrestled with many of the same questions, and much of what he said I have attempted to convey to friends, yet not half so well.

"We live in a continuous flow of impressions—from which one impression suddenly speaks to us in such a way that we must arrest the entire flow to let that *one* impress itself on our imagination. Because it is not a choice we make, but a choice the moment imposes on us, we take it for inspiration, and it inspires in us absolute devotion."

I nodded but did not dare speak.

"Of course, I stole that from Arthur Ransome," he said, with a disarming grin. "He calls it a promise we make to the moment, or it to us, and says that the real artist seeks only to be true to the original promise, and that with a good artist, we cannot discern with what he began."

I had to repress the urge to find an empty bench so that I could reflect on what he was saying.

"A painting captures a moment when we are most truly alive," he added.

I felt very much that way about *this* moment, sitting on a bench in Chicago with a negro who spoke with poetry in his voice. Life was presenting me with a moment in which I could feel with especial clarity what it is to be alive and to be an artist. I sat back and let myself enjoy the rhythm of his voice and the play of sunlight on his face.

As he spoke about the flow of time, my mind flowed back across the many moments that had brought me here, and I wondered what flow had brought him to this same place. I mused on chance, on the fact that I would not be sitting here if I had walked in a different direction, or come to Chicago a week later, or if Aunt Agnes had accompanied me.

I wondered where he had been educated. I considered his obvious intelligence and felt ashamed to have feared that he might speak some unfathomable dialect. I thought about his color, dark enough that I had immediately supposed he was a negro but light enough that he might have been a dark-skinned foreigner. How odd that a slight difference in skin-color can mean so much! I thought of *Pudd'nhead Wilson*, which I read at age eleven when it was first published, and that wonderful Kate Chopin story.

It was well into the afternoon before we returned to the exhibit.

The waiter has arrived with my shrimp Newburg. I think I might have a glass of wine to mark the day.

Tuesday, September 8

It is so hard to know what is happening in Europe!

The morning paper says the Germans are in a desperate defensive position. One article even analyzes how the allies would divide up the spoils in a victory. It all seems quite sensible: return Alsace-Lorraine, let Bosnia join Servia, etcetera—except that the Russians, whose attacks from the East loosened Germany's hold on France in the West, will want East Prussia and Austrian Galicia, though the people there have no desire to be under the Czar's rule. Apparently, everyone agrees that it would be an outrage, but everyone also agrees that Britain and France could hardly say "no" and that such an act would be a fragile basis for peace.

Wednesday, September 9

Lincoln's paintings are exceptional. His subjects are so different from anything I have seen that I cannot judge them, but he is a far more interesting artist than I could ever become.

Yesterday he took me to see five of his paintings that are here in Chicago. I shudder to think what Elizabeth and Aunt Emily would say if they knew that I had gone with a negro to a saloon and an apartment in such a neighborhood; but when he asked if I would be interested in seeing his work, his gentle, reserved manner persuaded me, and I realized that I was terribly curious. My only fear was that if I found them poorly done or terribly pedestrian, I would not be able to hide my reaction and would hurt his feelings. I needn't have worried.

We went by street-car, then walked a few blocks past idle men who spoke in a foreign tongue and stared sullenly at us. The architecture would not have impressed Julia Morgan. Toward the end of our walk, most of the people we saw were negroes or Orientals. The few white men looked rather rough, at best. I was glad I was not alone.

Despite our surroundings and our very different lives, we kept up a lively conversation. We are artists and also outsiders: Lincoln as a highly-educated negro artist in a rough-and-tumble world; and I, as an unmarried woman who paints and prefers the company of flowers and vegetables.

We stopped in front of a disreputable-looking saloon. Some of Lincoln's paintings were in the saloon, and some in the apartment above it. Of the five paintings, four were studies of people, mostly negroes in their environments.

The first was a portrait of a Negress surrounded by empty tables and chairs. She is sweeping the floor in a red dress that emphasizes her abundant figure and seems more suited to a soirée than to sweeping. Her face wears a dreamlike expression that says she is elsewhere. Behind her: a bar, a mirror, and shelves of liquor bottles;

in the corner, a piano. Rays of early-morning sunlight filter in through dust crystals.

The painting hung in a small sitting room in the apartment above the saloon. I studied it for several minutes. I could hear, smell, feel what could not be painted: the lively music, dense smoke, conversation, and laughter that had filled the saloon just hours earlier; and even, thanks to Bret's accounts, the exhaustion of the place itself from the raw emotions of its habitués. Finally, I turned to Lincoln who stood silently nearby and told him that I liked it very much.

He cocked his head, assessing my sincerity. "I *do*, truly I do," I repeated. He nodded after a moment, and then smiled and said, "I'm glad." I felt unaccountably happy.

The other painting in the apartment made me shiver with its bleakness: before a red brick wall a negro mother kneels, her arms protecting a small boy, both skinny as wraiths and dressed in rags. The boy's face is contorted in a scream while the mother stares fiercely off to the right. I could not guess what threatened them so, and doubted I wished to know; but I felt their terror and thought of Lucius. Then I thought of Father looking at me from his bed, near the end, and of Susan. How fierce could I be to rescue her?

Lincoln required no verbal confirmation of my obvious awe of the painting. He said nothing about it except that it had been moved upstairs from the saloon after customers complained that it dampened the spirit, which I could well understand, but suggested more artistic sensitivity than I had expected from negroes drinking in a saloon.

When we finally entered the saloon, it felt familiar. There were not yet many patrons. All were negroes. Lincoln approached the bar mistress, who appeared to be the model for his painting of the saloon after hours, and I wondered whether she was his wife, girlfriend, sister, or friend. She seemed to take offense at my very presence. Was it some foolish jealousy? A more generalized race hatred? I hung back until Lincoln beckoned.

He introduced her as Gwen, short for Gweniveer. He then introduced a bald man sitting at the bar as Curly. Gwen frowned and said she was pleased to meet me. Curly smiled and nodded in a friendly manner. Gwen asked whether I would have anything to drink, her tone hostile. Though a bit thirsty, I thanked her and said I'd have nothing just yet. She snorted and moved away.

Curly was watching me. "You white," he said in a neutral tone, possibly to explain Gwen's behavior.

I was unsure how to reply. On impulse, I looked down at my arm as if startled by this news, then looked at him and said that he might just be right about that. He laughed, perhaps a little harder than my witticism deserved. I remarked that he had a good sense of color and asked whether he too was a painter. That earned a deeper and richer laugh. Suddenly I felt almost comfortable.

Curly motioned with his drink to a painting on the wall to my left. He did not have to explain that it was Lincoln's.

A child dressed in rags was drawing (or writing) on a sheet of paper, his legs extending down through the missing boards of the front porch of an unpainted shack. He appeared determined to put onto this precious sheet of paper everything he had in him. Behind the boy, in an open doorway, his mother, with a rag tied up on her head, sat leaning forward and watching intently.

Lincoln had clearly captured something elemental, but my attempts to articulate my thoughts came out hollow and trite, and it seemed odd to discuss art in such a venue. He said that if I ever have the opportunity, I should view the work of Henry Ossawa Tanner, particularly "The Thankful Poor" and "The Banjo Lesson," to understand better what he was after. He said the paintings "exemplify the kind of painting in which the most telling moments of ordinary people in their daily lives become beautiful through simplicity and the play of light and shadow." He said that Tanner studied in Europe for years, and that when he returned to this country, "he used his mastery not to paint imitations of the French but to create powerful portraits of our own people." (I wondered that I had never heard of this Tanner.)

It struck me that two of the three paintings showed a mother and child in emotional circumstances. I said as much, adding that my mother had died when I was a child. In response, Lincoln told me something of his own background, his words flowing less fluidly than when he discussed paintings.

His father was a southern gentleman, a former officer in the Confederate army. A few years after the war, he took up with Lincoln's mother, a widow with one daughter, Gweniveer. They pretty much lived together, but he would not marry her, nor did he legitimize the children, of whom Lincoln was the youngest; but he educated them all, mostly at Tuskegee and a nearby negro teacher's college, and sent Lincoln to study art in Boston and then to London.

"My mother died in 1900. I was twenty-four and living in Boston. Her funeral was held in the small church I had attended as a boy. A modest building, always full of love. The preacher had known my mother well and spoke of her at length." Lincoln paused and looked away.

"Then my father entered the church, splendidly dressed and with all the dignity of his position in the community. He removed his hat and stood silently in the back. Everyone kept turning around to look at him. Even the preacher couldn't help looking at him every so often. The preacher understood that my father wished to say something and gestured to my father to come forward. I doubt any white man had ever spoken there.

"When my father reached the front row, he hesitated. I understand now that he was so full of emotion, he was like to explode, but you'd not have known from his face. 'You all know me,' he said. 'I'm Colonel Ashby. I won't take much of your time. This is Emma's time, and I know you all loved her.' His usually strong voice broke as he added, 'So did I. So did I.' I thought he might weep, and I guess he thought so too, for he paused, but then he went on with that splendid voice he had, accustomed to command, but speaking very softly, 'I loved her, and I have come here today to say what I was too cowardly to say during her life: Emma was my wife, as sure as ever man and woman belonged to each other; and these are our children.'

I can't describe the feeling that passed through me as he gestured toward us. Then he looked at the coffin, then at the preacher, then upward, and then back at the coffin, as if waiting for someone or something to tell him what to do next. Finally, he leaned over the coffin and whispered something into my mother's hair, then turned to the preacher and said, 'Thank you, sir,' and walked to the back of the church and sat down."

Lincoln fell silent. I heard a rush of sound from all around us, as if someone had opened a door—sound that had been there all along, but I was listening too intently to notice.

I fear I shall be late to the exhibit. My breakfast is now before me, and I had better eat it, yet I want very much to write down some of what I saw and heard and felt last night.

How to continue? My stomach is full, and my head is empty. What had seemed so clear before breakfast has blurred like a reflection in a lake rippled by a strong breeze.

I found myself in a wholly different world. Men, and a few women, drifted into the saloon. At times Lincoln and I were alone, but his sister's customers knew and liked him, and often our table was so full extra chairs were borrowed from other tables to accommodate everyone.

Sketch 1: We were joined by two men, Roland (whom I took for a white man) and Michael. During a brief lull in the conversation, Curly nodded toward me and remarked with a wink, "She white." Michael nodded, and Roland said, "I used to be white, once." Michael laughed, and Curly asked Roland, "Then why ain't you rich?" Roland leaned toward me and said that as I could see, his skin color was quite light, and that he had realized he could probably pass for white. One day, on impulse, he bought a ticket on a Mississippi gambling steamer, and ate his supper on the "Whites Only" upper deck with a group of white people and smoked cigars afterward with the gentlemen, just like a white man—though saying little and careful to conform his speech to the role. At first, he was delighted with his success and excited by the danger, but the conversation grew tedious. He could hear lively music from the lower deck where the negroes were laughing and dancing. "All a sudden, I just had to be where somethin' happenin'. Too boring to be white. So, I went on down there, an' I ain't never bin white since."

Sketch 2: Curly ambled over to the piano and sat for a moment, as if he were too tired to raise his arms or was trying to recall what the instrument was for. First his right hand and then his left wandered out onto the keyboard. He never seemed to "start playing," but soon his fingers were coaxing from the instrument sounds I hadn't heard before. He was truly "playing" the piano! I went and stood where I could see his face; he wore no expression. A lit cigarette dangled from his lips and his eyes were somewhere else, though he did nod at me and smile. He and the piano seemed a single creature.

Sketch 3: Gweniveer came by our table to see if Lincoln wanted more to drink and asked whether I would take anything. I told her I would take a lemonade, but when she set it down in front of me, I recalled the scene in "Traffic in Souls," in which the white-slaver puts drops of some sort into the younger sister's drink so that she will faint and can be taken discreetly to the brothel. I felt thoroly comfortable with Lincoln, but the girl in "Traffic in Souls" probably felt comfortable with the man who had charmed her. As Helen Smith must have with her Japanese. I decided my fear was nonsense. I was confident of Lincoln's character; and if these people meant me any harm, I was already lost.

Sketch 4: When I told Lincoln that he should have a proper show, he responded with this story: At the Centennial Exhibition in Philadelphia, the judges awarded a bronze medal to an artist named Bannister, whose landscape paintings Lincoln said I might appreciate. At the museum door, the guards turned away a negro, not realizing he was Bannister, come to receive his award.

When I said I had never heard of such a thing, Gweniveer, who had sat down with us, snorted, then scolded Lincoln for associating with a white girl. I could understand little, but she was clearly appalled by my ignorance, and offered it as proof that any thought of friendship with me was foolish, if not a betrayal of his people.

Lincoln sat silently through Gweniveer's tirade, an ambiguous smile playing on his lips, then said quietly, "Kate's here as my guest." This set off another Hotchkiss gun-burst of angry words, to which he responded, Kate's here as my guest." Gweniveer glanced at me, then at him, then shook her head. For a moment, no one spoke.

Frowning, Gweniveer said, "Well, you welcome, anyways." She followed her grudging words with a small smile and said, "Don' you mine me."

"I understand," I said.

"No, you don'. No reason you should." She sighed, glanced at Lincoln, and stood up, "You wan' a real drink now? A lil glass a wine?"

I told her that I thought not as I had still to get back to my hotel.

Now, looking around the hotel restaurant and listening to the conversations at the other tables, I am reminded of what Roland said about the white deck of the Mississippi steamboat. The people around me looked like wealthy corpses embalmed in their own manners and "standards."

At the next table, a man in a checkered suit read to his wife one of those humorous paragraphs that fill space at the bottom of newspaper columns. It was about a new colored maid who, when introduced to a metal bottle that could keep coffee hot or lemonade cold, stared at the bottle then asked, "How it gwine know if you wan' it hot or cold?"

Such "witticisms" are not my favorite form of humor, and this one particularly annoyed me. I thought of Lincoln, a highly intelligent artist who happens to be a negro. The people I had met in his sister's saloon have it all over these "upper-deck" folks in imagination, keenness of perception, mental quickness, and genuineness—everything except formal education and the informal training that constitutes "class" as most Americans understand it. Imagine the effect on my friends if I explained matter-of-factly that I had spent yesterday evening in a negro saloon, and found the company wiser and wittier than in my hotel the next morning. (How I wish I could share all of this with Father!)

Friday, September 11

Wrote nothing Thursday and perhaps should leave it so.

Twice now the waiter has asked if I am ready to order breakfast. Both times I was so deeply enmeshed in my thoughts that I might reasonably have convinced him that I am either an idiot or a foreigner. I do not yet see how to write of the past twenty-four hours, for the act of writing requires an attitude in the writer toward what is written, and—

After this third visit from the waiter, I contracted to inform him when I am ready to be fed in exchange for being left alone until that time.

I have done something I could never have imagined. I spent two nights with Lincoln.

I ought to feel ashamed, yet I do not. I feel—what *do* I feel? A strange inner glow mixed with fear that sets me trembling at odd moments. Fear of the sudden changes within myself; fear that someone might find out; fear that somehow, I have failed to take account of something important? Yet I feel more myself than I have felt for a long time, perhaps ever.

Various voices are clamoring inside me: Elizabeth's, Father's, Aunt Agnes', even Mother's, and the inner voice that speaks for society and all one has been taught about right and wrong, all asking *how* such a thing could happen. I cannot explain.

I do not "love" Lincoln. I do not see how I could. We have known each other but a few days and come from such different backgrounds.

Nor have we spoken of marriage, and we are not likely to. Yet there is between us much tenderness and much understanding, and not merely, as some might assume, the mutual satisfaction of animal appetite I had supposed I was without. Of that I can bring myself to write only that my experience with Richard seems rather limited. What has passed for virtue has been the timidity of a fool.

There is much I want to fix in my mind from these last few days!

Yesterday morning—an age ago, and but a minute—I awakened from one dream to find myself in another. I had been dreaming of the garden, but the flowers were so huge they loomed over my head like small trees. I was petting a very large grey rabbit, which then became an arm. When I opened my eyes, it was indeed an arm with skin noticeably darker than my own.

My senses sluggishly began to report my surroundings: peeling paint on an unfamiliar ceiling, and, inches from my eyes, strange hair and an ear on which my gaze lingered, tracing its lines as if it were an oddly familiar maze through which I would find my way; the deep scent, rather like popcorn, of another human being, a scent at once completely novel and deeply familiar, like an landscape one has visited only in dreams. I could hear the hum of the street below, a swell of indistinct voices punctuated by the occasional shout of a newsboy or a passing ice-vendor, mixing with the sounds of hammering, wagon-wheels, horse-hooves, and an automobile engine—a sound-painting of a busy, commercial street, quite different from the avian melodies and subdued activities of our residential street at home, or the tomb-like silence of a good hotel; and nearer, the sound of a another breathing.

I savored the novel pleasure of watching a man sleeping so close to me, with an intimacy and distance from the real world, I never quite felt with Richard. I should have felt guilt and fear, even horror, but instead I felt an inexplicable amusement, and as after a glass of wine, a sense of well-being. I lay on my side, watching him, my eyes tracing aimless paths around his face and body, as if I were a curious spider taking a stroll. He had awakened without my knowledge, and he smiled once he knew that I had caught him watching me watch him.

Then I did feel uncomfortable, looking into those eyes that now knew all of me. I had thoroly enjoyed our explorations of the previous night, but in daylight I should be too embarrassed to muster whatever strange mood had allowed me to do such things. Even as his widening smile and shining eyes coaxed an answering smile from me, and my rebellious fingers tentatively explored his face, I felt keenly that my body was mine and his was his, and that there should be no more tender acts. Yet, as his fingers explored my body as if they were the fingers of a ghost, tickling my ribs and belly as my mother had so long ago, I began to feel both the irresistible impulse to laugh and something more. I willed myself not to feel desire; yet the sensations were so thoroly enjoyable that when he ceased, I felt as bereft as a child told that the presents under the Christmas Tree were not for her after all. Lincoln laughed at my woebegone expression, as did I, and he soon elicited quite a different expression from me.

The poor waiter is hovering, although he has resisted speaking to me since we made our agreement. I had better eat and reassure him that my delay will not diminish this morning's income.

I awakened before Lincoln and knew instantly where I was. But for the call of nature, I should not have left the room. Returning through the kitchen, I found Gweniveer at the table, staring glumly into a cup of steaming coffee. A nearly horizontal shaft of light from the early morning sun crossed the well-worn tablecloth. The rich light, the frayed, checkered tablecloth, Gwen's hunched shoulders and downcast eyes—it was a painting I should have loved to make: "Negress at Dawn", or "The Next Morning." I had intended to return quickly to Lincoln, but now I sought to memorize the precise position of her clasped hands; the way her untended hair stood like tufts of prairie grass; the dark line of her skin through a hole at the shoulder of her grey nightdress; the paint peeling from the wall behind her.

When her eyes met mine, I started, as if caught in some shameful act. She glared at me as if she knew my thoughts, and they offended her. I wished that I was wearing more clothing.

"Good morning Gweniveer," I said.

"Good mornin' Trouble," she said with a tired smile. She picked up her cup and gestured. I should have preferred to return to Lincoln, and I felt uncomfortable alone with her, but I did not wish to offend her further. She rose, poured me a cup of coffee, and placed it on the table. I sat down.

"Thank you," I said. "How are you this morning?"

"Me? Oh, I be fine," she said. Then she smiled broadly. "How Lincoln?" she asked, in a tone that made me blush, as I think it was designed to do.

"He's asleep."

She nodded gravely, then said, "You *know* you be trouble for him, you stay with him long."

I had, of course, no intention of doing so, but her tone irritated me, and I said nothing.

"Maybe you ain't noticed he the color of your shadow?" She retorted. When I did not immediately respond, she grasped the skin of her forearm and pulled on it.

I felt the impulse to feign surprise and point out that my shadow and I had gone everywhere together for years with few disagreements, but I kept silent.

I wonder that I was not more alarmed by my surroundings, and more, by whatever within me had led me there. Gweniveer's words breached my calm somewhat: her concern that my association with Lincoln could harm *him* reminded me that our association could be dangerous for us both.

Gweniveer continued, "Maybe you so high-born you don' know what your folks do to a colored man, they see him with a white lady. Or don' it matters to you?"

"Do you mean lynching?'" I asked haltingly. "Such things don't happen in Chicago."

"What you know about it?"

"Not much," I started to reply.

She interrupted with, "No, I don' reckon you know much at all."

"Do you mean—"

"I means no good come of you bein' together. Maybe they don' lynch 'im, just beat 'im up real good. You think the police say anythin'? You think policemen in Chicago ain't white?"

I suddenly felt tired. Mustering as much courtesy as I could, I thanked her for the coffee and returned to Lincoln.

I must not return there this evening. Not because of Gweniveer's warnings. Nor from any moral concern. I need to clear my head. Perhaps too, like some woman who likes her laudanum, I must demonstrate to myself that I *can* resist temptation.

Saturday, September 12

Last night I had a moment of regret that I stayed away, but I also felt relieved to be alone. I read briefly, then slept soundly. This morning, I am excited to return to the Exhibition, despite the Saturday crowds. I am undecided about this evening.

How quickly and completely Lincoln has become not a negro but wonderfully himself! I enjoy the color of his darker skin, as I enjoy the laughter in his dark eyes, and the feel of his knotted hair.

Sunday, September 13

Saw Lincoln at the Exhibit. We did not visit the saloon; rather, we stayed up much of the night talking, mostly. How strange that the person who knows me best, at this moment in time, is the one person I am unlikely to ever see again.

I leave this evening at 7 p.m. He will not see me off. We have said our good-byes, without speaking of the future. We accept that we may never see each other again, but not without sadness, which has made us all the more determined to be as truly and honestly ourselves as we could.

Monday, September 14

When the porter came by, I spoke with him. Of course. Yet not at all of course. I asked him how he was, just as I might ask anyone, and while he was repairing the window, I asked him how many days he traveled consecutively, and the like.

He was clearly uneasy and shot me covert looks, trying to discern what I was about. There was in my tone something quite different from what he was accustomed to: that is to say, there was nothing—no condescension, no politely masked fear, no mockery. I was honestly interested, as one person speaking to another.

Initially, I attributed his uneasiness to the fact that he could not fix the window latch quickly. Now, having had some time to reflect, I wonder if his stiffness was a reproach. I had stepped out of my role.

What a difference language and diction has made to the lives of Lincoln and his sister. If Lincoln had been limited in his manner of speech, I probably could never have perceived the man I came to know. I see now the powerful wrong done to these people, not only in making their parents or grandparents slaves, but in refusing (even now) to educate them properly. Father, bless him, understood all of this. How I miss him!

Tuesday, September 15

Now that I am homeward bound, I am struck by the enormity of what has happened in the short time since I left Oakland. I have been intimate with a man, the first since Richard, and he would be considered by friends and family an "unsuitable" man. Had anyone suggested such an interlude could occur, I should have laughed uproariously, and advised him to see an alienist. (If anyone in Oakland finds out, I will be advised to see one! And yet, I do not regret any of it.)

Two hours later: My mind races, but any insights dissipate as quickly as the passing view. Have I, without knowing it, been seeking closeness to another—or has Father's death left me especially vulnerable?

An hour later, after gazing out the window, hardly thinking anything coherent: I have been contemplating the differences between Lincoln's manner of speaking and that of his sister and friends. Their speech was often beyond my understanding; a rhythmical and oddly appealing language bearing only a nominal resemblance to English. I felt as if I were traveling among foreigners and embarrassed by my ignorance of the language. Only when I ceased trying to capture each word, did I get the sense of what was being communicated.

Of course, Lincoln was raised in Boston and highly educated, while Gwen remained with their mother. When I mentioned his friends to Lincoln, he bristled slightly and asked why I assumed he was more intelligent. I replied that hardly a man I know, of any color, has his range of knowledge and insights, but as for his friends, well, I cannot always understand them.

"Here lies the iniquity of what our white countrymen have done to us: Because my friends do not speak as you do, you suppose they cannot think as intelligently, or have lazy minds."

My silence was a confession.

"What you do not see is how the negro has been systematically deprived of the opportunity to learn. Did you know that during Slavery it was a crime to teach a black child to read? That even now our children are not permitted to attend white schools, but inferior institutions with few books, and with teachers who themselves lack adequate education."

I mumbled that I had heard something of "separate but equal."

"Separate can never be equal when forced on one people by another. Where one controls all government, equality is as likely as a penguin on Chicago's streets."

I laughed, envisioning a penguin waddling past us, but nodded to show I took his point. "And it is getting worse," he added.

When I mentioned that President Wilson, as a former university president, must understand the importance of education, Lincoln replied, "He understands it thoroly, and thus knows he must keep it unavailable to our people, to imprison us in inferior positions." He asked patiently, as of a child, "Can you really not know that President Wilson is a virulent racist, and that white sentiment against us is strengthening?"

Wednesday, September 16

We will reach Sixteenth Street Station not long past 8:52 this morning.

As I spotted familiar landmarks, my heart swelled as if I were a child returning from a visit to the mountains. Then a profound unease overcame me. I have traveled much further than Chicago, and I am changed in ways I cannot explain, even to myself. Excitement at my homecoming is tempered by fears that my face or manner may betray me.

I know now that what I felt with Richard, I can feel with another. I am not convinced that I wish to marry, yet neither have I come to share Suzanne's views. (Perhaps Suzanne has more control of her heart.) I am not proud of what took place in Chicago; nor do I feel shame. I do not yet know what any of this means—it is likely that I will never again see the world as I did.

John Muir comes to mind as I watch the natural countryside give way to farms, roads, and stores. He described his first long period alone in Yosemite, starving and freezing but intoxicated with the beauty and peace. He said that when he came down from the heights to walk among other humans, he found himself unusually open to impressions, like a child. He saw more deeply and more clearly into people's hearts but took little joy in most of what he found there.

I wonder where Lincoln is this morning, and what he is thinking, and whether he misses me. I think I do not miss him, except when I let myself recall his smile, his voice, his touch. It is then that I feel that I have lost a dear friend. (Will we ever meet again?)

Went to see D.W. Griffith's "The Escape," based on the Paul Armstrong "problem play," at the Macdonough. It was not a movie I wished to see, but my claims of fatigue were brushed aside. The seven-reeler portrays slum conditions graphically and presents "a powerful argument for the science of eugenics." I found the movie's arguments muddled, and it reminded me of how far I have "traveled" since Chicago.

Apparently, Donald Crisp, to prepare for his role, spent weeks in New York's rough bowery neighborhood, haunting the east side dance halls and studying everyone as carefully as a detective. When Mr. Griffith told him to get a disreputable "Chuck Connors" hat, he searched for days and found one in a dirty little shop kept by a Polish woman. Taking him for a poor man, the shopkeeper argued with him in broken English, urging him to buy a better hat with which he could go out and get a good job, and telling him that if he bought the hat he wanted, he would get arrested and not to blame her if the police took him in. (I hope Mr. Crisp sent her a ticket to the picture.)

<u>**Friday, September 18**</u>

Peace in Europe may be possible—the Kaiser has suggested that President Wilson find out the terms the others would accept. Clearly Mr. Wilson sees some promise.

Whereas here we are deeply concerned to know whether the University at Berkeley will accept the women's resolution requesting an end to the ban on dancing the tango and the hesitation waltz, on condition that a paid censor be present to control orchestral selections!

Saturday, September 19

Morning in the garden, where I am truly home. "Home" seems sadly empty. I am more aware than before of how large and silent this house is without Father. It is as if Chicago was a dream, an intense dream.

Baron Von Schroeder has made it to the Front. Julia had a letter from him that makes his odyssey sound like a stage melodrama. The other Germans who left the Bay Area with him stopped at New York in fear of British warships. The British boarded his ship at Gibraltar and took off more than a hundred German reservists; but the Baron was disguised as an older man, an invalid. He is such an adventurer!

Much frivolous conversation during our Friday evening. Edward imitated Addison thundering, "Even the burlesque girls have a labor union now!" Suzanne had a letter from a friend recounting the furious search by the Swiss authorities at Basle for a criminal who had been giving at odd moments the regulation whistle for the departure of trains, thus putting the trains in danger of colliding with each other. The authorities finally discovered that a nesting blackbird inside the depot had learned to imitate the guard's whistle!

Were we sillier than usual? At first, I could not join in. Perhaps I was seeing my closest friends as Lincoln might see them. Perhaps I was feeling a lingering heaviness because of the war news. Yet once I joined in the fun, I was as silly as anyone, determined not to let troubling thoughts interfere, and glad to be safe among friends.

By the end of the evening, I was joking and laughing to detain the very guests from whom I had felt estranged just hours earlier.

Although I thoroly enjoyed my glimpse of another world, perhaps it was more of a strain than I realized, and I was reminded how, as a small child excited to be up past my bed-time, I could not cease giggling more and more helplessly as the evening passed, despite my determination not to attract attention. Perhaps too I did not wish to face my bed, my thoughts, my solitude, and the task of making home feel like home again. Thankfully, I fell asleep instantly, slept deeply, and recall no dreams.

Sunday, September 20

Disappointed everyone by reneging on our plans for the evening.

Words are inadequate to portray Anna as she sat in her home telling me of her experiences in Europe. She, her younger sisters, and her three children were visiting her sister and brother-in-law at Wilbeilen when fighting broke out between the Russians and the Germans. At first, they did not recognize the danger. When they did, she and her children found themselves separated from their party and in the middle of a battlefield. A Russian soldier pulled them into a trench, to safety.

Even so, the trenches were a living hell: intense heat from the burning houses, succeeded by cold and rain, shells and bombs exploding constantly. The rotting corpses of men and horses created a terrible stench from which there was no escape except through a wall of bullets. There was nothing to eat but rye bread and sour milk, and little of that. Her oldest son, just seven, grew ill with diphtheria. Anna buried him with her own hands. She got away to a town, but Amy, her four-year-old, died there. When she finally reached St. Petersburg (or Petrograd, as the Czar now calls it, so that it sounds more Slavish), she was taken for a spy, and saved only by the ambassador who gave her some money. She arrived home just yesterday.

At times she spoke of these horrors as one might read from the menu for a hospital benefit. Then suddenly she would stop speaking and look around, as if unsure where she was. Her haunted eyes begged me to contradict her and insist that Tommy and Amy were sleeping soundly in their rooms, that she had dreamt all this.

Once, after gazing into the distance, she shook her head, then remarked, "They would have grown up to marry and have children themselves, wouldn't they have? Think how many are buried in that one tiny grave!"

As I was leaving, she asked whether good mothers took their children to foreign countries. As I embraced her, I pictured Tommy sitting in the small dogwood with its one low branch that made an irresistible seat for a five-year-old boy.

I completely forgot about our plans to see a film, which now seemed absurd. When evening came, I pled a headache, rather than make everyone blue, and retreated early to my room with a cup of tea. Anna's account brought home how fortunate one is when the most pressing decision is between "The Virginian" and "The Barefoot Boy." If Mr. Griffith made a picture in which Mary Pickford or Mabel Normand experienced all that Anna Gibbs related to me today, people would say it was too horrible and too fantastic to be true.

Wednesday, September 23

This morning I painted Gweniveer.

As I worked, I did not think about what had led me to be in the company of this woman, although I felt a touch of the excitement and uneasiness I had felt. I concentrated thoroly on getting the likeness right, for Gweniveer demanded realism. Anything abstract would have felt unforgivably frivolous.

I painted her as she was that morning: seated at the kitchen table, a wisp of steam rising from her coffee, her eyes looking straight into mine. As her face emerged, I felt a twinge of fear, as if she might appear in the flesh and chastise me: for painting her likeness, for being a wealthy and privileged white woman, for having thought myself worthy of her brother's attention.

To my surprise, as I worked, I began to see Gweniveer: her toughness, her courage, her resolve. I like to think she would have approved, had she become flesh just then. She had spoken harshly to me, but I saw more clearly now that she sought only to protect her brother.

Thursday, September 24

For today's mass meeting against War, the street-car company added extra street-cars to accommodate the huge crowds and carried children free of charge. Mayors Rolph and Mott read resolutions calling on warring nations to lay down their arms: "You are present for the start of a great movement which will sweep across this country like a fresh wind, envelop Europe, and bring to a quick close this bloody conflict, the last such titanic struggle among civilized nations. I see among you, thousands of children. Our unanimous passion for peace will brand itself on their youthful minds, never to be forgotten. As they grow to succeed us in our various roles, they will know that they must never let such madness as this European War recur."

At times I was carried away by the hope expressed by the speakers, and then I thought of Anna.

Friday, September 25

Worked on the Gweniveer portrait. Missing the intensity of my encounters during my brief time in Chicago. No one here is as interesting to talk with as Lincoln.

Sunday, September 27

Visited Rockridge. That whole section beyond College Avenue and Broadway is now a city district. It seems but yesterday that it was mostly open grazing land, with no more excitement than a cow's tail swishing at a fly. There is an assortment of bungalows and larger homes, and the vacant lots are disappearing almost daily.

I find I am newly curious about the private lives of others. Do others find pleasure in a variety of ways, despite conventional wisdom? I cannot credit that those I see in church are so wholly without inhibitions, even in private. Still, some must be.

When I walked past Mr. Yamashita's workroom, it was closed and shuttered.

Monday, September 28

Dreamt I was a dog barking with other dogs. At one point, I barked from sheer delight at being alive. I understood what each bark signified. A nearby dog and I barked at each other, and our barks were a form of laughter. A third dog intruded, barking almost angrily, as if to warn us of the danger of barking together so freely, a danger we had lost sight of in our mutual delight.

Upon awakening, I recalled a moment with Lincoln in which, overcome with joy, I barked at him like a little dog, and he responded in kind, and then we laughed together like children. To my memory, I had never before barked like a dog, unless perhaps to amuse a child; yet I had the disquieting sense of having done so before. Later, I recalled that when I was four years-old, and visiting with Grandfather in his office, he and I barked at each other. It delighted me all the more because he always seemed so stern and serious.

President Wilson has made Annette Abbott Adams Assistant United States Attorney in San Francisco. She is the first woman to hold such a position anywhere in the country!

Tuesday, September 29

Received a letter today from Charles Hall.

Penchard
Friday, 4 September 1914
Dear Miss Willard,

Let me first apologize for having taken weeks to write you this letter. I make no excuses other than the obvious: that to write this letter forces me to face the finality of its contents and the delay has left you in pleasant ignorance. It is oddly cheering to know that those who loved Lester happily suppose that he is puttering about with brushes and canvas in his studio.

Communication with the outside world has been fitful, particularly since the Germans crossed the frontier. (Chance has played a most curious joke on us, letting our long-cherished dream carry us to this lovely countryside at just this moment.)

While it was frightening to realize that War was truly imminent, it has also been invigorating to witness the French response. Loud with political dissent only weeks before, the nation rose as one. Raw recruits from the peasantry marched proudly past with bayonet-set muskets, while women waved tri-colored flags, and every voice that was not singing the "Marsellaise" was shouting "Vivre La France!" We witnessed many tearful partings. Meanwhile, our letters began arriving opened, confirming the imposition of censorship.

Still, we did not believe war would come to us. Then early one morning, the garde champetre (the closest we have to a policeman here) marched up the road, beating his drum and pausing at every crossroad to read an order. He pasted two bills on the board outside the village hall: an order of mobilization and a bill requiring all foreigners to report to the mayor's office *tout de suite*.

The next day, we heard aeroplanes flying between Paris and the border. Two met right above our garden and circled around each other as if signaling, then flew off. ("Like two old friends who have met by chance and repair to a pub," Lester said.) But they were *not* old friends going off to get tipsy. Rather, as Lester remarked, it seemed as if we had stepped into Wells's "War in the Air." We felt old, reflecting on how quickly the aeroplane has become a weapon of war, and were reminded of our visit to the old *Galerie des Machines* at the 1900 Exposition, and contemplating with a friend (an engineer from New York) a huge model flying machine hanging above our heads. It had never been flown, of course; but its inventors claimed that someday it would. A few agreed, but most scoffed. Tom (the engineer) gazed up at it and said, "I'm sure such a thing will fly; but I doubt I shall live to see it." And he was quite young.

Aeroplanes have changed the nature of war. Neither side can make big surprise movements, since both sides will have spies flying about the countryside.

But I digress.

Traveling into Paris required us first to visit the office of the mayor, who could not even give us the paper we needed until he consulted one in a set of huge, dusty books that we had always supposed were merely for show. When Lester made some frivolous remark, the mayor advised us solemnly that two German spies had already been caught and executed in the next village. And near Meaux they caught three Germans disguised as Sisters of Charity thanks to a boy who noticed their gloveless hands.

Along the roads we found armed guards, either in uniform, or wearing a ca, or a numbered red armband to signify their authority. Their clothes may have been patched, but they had stern faces and wary eyes. At the railway station, even the French were required to produce proper papers before entering the city. Chance spared us that. There were almost no porters, and Lester, noticing a nurse standing beside far more baggage than she could possibly carry, quite naturally picked up two Red-Cross sacks to assist her. I took one as well, with the unforeseen result that we were taken for doctors and allowed to pass with no more attention than a quick salute.

Passing through the streets, Lester paused constantly to sketch it all: two recruits aping "military" bearing; a tearful woman standing in a doorway nursing an infant; the town-crier beating his drum, his face grave as he mixed news of the mobilization with the usual information on public auctions and such; and the concerned faces of citizens staring upward and arguing over whether German aircraft could indeed reach Paris.

In Montmarte we visited a friend from Lester's student days who runs a photography studio. A young woman who had entered the studio in a rush burst into tears upon learning that the photographs she had ordered would not be ready in time for her to give them to her young man to carry with him to the Front. Lester lost no time in sketching her. As he tore the page from his notebook and handed it to her, her tears gave way to a startled laugh and a grateful smile. Even

M. Godot's wife, who had always seemed to disapprove of his friendship with us, rushed to embrace Lester, turning him red as a beet.

We checked in at a hotel, then went out. After walking nearby streets and sitting in the square (where Lester sketched British soldiers and a street urchin), we made our way back to the hotel. Lester paused outside to buy fruit, while I mounted the stairs to the roof to survey the view. As I stood quietly smoking, two men in uniform appeared and advanced upon me, weapons drawn. They ordered me to stand still and demanded the drawing I had made of the town's fortifications. I was puzzled at first, then quickly realized that they must have received a report from someone who had seen Lester sketching. I said that we were Americans, Lester an art professor. As they were apologizing, we heard a loud shout from below.

Two young soldiers, peasants perhaps three days removed from the fields, were nervously accosting Lester in the street. One of them suddenly reached for Lester's sketchbook, and when Lester instinctively pulled it back toward his body, the startled soldier shot him. (I could not tell whether the boy had willed the shot or had fired accidentally.)

Lester immediately slumped to the ground, still holding his sketch-book. Providence, as absurd as ever, had placed the shot where it proved instantly fatal. The boy who had fired stepped back in shock. His companion was physically sick near the curb. One of the uniformed men beside me shouted down to them that Lester was an American artist, as if an explanation could alter anything now.

We buried Lester the next day. I have tried to tell myself that it is the best thing that could have happened: His last days, despite our concerns, were happy ones, spent arranging his studio and wandering through the country he loved, talking with people and sketching them. The end came so quickly he can hardly have understood what was happening.

Moreover, he will not see whatever is to come. He will not have to decide whether to stay in our new home and hope the war will pass, or retreat to England (or America) and witness through news dispatches the madness and violence engulfing his beloved countryside. He will not have to sit in some hotel and mourn the destruction of his studio, his home, the walled village of Crecy, and the fate of the young soldier who carries (still?) Lester's sketch of his girl next to his heart. He will not have to grow old and querulous, wondering at man's depravity.

I am sorry to send you such news. I can see you quite clearly, sitting in your beautiful garden as you read this. He loved you most of all his students.

I regret that I am unable to deliver this letter in person. I shall remain here. I am too old to fight and have no such skill. There is, after all, nowhere else I wish to be. Besides, I have heard that the roads are so full of refugees that no one can move in either direction. Likely a marauding band of soldiers will destroy the farmhouse, with me in it; until then I shall keep repairing it, and furnishing it, as we had planned. Perhaps there will come a time when I will be able to share with you Lester's vision.

Yours,
Charles Hall

Poor Charles. He must feel utterly lost.

I was not in the garden when I read his letter. I was standing in the front hall, then I went and sat on the stair. After quietly shedding some tears, I retreated to my bedroom.

Wednesday, September 30

While Europe slaughters itself, the City Council is battling the Superintendent of Schools over the signs he put up. The Council says that "DRIVE SLOW" will teach children poor grammar, and that the signs should read "DRIVE SLOWLY." The Superintendent replied, "Allegations that the signs were having a bad influence on the education of the children are possibly true, if the effect of the sign on the children is more desired than its effect on the automobile drivers." He added that the Century Dictionary gives "slow" as an adverb and noted that even Shakespeare writes in *Midsummer Night's Dream*, "How slow / This old moon wanes." The mayor's response cited Webster's to the effect that, despite the Bard, the primary use of "slow" is adjectival, and that "Mr. Webster denominates 'slowly' as a pure adverb, and therefore, if Webster be correct, and he has been an authority for many more years than the superintendent of schools is old, the adverb 'slowly' is the correct word." (How Father would mock such trivialities at such a time. And yet, Father, it is a distraction from the world's horrors.)

October

Thursday, October 1

A boy died in San Francisco this morning from a concussion sustained in a prizefight last night at the Eighth Street arena. The arena owner has disappeared. Police are seeking him and the referee for manslaughter. Jack and Bret say the San Francisco people are notoriously indifferent to the health of their boxers. I doubt that the Oakland promoters are any less cynical. They will all risk a boy's health to make a few dollars. No man has ever explained to me why the whole game cannot be abandoned.

Jack insists that a fair fight between two well-matched professionals is quite different from men like Coffroth putting unfitted youths in with huge brutes so that customers can watch what amounts to a simple beating. We must outlaw all such events next month!

Friday, October 2

Dreamt I was walking around Merritt's Lake as the full moon was rising, wearing a veil and a lacy white bridal gown, the train trailing thirty feet behind me. Everyone was dressed in odd-looking clothing. Some rode what I took to be strange-looking bicycles. The women looked almost indecent, as if they had rushed from their homes half-dressed. Several people spoke loudly to themselves. All stared at me, the abandoned bride. Some even laughed.

I was to meet the groom at Jack London's house, but I found the front door locked and the interior dark, and when I spied my reflection in the glass, it was the wrinkled face of an old woman. I turned away and descended the steps to the street, and a little negro girl approached and shyly pointed out that the train of my dress was soiled.

"Are you sorry?" she asked.

"Everything comes from dust, and returns," I replied.

In the street, the poet Joaquin Miller stroked his long beard and said, "I love; therefore, I am," as he made the sign of the cross.

Oakland's high school teachers and ministers are up in arms over a sacrilegious poem based on the 23rd Psalm which was published anonymously in the school newspaper:

"The motor is my auto, I shall not want. / It makes me to lie beneath it in green pastures. / It leadeth me into much trouble. / It draweth on my purse. / I go into the valley of death for its sake. / Yea, though I understand my auto perfectly, / I shall fear much evil, / for the radius rod and the axle breaketh easily. / It hath blow-outs in the presence of mine enemies…"

I hope that whoever penned this will put their cleverness to better use someday.

Saturday, October 3

I grow more and more fond of Lucius. What does his future hold?

Lincoln has taught me that the world will do its best to crush Lucius's warm heart, bright eyes, and eagerness to learn. Thinking of Lincoln and Gweniveer—even an Irishman like Sam McClure rising from poverty to edit a fine magazine—I better understand how vast a difference a good education (which I accepted as my due) can make.

Lucius has ability. If encouraged, he might have the ambition of a Sam McClure or a Booker T. Washington to undergo the suffering and indignity of getting an education as a negro. How many others of his ability but without the fight fall by the wayside? I am determined that his path must not be so arduous. I know that Father would approve.

Sunday, October 4

Bret stopped by with an unusually silly story about a friend in Richmond who wanted to catch the thieves raiding his pumpkin patch. One night the friend dressed up in old clothes partly stuffed with straw and stood leaning against a post in the garden, motionless as a scarecrow. When the culprits appeared, they took no notice; but their bull terrier wasn't fooled. It went right for Bret's friend, biting his leg. Once free, Bret's friend ran straight for his house, with no further thought of capturing the thieves.

Aunt Agnes says she's longing for the vibrant colors of New England—Autumn being her favorite season. She says that the leaves remind us of death, decay, and the passage of time, and make us more aware of life's fragility. I should like to visit New England to marvel at the brilliant colors I have seen only in paintings.

I also feel a kinship with this season. Evening skies darken earlier, as if resting after the excesses of summer sunsets. At thirty-three, many of my enthusiasms have faded, like snapdragons have faded. Yet I am finding more quiet pleasure in each moment, just as warm days seem more precious as winter approaches.

Monday, October 5

I have several times passed Mr. Yamashita's shuttered workroom. Today I knocked on the door of the main building. A young woman came to the door, and through gestures I inquired about Mr. Yamashita. A young man joined her, listening with arms folded and a frown. He told me that Mr. Yamashita died in September. I expressed regret. He asked the nature of my relationship with his grandfather. I spoke of the beauty of Mr. Yamashita's hands, how he worked with his plants, and of his eloquent eyes. The young man nodded, but I doubted he understood. When I ceased babbling, he turned to the young woman and spoke to her in Japanese, as rapidly as a Hotchkiss gun. He sounded angry. I felt like a fool.

The young woman looked from him to me and back to him, and then pointed toward the shed where the old man had worked. The young man asked a question. Their communications shortened to a few syllables apiece, as if they were clarifying a detail of some negotiation. I stood there wondering why they had not simply dismissed me.

At last, the young man turned to me and said, "You come. Please," and beckoned me to follow him to the shed. He came out holding a miniature cypress tree and handed it to me with both hands, making a slight bow, the way Mr. Yamashita had during my visits. I bowed in return, then wondered if it was customary for women to bow. He gave me a few simple instructions on caring for the tree saying, "I am not expert, but Grandfather, he teach me little bit. Any trouble, please, you come ask."

Tuesday, October 6

Uncle Thomas and Tub are furious that next Sunday's big celebration of Columbus Day is off. The committee announced that with nine nations engaged in a death struggle, and so many citizens grieving for relatives and friends, it would be tasteless to hold a massive festival. I agree. They will start the pageant next year and hope it will equal or surpass the Pasadena Tournament of Roses and

Seattle's Golden Potlatch. Uncle Thomas suspects business interests from San Francisco are behind the cancellation.

When Elizabeth expressed her disappointment, I looked at her fine clothes and thought of the women and children begging in Paris. I have read of the quavering voices of the former rich who have joined the ranks of the city's street singers, accompanying themselves on guitars, violins, even harps. I tried to imagine Elizabeth singing for her bread.

Not to be outdone, Jack chortled over the French trick at Verdun of removing their wounded from hospitals and replacing them with German prisoners as the German aviators began bombing the hospitals. I agreed that the Kaiser might deserve such a trick, but not the forty Germans who died in the bombings. Jack says that it will teach the Germans a lesson. Does the Kaiser care about a few more casualties? Do any of them?

Thursday, October 8

Find myself musing on that fashionably dressed lady in her fifties who rented a furnished home in Albany, apparently for the sole purpose of killing herself! They still have no idea who she was—she had torn out the tag identifying the maker of her long, black coat. All her clothing was of excellent quality but for an old straw hat. She dragged a rocking chair into the kitchen, placed it beside the gas range, turned on the gas, then took up a book and waited to die.

Is it macabre of me to wonder what book she took up?

What would I choose to read in my last earthly moments? (Father would have been delighted to take up this question.) Nothing political, nothing that would anger me. Nothing full of exciting new knowledge. Why introduce new facts into a mind I would shortly destroy? Like buying new furniture before burning down the house. Not a novel. I would not wish to spend my last moments straining to delay death long enough to see how it ends. Browning? Wordsworth or Keats? Definitely not Byron.

Friday, October 9

It seems terribly ironic that Fremont Older, the man most responsible for putting Ruef in San Quentin, is the leading proponent of his parole, while Congressman Knowland is trying to explain away his old association with Ruef. I have never cared for Mr. Knowland, particularly since he refused to say something for women's suffrage during the campaign of 1911.

Will having Mr. Heney and Mr. Phelan in the same race lead to Mr. Knowland's election as Senator? I will vote for Mr. Heney. He and Mr. Phelan both helped clean up San Francisco.

Such a novel waits to be penned in the intertwined stories of Ruef and Franklin Lane and Phelan and Heney and Governor Johnson: Ruef, Lane, and Heney are pals at Berkeley, then young reformists in San Francisco. Ruef becomes the boss who controls San Francisco, while Lane remains a reformist. Lane makes his career fighting the railroad, while Ruef comes to terms with it—profitably. When Ruef falls, he is prosecuted by Heney. But for an assassin's bullet, Heney would now be California's governor and Hiram Johnson an obscure lawyer. While Heney lies recovering, Johnson steps in to prosecute Ruef, and becomes the darling of the public. Now Ruef is a prisoner, and Fremont Older, who exposed him, is championing his parole effort. Governor Johnson will surely be re-elected; and Heney is running for the Senate. Lane, now in President Wilson's Cabinet, is supporting Phelan against Heney. If Dreiser or Brand Whitlock had written something like it, would we find it credible?

Likely there is more in all this than we will ever know. (I cannot imagine what Father would have made of it all.)

Jack was ecstatic because the Boston team beat the Athletics 7-1 in the first game of the World Series. He had bet $500 on the Braves. "I don't often bet so much on things I have no control over, but how could I resist two-to-one odds?"

He explained that the odds were based on the Athletics' reputation. "If the odds were based on the relative strengths of the teams, and not the fact that every fool with a newspaper knows Connie Mack's name, odds would be more even. I could not resist the difference, given what the Braves have done in the past couple of months." I had not the heart to tell Jack that I could hardly care less about any of it.

Saturday, October 10

Helen and I are going to the student play at Mills tonight. I remember only too well how exciting Opening Night can be. Performing was such fun, yet nothing in me longs to act again. Daily life involves ample playing of roles.

Helen quite exaggerated my abilities when telling Suzanne of my "thespian" days. By her account, I could have put Maude Adams and Julia Marlowe in the shade by now! Helen and Suzanne were looking at me. I had been asked something and had failed to react. (Does that happen more often these days?). Helen had been telling Suzanne of my performance in "Taming of the Shrew." "Don't you remember, that was the spring when we went around barefoot in imitation of Isadora Duncan."

1903, eleven years ago. Or eleven centuries. If we had not met Clara Morris, might I have tried it? How blunt she was when I asked what chance I had. Her eyes looked straight into mine as she replied somberly, "None," then added, "Coming straight from private life? Only three keys can open the stage door: great wealth, great influence, or great beauty. You are a lovely girl; but for beauty alone to secure an engagement, it must be a remarkable beauty."

"But you knew no one and succeeded without money or influence," I observed.

She laughed. "Without remarkable beauty you mean?" I started to apologize, but she smiled and touched my hand. "Perfectly true, on all counts; but in those days, the public did not hold the stage in such esteem. People supposed actors to be drunkards and actresses immoral. The more charitable thought us buffoons."

"You are beautiful, talented, and well-educated." Pausing and gripping my hand, she added, "You are also comfortable. Think of the unemployed actress who suffers from actual want. Would you take the bread from her mouth to satisfy your vanity?"

I must have looked unconvinced, because she added, "To do so could be justified only by the conviction that you brought to the stage a singular genius."

That all seems so long ago.

<u>**Sunday, 11 October**</u>

Seeing "The Sad Shepherd" at Mills last night revived memories of our time there. During supper, Edward and Dan (Josephine Cole's husband) had to listen to so many silly stories that both marriages would surely end in divorce if we went every week to a student play.

The play, I enjoyed, yet my mind often wandered.

One forgets that Johnson (the satirist) could also set a pastoral scene among shepherds with magic a central theme. Katherine Scudder was lovely as Marian, and she and the girl playing Robin Hood worked well together. And Miss List, playing the witch, had a wonderful time trying to fill us with fear and horror.

During intermission we talked with Amy Andersen. She and two other girls were touring Europe and studying languages when the war broke out. They woke up one morning to find that the old chateau in which they lived was surrounded by soldiers with guns and bayonets. Their flight to Switzerland was an adventurous dodging of guns, and they were horrified at passing bands of wounded soldiers returning from the battle field. Amy came home on a British ship. Just as she began to feel comfortable, a German warship appeared and chased them for much of the day, until at sunset, they entered a bank of fog. The captain changed course for a time, and they never saw the Germans again.

Afterward, we might have gone to the party for the cast, but I begged off.

Late this afternoon Aunt Agnes was looking at my recent work. (I had hidden the painting of Gweniveer behind some older work.) She quite liked the portrait of Mr. Yamashita with the miniature tree, so I told her the story, and that I intended to give the portrait to his grandson. When I said I would do it tomorrow if we did not have to go to Kahn's, she replied that Kahn's is highly likely to be on Tuesday precisely where it is now.

Monday, October 12

Delivered the portrait.

I had put it off from shyness. There is a necessary arrogance to art—How else could one presume that one's vision would amuse or instruct another—but I lose that arrogance the moment I complete a painting. Is there a kinship between the unusual state in which one undertakes a work of art and the unusual state in which one loves?

When the young woman I had met earlier saw that I had brought a gift, she shook her head, then giggled and shrugged and disappeared to fetch the young man.

When they reappeared, the young man bowed and said, "Thank you, but gift not necessary." I replied with a bow, "This belongs with you," and rested the painting against a footstool beside the door and undid the cloth covering it. I looked away and heard a sharp intake of breath, and still, I could not look at them. When I finally did so, the young man was staring at me as if he wished to ask a question; but whatever it was, it remained unasked. He said, somewhat formally, "We are deeply grateful," then added, "You will stay," before he turned and left us.

The young woman and I looked at each other. She giggled, causing me to do the same. For a moment we were two schoolgirls. She pointed at the portrait and nodded her head vigorously in approval. Soon he called to us, and we joined him in the dining room. He gestured to the painting, which she had brought with us, and rested it on a sideboard.

The table was set for tea, and he, rather than she, made the tea in lovely fashion, almost as if it were an art. I wondered if tea had a special meaning in Japanese culture but did not wish to interrupt. We sipped tea in silence. The silence enhanced the mood and felt surprisingly refreshing. They had little of anything in their house, and I wondered whether they are poor. Then again, I have heard that the Japanese are fiendishly disciplined at saving money and living modestly.

Tuesday, October 13

Heney made ten speeches yesterday, said to be a record for a single day! I hope he prevails.

This morning, after touching up a view from Mt. Tam, I stared at the usual blank canvas, uncertain what I might do with it. Then I took up my sketch-book, which quickly found itself creating a scene with young actresses in a green room, their faces, hands, and postures expressing various mixes of anticipatory excitement, pride, chilling fear, and other emotions.

Wednesday, October 14

I have not "fallen off the roof," as we used to say at Mills. Should have come the 9th or 10th. With each day, I feel more certain that I am to reap what I have sowed. Still, I maintain some hope that it is merely my conscience giving me a vivid warning.

Thursday, October 15

All last night, ominous dreams seethed in me like a boiling pot. This morning I lack the energy even to think coherently. I have wished a thousand times already that I could discuss this with someone, but I must keep my own counsel. I have wit enough to know at least that.

Certain of my friends would advise me to "do something" immediately. One dear friend would remind me of the firmness with which I gave *her* that advice, horrible though it seemed at the time. She would point out how right it was—now that she is happily married and has three lovely children.

Despite uncertainty about what to do, I feel a pervasive contentment spreading throughout my body—like a fever, but *sans* fear or confusion. I have never felt its like. Nor, I think, is this usual. I have seen several friends through their first, and although they manifested pride in their condition and expressed fond hopes for the future, they also complained constantly about how miserable they felt.

This I know: I could no more end this than a selfish child could give her last chocolate to a dog. When a delphinium has taken root, it is determined to flower and reproduce. In late spring, if snails damage the main stalk, another grows; if it flowers and is pruned, a new spike of color will surge upward in its place before the fall, determined to go to seed. (Are we so different?)

Dined with Elizabeth and Tub. Much discussion of the business interests abandoning Captain Fredericks for Curtin as their best hope against Governor Johnson. Tub admitted their desperation but failed to share my delight.

Dean and Ellen Allen were also at table. Her automobile crushed a five-year-old boy Wednesday night on Tenth Street. She was said to be quite distressed and to have carried the boy to Dr. Parrish's office in her car. She insists the boy ran into the side of her machine and denies that he was injured as seriously as the newspapers claimed. She seems chastened but hardly distressed. I resisted pointing out that the foolishness of children should be no great surprise to automobile drivers, who might drive more cautiously, rather than advance children's foolishness as an excuse. Perhaps my face gave me away, as she avoided looking at me.

Friday, October 16

I am finding it difficult to sustain interest in what is going on around me. Headlines scream that the allies are in desperate straits, and that Arizona's use of the militia may force the U.S. into war with Mexico—and they might as well be so many religious tracts in Persian.

This morning I wandered through the house, picking up various objects and contemplating the memories that flowed from each. Their reassuring familiarity tinted with sadness at Father's absence. The scent of his pipe rack and pipes, the portrait with General King, his old house slippers on the floor near his desk. I opened a drawer of his desk and found his revolver and felt both an instinctive fear of the thing and an intense curiosity about his soldiering days and the man he was then.

I picked up the telephone, and held the mouthpiece against my cheek and lips, moving it back and forth absent-mindedly as a child might do in play. Feeling its hard, cold surface against my skin, I silently named those to whom I could place no call: Father, Mother, the Admiral, Richard. Lincoln. I wished to hear a warm, reassuring voice, but there was no one I could call. No one could kiss this ache away and make me well.

I moved the mouthpiece away and stared blankly at it, feeling Father's death more completely than ever before. Whether, because I now have no "parent" to whom I could defer, or because I may know all too soon how it is to be a parent, I felt truly grown—and wholly alone.

Everyone gathered at Elizabeth's. I did not stay long as I was still feeling quite distant from it all. A German submarine has torpedoed a huge British ship. Something like 500 dead. While I contemplate new life.

Saturday, October 17

The boy Ellen Allen ran down has died. He was the third child crushed to death by a reckless automobile driver in Oakland just this week! Meanwhile the state has just announced that towns cannot pass ordinances setting allowable speeds lower than whatever is in the 1913 state law. All those "Automobiles and Motorcycles - Slow Down to Ten Miles an Hour" signs are bootless, at least where state law allows higher speeds. The attorney-general says drivers may ignore them.

With children dying in the street, and senseless prize-fighting deaths, we seem to value life very little now. Has the carnage in Europe affected us—or are we so intent on our amusements that we are as unconcerned about harm to others as a herd of buffalo? (Is it that *I* am growing more sensitive to such things? Certainly, I am feeling keenly life's fragility.

Sunday, October 18

Tub complained that the city is ignoring the attorney-general's ruling on speeds, and the flying squad is still arresting people for driving 20 miles an hour in a residential district. (Well done!)

Charles says the disparity has police courts all in a muddle. Judge Smith fined several speeders yesterday, but Judge Hennessey said he would follow the state law, not the ordinance. Politicians on all sides are making a game of this—what of the victims?

Monday, October 19

Saw "The Wages of Sin" at the Broadway with Helen and Edward. We guyed Edward about deigning to accompany us rather than going to the Wheelmen's Club to watch the fight. (They had no idea with what feelings I watched the picture!) They are both delighted by Helen's pregnancy, although it is beginning to limit her.

When Helen confides in me her hopes and fears, I listen without confiding my own hopes and fears. If I am correct, as each new day suggests, and if we are not cut by all and sundry because of the obvious, the children may crawl about the floor together, play baseball or have tea parties with their dolls, and be lifelong friends, like their mothers.

Thursday, October 22

Odd how fashions in names change. The newspaper's "Twenty Years Ago Today" column listed the officers from some 1894 organization, and the president and vice president were both named Mabel, and the secretary was named Maybelle. I can't think of anyone in our generation who has named her daughter Mabel.

Beatrice McCall says Judge Frick has filed his final brief for the appeals court on behalf of Hazel Lux. Poor Hazel!

Friday, October 23

Intended to go to Governor Johnson's rally at Dreamland Rink but lacked the energy. After a brief visit with friends, I am retiring early to enjoy some solitude before slipping beneath the bedsheets.

Bret said the stabbing Wednesday was over a girl, which is no surprise; but the girl had passed away in China last month while visiting her family. The Chinese say her spirit found its way back to Oakland, visited her lover but refused his advances, and made friends with another Chinaman. As the lover was sleeping, he apparently jumped up and knifed the other man to death. Love does make one do surprising things!

I asked Ah Fong whether opium truly makes men have such dreams. He smiled and shook his head (in wonder at his countryman's conduct or at my question?) and said he didn't think so. He added that he knew nothing of such things, and we both smiled at his white lie.

Saturday, October 24

Edward said Governor Johnson drew a great crowd. He seems certain to win. As for Senator, the *Enquirer* insists Mr. Heney is way ahead—but Knowland and Mr. Phelan each say that the race is between the two of them.

Sunday, October 25

Elizabeth said that they are starting up the "dansants" at the Oakland Hotel next month. I cannot hear of "dansants" without seeing Father guying her about serving liquor while trying to close saloons for workingmen. How long ago that seems. How much I miss him!

Monday, October 26

Despite my fears, the world feels far richer than it did just months ago. This afternoon as I awakened from a nap, my returning spirit seemed to hover just outside my body, regarding the motionless form on the sofa with interest, and no real connection to the body—or its problems.

All at once, I could see the full panoply of possible courses. At one extreme, I might rid myself of this complication. Women do. I have realized that I am not one of them. I have come to understand, somewhat to my surprise, that despite being the most rational course, I could not stop this life from becoming. At the other, I could go on about my life, here on Tenth Avenue, letting people say and feel what they will. I do not think I am that woman either, though I should admire her greatly. Fortunately, I have other options. (I doubt they include marriage, for the obvious reasons.)

I saw clearly that it would be entirely possible for me to leave Oakland and live elsewhere, painting and living a very modern life, independent of common (Aunt Emily's and Elizabeth's certainly) notions of family. I might attend lectures and join in heated discussions of art and ideas in coffeehouses. There are such women. They are not considered "respectable," but they survive and even flourish—and so should I! My financial circumstances permit me to do so (Thanks to you Father!), and if I might eventually be required to take on paying work of some sort, I do not fear that possibility.

I should now devote what energy I have to arranging as gracefully and profitably as possible to sell this house and live elsewhere.

Tuesday, October 27

UNCLE ARRAIGNED ON GIRL'S CHARGE

Antone Lopez, charged with a statutory crime in connection with his 15-year-old niece Cara Dutra, was arranged in Superior Judge Ogden's court this morning and pleaded not guilty. The case was set for November 5 for trial.

The girl complained to District Attorney W.H.L. Hynes that she had been mistreated by her uncle, being afraid to resist his advances. Lopez is a wealthy rancher of Niles. He is alleged to have taken the girl from her home in the Azores Islands upon the promise to her mother to care for her.

How simple the newspaper report makes it sound. Sandwiched between "Vienna, A City of Lost Hope" and "Commerce Chamber Will Consolidate."

Father would howl at the misspelling of "arraigned" as "arranged," which might be apt if the names were Thomas Fairchild and Susan West: "Fairchild is a wealthy banker and business leader in Oakland, where his bank holds mortgages on Mr. Hynes's and Judge Ogden's homes, and where he has contributed to the campaign of every judge on the bench. His wife Emily and Mrs. Ogden serve on charitable boards together and play bridge Wednesday afternoons. Fairchild is alleged to have taken the girl upon the promise to care for her."

The newspaper says nothing of the girl's tears and embarrassment; her fears of the reprisals her uncle threatened if she told anyone; or society's snide references to "that West baggage;" nor the likelihood that the district attorney might disbelieve such a charge because of her uncle's stature and reputation in the community; or that an entire family might be destroyed. No report of the interesting questions the girl will face from the uncle's sharp attorney.

Wednesday, October 28

The Oakland Political Protective Club has unanimously endorsed Governor Johnson and Mr. Heney. (I doubt that item would have caught my attention a few months ago.) I did not know that Oakland had a club for the protection of negroes' civil and political rights. How much protection do they need in California? Yet I feel reassured that such a group exists.

What once passed without my notice now irritates me beyond words. Mr. Archer berating his son the other day: "Will you never learn to eat pie like a white man?" The short story in *Munsey's* about the comical inability of some southern negroes to comprehend the War of Nations, with sentences such as, "Colonel Gaitskill knew the big nigger was not engaged in thought but had merely sunk into that idea-less inertia which only animals, negroes, and very small children can achieve."

Once I should have thought little of such a story. I might have been mildly annoyed by the use of vulgarities, such as "nigger"; but unless real hatred was expressed, I should hardly have noticed. Now I cannot read or hear such things without thinking of Lincoln reading or hearing such things—and what of Lucius and other innocents?

Friday, October 30

Must abandon Oakland. Quietly sell the house and disappear. But I cannot sell the house without consulting Aunt Agnes. I shall need to give some explanation, even if it bears little relationship to the truth.

Meanwhile, the young women we once were are preparing to dance gaily about the ivory ball room of the Hotel Oakland at the opening ball of the Winter Assembly. Befrocked in all the colors of the rainbow, they will cavort beneath pumpkins and black cats—while I sit here worrying like a witch who has run out of spells.

<u>Saturday, October 31</u>

1. ~~End condition?~~
2. ~~Marry?~~

Would he? Could we? I could bear the world's scorn, but not for a child. What Gweniveer said about trouble… Such couples pay a huge price. (Per *Following the Color Line*). Marry someone else? Not R, J? Does he still want to marry me? Would he accept me as I am, could I bear it? B? Too much a friend, almost a brother.

3. Go away? Alaska? New Mexico? Boston? Not Chicago! Live a different life?
4. Adoption? Would probably be best for all… but could I?
5. ~~Eternal rest in the Bay~~? Romantic, I suppose; but not for me.

NOVEMBER

Sunday, November 1

Mrs. Easterbrook stopped for tea with Aunt Agnes. She says Germany is on the verge of a huge revolution that will throw the Kaiser out and create a republic patterned after our own. She and her husband have spent a great deal of time there. They left Germany when the war broke out, then lingered in Norway and came home on a neutral steamer that sailed by way of Newfoundland to avoid the mine zones.

German officers are throwing away their swords. Apparently, swords are useless in modern warfare—and even dangerous. When a charge is sounded, and officers spring forward, their flashing swords identify them as officers to enemy marksmen. Bret says our army officers discarded their swords long ago, except as dress parade ornaments, but German officers held onto them as badges of rank.

I alternate between fatigue and buoyancy, almost joy. Yesterday, Aunt Agnes called me "glowing." Still, many mornings I feel ill, and my breasts are tender.

Monday, November 2

I have been staring for several minutes at one of the few trees that changes color here and wondering whether the soldiers in Europe notice the flaming leaves. In the current *Mirror*, George Reedy muses on "the beauty of the season and the stupid violence of the war," in discussing the odd letter he publishes in the same issue from an American-born woman living in Munich. She wants Germany to win, of course; but also writes:

> I'm for this war, anyway—strong! — not from the mere political point of view, however important that aspect may be to the nations involved. The war was necessary; spiritually necessary. The soul of the human race has taken on fat and grown sleepy. Europe has become one vast bourgeoisie: proletariat, peasantry, middle class, aristocracy alike. A huge bourgeoisie: content and slothful. No matter what the catastrophe; death, destruction, hunger, pillage—*the war is necessary.*
>
> The awakening will pay for all. And I hope and pray (for this same reason) that America may be drawn into it!
>
> All of which sounds very absurd to you, no doubt, but the world needs a thorough house-cleaning!

Weeks ago, Jack expressed similarly beastly thoughts, and Bret told him to volunteer. I tried then to understand Jack's thinking. Now I feel no such patience.

Tuesday, November 3

General Election today. Went out early to be one of the first to vote and found a long line. Many women, even whole families. Voters talked most about the Prohibition amendment. Huge ballots and small voting booths. A man in front of me took 20 minutes!

The streets are full of wagons bearing placards urging people to vote against the water commission law because "the farmers" oppose it—as if California farmers who depend on irrigation would take such a position. Obviously, the water trust hired the wagons to fool people.

This is a particularly important election, and the choice is clear. Governor Johnson has accomplished a great deal of progressive legislation in a short time and helped gain back control of California from the railroad. Curtin has opposed everything. Can anyone believe the claim by Curtin and Fredericks that *they* kicked out the railroad when the railroad's newspapers constantly attack the Governor? One could do worse than a flat rule of "See whom the trusts support—and vote the contrary!"

I fear for the Senate race. If only the Progressives could have stood united behind Mr. Heney or Mr. Phelan.

Clair Starr was out driving her own car and carrying women voters to the voting booths, with signs all over the car for George Gross and M.J. Kelly. I almost wished I possessed a car to do the same.

Wednesday, November 4

Tea with Adeline Gardiner. The baby boy who magically appeared on her doorstep in February was crawling about the floor, drooling, and laughing. I *had* imagined that I might go away on an extended vacation, and then deliver the infant to some bereaved woman, such as Adeline, longing to nurture a child. The child would find a loving home and be spared the ugly brand of illegitimacy. Might not that be the best for all? If one could only be certain!

Phelan has won election to the Senate! Prize-fighting is banned and the Red Light Abatement law passed.

Beyond California, Progressives fared poorly. Women's suffrage was defeated in North and South Dakota and Ohio, and may just squeak through in Nebraska, where I should have thought it would do well. Montana and Nevada have probably adopted it.

There seems no end to the ways Evelyn Nesbit Thaw will exploit her notoriety: The Broadway is to show a new motion picture in which she appears with her little boy. The advertising claims that the New York critics admired it greatly, which I doubt. Even Elizabeth is not interested. (I must not be so hard on Elizabeth.)

Thursday, November 5

How can a helpless creature control the mind and heart so wholly? I suppose some ancient pattern is quilted on the soul. As with plants, there is in us some instinct, to which all else kneels, to bring forth the seed growing within. I have no choice. Curiously, I want none.

The result of Nebraska's suffrage vote will not be known for days. Pauline said we should take heart from adding Nevada and Montana, rather than despairing over failure elsewhere. One-fourth of the states are now for equal suffrage! Gaining suffrage by amending the federal constitution seems the more promising course.

Four western states have gone dry. Sarah said her mother and the dry leaders are determined to put the question to California voters again in 1916. Ann laughed and said they had better improve their arithmetic, as Amendment 47 appears to have passed, forbidding further prohibition elections here for eight years. Sarah said that it will be declared unconstitutional.

Friday, November 6

This evening felt almost like "old times." Robbie took some guying over his mother's purchase of a monogram panel for her motor car. Elizabeth said a friend in New York ordered a monogram with garnets and rhinestones encrusted in a gold setting. (How Father would mock yet another foolish imitation of European aristocrats.)

Jack said the Anti-Boxing Amendment will be challenged in court. When Julia spoke up for it, Jack nodded gravely and said, "We do need to protect people from such things. And let us prohibit motion pictures, too. Seven 'movie' actresses were hurt this week when a four-horse stage careened out of control after a sensational run, in front of the camera. And a university rugby player cut his foot and died from infection. Best put rugby on the ballot as well."

"And women's hats, if feathers and plumes get longer again," added Robbie. "Always looking to poke a man's eyes in the street-car." Elizabeth said nothing but looked annoyed.

Tub leaves tomorrow morning for Los Angeles. He was grinning like a boy about the desert automobile race to Phoenix and speaking of Barney Oldfield and Louis Chevrolet like a ten-year-old awed by Frank Chance and Honus Wagner.

Suzanne and I are going out to the Edmonds farm in the morning! Jack asked if I wanted to go with him to the exposition grounds on Sunday to see Lincoln Beachey do his thousandth "loop-the-loop", then stage a fifteen-minute air battle and blow up a "battleship." I told him we will not return until late Sunday afternoon. Jack could not see the attraction in visiting the farm, which made me anticipate it with greater delight.

Saturday, November 7

Pleasant drive on a lovely afternoon, and a marvelous sunset, which I tried to capture with paints while Suzanne photographed two horses and their long shadows. She laughed when I reminded her that she claims not to care for the "art" in photography. "I feel no need to burden what I do with such a high-fallutin' label. Jenny and I are merely a creature that feeds through the eyes. And we delight in a varied menu." After we got ourselves back through the stile in fading light, our skirts and tools in hand, Suzanne asked, "Are we really any different from children playing in a mud-puddle? Adults have been trained what to say and how to see. Painting carries you back to a time when your curiosity was unimpeded by rules, as photography does so for me."

Supped with Mr. and Mrs. Edmonds, Antonio, and the children (two granddaughters and their youngest son, Frederick). I ate too much but enjoyed a warmth I have missed without knowing it. There was much good-hearted teasing and laughter about simple family matters. Mr. Edmonds and his wife call each other "Ma" and "Pa," with self-deprecating humor. (He went to university and has a far wider perspective than farming might provide.)

The children took as much a part in the conversation as anyone, and I found myself paying closer attention to them than was usual. The little girls are already quite distinct: both bright, and as cute as two buttons; Elinora peppered us with questions about Suzanne's camera and the city, her eyes as big as saucers, while Miriam was kittenish and playful, and wished no one (particularly the men) to lose sight of her for a moment.

As we mounted the stairs to our rooms, Suzanne said, "Just think, we could be starting home through the streets of Oakland from 'Disraeli' right about now."

There is a special scent to a farmhouse where life has been lived simply and well. A scent brewed from sun-baked wood, dust, animal smells, Bon Ami, and the sweet clematis vines climbing the exterior walls.

As I write, I hear only occasional neighs, the loud hoot of an owl, and the wind through the trees. Not that home is noisy, but the farm *feels* truly silent. Beyond two hired men sleeping in a shack, there *are* no other neighbors.

As I stood on the well-worn rug, turning down the very old quilts on the narrow old rough-hewn bed in which I will sleep, I felt a sudden wish for just such a home and just such a family.

Have I misspent my life?

<u>Sunday, November 8</u>

Dawn brings a symphony of bird calls and an early morning walk.

Breakfast conversation concerned tasks—rather than movies and gossip and the news.

Mr. Edmonds seems almost fatherly toward Antonio. When I said something to that effect, he smiled, a little embarrassed, and said that with American boys so unwilling to work on farms these days, he was lucky to have Antonio and would be sorry to lose him.

"Is he leaving?" I asked.

"Not today, or tomorrow, or next week, but he is not a farmer. He has done well at making himself a farmer, but even I can see it would be a right shame if that's all he ever does."

"You sound as if farming were unworthy work, yet you've spent your whole life at it!"

"Well, not yet I haven't," he grinned. When I looked confused, he added, "I ain't lived it all yet," and acknowledged my laughter with a nod, then continued, "Yes, I have indeed made a life of farming, and Antonio would not be miserable if he continued so. The older I grow, the more it seems that being happy or unhappy depends little on what's going on outside, but comes from inside. Still, deep down, this life wouldn't suit him."

I asked what would fit Antonio.

"You know he was a teacher."

I nodded.

"I never found near as much in Plato, Gibbons, or Wordsworth as in seeds sprouting, or a foal birthing on a foggy morning. But I think Antonio misses that side of things."

Feeling lazy after the meal, I sat contentedly drinking coffee and listened to "Pa" discuss how farmers would be affected by the parcel service's new policy to help them distribute agricultural products to city folk. After a while he downed the last of his coffee, winked, and said that while some folks might be on holiday, others had work to do.

My only "work" was to take a stroll through paradise, sketching what caught my eye.

Suzanne made photographic portraits of everyone, and then photographed Antonio rubbing down a horse and repairing a fence. She watched his work on the fence as if his hands were dancers and she a ballet critic. Then she walked slowly along the fence, stopping occasionally, and studying it from different angles. Finally, she retrieved her camera, inserted a plate, and returned to a spot where she set up "Jenny," then asked Antonio to join her, showing him where to put his hands. She seemed to be making a plate in which only his hands and the pattern of the fence would be seen. I moved closer, curious about what had intrigued her.

Antonio bore it as placidly as the horse grazing nearby. "Be glad it's not thirty years ago, when it took twenty minutes to expose a plate," Suzanne said with a grin. Antonio nodded. "Yes, this very hard for me, to have little rest. And terrible, instead cows, I see pretty ladies."

After lunch I talked alone with Mrs. Edmonds. I had met her only once before, in Oakland. A musical evening. Despite her shyness, she sang rather well.

She asked about my painting, saying it must be cumbersome to carry easel and paints into the countryside. I learned the names and locations of her children, their professions (or their husbands'), the total number of grandchildren, Elinora's and Miriam's ages (5 and 4), and much else. Speaking of children and grandchildren brought out a smile, like the morning sun burning off the mist. I guessed that life was good with her. Curiously, she replied when asked, "God has been kind to us, kinder than we deserved, then added, "You never have married." I nodded. "Have you never wanted children?" she asked, tentatively.

"Not really, although I enjoy them," I replied, hoping to sound as casual as I might have months ago. I then mumbled something about never knowing what the future might bring. My evasiveness made me uncomfortable. I suddenly wished I could tell her the truth, and perhaps solicit her advice. What would she say? I considered her ready warmth and acceptance of Antonio, but also her regular churchgoing and protectiveness toward her grandchildren.

"I wish I could paint what I see in your eyes when you speak of your grandchildren," I said. This, at least, was true.

There ensued a silence. We had climbed to a plateau of intimacy (despite the lie) and were content to rest, each uncertain whether to continue our ascent or enjoy the view in silence before returning to the world below.

Late afternoon, I watched Suzanne make another photograph of Antonio, this time kneeling in a row of broccoli. He endured it with good grace, laughing. I had never seen him in conversation with any of our set. Some would not enjoy him as Suzanne seems to. Jack mocks his accent and complains that Sicilians and Greeks are taking jobs away while Elizabeth ignores him. Antonio must have said something funny for Suzanne was laughing so hard that her body shook, and her head bobbed.

Mrs. Edmonds was watching her grandchildren at play and contemplating the distant peaks. When I remarked that if not for us, she might have watched the peaks change color without interruption, she laughed and said that she'd hardly have interrupted her work, and she was grateful for the respite we provided.

I told her how much we enjoyed the farm and asked how she felt about living there.

She nodded at "Pa" Edmonds, who was re-attaching a plow handle, and said, "This is what he wanted. I wanted him. And them too, though I didn't know that then," with a nod toward her grandchildren. She smiled, then waved her hand at the scene before us. "*This* was not what I had dreamed of. There was no 'back-to-the-farm' movement just yet. Nor would I have been likely to join one." She laughed. "But this life has grown comfortable as an old coat."

She stared hard at me and added, "Life here has not always been easy. So isolated, I felt lonely at first. The telephone, and now the motor-car, have made it easier, but for many years we had to work everything out for ourselves. If you didn't know how to make or mend something, you found a way. If you forgot to buy something on Saturday, you did without it for the week. There was no going round to the nickelodeon when your spirits flagged. Well, there was no nickelodeon yet anyway, but the theater. Or a ball. No dances, no whist. No afternoon teas. If I wanted conversation when Pa was outside working, or in a mood, I learned to imagine the hogs were as witty as Mr. Twain, and the cows as creative as Mrs. Atherton."

Mrs. Edmonds's father was a San Francisco merchant. A member of the Vigilance Committee. She had been raised to marry well and had lived a cloistered girlhood with her quilt-making, dancing lessons, and piano. Her father's secret love was the violin, and evenings were often given over to playing music. Recalling those evenings, she glowed.

When I asked how she met Mr. Edmonds, she said that he had been at university with her brother. "You might not think it now, but he was quite the hero. Even before I met him my brother spoke of him with awe. Stories of John surviving some foolish exploit on a horse or leading them in some mischief. He once won a bet with other students by shooting out the spots from the five of clubs with his revolver, then using the sixth bullet to drive in the tack they had used to hang it on the wall! He could hunt like an Indian and swim like a fish and became quite the skillful fencer as well. And believe it or not, he was always in plays. They didn't have so much of a student theater then as they have now, but he was its Joseph Jefferson."

Sitting there, the farm spread out before us like an old oil painting on a museum wall, I did not wonder why such a man had chosen to withdraw to such a place. But now I do wonder if there was something she did not tell me, something that she might have wished that she could confide, as I wished to confide in her.

On the drive home, I guyed Suzanne about setting her cap for Antonio. After a quick laugh, she said with unwonted seriousness that although she had no such interest in him, she found him interesting. “I’ve not forgotten that remarkable story about the bird-calls, and I knew that *you* talked with him. Otherwise, all I knew of him was Jack’s imitation of his accent.”

“You could work on his accent with him,” I teased.

“No,” she said thoughtfully, with neither a lover’s embarrassment nor the abruptness designed to cover such embarrassment. “But one could do worse, and most women do.”

I asked what she meant.

“He is manly, yet gentle. He listens well, and when he speaks, one cannot doubt that he means what he says. He does not say what is “smart,” or what he supposes one wants to hear. He says what is in his heart. I have the impression that he has read a lot. He is not frivolous, yet he can be playful and amusing. And his ability to maintain a childlike sense of wonder rivals only yours,” she finished, with a laugh.

I felt as pleased as when I was a girl, and two of my dear friends finally met and immediately liked one another, and I realized how much I liked Antonio even though I had not thought of him as a friend, so much as a… A pleasant appurtenance to the garden?

We were to have gone to the Oakland to see Mary Pickford, that is if we had returned in time; but neither of us much cared for the idea. When I telephoned, Elizabeth laughed, and remarked that having spent the weekend at a quiet farm we’d likely not care to see a picture about another.

Monday, November 9

Poem by Webster Ford about the German woman returned to mind several times recently, until finally, I searched out the page onto which I had pasted it.

How differently it reads now. I suppose that in her place I could do as she did—if I were poor and penniless. It would be selfish to suppose that struggling through a difficult life with the mother would be better for a child than to be raised comfortably by a stranger who could provide books, clothes, and toys. And Elsa's son *was* with his father. If I were to tell Lincoln, and he chose to raise the child, then instead of thrusting the child upward to be raised in the bosom of a marriage and family, I should be pushing the child downward, to be raised by a class of people who are looked down upon, universally, even by some of their own.

Went to hear Mrs. Herbert Clark Hoover of the American relief commission. Everyone is upset to learn of the Belgian suffering, even people who rarely notice anything much beyond their noses (Elizabeth). In addition to the huge benefit ball Saturday night, the women at the University are abandoning teas and using the time to make clothes for Belgian babies. (There are women and children in far worse straits than I.)

Under the headline "Negress Proves Alameda Puzzle," the newspaper reports that "Mrs. Annie Benson, a negress, who has a half dozen times been arrested on complaint of residents of this city that she was acting in a queer way, was last night again taken into custody, only to be released upon her showing that she is not insane. The police are puzzled as to the disposition of the woman's case. "She wanders apparently without aim about the city but has never offered to molest person or property." Well, I "wander apparently without aim about the city," without offering to molest anyone, and no one is bothering to inquire if I'm in my right mind!

<u>**Tuesday, November 10**</u>

Some men brought the sundial today. (At last!)

I had just finished a surprising sketch. Surprising to Aunt Agnes, certainly—but also to me, as I have not let my thoughts linger on my time in Chicago. Without conscious thought, I started drawing Curly at the piano. When I finished, I was smiling, recalling how Curly played the piano with the same reverence Antonio showed for the garden. (How I miss Lincoln. Am I making yet another mistake?) Aunt Agnes quite liked the sketch, and when she marveled at my "fertile imagination," I just nodded and smiled.

After Aunt left me, I sat and looked at Curly and thought of Lincoln, and how rare and precious our sudden closeness was. I have regarded Chicago as a comet flashing through my life. Could we ever become two moons revolving around a child? Despite Gweniveer's grim warnings against attempting any such alliance this side of Paris? How quickly and clearly and fruitfully our minds and hearts (and more) had met. Ours was a union that needed no reason, no history, no logic. Do I owe it to all of us to reach out? Could not we lead a fruitful life, full of art and talk and laughter—somewhere! If I knew the telephone number, I should have called right then, I believe. Let him choose our course. Except that he would not view it as a choice. He would do as he thought he should, whatever he truly felt.

Wednesday, November 11

Pen poised in mid-air, I noticed yesterday evening's paper opened to Kahn's full-page advertizement, including numerous baby items: infants' crocheted bootees, dainty patterns, special at 19 c; infants' dresses of fine nainsook, trimmed with lace or embroidery, special at 43 c; and hand-embroidered cashmere shawls and crib blankets. Yesterday, my eyes brushed past those items to read of the Missouri Suffrage League's confidence regarding Amendment 13, but I may soon be reading such lists closely. It is as if I had been told that soon I shall be reading the news from some Japanese fishing village instead of from Oakland. Not to mention that the child will look quite unlike the light-haired infant sketched wide-eyed and smiling beside the booties, bibs, and bonnets.

I find I feel a touch of resentment, but at whom? My life has not been all it might be, but it has been wholly my own.

Thursday, November 12

Awakened long before dawn. The full moon was falling toward its rest, swelling as it approached the horizon, as if with fatigue. The mild morning drew me out into the darkness, without intention or destination. I walked to Trestle Glen and sat among the oak and laurel, sheltered from the world. This had been a favorite place of my parents, even before my birth.

The oaks were like tall dancers, caught in mid-pirouette, reaching toward the darkness above. Their mere presence reassured me, as the silhouettes of my parents standing in the doorway once comforted me in my crib. While Lizzie and I held absorbing conversations with our dolls, before and after giving in to heavy lids, my parents knew all and had everything in hand.

I felt secure in a way I have not of late, sitting among the towering trees, their branches touching above my head. These giants had watched each other grow for decades. Long before they grew tall enough to touch, did they sing to each other in the night? Did they long to reach out to another as they do now? Did they mourn their cousins, felled to permit construction of the trestle, then rejoice when the trestle itself was torn down? Did they gossip about the strange doings of the small, two-legged creatures who wandered among them? Were their waving limbs and rustling leaves a language, rather than the vagaries of the winds? I felt they would understand me if I spoke to them. Then laughed aloud at my foolishness.

Throughout all our grief and laughter, these trees have continued to grow. Whatever I do now, they will continue. If the child wanders here a decade from now, perhaps with a dog, or two decades from now, perhaps with a lover, or three decades from now, perhaps with their own child, these trees will be looking down at them just as reassuringly.

I began saying aloud what was in my head. I spoke of Father. Their silence gave me leave to continue. I spoke of the new life growing inside me. I told them that I loved them. That Mother and Father had loved them. That the child would love them—and they him, for he would be as gentle and creative as his parents. I told them that they were beautiful and good. I told them that no one else would listen so patiently to such nonsense at such an hour. Had anyone chanced to pass, I might have been locked up in an asylum.

This morning, Aunt found me in the studio and saw the portrait of Gweniveer. She studied the painting for a while, then said, "It's very effective, even moving," and looked pointedly at me. She asked nothing about how I came to paint such a scene. She certainly could not have guessed, and likely would refuse to believe it, if told. My own attitude toward the portrait might have revealed to someone who knows me so intimately that something important lay unspoken.

Spent the evening at a meeting of the Women's Protective Bureau. We have determined to ask Governor Johnson to pardon Hazel Lux. That would be the fastest way to free her. He may be sympathetic, but if he declines, we will help her seek parole or a new trial.

The jury could not agree in the case of the rancher from Niles and his niece. Although he had admitted to several men that he was her child's father, two jurors voted not to convict. His lawyer claims the niece's uncorroborated testimony could not be allowed because if there was any crime, she herself would be an accomplice. The law is utterly baffling!

So too is Judge Ogden baffling. That Randolph man was sentenced to mere probation after conviction of statutory rape! He claimed that Loomis, who pled guilty, had sent the girl to his room while he slept. The 'paper says that in giving both men probation,

Judge Ogden said to Randolph, "A man is a man, and he would be a pretty strong man if he could escape the effects of such temptations as you were subjected to." Can Judge Ogden believe that the young girl merely appeared, without any indication by Mr. Randolph that he sought company?

The wealthy rancher may have his way with his young niece because his own misconduct makes her a criminal who cannot testify against him; and Randolph may have a young girl sent to his room, without real consequences, if he testifies that he was asleep when she entered. If this be justice, we may see the Mad Hatter appointed Chief Justice of the Supreme Court. (Father, you must be turning in your grave!)

Friday, November 13

Made a decision. More precisely, I recognized tonight a decision that instinct had made for me immediately.

Jack and Elizabeth were going on and on about saddle horses. Jack said thoroughbreds were too nervous and excitable, had no stamina, and lacked the trotting action to become a good harness-horse. Elizabeth answered the stamina charge by pointing out that thoroughbreds ran steeplechases, were marvelous hunters, and served all the cavalry of Europe in wars. I could not feign interest and quietly contemplated my private concerns.

To prove her point, Elizabeth looked out a back number of *Century* in which some authority compared thoroughbreds and trotters. After reading aloud a passage, she tossed the magazine on the table, and I picked it up.

"You must at least admit that the thoroughbred's shoulder is both more pleasing and more useful than that of other horses," Elizabeth went on. "You never see such a shoulder on a horse that isn't thoroughbred, or nearly so; but on a thoroughbred you see it even on some old screw pulling a grocer's wagon."

I glanced idly through an article on fraternities in women's colleges, reading with amusement that a would-be chapter of one group was nearly rejected because the photograph they submitted showed that they did their hair unfashionably. Then I noticed an article headed, "Is the Negro Having a Fair Chance?" by Booker T. Washington.

As Jack and Elizabeth nattered on, I read of lynching-bees and convict labor. While Elizabeth waxed eloquent about blood-lines, I wondered what she would say of the blood-line of this unexpected niece or nephew. As they debated the charge that trotters do not breed true, I wondered what a eugenicist would say of people who mix colors beyond the confines of a canvas. Jack said that although a thoroughbred must be the progeny of thoroughbreds, a trotter may become "standard by performance."

Can a "negro" child become "standard by performance?" Mr. Washington's account confirmed that this would be difficult. Although the Northern negro has the same opportunities as we do for education, once educated, he must choose between becoming an agitator or moving to the South. I should have supposed the North more sympathetic, but Mr. Washington writes that they are seldom sure of just what they may or may not do. If one is a stranger in a city, he does not know in what hotel he will be permitted to stay; he is not certain what seat he may occupy in the theater, or whether he will be able to obtain a meal in a restaurant.

Elizabeth said that thoroughbreds and hackneys hold their qualities more intensely and reproduce them more consistently than trotters. I wondered whether my forebears or Lincoln's would most influence the child's appearance. When Jack pointed out that the trotter's inconsistency created a productive variety in types and that they were known for their kind dispositions and intelligence, I recalled hearing people say that mongrels are the most intelligent dogs and felt as if someone had scored one for my side. While Jack and Elizabeth traded names of famous horses, I read: "The constant fear and expectation of rebuff which the colored man experiences in the North is often more humiliating than the frank and impersonal discrimination which he meets in the South. Northern colored youth, educated as they are alongside white youths, taught by the same teachers, and inspired by the same American ideals, are not prepared for the discrimination that meets them when they leave school."

Suddenly I understood what instinct had known: I must not tell Lincoln. If the child's appearance permits, he must not be a "negro" to the world. He must not suffer such cruelty. I could not bear it.

Saturday, November 14

"Starving Belgian Benefit Ball" at Hotel Oakland tonight. I made a donation but do not care to attend.

This morning I felt a strong urge to sketch Lincoln's portrait but shied from the intimate recollections that would accompany attention to his face. I considered instead the bar, but he had painted that so memorably. I had also a sense that depicting what I could recall of that world might undermine my resolve, and I retreated to the garden.

Sunday, November 15

Everything feels so different from moment to moment that I wonder if I am going mad. This morning, restlessly waiting for Aunt, I glanced through the fiction in the August number of *Everybody's Magazine*. In Beatrice Grimshaw's "To the End of the World," a man and a woman, married to others, elope. As everyone cuts them, particularly the woman, they move to some island in the South Pacific, but even there someone shows up on a packet boat who has heard their story. Finally, the woman, recognizing she cannot escape condemnation, flees to a convent to free her lover from their isolation. I shivered, reading the lines that haunt her: "Down the road you've followed there is no returning. / Mary, pity women! But you're late in learning."

In Traver's "The Dollar," a young journalist meets a girl who has been abandoned by the rotter who talked her into eloping with him. The reporter has with him a dollar he received, amidst much laughter, at the end of a poker game. He gives it to her to purchase a night's lodging. The next day he goes to the lodging house, but she is gone. A fellow journalist tells him there's a "floater," and when they go to the morgue, he recognizes the girl from the night before. At that evening's poker game, he is joshed about the dollar, and learns it was lead. The girl, unable to spend it, construed his false gift as fate's last joke on her.

Two women driven to self-destruction for defying social conventions. It seemed as if every story (contrary to the contemporary rot about it being "past sex o'clock") has been designed to remind me of women's vulnerability and men's freedom. I closed the magazine and pushed it away. I suddenly felt as if the walls were pressing in on me, that wherever I turn, a hard lesson awaited. For a moment it was difficult to breathe. I wanted to strike out at someone, or something. How can it be, always and forever, that Douglas is invited to supper on the boat, yet the women will not let their men go home to tea with him and Grace?

Monday, November 16

Cold, dreary morning. A harbinger of winter. Ominous grey skies, violent winds, and some rain.

Sat at the breakfast table for a long time, chilled by more than the weather. The wind rattled the windows and sent a large tree branch crashing to the street, reminding me how little control we have over anything. Retreating to this journal, I read the first few entries. The women being herded like cattle from the District never thought they would end so. To what unforeseen future will my heedless behavior lead me? Only money saves me from the sort of life Hazel Lux led, and money can be lost all too easily.

Aunt joined me, and we exchanged pleasantries as she prepared to go out. She laughed about the rain, which she said had not dissuaded her from her mission one whit. She seemed as cheerful as always, yet I have noticed that her skin seems to have sagged and her eyes dimmed since Father's death. Her life has consisted of good works (appreciated neither by the poor, who often resent her, nor by the well off, to whom she is a living reproach), her family (dwindled now to Aunt Emily, Elizabeth, and me), and her reading. What inspires her to go on?

More urgently, whatever am I to do about this strange creature growing inside me—and about the strange creature that I am becoming? I sift through my options as if they were stale buns at some benefit, reaching no conclusion.

When I finally ventured out for the mail, old Watson passed, his wagon well-covered against the rain. I thought of the dream. How vulnerable we are. How weak and pitiful I feel. I must cease dithering and remove Susan from that house—somehow!

Tuesday, November 17

The sky is a lighter grey today, and my gloominess has lifted too. (Yet like the weather I may turn at any moment without warning!)

Wandered through Father's library, in search of something diverting to read. The room, filled as it is with his books, pipes, and pens, both comforts me and renews my sadness. My fingers found the worn green cover of *The Woman Who Did* before I realized what it was. I sat for nearly two hours in Father's chair, reading it through for a second time, and was glad I did. (I had forgotten how well Grant Allen wrote.)

I shuddered at how society viciously breaks Herminia's daughter's heart. Even before Dolores longs for the upper-middle class life and status her mother sacrificed for principle, I sensed that she would desire the fine things denied her by social isolation and relative poverty and would seek in *things* the self-confidence refused her by the whispers about her parentage.

Not so for this child! I don't care a pin for society's view of *me*, but I tremble at the thought of arming it to hurt a child. We are twenty years further along, but illegitimate birth is still a terrible handicap. Too, if I am honest, while I agree generally with Herminia's philosophy, I am not so advanced as she—as indeed, few were then, and few are now. (Perhaps Suzanne?)

"No woman is truly civilized until she can say… 'Give me what you can of your love while you can, without grudging, but don't think I am so vile and selfish as to desire to monopolize you.' When men and women can say that alike, the world will be civilized." Fine words, but my heart, like some skittish horse, rears up and whinnies in fear, refusing the jump. It wants no man—or all of him.

Wednesday, November 18

Dreamt this morning that I stood looking at the garden with the new sundial.

At first, it was a huge painting at an exhibition, in the pointillist style of Seurat. Figures sat and strolled, a few familiar. Then I was *in* the garden, which was no longer a painting. As I approached the sundial, a small boy, dressed like a cherubim in a medieval painting, brought me the sundial, now small enough to be held in his chubby fingers. As I read the motto, the sundial became a small, glass ball, with figures and a snow-scene inside, like a paperweight.

The entire garden was inside the ball. Father was sitting in an indigo upholstered chair reading his newspaper, wearing the suit in which we buried him. Luther Burbank sat by the old-fashioned rose bushes, which were blue and then green. In a corner stood two men in black coats, the German damaged-dogs man and Dr. Malkin, the fellow who operated on ________. (My hand will not write her name, for that is *her* secret.)

Everything in the ball was just as it was outside the ball. The tiny Kate inside was inspecting the ball, just as I was outside the ball. When I approached Father, it all felt quite natural, until I recalled that he was dead. I wanted to ask him how dying felt, but I feared that reminding him would shatter his illusion that he was alive, and he would disappear, and I did not wish him to look up and see the boy.

The boy had Lincoln's face, though a shade lighter, and his forehead bore the scar that Father had retained from his youth. He was wearing the little cap that Lucius sometimes wears. When the boy smiled, I smiled back, then realized that he was smiling at a dog. He started to throw the glass ball for the dog, and I became frightened. Fortunately, Mrs. Livingston, whose dog it was, called it away. I sensed that the destruction of the ball would destroy us too.

Jack was there, smiling broadly, his clenched teeth holding a cigar, as he pounded a baseball glove, inviting the boy to have a "catch." The boy managed to toss the ball to Jack, and to catch it, even though Jack threw it much too hard. When the boy tried to throw it a second time, it slipped out of his hand and went straight up in the air, and would have fallen to the ground, except that Antonio, nearby, managed to catch it. He stared at the ball, and was about to hand it to someone, when I awakened, damp with perspiration and somewhat confused.

Recalling the dream makes me wonder at the unconscious mind. A child is indeed in control of my life, and where he throws us, we will hopefully land safely, and pick up life anew.

<u>Thursday, November 19</u>

From this morning's post:

November 11, 1914
Dear Kate,

I imagine you will be surprised to hear from me if this reaches you at all.

Say hello for me to Elizabeth and your father, and to your Aunt Agnes, although she never much cared for me. Helen, too.

I will not recite all that has happened since I last saw you. If you are interested, there will be time enough; and if you are not, why strain your eyes reading a lengthy and tedious history? Probably you have married, or left Oakland, or you will toss this letter away in anger.

I worked as a newspaperman on the East Coast, building a reputation and having fun, particularly on my semiannual binges, when I drank everything in sight. Didn't seem to do any harm at first. This is no excuse, but in newspaper work one drinks to be a good fellow, to loosen the tongues of officials, to relieve the pressure after meeting deadlines and avoid thinking too much about some of what one sees. One is both plunged daily into such close contact with strangers' crises and yet curiously removed, solitary, isolated.

Frankly, I became a drunk, the sort of fellow we used to see (and I used to laugh at, much to your annoyance) on certain streets in Oakland, sitting in some darkened saloon with his head on the table or lurching down the street. I don't know just when I lost control of it, but I did.

You know me, I was too stubborn to listen to the judges, social workers, and assorted do-gooders who offered help. I was given plenty of chances, and enjoyed the hospitality of various institutions, usually by judicial invitation; but I was damned if I'd let 'em break me. After a while, everyone gave up and wrote me off as one more walking dead man cadging nickels on street corners. I was glad. I liked being a drunk. No more endless questions and rules. But then I thought, if they think I'm so damned worthless, maybe I ought to show them different.

You will likely not have heard of Andress Floyd and the Self-Master Colony. Mr. Floyd was a big broker, but lost all his money about ten years ago. Many other families went broke too. He and his wife help homeless men, many of whom are drunks. He has a large colonial mansion on fifty acres. From across the road, in a country saloon named McKeen's, it looked forbidding—and very dry.

It may seem odd to have a saloon across from a place where men learn not to drink; but I think Mr. Floyd found it convenient. He knows that a man who's lost his grip on life can't regain it unless he becomes his own master; and if alcohol is part of the problem, he'll run across plenty of saloons to tempt him once he leaves the Colony. He might as well start learning to resist straightaway.

When I ran out of money, I stumbled on over to the back door of the Colony. It was nearly dusk. I could smell coffee brewing and food cooking. In the yard, a bunch of men were washing up at a well. Everything was wonderfully quiet and orderly, even more so than a jail, because the quiet was *inside* the men. Someone pointed to the kitchen steps and told me supper would be ready soon.

I knew Mr. Floyd right away. He was tall, clean-shaven, and neatly dressed in a close-buttoned frock coat and a large fedora. He was friendly but reserved. He studied me carefully, though he asked no intrusive questions.

Mr. Floyd doesn't preach. His idea is, become your own master. He doesn't talk about it, he just lives that way, and his calm self-control soon affects others. Sensing the peace inside him makes you want to emulate it.

My main memory of that first supper is of looking into the inner dining room the way a ragged little boy might watch a moving picture about Christmas. There are three dining rooms, and men get shifted from one to another based on their conduct. I was in the third, which was in the kitchen. I could see into the inner one, with Mr. Floyd at the head of the table and Mrs. Floyd at the foot. This probably sounds foolish. In the old days just a lady and a gentleman and their guests holding polite conversation would have seemed laughably dull. But I had fallen so far that a quiet, cordial atmosphere seemed miraculous. I resolved that I'd soon be eating in the inner dining room.

The cook said, "If you want, you can scrub the kitchen floor." You would think I might have gotten angry, but I just started scrubbing. I'd never done that before, and you can imagine how much work it takes to clean up a kitchen where they cook for forty men, but I was determined. Maybe it was the glimpse of that dining room, or the way the cook's casual "If you want," left the choice to me. Treating me like a man, not a prisoner. At first, I figured to get the scrubbing over quickly, but then I found myself almost enjoying the work, determined to do a bang-up job.

The next morning, the men went to their jobs. I sat around feeling weak, and desperate for a drink. Even after two good meals, I felt sluggish. I stared at McKeen's and figured a drink or two might help. Mr. Floyd came up to me after a while and asked whether I wanted to stay. I didn't tell him that what I wanted above all was to belly up to that bar, but I think he knew. Mostly to be polite, I told him I wanted to stay.

He said I could stay as long as I wanted and could leave whenever I chose. If I stayed, I'd be treated like a self-respecting man, and be expected to work and contribute my share to the life of the place; and I'd get paid a small wage. So long as I behaved, I could stay; but if I didn't, I'd have to leave. "Allowed to stay" and "told to leave" are not phrases you hear in prisons, and I sensed there might be something worth staying for. He told me to rest up, and that he'd assign me a job the next day.

He even said that if I absolutely needed a drink, I could get one from Mrs. Floyd! I nearly fell over at that, but I damned sure found Mrs. Floyd, and got that drink. It helped to know that if I needed a drink desperately, I could get one. But knowing that it was all up to me was powerful medicine. Being trusted, after so very long. And starting to see that if I worked at it, I could grow stronger and might not need that drink so desperately after a while. No one had treated me that way for a long time.

I did go see Mrs. Floyd sometimes. It took weeks before I could get through a whole day without. After much longer, one day I suddenly realized that I could look over at McKeen's and pay it no mind. What a wonderful shock!

Still, it was tough going. I don't know as I'd have stuck it out, except that I had a real good view of dozens of other men fighting the same internal war, and this seemed my last best chance. Men came to the door, got a meal and a kind word, then were sent on their way because there was no room. I didn't want to fall back to sleeping out in the weather.

Leaving still worries me. I'm like an injured wild animal that's been taken care of for a spell by kind people but is not quite ready to return to the wild. You may not credit this, recalling how willful and independent I was, but it's been a long time since I did anything that took any initiative. I don't feel confident yet, but I get closer every day.

I'll leave soon. Mr. Floyd said he'd arrange a quiet, simple job for me. That's all I want for now. Just to be some kind of a clerk and get through the day, and then the next, until I feel more sure of myself. I'm not the man I was when you knew me, Kate. Likely you see that, if you've read this far.

You may be wondering why I'm writing to you. As you read this letter, you are probably sitting in a garden, surrounded by laughing children. Maybe you have forgotten me, but I suspect you were angry at first when you didn't hear. I'm sorry for that. (Don't worry, I am not planning to go out to California to see you. Seeing you would be grand; but I have no illusions that I am still a man you would want to know.)

I needed to write you because I did love you, and I think you loved me, and telling you my story might help me regain control of my life. I dislike admitting to you that I'm a weakling; but that is the truth; and if I want to hold onto what I've gained, and continue to get stronger, I can't blind myself to who I was and what I am.

I hope this letter doesn't trouble you unduly. If ever I do pass through Oakland, I would like to suppose I might stop and have a cup of tea with you and your family.

Yours,
Richard

Friday, November 20

Slept only an hour. Then I lay in the darkness fully awake, my mind trying to puzzle out the right course, sifting through the possibilities as through grains of sand.

Yet even this was better than the nights on which I seemed to sleep, but did not, my dreams vague and ominous. Always I am struggling to accomplish some task: desperately trying to find a certain garment by playing the right card at whist; in a balloon that has taken off inside a building, and to fit through the door, I must memorize a poem; trying to buy a train ticket to New Mexico from a clerk who demands that I first tell him the child's name.

How strange to hear from Richard—now! (A sign?) Richard and I, each older, sadder, if no wiser, and both wounded in our different ways. Could we find in each other a quiet solace as precious in its way as the joy we once shared? He might yet make a fine husband and father. Always he had charm and intelligence. Sorrow and failure may have tempered his manly vigor and taught him patience, humility, and understanding. Perhaps even wisdom.

We are familiar with each other. We could marry, quickly, and give out that we had met at the Exhibition, so that those who wondered about such things (Aunt Emily, Elizabeth, too many others) would assume that we had been intimate while in Chicago.

What if the child is dark?

Saturday, November 21

Ever since my most recent reading of *The Woman Who Did*, I have felt differently about what I write here. How might my thoughts and dreams and actions appear to my child, decades from now? I cannot escape my new awareness regarding what had begun as the private, harmless, scribblings of an old maid.

I remain uncertain of my course. Yesterday, I decided to pose as a widow and teach children in Alaska. Today, I will move to a small town in New Mexico. Tomorrow, I may consider taking prussic acid. My situation chills me; yet I also feel a sudden lightness. Like Richard, I must change my life; and with that change comes a certain freedom from what was. (Settlement worker in Chicago? Painter in Paris?)

Ultimately, I will do what is best for the child. I may fail terribly, and one day I even may be compelled to present this otherwise embarrassing record of my dithering as evidence of my good intentions. (After writing this last, I sat silently with my hands on my stomach, waiting for a response. Let the record show that you offered no opinion that I could perceive.)

Sunday, November 22

Richard's letter lies on my writing table awaiting an answer. I have mentioned it to no one. Twice I have sat down to respond without writing even the salutation. (Helen would be astonished.). My hesitation is not from uncertainty. I shall answer politely, warmly, but sans encouragement. It is not that I respect him less because of his trouble, nor do I feel superior. Quite the reverse: He has lived the life he wanted to live, and if for the moment he has fallen, he will rise again. By contrast, I have hardly lived. I have existed, like a museum piece: "Jilted Girl, America, early 20th Century." If that description is a trifle unfair to me, it does not miss the mark by much.

Nor did Richard's long silence embitter me. I feel nothing of that sort, although sadness steals over my heart like the fog on the bay when I think of what might have been. His letter does not explain why he never wrote. If he feels for me as his letter seems to say that he does, why did he never send for me? I wonder, but I will not ask. It no longer matters. To ask might inspire hope where none should exist.

Monday, November 23

Dreamt I was in a pension in a small village in Germany. There was a fire in the fireplace, and the wind kept nearly blowing it out. The men (Bret, Richard, and others) kept interrupting their conversation to tend the fire which was keeping us warm. Outside, a group of women were gathering. Someone said that one of the women was Emmeline Pankhurst and that another had destroyed a famous painting. Jack was laughing, but the others seemed worried, as if we might be attacked.

I urgently desired to paint a famous waterfall, but my friends warned against walking there alone. I approached the women in the street to inquire about a safe route. They were standing in a grove of five linden trees. (The hotel was named for the trees.) Bret and Richard were playing at tennis nearby, cheerfully insulting each other and laughing. Antonio was watching them from behind a wire fence. Richard handed his racquet to Antonio. When I looked again, he was talking with three women. I was pleased and hoped one of them might become his wife.

The women in the street, though not unfriendly, gave conflicting advice. One said that the town was thoroly safe; another shook her head and advised me to walk only through the well-lit center of town; and a third said the town center was dangerous at night. One of the women wore an aigrette very like one I had seen Elizabeth wear; another wore a silk scarf of Suzanne's; and a third, very stout, wore eye-glasses like those of the settlement house woman.

It was understood that if I went to paint the waterfall, I might be away for a very long time, perhaps forever. I began walking, and when I glanced back, Antonio was playing lawn tennis brilliantly, somewhat to Bret's surprise.

Then I was on a hillside with a fine view of ancient ruins, with columns, and massive stones lying about. I tried to set up my easel, but the ground sloped too steeply, so I sat and watched the full moon rising behind the ruins. I heard soft footsteps behind me. I did not know whose yet felt no fear. I thought it might be Richard. Then I felt gentle hands on my shoulders. His scent was not Richard's scent, yet it was familiar. I turned, and behind me was Antonio.

Then we were in a vast garden with lilies and well-tended rose bushes. I was dressed (if it could be called that) immodestly. Antonio was communicating with the birds. I would have liked to hear what he and the birds were singing to each other, but I did not wish to disturb them. I had given Lucius's mother my clothes. I felt no shame at my state of undress, but I supposed it might be unwise to wander about so in a garden with strangers, and I asked Antonio for his shirt.

The howling wind outside awakened me. Despite the strange dream, I felt oddly cheerful. This was the first time I had dreamt of Richard as a friend rather than a lover; and I did not awaken agitated. I wish him well, but I know now that I want nothing from him.

Wednesday, November 25

I now understand why I could not answer Richard's letter immediately. I needed to be certain my lack of interest was not because of his weakness.

I have grown beyond Richard, as he has undoubtedly grown beyond me. Perhaps I had done so quite some time ago, without realizing it, yet held to my "love" as some sort of amulet, to ward off other . . . connections. I feel no temptation to reach for Richard in my present uncertainty. I must go forward now, not back — if I can only discover what on Earth that means!

Dear Richard,

I was pleased to hear from you, sad to hear of your difficulties, and glad that you are on the path toward transcending those difficulties. I read your letter as that of a man who has been seriously ill and has nearly recovered. Wherever your life now takes you, you will be a stronger and better man for having experienced and surmounted your difficulties. To have climbed back up from such depths will give you a special insight. Moreover, you ~~seem~~ are less than ever inclined to turn away from self-knowledge, ~~and such courage is~~ a rare and admirable trait.

I thank you, too, for satisfying my curiosity about where you were and what had happened to you. I will not pretend that for some time after your departure I did not hope that we would be together again. Even after the passing years extinguished that hope, I continued to wish you well, wherever you might be, as I do now.

[I shall include news of Father's death, Elizabeth's and Helen's marriages, etc.]

If someday you ~~happen to~~ visit Oakland, ~~I would welcome your presence at my door~~ do feel free to call on us. And ~~let me know~~ know that I do care how your fight progresses – toward ~~what I feel sure will be~~ a successful conclusion.

It is not an entirely honest letter. It omits how long and foolishly I pined for him; but it states clearly how we stand now: old friends, if he likes, with no impediment to our meeting as such.

Thursday, November 26

Thanksgiving Day. Father always called Thanksgiving Day "our most fatuous holiday," because it purported to celebrate the kindness of a people we thanked by destroying. (How I miss you, Father!)

My contribution to our feast this year was the cream cheese. A simple enough chore: Crush two cream cheeses; mix with salt, cayenne, and a little cream; chop a cup of black olives very finely, and a half-cup of walnuts a little less finely; press mixture into a mould; slice; and lay the slices on a bed of Romaine cos lettuce. It is important to Aunt Emily that I contribute something, but she knows I am no cook, so we have settled on this simple but essential dish.

As for the rest of the meal: Grape fruit with white grapes; consommé a la Royal; celery hearts; olives; oyster patties, and of course a huge turkey, roasted, with mashed potatoes and onion souffle; then cranberry sherbet, lettuce salad, pumpkin pie, ginger ice cream, and the cream cheese. (Although I relish olives, I could not abide them today and avoided eating the cream cheese.) Lastly, little cakes no one had room to eat, and coffee.

Our giving of thanks was unusually solemn, and not merely because we missed Father's presence. The plight of the European countries reminds us daily how fortunate we are not to be amid their deadly quarrels. We are grateful now for blessings that formerly went unnoticed: We do not live in terror of any enemy, and our young men are not enjoying a last supper before being sent off to battle.

Father Armour, saying grace, added an important point: that in granting us dispensation from war's horrors, God expects from us in return something more than mere thankfulness. If we merely give thanks for our oceanic barrier, we will fall far short of His expectations. We must view our good fortune as a spur toward helping our less fortunate cousins across the sea.

I was preoccupied with a much more local concern: Susan's pallor and withdrawn manner.

Friday, November 27

Went for a long walk this morning determined to think out some plan regarding Susan. At first, I neither knew nor cared where I walked, my mind flooding with images of Susan: swinging her thin legs from the kitchen stool; the disturbing drawing she showed me; her look of horror, months ago, and my fears that Uncle might be behaving as he did with me, and worse; her increasing timidity. How can I have delayed so long? Neither Father's death, nor the child is any excuse.

My feet had taken me to the spot on the estuary where the Admiral and his family had lived. To a place before the loss of Mother, where I had been a strong child, my mother's child. Where I had known friends to whom I could look for loving guidance. The boat was long gone. The Admiral was not there with his confident smile. If I am not strong enough, … Nay, I *must* be strong enough. Standing by the water, I said aloud, "You fool! You cannot but be strong enough, with all the wonderful people you carry inside you: Mother and Father and the Admiral and so many others." I thought too of the child and knew that I must somehow do this.

Sunday, November 29

I have decided how to deal with Uncle Thomas. A desperate gamble indeed! Yet, if I succeed, is it wrong to bring Susan to live with us when my own future is uncertain? I might bring her here only to take her away or leave her in Aunt's care. No harm that my situation can do to her reputation approaches the harm I fear he does to her each day.

Monday, November 30

Only today did I hand the mailman my letter to Richard. Was I uncertain in my heart?

DECEMBER

<u>Wednesday, December 2</u>

Awakened early, as I made an appointment to meet Uncle Thomas in his office at 9:30 a.m. I felt cold, and when I lifted my coffee cup to my lips, my fingers trembled. My stomach was upset, as it has been of late. I have eaten no breakfast the last few days, but this morning the need for strength forced me to risk eggs on toast.

After several fruitless minutes contemplating the page, mostly to distract my mind, I leafed idly through pages I wrote months ago. Smiling at mention of Lucius. Nodding sadly over Father's sudden decline and death. Wonder at Chicago. This has not been the year I expected!

(Each time I read Susan's name, my mouth tightened with anger at myself—for my obtuseness and for my timidity.)

Not two hours later, I arrived home, exhausted. Aunt Agnes was out, thank goodness. I needed to sit quietly with a cup of tea and collect my thoughts. And my feelings, which more urgently need collecting.

Where to start? Uncle greeted me kindly, assuming I sought his counsel on financial matters. Before we went into his inner sanctum, I asked him to instruct his secretary to hold any telephone calls. He demurred, saying that his people did not interrupt him in conference; but I insisted, my voice tremulous, and he mistook it for girlish nervousness and complied.

The dark wood of his office spoke of wealth and power. The chair in which I sat had new upholstery. Uncle always seems taller sitting behind his desk; his many plaques, awards, and commendations behind him, and of course McKinley's letter.

Then it was tim. For a moment I could not speak. The pleasantries had ceased a moment too soon. My mouth was dry, my chest constricted. Frantically, I looked out the window.

"Come now, I know that your father has left you reasonably well off," Uncle prompted.

His voice was as smooth as when he had tried to persuade me that his late-night visits were some mystical adventure. A surge of anger loosened my tongue. My face must have hinted at the loathing I felt. I said I had not come to discuss finances.

He *must* have realized what I meant to discuss, but he appeared puzzled.

I wanted to shout, "Do you ever think what you are, what you've done to us!" Instead, I said calmly that I thought it would be better for Susan's development to live with me and Agnes.

He looked at me, open-mouthed, and I realized I had caught him off his guard.

I said that I recalled vividly the time I had spent in his house when I was Susan's age, particularly during my sister's absence; that although I did not then understand that his unspeakably vile conduct was criminal, I knew that he was acting in a vile manner with Susan and was determined to put a stop to it.

The room seemed to contract. My eyes locked with his. His wore a mask of polite disbelief, but his eyes moved wildly about.

"I can't imagine Susan could possibly have said such things," he whispered. "Are you saying she told you that I...?"

"She has told me enough," I replied.

He pounced on my vagueness, rising, and leaning over the desk like an angry schoolmaster. "She has made no such statements then!"

"She has showed me, and told me enough, and must be removed from your house," I said.

"If I do not agree with this absurd demand?" he asked.

"I am prepared to make all of Oakland aware of your true nature."

"By speaking openly of these terrible things you claim?" He leaned toward me as he sat down, then said, "I am not so sure you would enjoy that. Such tales would hardly enhance your marriage prospects, and no one who matters would believe you. They would infer, as I now have, that your father's death has unhinged your mind. They would wonder about your silence, assuming that any decent girl, whose father not only had the bully-pulpit of his magazine but was once one of the State's most ferocious trial attorneys, would have acted more seasonably if such accusations were true. You would succeed only in hurting Aunt Emily and making yourself into a pathetic creature to all who know you."

Despite his harsh words, I felt calm. I agreed that some might react as he suggested, but that quite possibly many would not; and that some would be disinclined to continue doing business with him. I said that those who knew me thought me a sensible person, not given to tall tales, and that although it was too late for *me* to bring legal charges, Susan would speak to the police, if necessary, and my testimony would back her up.

"And would destroy your standing in the community," he said, almost snarling.

"Quite possibly." I replied.

He looked startled and sat back in his chair as if we were chatting and said, "Of course, if asked, I would recall, reluctantly, that you were always a very strange girl." (He must have recognized that I was perfectly prepared to risk disaster and had no profits to protect.) Then he put his palms together and tapped lightly against his chin with his index fingers. "I would also recall that in your loneliness and grief, and anger at your father, you were driven to win my love, in ways no man would imagine a young girl acting and resented me for discouraging you." His tone was almost sorrowful. "Furthermore, until the loss of your father, you have been well-behaved and even dined with us frequently—which no one could imagine you doing if these appalling allegations had merit. If fresh grief deranges your mind, as it did in your girlhood, perhaps some sort of confinement would be best. For your own good."

A smile flitted across his face. "No," he said, looking intently at me, "Even if you did not know so well my standing in this town, did not know how close I am with our political leaders, with Father Armour, with all of the leaders of civic and charitable institutions, I do not think you would dare to publish these terrible slanders."

"I have begun already," I said.

The confidence drained from his face. He shook his head. "I would have heard of it."

"Call your secretary to bring in your telephone messages."

"I am not accustomed to being ordered about so! In my own office at that!"

"Nevertheless, it would be in your interest to call her in," I replied firmly.

He stared at me, as if his eyes were two cobalt-blue revolvers leveled at my head. I stared back. Curiously, I thought of Mother.

Still, he did not move.

"Very well, then," I said. "Let me read your telephone messages for you." Picking up an imaginary slip of paper, I feigned reading: "Art Sullivan called to request a personal interview for an article on respectable men who commit statutory offenses." As I repeated the pantomime with several more "messages," Uncle started twisting his fountain pen. "My good friend Bret Lyons has left a similar message. Ann Swinburn called to advise you that she and the women who work with her are prepared to march outside your office, like labor strikers, starting tomorrow if Susan is not yet in my custody. Mrs. Earnest of the Lakeshore Improvement Association—the people who protested a few months ago when the school fired the woman principal to hire a man; Charles Powers, the attorney, regarding the legal papers he has drawn up, asking the court to remove you as Susan's guardian."

There was a snapping sound as the pen broke open, spilling ink onto his desk.

"Oh, yes, just one more. Suzanne Coolidge called to arrange a time when she may come and take a photograph of you to accompany Mr. Sullivan's magazine article."

Uncle cursed and raised his ink-spotted right hand, then stood up looking about for a towel, and started for the door. "After you clean up, you might ask your secretary whether or not anyone has 'phoned," I suggested again, sounding more composed than I felt.

My blood seemed to surge through me. I hoped my friends had not been delayed from making their telephone calls at the appointed times. What if Uncle 'phoned one of them back before returning to his office? How smug his face would look as he told me that he would be delighted to spend an hour explaining the new banking regulations with Art Sullivan.

I did not think he would dare call anyone, but if he did, I would explain that this was a dress rehearsal, that he could not doubt that these people, if I confided in them, would act just as I suggested, and I was offering him a last chance to spare himself, Aunt Emily, and the family a tremendous public humiliation.

When he returned to the office, he walked round his desk, searching out an unsoiled place where he could lay the message slips. I realized that he had not sent anyone in to clean the ink from his desk.

He resumed his study of me as he sat down.

"Would you like to use your telephone?" I inquired.

He laughed. "You are quite a woman, Katherine," then added carefully, "I recall no such events as those you claim. Nor can I imagine engaging in such conduct." He shook his head. "We both know your mind was troubled by your mother's accident and your father's long absence. Now, however, you are a grown woman of strong character." He coughed. "Perhaps stronger than I had realized." He looked down at the spots of ink, as if reading his fortune. "You might be a fine influence on Susan."

"Thank you," I said, unable to speak in much more than a whisper.

"I have one concern that we must discuss." His eyes darted up to confront mine. "If I am to consider allowing my ward to stay with you, I must know that these delusions will not affect her; that you will not influence her."

(He feared the possibility of criminal charges!)

I started to promise him that there would be no such charges. Anything to get Susan out of his house. Then I thought better of it. "Unless you make it necessary, I do not wish to see Susan dragged about the courts, subjected to newspaper articles and whispers and sniggering about town, and whatever else your attorneys might concoct for her at a trial."

He nodded.

"However, I can promise nothing on Susan's behalf. You have committed crimes against her, and you know better than I whether she will wish to have you brought up on charges. I will not suggest it, but if she mentions such a thing, I will neither encourage nor forbid her."

We looked at each other in silence, Uncle trying to gauge my sincerity and perhaps calculating how certain he was that Susan would do nothing. After several seconds, he nodded. "I take it that I need not respond to these?" he said, pointing at the telephone messages.

I could not resist smiling. It needed a moment for me to be sure of my voice. "I believe I can undertake to do that for you."

I made a mental note to suggest to Art that he delay the banking story for a few weeks and to tell Suzanne that I have decided not to surprise Aunt Emily with a photographic portrait of Uncle Thomas. If he someday learns that these calls were thoroly innocuous, I think he understands that I am willing to risk what I must.

I am to fetch Susan this afternoon after school. Uncle will explain to Aunt Emily that I required Susan's companionship out of grief, and that he believes Aunt Emily needs a rest. (I have no idea how much Aunt Emily knows. Nor do I wish to know.)

Thursday, December 3

Susan is such a dear child. When I told her that she would be staying with Agnes and me, her eyes got big and she looked pensive, and then she smiled. "Forever?" she whispered. "Until you grow up and marry or go off to study and become a doctor," I replied. She laughed at that last and was visibly relieved to be leaving that house. She did not ask me why she was coming to live with us, and I sensed that she did not wish to discuss it. (As I would not have wished to do!) We talked briefly about which of her things really matter to her. She wants surprisingly little from that house.

With Susan off to school, I reflected on how my new responsibility will affect my own course. To stay here, unmarried, not only would tarnish my reputation, but Susan's too, and could result in her being taken from me. (I cannot risk her falling into his hands again!)

Yet leaving has also become more complicated. I had harbored some vague, romantic vision of us living in a bohemian neighborhood in some distant city; I would have my painting and Susan a new start in a new school—both of us living a life that would show her that women have choices and a say in how their lives turn out. I could pass myself off as a widow or simply make no explanations. I have since realized that Susan might find it difficult to be suddenly separated from family *and* friends *and* from everything familiar; and such a home would necessarily feel unsettled, perhaps even chaotic, which is not what she needs.

Meanwhile, since the visit to the Edmonds farm, a new idea has been growing inside of me. I declined to recognize it at first for obvious reasons, but I think I had felt a hint of it months ago without quite knowing what it was exactly I was feeling. Now, how to explore the possibility is the question. Am I mad to hope that…?

Here is Susan, home from school.

Friday, December 4

Susan went walking with me this afternoon.

We passed the old Japanese man's house. I rarely walk that way of late. His death saddens me, although I knew nothing of him. Time is speeding past us, and through us, and we rarely grasp hold of our lives and gain from them all that we might. That the death of an old man with whom I never exchanged a word should weigh on me so, when Father is also recently gone, seems odd; but Father's death is too large and near for me to see it clearly—as I might comprehend the form of a tree better at a distance of twenty yards than I could do if the tree were a hundred feet tall and right before me.

Of Mr. Yamashita, I know only that his face expressed such wisdom, and that whatever I might have learned from him, I had not the time. He is also a signpost warning me how foolish it is to be too timid or too preoccupied to do what matters!

Saturday, December 5

Spoke with Antonio today.

Sunday, December 6

Having Susan here is like having a little sister (though she could easily be my daughter). She is slowly emerging (like a delphinium) and already acts more spirited. She seems glad to be here but cannot quite trust that this is her home now. She has said nothing of her life previously, and I do not ask. Uncle Thomas's conduct and Aunt Emily's example have left her timid and tentative and frightened of becoming a woman. She watches Agnes and me with great interest.

Church was awkward. I could see the tension in Susan's face before we left the house. Afterward, we spoke briefly with Aunt Emily who asked how she was doing and appears to miss her. I made sure to thank her profusely for letting Susan stay with me.

I have assured Susan that we need not dine with them other than on important occasions, and she may remain at my side throughout any such visit. She seemed relieved.

I have arranged that Susan will accompany Aunt Agnes when she visits a friend in Santa Rosa next weekend. (The visit being essential to my madcap idea.) Susan seemed uncertain and asked several times whether I might go as well; but she seems to be coming round.

Monday, December 7

Aunt cross-questioned me this morning about Susan. Emily had mentioned my extreme grief over Father as the reason for Susan's change of residence; and Aunt knows that while I grieve deeply for Father, I am bearing up fine.

I told Aunt that Thomas was not a good man for a young girl to be alone with and that Susan needed a loving and safe home. Obviously shocked, she asked how I had learned of this. Had Susan confided in me? I told her that when I taxed him with it, he as good as admitted it. After a moment, she said sharply, "But you yourself lived in his house for more than a year!" "I did indeed," I replied in a tone that confessed all. I said nothing of my confusion when he began coming to my room at night, or of the fear thereafter about when he would return, which lingered even after Elizabeth joined me; or of Aunt Emily's blindness to it all.

Aunt's face registered several emotions before she hugged me, tears in her eyes. "I'm sorry," she whispered. "I am so sorry." I thought she would ask why I hadn't told her, but she did not. She shortly 'phoned her sister and made some excuse for not supping there tomorrow.

Saturday, December 12

Supper with Antonio this evening, tete-a-tete. Now that I have managed to empty the house of all but Ah Fong, who will leave after he prepares our meal, I almost wish my efforts had failed. How am I to say to Antonio what I must? We have lived entirely different lives, and I have had but the slightest sign from him that he has even noticed that I am a woman.

Sunday, December 13

Broke into giggles all morning like a school-girl. Whether I laughed from delight or nerves—I could not say. I have never known myself so little, even when I was in Chicago. Is this new tenderness I feel toward Antonio partly relief that I need not face various imagined hells? Do I suppose I "love" him because thinking so eases my mind?

Here I sit, smiling at nothing, and everything. Perhaps I *am* going mad after all!

Stick to the facts, like a newspaperwoman, Father would counsel. Antonio arrived promptly and was startled to find me alone with supper prepared for two. He looked round warily, and I wondered if he understood that I planned to seduce him, in a fashion.

I repeated that I wished to talk with him about a serious matter, and that I trusted him to keep our conversation thoroly secret. My serious tone quickly punctured any illusion that I sought merely a night of passion. Yet he could not imagine what was in my mind as I could hardly imagine it myself! Nor could I imagine how to begin, although I had thought of nothing else for days.

I asked if he was hungry. He answered, "Yes," then smiled sheepishly and said, "No, this moment, no." His indecision seemed to amuse him, and his lips danced boyishly. Then, dressing his face in its Sunday-best solemnity, he said, "Tell me, *per favore*, what troubles you."

It was hard to meet his eyes at first, but then it was impossible not to, as if our eyes meeting might help my stumbling words. "I fear what you will think of me, but I have an idea that you and I can help each other. It is a most unusual idea and involves the head and the heart." I paused and placed my hand over my heart. (In my mind, the words had flowed more gracefully.) Antonio nodded encouragingly. I continued haltingly, "I think you are a good man. You have a good heart. We have not talked so much, but I can tell, I know that you are a good man, a man of many skills, a man with a good heart. I paused and looked away and took a deep breath before stumbling on, "I have a situation. I am going to have a baby. The man does not know. No one knows."

Antonio was looking at me intently. Then, for a long moment, there was nothing but our breathing. I felt suddenly frightened to have put myself in the hands of someone I knew so little of and paralyzed by what I still had to say and the need to say it with great precision. My words were coming out awkwardly, and I sounded confused even to myself. Antonio's brow was furrowed as he struggled to understand, but his calm gaze allowed me to continue. I said that for an unmarried woman to have a child, as he must know, was no good and that I had been thinking about what to do; that I might leave Oakland; that I might marry someone, a friend perhaps. I saw the question in his eyes and shook my head and said that I could not marry the child's father.

"Now perhaps you begin to see why?" I looked at Antonio hopefully. "I like you. I do not know you so well, or how we would get on, but I have thought that you and I might marry." I paused, and Antonio opened his mouth, but I rushed on before he could speak as there was more *I* needed to say, and I feared what *he* might say.

"If I were not with child, I would not ask this of you, but I do not ask *only* for this reason. I have other friends I *could* marry, but I will not ask, and I have other choices. I think there is a good chance that we could make a family together… that in time… ours could be a true marriage." I paused and looked away and took another deep breath before continuing, "I cannot know. We cannot know. I could help you finish your education, to teach if you wish it, or to begin a business, or a farm... I am not rich, but I am not poor." I paused again, my throat dry, my lips like parchment. The house was so silent. I was more embarrassed even than I had feared. I thought of how I must sound: A wealthy woman trying to buy a husband to hide her misconduct.

"I have more… but is this something you...?" Before Antonio could open his mouth, I added, "If you find this entire matter distasteful, you must say so at once, and we will talk no more of this. We will sit down to supper, of course. I trust you will keep silent." Again, before Antonio could speak, I added, "If you are offended, I am truly sorry, *sono desolata*… You understand?"

"I understand your words," Antonio said after a brief silence, in which all I could hear was the pounding of my heart. He fell silent again before continuing. "I not know I understand your heart." More silence. "I not know … what I do." For the first time he looked away, then he looked back at me as if he had made an important decision. "Have you some wine?" He asked.

I laughed out loud with relief at his question, quite the most sensible thing that either of us had said. "Yes!" I shouted through my laughter, wondering if he thought me mad; but he laughed too.

I fetched some wine and a corkscrew and began to open the bottle, but he gently took both from me and opened the wine in a graceful, practiced manner. Perhaps he had noticed my hands shaking, or perhaps he just wanted a glass of wine faster than I seemed likely to provide it.

I set out two glasses.

"I not drink *tanto*, so much," Antonio said gravely, which nearly started me laughing again, although I was pleased to hear it. (I was reminded of the letters to the *Munsey's* "spinster"— "don't smoke and detest whisky, drink glass of beer in the summer sometimes.")

Antonio poured the wine, and we drank in silence.

"Thank you," he said. He seemed more relaxed. "I understand what you say. You ask me, am I offend? No, I no offend. I insult you went with man? No. If we, you say 'sweetheart', if we marry, and you go with man, is different. But you no promise me anything. Do I think you are *bellissima* woman? Yes, you are beautiful woman with beautiful heart. I see you with Lucius, the black boy, and I think, you are a kind person, beautiful and kind. I see you with friends, I think you are strong woman, strong in your mind. And I see you paint, you have artist heart."

I held my breath, watching Antonio's dusky, honest face and listening to his musical voice, fearing that his kind words prefaced a courteous rejection. I lifted my glass to take more wine but could not. I had not foreseen how deeply I might care what he said!

"Marry? This I no think. No, I no think to marry with you. Impossible for me, no money, no… So… now. I have questions, I need to understand, how to ask?" He brought the wineglass to his lips and kept it there for a moment, then asked, "What is idea? Marry, be man and wife? Marry, but…?

I tried to keep my voice steady. "If we marry, we will be man and wife." I spoke slowly, trying to read in his eyes whether it could be true. "In every way, man and wife." (How could I be saying this? We have never even kissed!) "We…" Flushed and flustered, I could not finish; I dared not speak what was in my head.

In truth, I did not know what I wanted. Of course, I hoped that we would someday feel love for one another; but hope could hardly make me *feel* so, let alone command another to feel so. Might Antonio agree to marry me without knowing whether or when we would be fully man and wife? (Why would he? To be kind? For money? In the shared hope that we might grow to care for one another?) I had thought myself prepared to embrace him tonight, but my fear and embarrassment outweighed any curiosity or excitement.

Suddenly it all seemed terribly complex. I suppose I had envisioned something out of a magazine story, where everything magically works out. Suddenly, this very handsome man sitting in front of me seemed more thoroly a stranger than he did the first time we spoke. What had I been thinking? *Had* I been thinking? How little we know of each other! I did not know how to continue. I knew what I had intended to say… I feared I might weep. Then I thought about the child growing inside of me. Giving myself to Antonio was nothing compared to what some women experience, and I knew him to be kind, intelligent, and no drunkard.

"I would not ask you to be... with me and not with me. I know how strange this must be for you—a woman proposing marriage, a woman to whom you have never said one word to suggest such an idea. You may wonder if I am... willing. We are alone."

"You want that we be as man and wife now? This night?"

I nodded. Antonio smiled sadly as he stood up and approached me and pulled me to my feet. When he put his hands on my shoulders, my body flinched with sudden fear, but then I felt the gentleness in his strong hands and recalled those hands carefully setting plants into the soil. His fingers stroked my shoulders. I looked up, anticipating the kiss, determined to kiss him back properly. I closed my eyes.

Instead of being pulled into his arms, I felt his fingers on my chin, gently shaking my head, as if to wake me. When I opened my eyes, he said, "In English, my words no say my feeling, how much I… First, I say: Of course, I marry you. You are *esatto*. I no think to marry, but I watch you. I like you. I wonder… This thing no *possibile*. You are rich woman, you are American woman, you are beautiful woman. So yes. I want. You stand here, we are *da solo*, I am only me *molto tempo*. You say this thing… how much I want, *pero no*. I touch, body jump like fire. Face like deer. How to say? You are… willing, not want, I think."

I felt relieved, surprised, and disappointed, all at once. I had been determined that if Antonio was willing to consider my mad idea, I must do my part. I had thought he might reject me but had not imagined he would accept my offer with such delicacy.

I reached up to touch his face, my fingertips exploring it like a blind woman's.

He stood motionless, smiling. I thought of a cat purring. Then he shook his head and gently pulled my hand from his face. "Please, remember… I am a man."

"Yes, you are," I said. (And I am a woman! I thought, before also thinking that this is not what we are taught in school about how to act.)

Enough. My hand is tired. My head is tired. Anyone who reads this need know no more.

In the end, Antonio's gentlemanly scruples went for naught. Perhaps he could have maintained his resolve, but I—rather to my surprise—would not have that.

Monday, December 14

Feel like A.H. Wagner, the automobile man, who cast dice at the Hotel Oakland bar to determine whether to follow his wife to

Hawaii and murder her. I mean no harm; but I too have cast my fate onto the winds of chance and feel a curious freedom having done so.

Much relieved that Antonio seemed unconcerned about the child's appearance, showing none of the disdain most men would have expressed about my intimacy with a negro.

Must tell Aunt Agnes of my plans. I do not suppose she will approve; and it will seem quite sudden. Let her guess (as she surely will) that Antonio and I have been lovers for some time. She has noticed nothing, as I have gained little. I had thought of telling her after the ceremony, delicately hinting that passion accounted for our haste. It would be far easier to talk about the marriage as a *fait accompli* than to discuss why we will not be having a church ceremony. However, it would pain her not to be included, and I owe her too much, and love her too much, to leave her out.

Tuesday, December 15

Much to plan just when I am feeling least capable of doing or thinking. Still, I am excited, despite feeling faint occasionally and a burning sensation if I eat too much, which is thoroly irritating as I seem always to be hungry. At least the nausea seems milder of late.

Thursday, December 17

Sitting in the garden this morning, I let my thoughts drift like falling leaves and wondered whether in some corner of my heart I have been drawn always to Antonio but could not permit myself to recognize the attraction. Am I so shallow? Perhaps I am. Desire, it appears, when unable to overrun our fear and timidity, eventually outflanks them. Are the conflicting forces within always in formation on some inner battlefield, quite as invisible to our conscious minds as a battle raging in Juarez?

Was I coming to love Antonio these last few months? Or did my determination to avoid disaster alter my perception, as an artist might improve a portrait with a few deft strokes?

How I miss your gruff wisdom, Father!

<u>**Monday, December 21**</u>

It is done.

We married at City Hall rather than St. Paul's. The simplicity suited the circumstances. I would not have enjoyed dozens of pairs of eyes on us, all the chatter, and then introducing Antonio to… everyone. Nor could I have brooked long discussions with Father Maines or Father Armour about our haste, and our different religions, and the inappropriateness of celebrating a marriage while in mourning. Too, as an "impure" bride I should have felt as if I were lying. Making the promises we made to each other in a civil office felt right and true.

Elizabeth would have been appalled. There was not the music and celebration of which young girls dream, and that others were waiting to marry could have made it seem less special—yet as I covertly observed their joy, hope, fear, and excitement, I felt cheered to be among these strangers. I almost wish we could all meet again, in a year or five or ten, like graduating classmates. (Could the plainness of our surroundings better ground our marriages in the realities of everyday life? I can only wonder.)

The conversation with Aunt Agnes was difficult—and curiously rewarding. How does one say, "Might we stop at City Hall on the way to the fish market so I can get married?" I asked whether she had plans and said that I wanted her to accompany me somewhere, and that I hoped the surprise would please her nearly as much as it did me. I apologized for not letting her in on my plans earlier, that I had wished to be sure before telling her that I intended to be married at City Hall today.

"To anybody in particular?" she asked with raised eyebrows.

"To Antonio Bonifacio. You have met him. He is a wonderful man. He was a teacher in Sicily before coming to live here."

Aunt did not remark that he was hardly a teacher *here* or ask how we had come to know each other so well. She studied me quietly as our eyes met and held. I willed her to understand, or at least to accept. After what seemed a terribly long time, she picked up her teacup and remarked that there was a crack in it. From her abrupt change of subject, I might have assumed that she was offended or displeased, except that her lips, tight at first, curved into a smile.

"You do not wish a church wedding?" she asked lightly.

"No. Not so soon after Father's death," I replied quickly.

She said she would be pleased to go with me and offered no further comment.

Her reticence was striking. I did not construe it as disapproval. Yet I had anticipated a deluge of questions and advice, and her response was so thoroly the opposite that it pulled me off-balance. Having feared what she might say, I now found myself asking what she thought.

"I am surprised. I do not know him, but you have obviously found something in him that you have not found in others. I have no opinion, or at least none worth hearing. I will say this: I love you very much; you are not a fool; and I look forward to coming to know him."

Thursday, December 24

I have begun to see in human lives the same imponderable, intricate pattern I see in nature. If Mother and Father had left us with the Admiral and his family, I might never have recognized the need to rescue Susan from that house. If the brief interlude in Chicago had not left me in a quandary, I might not have found myself growing to love Antonio. If not for Mother's death, and if not for Father's absence, and if not for our stay with Uncle Thomas and Aunt Emily... would I have grown into the person I am? If not for Lincoln, would I have confronted Uncle Thomas? Would I have wed Antonio? If not for Father's boyhood involvement in the Underground Railroad, and if not for my friendship with Lucius, would I have seen the person behind Lincoln's lion-hued skin?

Life flows as it must! Here we are, a strange and wonderful new family welcoming Christmas: Antonio, Susan, dear Aunt Agnes, and the unborn child. I only wish Father were here to share it!

Friday, December 25

Christmas. What a full and remarkable day! I am too tired to write more just now, and my new husband (Antonio is proving to be a most extraordinary gift to us all) awaits me in our bed.

Saturday, December 26

Boxing Day. Many callers. I overheard Mrs. Livingston sniff, "I have heard that 'love levels all ranks.'" I would have been tempted to show her the door if Antonio had heard her.

Sunday, December 27

Today, I was particularly eager to attend services as I wished others to see our strange and wonderful new family.

It has been instructive to watch the reactions of friends. Jack was coldly courteous. Bret laughed and said that he could not imagine a man better suited to me. When I asked why, he replied that Antonio appears equally at home with the natural world, then added, “Antonio is an intelligent man who could be doing much more than he is. You are a talented woman who should be doing more than you are. I hope and trust that you will encourage each other.” Suzanne commented, “Antonio is often silent; and his silence reminds one that much of what we utter need never have been said.”

Elizabeth and Tub dined with us after church. Tub smiled politely throughout and made no effort at conversation with Antonio, while Elizabeth spoke to him as if it were an exercise assigned her by a schoolmaster.

I have several times entered a room to find Aunt talking quietly with Antonio. She appears determined to know him better, and he says that he likes talking with her. (I am much relieved.)

As for Antonio, he is wonderfully patient with my friends because they are my friends. He seems neither determined to impress nor jealous of my easy ways with them; and although curious, he appears indifferent to what they may think of him!

Monday, December 28

John Muir is dead. A shock, despite his age. Redwoods grow old too, but they rarely topple over. It never occurred to me that John Muir could die!

Although I met him but thrice, two of those meetings are among my most vivid memories. Will future generations even recall him? When I asked Suzanne, she replied, “Perhaps he will be wholly forgotten because everything he stood for, which the rest of us are just now learning, will someday seem so obvious that nothing he said will need saying.”

“Why would he be forgotten?” Helen joined in. “Everything Jesus stood for seems obvious now, but we haven’t forgotten Him.”

Suzanne smiled and replied, “If the world treats John Muir as it has treated Jesus, we will build statues and shrines in his honor, and railroads through everything he tried to save. We will insist schoolchildren memorize his words, but mock anyone who truly follows them."

Helen and I laughed. It was thoroly true and not at all funny.

Tuesday, December 29

Last night, I stood by the window before joining Antonio in bed, and I saw not our garden but the wilderness; and I heard John Muir telling us about being asked in his youth where he was going and answering, "To any place that is wild!"; and I whispered into the night, "I hope Heaven is wild."

As I sat with Susan while she breakfasted, I was reminded of her fascination with the miniature tree. I think she is a little afraid of it. Does its helplessness against man's whims strike a chord in her heart? After she left for school, I sat gazing at the tree and felt a kinship with it. I too have felt at times restricted from normal growth. Yet the tree has managed to thrive, and so I suppose have I. We are trained by our families and our experiences, as the tree was trained by Mr. Yamashita—and as a tree in a forest is shaped by light, rainfall, wind, as well as by lightning, fire, and surrounding trees.

I think of Mother often. Soon there will be a new person for whom I am everything, as she was to me. As I drew from her certain strengths, the child will draw from me certain strengths—and weaknesses. Having no way of regarding the world, the child will look to me and imitate me; and as his gaze widens, to Antonio, and then to Susan and Aunt Agnes, this is how he will acquire the seeds from which his own attitudes will grow.

I have not wanted to admit to my wounds, preferring to forget or to refocus my mind, and I do not know what all this means, except that if I can be strong and kind and honest, our child may be so. If I am craven and wounded; if my mind and heart contain rooms I fear to enter, or if there are those whose eyes I dare not meet, he will see that and learn to look away when meeting the world—and himself.

I am frightened and strengthened by this understanding, and deeply grateful for Father and Mother, Antonio, Susan, and Aunt, who have helped me endure with their light.

Thursday, December 31

I have kept this journal now for one year.

I am glad I have done so—but for reasons I could not have imagined a year ago. I did not suspect that Father would die; and I should have been beside myself with laughter if someone had foretold the events in Chicago, my marriage to Antonio, and Susan's move to our home.

Yet only this year have I become myself.

We could have joined our friends at the Oakland Hotel. A gay gathering, I am sure, but we preferred a quiet evening at home.

Last night, I realized that I did not know where Antonio had gone to. I found him in the garden reading the motto on the sundial by moonlight. I had not read the silly thing for months myself. He seemed absorbed by the words. I stood beside him and read what I had written—with no idea that before the year's end an unborn child would hold me in his hand, tossing my life in this direction and that.

Time's finger writes but letters in the sand / The earth's a ball a child holds in his hand / Yes, pause and glance and say you know the time, the way a child repeats a silly rhyme / And let the garden's dancing hues beguile / you back to childhood for a little while.

"It pleases me," Antonio said softly, then added after a moment, "It speak true. We think we know time, and we think we know life, *però probabilmente no. Però* we think it, we feel more… how you say *confortevole*… comfortable."

I took his hand in mine.
"You have made a good garden," Antonio said.
We turned and walked back to the house by moonlight.